FLESH AND THE DEVIL

FLESH AND THE DEVIL

DEVYN QUINN

APHRODISIA

KENSINGTON BOOKS

http://www.kensingtonbooks.com

APHRODISIA are published by

Kensington Publishing Corp.
850 Third Avenue
New York, NY 10022

All Kensington Titles, Imprints, and Distributed Lines are available at special quantity discounts for bulk purchases for sales promotions, premiums, fund-raising, and educational or institutional use.

Special book excerpts or customized printings can also be created to fit specific needs. For details, write or phone the office of the Kensington special sales manager: Kensington Publishing Corp., 850 Third Avenue, New York, NY 10022, attn: Special Sales Department, Phone: 1-800-221-2647.

Aphrodisia and the A logo are trademarks of Kensington Publishing Corp.

ISBN-13: 978-0-7582-1653-3
ISBN-10: 0-7582-1653-X

First Kensington Trade Paperback Printing: April 2007

10 9 8 7 6 5 4 3 2 1

Printed in the United States of America

To Hilary Sares, my fabulous editor.
And Roberta Brown, my equally fabulous agent.
This book would not exist without these two ladies
lending a helping hand and their expertise!

Acknowledgments

A big thanks to my test readers, who were willing to look at the manuscript in its rawest form and render their opinions and reviews. This book came together with the support of Vivi Anna, Marianne LaCroix, Kelley Hartsell, Valerie Bongards, Serena Polheber, and Jaymi Egerstaffer. Your input and comments were priceless. And to my friend, Sara Reinke, who kept the cheering squad going.

Not to be forgotten are the ladies of Wild & Wicked, my online support group: Tyler Blackwood, Marianne LaCroix, Adrienne Kama, Rian Monaire, AnneMarie Ortega, and Desiree Erotique. These girls hold me up when I am down, encourage me when I am discouraged, and give me a boot to the butt when needed. I am proud to call them friends and cohorts. Visit us online at www.wildauthors.com.

1

*T*aste the forbidden. The hunger was there.

The game he was playing was dangerous, but Brenden Wallace couldn't help himself. Part of the thrill of working undercover vice was the ability to live out the erotic fantasies he'd never risk trying in real life.

Brenden hardly dared to move. He didn't even breathe. Closing his eyes, he relished the smooth glide of silk circling his wrists. The soft bite of the fabric into his skin sent a chill whispering down his spine.

The touch of a fingertip tracing the curve of one ear caused the fine hairs on the back of his neck to rise. A voice of smoky rich timbre drawled, "Too tight?"

Brenden licked parched lips. "Tighter, honey. I want to feel the burn."

A tug on the scarf answered. Tightening. Binding. "Better?"

Arms stretched around the back of the chair he sat in, Brenden tested the strength of the knots. They held, solid and unyielding. The material chafed, a not-so-unpleasant sensation. "Yes."

His captor reappeared. The woman was a paid escort, hired

for the evening. The service she worked for charged three hundred dollars for the pleasure of her company. He knew her business, didn't know her name, but by the look of her, she was worth every penny.

A muscle twitched in his jaw. His penis stirred, cramped in the confines of his tight jeans. How far would this one go to *entertain* a lonely man? Having kinky sex wasn't illegal in Louisiana. It was only criminal if cash traded hands for erotic favors. Then it was prostitution.

And someone had to get arrested.

Looking at her, his thoughts veered from professional to personal. Tall and slim, she wore a tight, red dress, clinging to every lush curve and perfectly matching her bright red stiletto fuck-me pumps. No longer tied up with the scarf matching her outfit, her black hair cascaded around her shoulders like the spread of a raven's wings.

That scarf was around his wrists.

Taste the forbidden. To play his role believably, Brenden had to live it.

She smiled. "You like playing dangerous games?" Her parted lips revealed perfectly white teeth. The cuspids were slightly elongated and came to neat points, enhancing her hovering feline quality even more.

Heavy awareness pulsed through his veins. "It's part of the thrill that makes life worth living."

His words seemed to amuse.

She bent, parting his legs. As if lit from inside, she radiated heat that practically screamed *wanton female*. Screamed it loud enough to arouse the male animal in him to an unbearable degree. She wasn't wearing a bra and the thin fabric of her dress clung to her nipples, outlining their prominence.

Her warm palms moved up his inner thighs. "Maybe. Maybe not. The things we think are deadly sometimes really aren't." She guided the tip of her tongue to tease an incisor. "And the things we think safe are sometimes most deadly." Her words were menace cloaked in crushed velvet.

The intimate contact jarred. She was so close Brenden could smell her heat, the scent of her arousal. Potent and mysterious, the cloying odor was enhanced by the addition of some exotic oil. His erection pressed, thick and hard, against his tight jeans. Closing his eyes, he shifted in his seat, letting a ragged breath escape. Say one wrong word, make one false move and the entire investigation would be blown.

Concentrate, asshole.

Brenden opened his eyes, ready to take the plunge. It was all or nothing. "I'm willing to take that chance."

Pleased, she moved closer. Eyes the color of the sea shimmering under a midnight sky drew him in. Her fiery cinnamon lips were just inches away, slightly parted, moist and utterly enticing. "Are you really?"

"I'm ready for anything." He imagined her teeth raking down his most sensitive flesh. He had the feeling she could cause a lot of pain, and make it last in the most delicious of ways.

She glanced toward his crotch, his obvious arousal. "Do you want me?" Her hands were close, but not close enough to make contact. She was playing the tease for all it was worth.

"God, yes . . ." Why lie? His body betrayed him. He'd already gone too far, torching every rule in the book. The lines between legal and illegal were blurring, the raw and open connection between them growing personal. What was wrong was beginning to feel too enticingly right.

She leaned in closer, pinning him down with an intensity that caused his skin to prickle. Brenden felt as if he was not just being probed, but explored. Every breath he drew singed his lungs. "I know what you crave." Her fingernails dug into his thighs, marking him as her own. "That secret desire gnawing at your heart is unsatisfied. I feel it inside you, waiting to be freed. Your soul is crying out for a fulfillment you dare not ask for."

Her words were spellbindingly, achingly true.

Feed the fetish. Aching with the need to climax, the notion was there. Hovering. Tempting. Beckoning. *Taste the forbidden.* His own secret mantra thundered through his skull, pressured by the painful hammering of blood driven by lust. Body shuddering with excruciating sensitivity, he lost his grip. Want exploded into need. There was no turning back. "Show me how."

"You start like this." Her lips brushed his, tongue sliding easily past his lips, melding them together.

Protest died an easy death as control slipped through his fingers like grains of sand.

Lost in the liquid pleasure, Brenden parried her thrusts, enjoying the tangle of mouth on mouth. Who was kissing or being kissed, he didn't care. No matter the consequences, he knew he'd wanted this to happen since she'd walked through the door, wanted this woman more than anything. Even his career.

Her tongue speared again, claiming and conquering, exploring every crevasse.

Brenden's cock surged, all molten heat and devouring hormones. Penetrated to the core. Pleasure gripped and squeezed him. Given free reign, carnal desire overrode his sanity. Everything missing in his life suddenly solidified into one defining thought: he needed this woman. He made the decision, prepared to sell his soul for a single night in her bed.

His hired escort wasn't buying. Murmuring something against his mouth, she ended the kiss. Warm lips trekked across his cheek. Her fingers brushed his long blond hair away from his ear. Her sharp tone shot a quick barb. "The only one getting fucked tonight is you."

Astonishment struck a sledgehammer blow. His stomach clenching around icy shards, Brenden's heart plummeted. Anxiety tied him into knots tighter than those around his wrists. *Oh, Christ.* Surely she hadn't . . .

She had.

Brenden forced himself to meet her steady stare. Her face grew rigid, a smile of bitchy amusement frozen on her lips: half mischief, half naughty dominatrix. "The next time you want me to tie you up, Officer, ask for it on your own time."

Brenden sat for a moment, stunned, struggling to make sense of her words. When they finally did sink in, he started to rise. The chair came with him. Muttering a curse under his breath, he sat back down. Game. Point. Match. He'd been bested by a pro.

Stepping back, she pivoted on one slim heel. Claiming her purse from the nearby bureau, she walked to the door where she paused and turned. Her nose crinkled and a smile edged around the corners of her mouth. "I believe you have my number."

2

Brenden sat in the hotel lounge, nursing a double Jack on the rocks and his wounded pride. Cutting his shift short, he felt a little misery drinking would be appropriate. He reeked of disillusionment from the sting gone so badly awry. Right now he was the laughingstock of the vice squad—a cop one-upped by a savvy prostitute. How could she have possibly known he was the law?

He finished the whiskey in a single gulp, motioning to the bartender for a refill. The night wasn't going to get any better. He was off duty, so he might as well drink. Change from a fifty-dollar bill lay in a stack in front of him, a bowl of peanuts at his elbow.

Brenden glanced at his watch. One in the morning. He was too keyed up to go home. After encountering a female who set his nerves on edge, he wasn't exactly looking forward to the empty bed waiting there. Every song playing on the jukebox was some country and western standard about broken hearts and long, lonely nights under cold sheets. Those sort of songs were guaranteed to depress the hell out of him.

The bartender delivered his second drink with a smile and wink. "Here you are, sir." A not-so-good looking chick with frizzy blond hair and way too much eye makeup filched a ten-dollar bill from his stack and returned four dollars.

Brenden gave her the eye, wondering if she'd get better looking by time the lounge closed. Her face wasn't so pleasant, but she did have a killer set of tits, which helped balance out the roll of fat around her middle. In the night, in the dark, any pair of spread legs would do—especially for a man who hadn't had sex in over a year and was about ready to explode.

He exhaled in frustration. Hitting on the bartender wasn't going to be the solution to his problem. She wasn't what he wanted. A change of venue wouldn't help either. He could always go to a bar where cops hung out when they weren't on duty. Plenty of civilians, both male and female, flocked around to make time with Dordogne's finest in—and out of—uniform. To some, the lure of a gun, a badge and a pair of handcuffs was irresistible. He could have his pick of the groupies.

Damn. He was truly feeling desperate.

Brenden closed his eyes, rubbing them hard with two fingers. The sexy woman with dark hair and stunning figure filled his mind. Just the thought of her sent a pulse of heavy awareness through his veins. He rubbed his eyes harder against the tremor her image invoked. For some reason, this exotic goddess had affected him on more than the physical plane. Handling this woman, he was sure, would be like handling dynamite. Dangerous and highly explosive. He couldn't easily shake the thought of her, the way she touched him. Then again, he didn't want to. He wanted to hold on to her memory, imagine again what it would be like to make love to her.

The sudden hitch in his breathing caused his heart to skip a beat. A shiver took hold, one of pure desire. He glanced at his hands. They were shaking, an unfulfilled sexual energy vibrating through every inch of his being. He cursed under his breath.

Giving the eye to another dude at the end of the bar, the bartender glanced toward him. "You need something, sir?"

Brenden waved a distracted hand. "No, nothing."

The bartender nodded and went back to her chat.

Brenden swore a second time. He hadn't eaten much today and the booze was going to his head. He popped a handful of peanuts into his mouth. His stomach rebelled. The peanuts felt like rocks hitting his gut.

He sighed. He was thirty-two years old, newly divorced, and on the edge of a serious burnout. Downing more whiskey, he wondered how much longer he'd be able to hang on. His sanity seemed to be slipping away, just as the best years of his life were passing him by.

Working double shifts? Check. Zero time to sleep? Check. All work and no play? Check. Sex life nonexistent? You bet. He wasn't living anymore. He was existing. He wondered why he even bothered.

He thought about Jenna. His ex-wife had quickly moved on with her life, barely looking back and shedding few tears after he'd signed the divorce papers. In fact, she was about to remarry, and with good reason for her haste. There was a bun in her oven, something she'd never been able to achieve with him. Not that he wasn't able to father children, thank you very much. He simply wasn't around enough to start a family.

Regretfully, it was too late to turn the clock back on the last decade, rearrange a few years so the story of his marriage would have a happy ending. In this world, "happily ever after" was for fairy tales. Divorces were for cops who paid more attention to the intrinsic union of badge, gun, and shield than to their marriages. He would always be one of those types. Police work was in his blood.

Brenden's mind returned to the blue-eyed angel who'd walked into his life tonight. Reaching into the pocket of his jacket, he pulled out the red scarf she'd worn in her hair. The color of passion, the color of heat. He fingered its softness, briefly pressing it to his face. The scent of her cologne lingered on the fabric, marked by its owner with her unique fragrance.

A lightly accented voice broke into his musings. "I see you still have my scarf."

Brenden's head swiveled to the left in time to see his former date slide onto the empty barstool next to his, her move one of sheer grace. Lost in his own thoughts, he hadn't heard her walk up.

The bartender came over. "Something to drink?"

She nodded brightly. "Wine, please. Red."

The bartender returned a few moments later. Placing the long-stemmed glass on a cocktail napkin, she slid the wine toward her. "You paying for your lady friend?"

Pride still stinging that she'd played him like a goddamn violin, Brenden gave a sullen nod. "Okay." Another ten was filched from his stack. The bartender returned a few dollars and loose change. He suspected she was tipping herself liberally for her services. He considered letting her know he was on to her game.

"Thank you." His new companion lifted the glass to her lips, taking a sip. "I've been dying for a glass all evening."

Brenden grunted and took a drink of his whiskey, relishing the burn. Ice clinked in the glass when he lowered it. "I'm surprised you're still hanging around here."

She gave a confident smile, leaning so close only an inch separated their shoulders. There was a small freckle at the base of her throat, right where a man would nibble her pulse. Brenden couldn't help but wonder if that freckle would taste like milk chocolate, or exotic dark chocolate.

"I'm not what you think I am, Officer. You're the one making the judgments." Voice husky and low with intimacy, her warm breath tickled his ear. "Remember, it's innocent until proven guilty."

Brenden shrugged. "When a lady shows up to a strange man's hotel room, she ain't no lady." He turned to face her. "Know what I mean?"

At his biting tone, she stiffened in her chair. Her eyes clouded, then cleared just as quickly. He had meant the words to offend and they did. "I don't claim to be a lady. But a girl must work if she wishes to eat. The services I offer are . . . unique."

"Ah." He fished out a piece of ice, popping it into his mouth. Suddenly he didn't want anything else to drink. His attention was focused on the woman sitting so enticingly close. Every dirty thought he'd entertained about her came back to mind. "And may I ask what your services are?" Not caring he was ogling, he let his eyes linger on her face before sliding his gaze down her slender neck to the pert breasts hovering over her slender waist. The hem of her dress had come up, exposing a fair amount of her skin. Another inch and he'd be able to see the silky panties covering the gates of heaven. The color of those panties and the hint of what lay beneath was almost more than he could take. She was a piece of work, oozing sex appeal from every pore. Were he to sculpt the perfect woman, she would've met all the requirements.

Amusement waltzed in her gaze. She tilted back her head, freeing a laugh. "No. You may not. I'm not here to talk about my work."

"Then why are you here, if I may ask again?"

Her head came down, pinning him under a laser-beam stare. "I came because I could feel you were thinking about me." She arched an eyebrow toward the scarf he still held. "And you have something belonging to me."

The fine hairs on the back of Brenden's neck rose. Given her mysterious accent and air of perceptive mystery, he was almost inclined to take the words as the gospel truth.

Seeing the look on his face, she drew back with a light, teasing laugh. "I've been watching you," she confessed, taking another sip of her wine.

His brows shot up in surprise. Internal Affairs? He wondered what he might have done to land himself under the eye of heavy heat. Of all the departments on the force, Vice was the one where the dirtiest cops on the take usually operated. Their immersion in the seedier side of drugs, gambling, and prostitution offered plenty of chances to skim off thousands in return for developing a case of hear no evil, see no evil.

He wasn't on the take. Never had been. His partner wasn't so judicious, however. He hoped she didn't want him to rat out Montgomery Blake. "You were following me? Why?"

His concerns were soon dispelled. She leaned closer, propping her elbows on the bar and giving him a fresh whiff of her perfume straight from the source. Her stare narrowed subtly. She reached out, stroking the soft skin under his left eye. "Your eyes fascinate me. There's something deep inside them, waiting to come out, a passion you haven't set free because it scares you." Both of his irises had streaks of amber through their lower half, as though someone had taken an eraser and begun to rub out the green tint and replace it with another. People, especially guilty ones, were frequently unsettled by his odd eyes, something he used to good effect when employing his best crazy-cop stare.

Her words sent a shiver of awareness straight into his cock. Strange how discerning she was of his character. She seemed to see the pieces he kept carefully tucked away from all others. "A passion I haven't let out yet?" It was true she affected him on more than a physical plane and his attraction was starting to get dangerous. The sensual combination of her skin and her exotic scent reminded him of temptation and the trouble he could land himself in by mixing things up with a working girl. But if his tingling nerves and rising anticipation were any indication, he wasn't going to be able to resist her much longer. "You see that in my eyes?" He shook his head. "That's a lot, considering you don't even know my name."

"Nor do you know mine," she countered.

Of course. Too busy playing bondage games in his mind, Brenden hadn't even bothered to ask. Obviously the trained investigator at work. Right . . . There was silence, then he offered, "Wallace. Brenden Wallace." No reason to lie. His cover was blown.

"My name is Líadán." Again, the parting of the lips in a smile that would melt steel. She gave no last name. Slick.

The determination to resist reared its head, backed by the return of his sanity. Thinking with his cock had already gotten Brenden into hot water with his partner. He didn't need any more trouble if he wanted to salvage his job.

He tossed off another shrug. "Whatever you think you feel, lady, it isn't there."

Líadán placed her hand on his arm, the heat of her touch seeming to burn through his shirt. Her fingernails were long, painted in a shade matching her dress.

Opposition melted like wax under the flame. Brenden could imagine those nails raking down his back as he took her, creating the most exquisite pain. He thought about the scarf. No, he'd lasso those claws above her head, give her a little taste of what it felt like to be controlled.

"You're wrong." She paused a beat and then rushed on. "I feel there is something between us, drawing us together." She moved her hand up. Her fingertips brushed up the back of his hand, his fingers. She traced the ring on his third finger. "But I see you are already taken. My loss." The last two words came out as if the heartache she felt would slay her.

Brenden glanced down. The plain band almost seemed to be a part of his finger. He hadn't taken it off since the day he and Jenna exchanged their vows. He wished he hadn't worn his wedding ring, though at the time he'd believed it would give the impression he was a man looking for a little action away from home. His marriage was over, but suddenly he didn't want to convey the image he was a cheat. Why this small detail should bother him now wasn't so clear, but it definitely centered around this very alluring female.

Brenden slid off his ring, setting it on the dwindling pile of change. He'd figure out what he wanted to do with it later. Right now he didn't want to think about it. His finger felt naked, as though a piece of his soul had been stripped away with its removal. It didn't belong on his hand anymore.

"I'm not married. It was just for work."

Líadán laughed and gave a slight shake of her head. "It sounds crazy, I know. I am a woman who has known many men, yet I feel there is something about you I must explore." She pinned him down under an intense, probing gaze, blue eyes shimmering with something akin to what he perceived to be hope—and a sexual signal he couldn't possibly mistake. "I sound like a fool, don't I?"

The tremor of excitement her words ushered in was hard to suppress. She was making it clear she desired him.

There was no doubt Líadán could fulfill his every fantasy. Her presence alone sent his sexual awareness soaring. His emotions warred inside. He was a cop and cops didn't commingle with suspected prostitutes. Innocent until proven guilty. He tossed the argument against her out of his mind. He wanted her so badly he didn't care that the lines between their opposite professions were dangerously threatening to vanish.

Brenden licked his lips again, her gaze following the movement of his tongue. She wasn't cutting him any slack, not giving him any reasons to refuse her. "No. You don't sound like a fool." He barely recognized his voice as his own.

She nodded. "Good." She snapped open her clutch, pulling out a key card. "I have taken the liberty of reserving a room for myself." She slid her scarf from his fingers, making sure he felt every inch slip through his grasp. Her lips curved up at one corner and her voice lowered to a seductive huskiness. "Would you care to join me there?" She threw out the words as a challenge, waiting to see if he would back away.

Brenden felt his heart hammer his chest. This was a woman with the capability of getting inside his very soul. But to give her that chance? The risk could taint his career. Pursuing his attraction after hours, getting to know her for his own reasons—the idea was crazy. But Líadán fascinated him in a way no other woman ever had. He wanted—no, needed—to know why.

3

Líadán touched Brenden's mouth with one finger. A spark traveled between them. "Don't say anything. Come with me."

That settled it.

Brenden nodded. He wasn't sure how she knew his decision had been made, but the rush of excitement flooding his senses told him there would be no turning away, no backing off and disappearing out the door and to the safety of home. A tremor rippled through him as he realized the implications—and then ignored them.

Abandoning his change to the bartender, Brenden followed Líadán to the room she'd rented. Whether by jest or by chance, her suite was across the hall from the one the police occupied earlier.

After they stepped inside, Líadán closed the door, locked it, then turned to face him. She'd obviously been present earlier. The lights were turned low. A second scarf matching the one she carried draped across the edge of the bed. She knew what she wanted. And she knew he wanted it, too.

Just looking at her caused a fluttering sensation in his groin.

A delicious warmth spread down his penis. In his fantasy, he'd imagined himself being in control of the situation. The last thing he felt, though, was like a man in control of his own sexual gratification. He felt like a fumbling fifteen-year-old, sneaking off for the first time with his girlfriend to have illicit sex.

"I don't do this often." Nervousness twisted his guts but didn't manage to quell his desire entirely.

A smile tugged at her lips. She started to say something, hesitated, then changed her mind. He raised an eyebrow. Her gaze locked with his. Her eyes lingered on him with what felt like a heated caress, yet she hadn't lifted a hand, hadn't touched him since they had entered the room. "Neither do I. I have never . . . pursued . . . a client on a personal level."

"Why me?" She was so close. Tense. Hot. And seductive.

"I don't know . . ." Líadán stepped nearer, her body inches from his. Her steady gaze never veered from his when she reached up, cupping his face to draw it closer to hers. She joined her lips to his, tasting him, drinking him in, as if needing to take all she could as fast as she could.

Brenden's arms circled her slender waist, drawing her closer. She tasted of tart red wine and cinnamon gloss, a heady and delicious combination uniquely her own. Her breasts crushed against him as their bodies collided, the hard peaks of her nipples grazing his chest. His penis came instantly to life, arching and straining within the confines of his jeans, pulsing with a need yet to be fulfilled. His hands moved under her rear, bracing her body and lifting her up onto the tips of her toes, letting her feel every inch. He moved his hips against hers. She responded to the hardness of his blooming erection. Judging by her flushed face and uneven breathing, she wanted him, too.

The intense, forceful passion of their next kiss sent a wave of electricity humming through his body. He'd never known something as simple as a kiss could be so bluntly intimate. The feel of her tongue lashing hungrily in his mouth was so sensually hot his limbs began to quiver, his senses to quicken. The intensity of her body's heat fused to his length, settling into the center of his soul in a personal and intimate way. Her bold, aggressive moves were staggering, rendering him aware of nothing but sheer sensation.

Between the bust gone bad and the sexual tension throbbing inside, Brenden was wound tighter than a cheap watch. "I want you."

Líadán closed her eyes and leaned into the hard plane of his chest, her fingers digging into his shoulders as a soft moan escaped her lips. "Tell me what you need."

The glimmer of unfinished business came to mind. Brenden wondered what it would feel like when they were naked, flesh to flesh, bodies pressed together in glorious joining. But there was something else they'd started, a bit of unfinished business between them.

"The chair. Finish what you started. Only this time take it all the way." Hearing the words spoken, his body heated up all over again. He couldn't believe he was requesting she tie him up and have her way with him. The idea of putting his pleasure into the hands of this woman wasn't so farfetched. Men usually had to do all the work—the seduction, the sex act, the aftermath. To relax and hand the reins over to a lover was intriguing.

A whisper of a smile touched her lips as Líadán pulled away from his embrace. Crossing to the desk, she retrieved the chair. Placing it exactly as she wished, she extended her hands in invitation. The tremble in her arms and her ragged breathing offered a sense of comfort. She was just as nervous as he was.

Brenden sat—waiting, imagining, more than a little bit eager. In a change of routine, she settled the scarf across his eyes. All light was completely blocked out. Blind, he would have to rely on other senses.

Brenden couldn't see her, but he could hear her as she walked around. The sound of sharp heels sinking into the plush carpet made a sensual rubbing sound, one heightening his urgency to red-hot levels. He could picture her claiming the second scarf. A moment later, he felt it wrap around his wrists, this time binding his hands tightly behind his back. He reminded himself to breathe, savor the sensations.

He heard Líadán move. She parted his legs and knelt down between his spread knees. His shirt was again unbuttoned. Her hands explored his bare chest, hot against his already burning skin. She played with his body as if she were a connoisseur of the male physique, flicking her tongue here, tracing her fingertips there. His muscles jerked under her hands.

"Does that feel good, my sweet?" Amusement played a lazy note in her rich accent. Her strong hands worked his inner thighs, finding every knotted muscle, untying the tension, making him groan with pleasure.

Brenden wiggled, shifting his body into a more comfortable position. Every breath he took was reinforcing his emotional and physical awareness of her. "Excellent," he gasped, brain fogging deliciously.

Líadán methodically worked her way higher. Her hands moved up, expertly undoing his belt and the top button of his jeans. He heard the crunch of the zipper when she lowered it. Her warm fingers wrapped around his swelling erection. "I regard oral sex as the highest form of expressing love between two people."

Oh, Jesus. This is every man's fucking dream, a woman who likes sucking dick. I've died and gone to heaven . . .

With his erect penis pointing toward the ceiling, Líadán cupped his balls in one hand and gently, using only her tongue, licked softly along the entire underside of his erect organ. Brenden felt her fingers massage his sack, playing with him, tugging. She placed his stiff cock inside her mouth, but didn't tighten her lips around the shaft. Her head began a circling motion. His penis slid to different places in her mouth as she moved clockwise and then counterclockwise in a slow, purposeful manner.

Brenden damn near climaxed. As she touched him, his body trembled, vibrating almost to the sensitivity of her touch. He loved the sensation of her soft, warm mouth against his hardness. Gritting his teeth, he fought to hold back from orgasm as her skilled mouth worked. Yes, she was definitely a whore—a very talented whore.

Líadán found the underside of his balls, licking in an upward motion to the very top of his crown. Reaching the tip, she took him into her mouth, sliding her moistened tongue lovingly over the head until her lips closed around his shaft at the point just behind the corona. She encased his shaft with her hand. In an odd move, she twisted her head from side to side, her moist lips staying in contact with the coronal ridge. As she did this, she gently moved her hand in an up-and-down stroking motion.

Body trembling, drenched in sweat, Brenden fought against the pressure building deep in his loins. His cock pulsed; he could feel an intense tightening, warning him explosion was near. "I don't know how much longer I can hold off, honey."

Líadán laughed and drew back. Her fingers teased back up his body, touching and kissing him all over as she slowly removed the blindfold and let it fall to the floor.

Brenden tried to clear his mind, think logically and calmly, but he was too dazed with desire. Heart beating fast in his chest, his need for her was driving pure adrenaline straight through his bloodstream, sending his system into lascivious overdrive. He strained against the scarf binding his wrists, wishing he possessed the sheer brute strength to tear it in half. Once free, he would throw her to the floor and fuck her until she cried out his name.

Carnal cravings burned fiercely inside him. She'd given him

a taste and he wanted more. "Untie me! I don't think I can take much more." Suddenly the room felt closed, claustrophobic. Air was in short supply.

"Not yet, my sweet."

Líadán lifted one high-heeled foot, planting it firmly between his spread legs, the tip of her pump just inches from his straining hard-on. Balancing on one leg, she slowly lifted the hem of her short dress up over her hips. She had gorgeous, long legs, and her thighs were shapely and firm. She pulled the dress up around her hips until she uncovered her white panties. *Something in her movement was so sensuous*—and so very dangerous. He found himself struck anew by the power flickering around her like an aura.

Brenden stared at her panties, feeling his penis twitch like a hooked fish. He could see the outline of her most sensitive petals. By the wetness spreading across the material, she was clearly aroused by her power over him. He wished to God he could rip those panties off her and slide his tongue between her legs.

"You're so beautiful," he choked out, not caring if it sounded inane. At this point, if she had put a gun in his hand and asked him to rob a bank, he would have.

"You think so?"

"Yesss . . . Oh, honey . . . yes . . ." Brenden savored the delicacy of her bone structure, the high arch of her cheekbones, her long, slender neck, and the pulse fluttering at the base of her throat. Most of all, he savored the shocking, electric light in her blue eyes when she looked directly at him.

As if reading his mind, she hooked her finger in the crotch and pulled the thin material to one side. "You would like to be doing this," she whispered in a breathy voice. "Stroking my clit, seeing how wet you could make me."

Brenden caught his breath at the sight of her mound, shaved

and slick as a whistle. He fought to swallow the lump forming in the back of his throat. Unable to speak, he nodded, unwilling to take his eyes off her.

"You would like your cock inside me," she continued in a sultry tone. "Thrusting inside me, building toward the heat of climax."

Very lightly, she ran her fingers over her nether lips. She used her thumb and forefinger to spread herself open, her other hand moving so her index finger lightly stroked her little hooded clit. Sliding her fingers up and down, she began to caress herself, moistening her fingers with her own creamy juices and sliding them inside her depths. Eyes closed, lips slightly parted, hips rocking back and forth, she tilted her head back and moaned as she gave herself to her orgasm.

Brenden let out an agonized breath, feeling as though he'd gone over the edge with her. "Let me taste you."

Answering his plea, Líadán traced his lips with her sticky juices. Then, leaning over him, she cupped his face in her hands and kissed his lips softly. He accepted her kiss the way a man lost in the desert would welcome rescue. He inhaled her sweet fragrance as she pressed her lips harder against his. Her tongue thrust aggressively into his mouth and he felt a sensual stab of pleasure in his belly, as if she'd entered him more intimately.

A groan shuddered through him when he wrenched his mouth from hers. "Please . . . I can't wait much longer." Hands balling into fists, he started to shake. His whole body was aching with the need for release. He ground into the chair, trying to push his hips forward, growling with frustration. His skin felt luminous, glowing, and vibrant. With each beat of his heart, his passion grew heated—verging on the point of desperation. The need to slake his unbearable desire threatened to consume his senses.

With a teasing laugh, Líadán lifted her dress over her head, letting it drift to the floor. She gave Brenden a long, sly look, enjoying her power over him. She wore no bra. Her breasts were perfectly shaped to fill a man's hands. Her nipples protruded, topping her smooth mounds like cherries on a luscious sundae. She squeezed them, rolling them, tugging gently before sliding her palms over her flat belly to the flare of her hips. A thin gold hoop pierced her navel. Slightly to the left, a brand had been burned into the soft curve above her Venus mound. The symbol—a pentagram turned upside down and surrounded by strange lettering—was chilling but also highly erotic. Hooking her thumbs in her panties, Líadán smiled and teasingly lowered them over her firm ass.

Naked except for her red heels and a devastating smile, Líadán turned back to him, her pale, naked skin assuming a strange, glowing radiance. He wanted to touch it, flatten his palms along the curving planes of her breasts, her hips, her ass, touch his lips to hers, feel her body tense, then tighten. Those strange teeth of hers seemed sharper. . . . Longer. She didn't seem human, a creature of flesh. She seemed to be so much more . . . animalistic. If she'd had a tail, it would have flicked.

Straddling his lap, Líadán guided one nipple into his mouth. Brenden suckled greedily, his tongue rasping against the hard nubbin. He listened to her moans and felt her body rubbing against his. She wiggled and let out a little scream of surprise when he nipped at her soft flesh. She laughed, guiding his mouth to the nipple he had yet to taste.

Líadán whispered in his ear. "I promised you exquisite pleasure. I will take you to a place you have never known before, a place you will long to return to again and again."

Shifting slightly, she moved one of her hands between their bodies. He could feel her fingers encircle his hardness, hold him steady as she guided her hips down onto his penis. Her warm juices soaked his skin as her inner muscles clenched tightly around his surging erection. Her depth was molten—hot, fiery, inescapably drawing him in like quicksand.

They moaned together.

In an unhurried rhythm, Líadán lifted her hips until his erection was almost completely out, then came back down, taking him deeper with every stroke. She felt like silken bands around his cock, tight and unrelenting. Brenden gave a deep shudder, the smell of her skin lighting fires in his heart. He didn't like to get too emotional about anything, but something about this woman had caused him to throw all sense to the wind, something driving him with an urgency he couldn't understand, yet also couldn't deny.

Brenden moaned. His nerves were on edge, peaking toward the ultimate sensitivity. "I wanted you from the moment I saw you."

Their gazes locked, Brenden could see a strange fire in Líadán's eyes, the reddish-orange glow flickering behind them. "As I have wanted you."

Slowing her movements, Líadán settled for a final time onto his shaft. Tangling her fingers in his hair, she wrenched his head to one side. She lovingly nuzzled the hollow between his head and shoulders, her warm tongue tracing a moist trail along his jugular. Burying her face in his neck, she whispered something in a language he could not understand. And then, as if she could not control a beast raging inside her soul, her strange, sharp canines tore through his flesh, her amorous bite unmerciful in its penetration.

Brenden gasped, almost whimpered, shocked by the searing pain. Ricocheting through his senses, it seemed to brand itself on the walls of his skull. The prickle of some kind of primitive fear ran up his spine. He was paralyzed, body and mind. His body quivered brutally and he felt the warmth of his blood trickle over his unexpectedly frigid skin. The pain was strangely exquisite, almost as welcome as the pleasure he willingly gave himself to. She had taken him to the edge . . . and then over it.

Lost in the depths of her feeding off his blood, he gazed un-seeing into the floral patterned wallpaper across the room. He willingly let himself disappear into the all-consuming abyss of a demonic sexual deviation as Líadán drew not only the seed from his loins, but the very life from his veins.

4

Brenden arrived home at six-thirty in the morning. Squinting through a blurry haze, he struggled to put the key in the lock before turning the knob with a shaky hand and stumbling through the door. He wasn't sure how he'd gotten home, but he was relieved he'd made it from point A to point B in one piece without getting arrested.

The hours he'd spent in Líadán's arms were everything he'd ever dreamed sex with a woman could be and more: sensual, explosive, exciting. Every pull of his muscles reminded him of their strenuous lovemaking. After she'd freed him from his restraints, they'd moved to the bed, tearing up the sheets in a display worthy of a gold medal in sexual acrobatics. Thoroughly sated, they'd fallen asleep in each other's arms, curled together like two small animals seeking the heat of each other's bodies.

The sleep beginning in her arms was not to end that way. When Brenden woke up, Líadán's side of the bed was empty. She'd departed as she'd arrived, mysteriously and alone. He barely remembered dressing and stumbling into the sleepy dawn.

The house was silent, perfectly empty. After spending all

day in the grime and crime downtown, flying back to his own little roost was heaven. He lived in Villa Del Mar, a middle-class neighborhood populated with folks who liked to live quietly among manicured lawns and picturesque, tree-lined avenues.

Bear was barking in the back yard. The pitch of the dog's whine said he'd been left alone too long. Haze clearing from his head a bit, Brenden let the dog in. The big galoot almost knocked him down with eagerness. All wagging tail and licks, Bear was delighted to see his master.

Brenden laughed. "Get down, you big idiot." The dog was almost ridiculous with joy, body twisting in spasms fatal to objects the height of Bear's furiously pumping tail. Right now, Bear was the happiest creature on earth to see him. Once, there had been a wife waiting for him to come home. Only Bear waited now.

Reluctantly obeying, Bear watched with adoring eyes as Brenden filled a bowl with fresh water, filled his feeder with kibble, and offered a fresh rawhide chew. Bear ignored the chew and dived into his water, taking great slurps, sending droplets of water flying. Brenden felt guilty. Weeks had passed since they'd gone out on a run. He hated neglecting Bear. He promised himself he'd take more personal time. He had plenty in reserve and his two-week vacation was just around the corner.

Aside from Bear, the minutiae of everyday life escaped him. Unopened mail littered the counter, along with unread newspapers, and messages from friends he no longer bothered to call. Much different when he was half of a couple. Flying solo, it felt odd to hang out with his married buddies and their wives. He didn't want to see that look in their eyes, the one of pity. Avoidance was easier.

His cell phone was curiously silent. He checked his messages. Aside from a few work-related calls and a wrong number, the machine was distressingly absent of the one he found most important. He cursed under his breath. He was about to reach for the phone when he stopped his hand in mid-air. Dani hated it when he called checking up on her whereabouts. Even though she was crashing in his basement apartment, his sister was a grown woman. She had a right to her privacy.

Dani's need for privacy didn't stop Brenden from worrying. And it didn't mean he wouldn't be ready and waiting to jump on her ass. He was still her big brother. And she would always be the skinny little brat he teased unmercifully—knobby knees, braces, glasses, and all giggles.

Knowing he couldn't sleep until Dani came home, Brenden headed to the refrigerator. The pickings for something to drink were slim, milk, juice, or diet soda. He chose a soda.

Popping the top on the can, Brenden surveyed the cabinets. He was ravenous but didn't feel like cooking. He should have picked up a burger. Instead he fell back on the tried and true bachelor food, a frozen dinner.

Selecting one, he popped the meal into the microwave. In fifteen minutes, Salisbury steak in brown gravy, potatoes, and some kind of vegetable medley would be ready. Hardly the most nutritious thing to consume, but it would do. He made a note to himself to start eating better and get back to a more healthful lifestyle. He worked hard to keep in shape, hitting the gym when time allowed. Washboard abs didn't come from drinking too much booze and eating too much greasy junk food.

The microwave beeped. Brenden was prying the steamy cellophane off the plastic tray when Bear leapt to attention, barking at the back door. The dog heard what he hadn't. Danger discarded, Bear bounded to greet the newcomer, his excitement nearly knocking Dani down. Bear was big, weighing almost a hundred pounds to Dani's slight twenty pound advantage.

Brenden didn't turn. "You're home late." He glanced over his shoulder. "Where have you been?"

Danicia gently pushed the big dog away. "Down, Bear. Good boy." She flashed a guilty smile, looking much like a sixteen-year-old busted for sneaking around on a school night. "So? I wasn't aware I had a curfew."

Brenden dug a fork out of a drawer. "I thought you said you'd be home early."

Dani shrugged. "Didn't work out. I had things to do." She dropped her purse and gym bag on the floor before kicking off her tennis shoes. Bear snuffled the bag, making sure there was nothing strange lurking inside before padding back to his food dish.

Dani sat down at the kitchen table, rubbing her left foot. "God. I've got blisters an inch thick. Those damn heels are ruining my feet." She was dressed in a tracksuit, her pert face scrubbed clean of makeup, her hair pulled back in a loose ponytail. A teenager's braces had given way to straight white teeth and the thick glasses replaced with contacts. With a sprinkling of freckles across her upturned nose and long, naturally blonde hair, Danicia had grown up to be a knockout. The gym bag she toted carried her work clothes—not that there was much outfit to G-strings and pasties.

"You chose the work," Brenden sniped, in no mood to listen to her complain. "You could have left me a message." Without bothering to sit, he forked up a bite of meat, sniffed it, and declined to taste it. The soy-based patty swimming in a brown sauce of questionable matter was unappetizing. "You know—"

Rolling her eyes, Danicia held up a hand. "I know. So you wouldn't worry." Her gaze settled on the meal he'd rejected. "You going to eat?"

"Nope." Brenden set the tray on the floor. Bear attacked the chow, devouring it in huge gulps, veggies and all. Brenden took a sip of his soda. He hated diet drinks, but swallowed it anyway.

Seeing a way to weasel out from under the third degree, Dani picked up his hint. "Let me make breakfast since we're both hungry." Up and bouncing around the counter, she gave him a quick peck on one stubble-covered cheek. Catching a whiff of his cologne, she crinkled her nose. "You're dressed nicer than usual." She checked the collar of his white shirt. "And what's this? Lipstick?" Her eyes sparkled in delight. Her hands flew up, fingers wiggling in the air. "Looks like my love spell worked. My power's increasing, thank heaven. I was getting worried."

Anger evaporating, Brenden couldn't help rolling his eyes. "Oh, please. Love spell, my left foot."

Dani's lower lip came out in a pout. "Yes. A love spell. I got tired of watching you mope around, so I thought I'd give things a little jump start." She grinned smugly. "It worked quite nicely, I think." She edged his crimson-stained collar lower. "Damn . . ." She whistled. "Super-sized hickey you got there, bro. Did she mistake you for a sandwich?" She flashed a lascivious grin hinting of knowledge little sisters should not have.

Brenden made a disgusted chuffing in the back of his throat. An image of the raw sensual pleasure he'd felt as Líadán's teeth sank into his skin flashed and a twinge in his loins reignited desire. He took a deep swallow of his soda in an attempt to cool himself off. "If you don't mind, I'd like to keep my sex life private. I very much doubt any—" His hands flashed up, fingers bending in mock quote marks. "—'love spells' you cast had anything to do with what happened tonight."

Dani shook her head, clucking her tongue in amused disapproval. "It's all very well you mock me, but at least respect me enough to take my beliefs seriously." Like her maternal grandmother Brigit, Dani practiced an unorthodox religion and fancied herself a witch—or *Bandruai*—of some power. Her whole life was centered on her search to find the truth in the "invisible" side of existence, as she called it.

Brenden personally felt her beliefs were a load of mumbo-jumbo bull cookies.

He shot her an annoyed look. Dani never failed to try to

work in mention of a spell's success if she could. A love spell? Sheesh.... None of it made a damn bit of sense.

"How can you take such shit seriously?" he countered, remembering the thousands of times they'd had this exact same conversation. "All those things Grandma Brigit told you were spun out of thin air, an old woman's stories to entertain children. Use your brain! The idea we're somehow descended from some damn cult of Irish druids doesn't make a bit of sense. Magic doesn't exist in this world. If it did everyone would be waving their wands and casting spells."

Certainly if Danicia were a witch of any influence, she'd magic away her debts and conjure herself a million dollars. Her argument was classic—a soul was iniquitous to gain mammon through paranormal channels. Uh-huh. Yeah.

Brenden's tongue always went deeply into his cheek when Dani explained her beliefs. She insisted blessings would come through magic if a heart were true and the intent of the conjurer pure. She made sure he understood she only practiced "white" magic, as opposed to the "black."

Frowning, Dani met his incredulous gaze with a cool, unwavering gaze speaking of her absolute belief. "You don't see what goes on under the fabric of everyday existence like I do, Bren. There's a battle going on for lives . . . and souls." She angled her head, sending her long ponytail whipping around. Sparks flew in her intelligent eyes. "Sides are being chosen and names are being taken. One of these days you will encounter evil. And when you see it, you will know it."

Brenden sighed, rubbing his hand against his aching forehead. His day had been too long and he was developing a tension headache. Sex and magic spells aside, the only thing on his mind was food, followed by sleep. He understood none of Dani's obsession but tolerated days when the air reeked of incense and she wafted about in white robes, purifying the house of "hindering spirits." As crazy as it seemed, he supposed there were worse things in this world than having a witch in the family.

"I see evil every day I go to work, honey. It isn't the work of some supernatural force. Evil sprouts in the hearts and souls of mankind. It's my job to sort through it as best I can. As for the rest of it, I say kill them all and let God sort them out."

There was a knot of tension in his shoulders. Brenden tilted his head, absently rubbing his neck. His hand brushed the bite. It felt sore, irritated, but nothing life-threatening. Líadán had just gotten a little overexcited. And he hadn't minded a bit. Little prickles of sweat broke out on his forehead when he remembered the shape of her beautiful lips, the way his penis had slid into her mouth. He took a deep breath, feeling his cock stir in his tight jeans, his blood heating up all over again.

Get a grip, he warned himself, thinking a dash of icy water would be useful. Brenden swept his hands through his hair, trying to pull his mind out of his crotch. Now was not the time to be thinking dirty thoughts.

He rummaged around in his brain cavity for the crux of their original conversation. Ah, there it was, hiding between his irritation with the present conversation and the dirty thoughts he couldn't put away. He was jumping her out.

Back on track, he said, "Which is why I always get pissed off when I don't know where you're at." He lifted his hand in the motion of putting a phone to his ear. "Very simple solution, Dani. Call me."

Realizing Brenden was going to pull his bait and switch tactic to change the conversation, Dani let him have his way. She made a silencing motion with her hands. "Okay, Bren. Enough ass-chewing for one night." Her eyes settled on his abandoned meal. "You want breakfast or not? I'm half tempted to let you starve."

He groaned. "Just cook, please. I need food."

Dani punched his arm. "Jerk!" She gave him a playful push

toward the table, clearing the space he occupied. "Sit down, you big ape. I'll handle the chow and you can tell me all the dirty details." Taking down a frying pan, she fished eggs, sausage, butter, and milk out of the refrigerator, then a loaf of whole-grain bread from the cabinet, preparing to throw together something edible.

Brenden claimed the chair she'd vacated. "If you don't mind, I'd like to keep details to myself." He leaned forward on the table, propping his elbow in its surface. "You're too young and tender to know these things, sis."

"Young and tender, my ass!" Dani shot back, digging through the drawers for a whisk. She cracked half a dozen eggs, whipping them into frothy yellow foam.

Speaking of tender asses . . .

Despite earlier orders, Brenden's cock tingled. The feel of Líadán's lips laving the tip, her tongue rolling around and exploring the swollen crown, the sharp edges of her teeth brushing his most sensitive skin was enough to send his internal temperature soaring toward complete meltdown. His balls drew up tight, as if close to release.

Brenden laid his head on the table, hiding his face and releasing a silent groan through clenched teeth. Damn. Now that he'd experienced a walk on the wild side, he was hooked like a junkie craving crack. He'd never known it would feel so damn good, so explosive, to explore a secret fantasy. Repressing his deepest needs had made him a miserable man. A mistake. There was now no denying or ignoring his excitement and desires.

Breath catching in his throat, heartbeat echoing in his chest, Brenden already knew one thing was for sure.

He wanted another night with Líadán.

———————

5

Auguste Maximilian sat in a blue velvet chair, dressed in the last of the night's fading shadows. Stretched out with one foot resting on a matching footstool, he had a glass of wine in one hand and held a cigarette in the other. The rich scent of foreign tobacco mixed with just a hint of heady spices hazed the atmosphere around him. Lingering in a halo around his head, the opalescent smoke gave his frosty features an unreal, almost illusive quality.

Auguste Maximilian, sovereign of the vampyr legion.

Seeing him, fear knotted in the back of Líadán's throat, threatening to steal away her breath. She could feel his gaze raking over her, examining her from head to toe. Auguste had been waiting for her return, waiting the way a predator waited for prey, patiently and with much anticipation. His penetrating gaze under half-lidded eyes smoldered with barely concealed ire. She was hours late, lingering when she should have hurried. She hated returning to the old abbey feeling the desecration every time she set foot inside its stone walls.

Líadán had danced. Now she would pay the piper.

Saying nothing, Líadán put aside her clutch and wrap, then simply stared at him, waiting. She felt as though her heart were squeezing inward, threatening to suffocate her. No matter how well one had been trained to submit, there was always the specter of dread behind the striking hand delivering the discipline. She should bolt, run until she found a small, dark corner to hide in. The impulse died soon after its birthing. Of course, she could not run away. She had no other place to go. Auguste was the master who owned her, body and soul.

Auguste leaned back in his chair. His eyes had mocking glints in their depth as he studied her carefully. His face bore the imprint of cruelty, something hard and vicious lurking behind his wolf-like demeanor. A rough soldier of aristocratic stock and manner, he was a brutal and dangerous man, not only in looks, but in temperament. Taking a deep drag off his cigarette, he caught it between thumb and forefinger. "You are late, Líadán." His accented voice held a trace of annoyance.

Líadán bit her bottom lip, turning her head briefly away. No. Auguste would sense something was wrong. She called on a reserve of icy calm, absolute control, to shield her fear. Armored in pride, she refused to surrender it.

Bringing her chin up, she leveled an unflinching gaze at him. "I had to feed." A simple, direct statement. Also, the truth. Long ago, she'd accepted the forces the occult had levered into her life. That didn't mean she welcomed them.

As she spoke, Auguste studied her face. The slight curve of his mouth at one corner mocked. *I hate him.* Tense, she waited for his reaction.

Auguste's smile, so sinister and not entertaining a single ounce of mirth, chilled her heart. He nodded, as if turning over each word of her answer to examine it for truth or lies. "I am glad you have consented to take human blood again. The blood of animals is beneath us. Humans are our rightful prey." His tone was a purr of silk across stone, low and hinting of menaces spoken and unspeakable. His tongue snaked out, stroking one of the razor-sharp canines in his mouth, much longer than hers, more prominent.

Líadán indulged him with a taut smile. "I wish only to please you, lord." She offered a short, respectful nod of her head, as befitting a man of his rank and breeding. The frozen expression on his face made her cringe. She had aroused his ire. Her stomach felt as though a thousand tiny snakes were coiled within, wriggling and biting.

Minutes passed, each excruciatingly longer than the last. Auguste was taking his time, toying with her the way a cat played a mouse to exhaustion before coming in for the fatal strike. He enjoyed giving pleasure almost as much as he enjoyed inflicting pain. She dipped back her head and stared out the window past his shoulder, wishing she were someplace far away.

After what seemed an eternity, Auguste finished his cigarette, then drained the last of his wine. He rose from his chair, his movements ophidian and effortless as he crossed his sitting room, the strength of a cunning stalker entwined as one within his being. His boots didn't make a sound when he crossed over the expensive rugs covering the floor. Dressed impeccably in a creamy shirt under a white silk vest, he wore perfectly tailored white slacks and low-heeled boots. His penetrating stare under thick brows was intimate. He didn't conceal the fact he examined her closely, a slight smile and devious expression dancing in the depths of his gaze.

Stalking closer with feral grace, Auguste was the malevolence slumbering dormant in saner souls, the part of existence mankind wanted to deny—and feared. A hunter, a predator who harvested from the lost and devoured the proud, he would not be tamed.

Carrying himself stiffly erect, Auguste expected—demanded—absolute respect and utter compliance from those around him.

Like an untamed animal, muscles sinuous under his immaculate clothing, he made her shiver. His body was hard and brawny under his expensive tailored clothes—broad shoulders, narrow hips, and muscular legs. The ages and much exertion to bridge them had honed his figure to a sharp and strong degree. If he had been the first man created, the gods would have been well pleased with their efforts.

Líadán licked her lips, drawing in a quick breath, her cheeks growing warm under his critical visual sweep. Auguste was breathtakingly handsome from the rust-shaded hair spilling in a tangle around his face to his honey-dappled eyes guarding the answers to all the mysteries of the ages. His sideburns grew down his sharp jawline, assimilating into the thin, elegantly trimmed goatee ringing his mouth, part of the look enhancing his Old World manner and bearing. The long white scar angled at the corner of his left eye did nothing to detract from his looks, serving only to enhance the aura of danger enveloping him.

More than immortal, Auguste seemed everlasting—eternal. He'd bartered away his soul and in return had received the gift of the first jouyl to infect the earth. His eyes belied his heavenly beauty. A cold soulless creature lurked within the depths of his gaze, a feral beast of searing insanity he often unleashed to hunt and kill at will.

Were she any other woman, Líadán would have welcomed his attention, allowed herself to become easily mesmerized by his grace and charm. She, however, knew the fiend inside him well, had trembled under its wrath more than once.

Líadán concentrated on standing very still. Unfailingly, he would somehow strike her down, be it mentally, emotionally, or physically.

Auguste reached out, catching her hand in his. "Come to me, beloved. You have been away so long tonight." His grip was iron, close to crushing her fingers.

Líadán was always unprepared for his touch. The effort to endure brought a wave of nausea as he pulled her into his arms. She fought the urge to pull her hand away, willing herself not to flinch. In her misery she barely noticed the icy pallor of his flesh. Head sinking back, she couldn't help but look into his striking and cynically remote face.

Auguste studied through narrow eyes, his too-perceptive gaze piercing through her like the tip of a blade. "I smell another man on your skin." He dipped close, inhaling her scent. His hand came up to caress her nape. "You enjoyed him, I hope."

Fighting the urge to wipe her mouth as though her lips harbored a guilty stain, Líadán resisted turning her head. "Yes, lord . . . I fed well tonight." Her admission was true. She had more than enjoyed Brenden Wallace. She'd savored him like a fine vintage and found him very pleasing.

Auguste eased her forward until their lips were only inches apart. "Let me taste his blood on your lips, my sweet." With a desperate, angry sound, his mouth claimed hers.

Líadán's lips parted under the searching invasion of his tongue. She tasted rich tobacco and sweet red wine. His hands claimed her waist, pulling her to his hard, forbidding frame. Her body arched reflexively as one of his hands sought and fastened over her breast. His thumb slowly brushed back and forth across her nipple. A tiny shiver tingled down the length her spine.

She bit back on an escaping moan, drawing in a sharp breath as unwelcome erotic delight blazed straight down to her belly and beyond. She could feel the ache between her legs intensify; could feel herself grow wetter as her very being pulsed with tense, moist hunger. She strained against the growing sexual craving that warred with her abhorrence of his dominance. Confusion dashed down the paths between her head and her heart. Auguste was touching her with hands familiar with her body, and she had no defense against him. She knew this was a calculated act of persuasion and she loathed him for doing it. Her weakness to resist him was as much of a bond as if he had her tied down. Why, oh why, could Auguste so easily master her body when she despised his touch? Had centuries of abuse gone so bone-deep she couldn't even control her own body's responses?

Auguste's mouth left hers, traveling lower before he nipped with none-too-gentle teeth at the soft flesh of her neck. When she pulled back, he wrapped his massive hand in her hair. His tongue stabbed deep, the force of his kiss becoming painful to the point Líadán feared she would lose breath. He seemed to want to possess her, the touch of their mouths hardly enough to sustain him.

Auguste abruptly pulled back, a strange shadow crossing his face. "I can taste his passion, his hungers. You chose well, beloved." He grasped her earlobe between his teeth and tugged. The sting traveled straight into her nether region, but the empty, longing sensation remained.

Líadán's breath lodged in her throat as disgust battled the need to remain compliant. Her stomach coiled into a tight knot. Auguste could twist her around his finger as he wished and she could offer no protest. Not while his brand was burned into her flesh and the golden sigil looped into her navel remained in place, the bonds shackling her to serve his command.

Auguste drew back. His honey-shaded eyes were smoldering with a fervor barely fettered, his barely restrained lust almost an odor in the air. Shifting gears into a rougher frame of mind, he began to tease her, touching and tracing her cheeks, jawline and neck with his lips. His mouth settled on the warm pulse beneath her skin. He nipped at her jugular, sending a chill scurrying down her spine.

Líadán stiffened. Auguste could easily rip out her throat, tearing her apart with deadly incisors he could extend or retract at will.

"Tell me of your new lover." His expression twisted—the sadist relishing the deliverance of pain. "Did he take pleasure in the penetration of your bite into his flesh?" Another nip, harder, more insistent as his voice dropped to a sensual hiss. "Or did he whimper in pain?"

Líadán's conscience flinched, as if lashed with a strap. She took a quick breath for calm. "He welcomed the pain, giving himself to the sensations."

A rusty brow shot up in interest. "It pleases me you enjoyed him."

Looking up, Líadán's gaze collided with his. Auguste was probing, searching . . . seeking the truth. Her first instinct was to shy away, as though he could see past her eyes, read every thought in her mind. "I did, my lord. Very much."

Chilling calculation frosted Auguste's gaze. "It pleases me you hunted tonight." His soft voice sent an icy shiver down her spine. A sharp fingernail traced a path from the soft hollow in her throat, trailing higher until the tip reached her cheek. He tapped the side of her face. "Do not try to starve yourself again."

Líadán shifted uncomfortably. He was too tightly wound.

Without warning Auguste grabbed her face, digging strong fingers under her jaw. He lifted, levering her higher with effortless ease until the tips of her toes barely touched the floor.

Líadán stiffened in shock. In a moment of raw, black terror, her hands flew up, fingers scrabbling to get a hold on his hand in a futile attempt to relieve the agony and gain release from the intense pressure threatening to tumble her into a void. Fear smothered her thoughts. "Please . . ." She tried to speak, but the word came out only as a weak, incomprehensible gurgle. Her whole body shook with her attempts to free herself. She couldn't get loose.

"You grovel like the peasant you are." Amused by her struggle, Auguste's grip tightened, giving not a fraction. His cold eyes flared with amusement. His parted lips showed those deadly razorlike canines.

Realizing the harder she fought, the tighter he would hold, Líadán let her hands fall at her sides, dangling like useless stumps. There was absolutely no doubt Auguste could kill her right where she stood. If he so chose he could tear out her throat and toss her dead body aside like a rag doll. Frustrated by her inability to fight back, she closed her eyes.

Auguste's grip tightened, spreading an intense red-hot wave of agony through Líadán's body. Time reeled, sliding away in the horror and panic filling her. Her mind, her nerves, all her senses were screaming in desperate revolt for relief.

She heard a gurgle fall from her slack lips. Vicious pressure built inside her skull and the top of her head felt tight, almost as if her brains were about to overflow and leak out her ears. Molten blasts of light began to stab at her eyes, each brighter than the last, threatening to blind her with the intensity. She couldn't move. She couldn't breathe. Slowly all feeling was beginning to drain out of her body. . . .

6

The headache struck out of nowhere, a spike of pure lightning ushering in a blazing crimson flash. Heaving himself up, Brenden's hand flew to his forehead when another burst of skull-cracking pain exploded behind his eyes, the second barrage of scarlet-tipped bolts penetrating even deeper than the first.

Vision fading to darkness, his formerly pleasant thoughts disintegrated like sparklers burning out. "Damn." Where did that come from? A minute ago he'd been fine, not feeling like someone had used his head for a soccer ball.

"Is something wrong, Bren?" Dani's voice sliced through his distress, her words tinged with worry.

Regaining control of his senses, Brenden pressed the tips of his fingers to his temple, trying to will away the ache settling behind his eyes. Molten fire poured through every crevasse, attacking and burning out the cells in his brain. He shrugged, trying to act nonchalant. "Just a little headache. Food will fix me right up. I haven't eaten all day."

Dani frowned, clucking like a mother hen. "No food? Gee, Brenden, no wonder you feel sick. You need to take better care of yourself." She reached into the kitchen cabinet over the sink, taking down a bottle of Tylenol and delivering three tablets with a glass of water. "Take this. Breakfast is almost done."

Brenden swallowed the pills. "Thanks."

Dani went back to her cooking. "So when are you going to see your new lady again?"

Another shrug. "I don't know." Brenden didn't want to admit he'd spent the night with a suspected prostitute. Acting on an attraction, they'd had sex, then gone their separate ways. For all he knew, this was their one and only night together.

"Soon?" Dani prodded hopefully.

Brenden drew in another deep breath, then released it. "We'll see." He gave his stomach a rub. "Meanwhile can you rush the chow? I'm famished."

She saluted with her whisk. "Will do."

Sipping his cola, Brenden sat, watching her. She was graceful, moving with the assurance of a long-legged gazelle. Danicia worked as an exotic dancer at a nightclub called Faster Pussycats. As Brenden saw it, there was nothing *exotic* in being a stripper. He disapproved of her career choice. Dani just listened and laughed. She was dancing to pay off her credit card debts, but had recently begun talking of traveling to Europe to trace the family's roots and continue her studies with more advanced members of her craft.

Brenden was doing all he could to discourage Danicia's wanderlust. He didn't like the idea of her tramping around in a foreign country with a bunch of loonies who fancied themselves mystics. Cults could be a dangerous thing to those too willing to believe the spiel. Dani was young, still searching for her place in life. As he saw it, her future looked bright as a shiny new penny—if only she'd get out of the clubs, and if only she'd abandon her crazy idea she was a witch. She didn't understand both were strikes against her future.

Brenden toyed with his can. At least his headache was fading a bit. The medicine seemed to be kicking in. "So where were you tonight?"

Dani glanced up. "I went out with the girls after work." Her face took on an elfin grin. "We all went over to Peggy's house." She waggled her eyebrows. "Did a little chanting, studied some spell work, had a few margaritas, and now I'm home safe." She grew serious again, a frown replacing her smile. "Do you have to know where I am twenty-four hours a day?"

Brenden set the empty soda can aside. "I can't help worrying, Dani," he said quietly. "All I need is a few words letting me know who you're with and where you're at."

Dani crossed her eyes and stuck out her tongue, a habit of childhood. "The cop in you, I suppose."

Any time Dani was in trouble, she played the clown. An effective plot, but not today. Brenden shook his head, all seriousness and brass tacks. "No. It's the brother in me. I worry. I know the line of work you're in isn't safe. I see girls getting beat up and raped all the time because some freak crosses the line."

His tone sobered her. "I know. Give me a bit more time to get things together, then I'll quit. I promise."

"I'll loan you the money."

She cut him off with a wave of her whisk. Egg goo splattered the counter. "Giving me a place to crash is enough. I'll get my finances straight. I just went a little crazy with the plastic." She shrugged. "What can I say? I love to shop."

"It's there if you need it," Brenden said, letting the conversation drop. No reason to push it. His own financial security was a blessing.

Setting the eggs aside, Dani sliced up some sausage patties and set the meat to sizzling. The aroma of frying pork elicited a rumble from his stomach. The food smelled wonderful. He was glad she'd offered to cook.

Danicia finished the meat without further comment, then

quickly scrambled up the eggs in the sausage grease before buttering the toast and slathering it with strawberry jam. She set the table for two: a glass of whole milk for him, orange juice for her. Loading down their plates with all the fixings, she set breakfast on the table before taking her own seat. Bear sat on the floor between, scoping out the table in case a tasty morsel came his way.

Since he was ravenous, the food was welcome. Brenden usually ate to keep his body nourished, but now he savored every nuance of the food. Being with Líadán had somehow awakened all his senses again. Everything tasted wonderful—eggs soft and fluffy, toast crunchy and sweet, sausage particularly tangy. He emptied his plate in a few minutes.

"Seconds?" he asked hopefully.

Dani took his plate, filling it with the rest of the scrambled eggs and sausage, adding two fresh pieces of hot toast. "It's been a long time since I've seen you eat like this, Bren. I like the change. Whoever you're seeing, keep seeing her. She's good for you."

Shoveling in a bite of sausage, he wiped his mouth. "I would like to see her again."

I hope I can came the silent follow up. He had only a phone number, a first name, and not much else. Catching sight of Bear's baleful eyes, he picked up a piece of sausage, holding it out. The dog gobbled it down. He tore off a piece of toast. Bear devoured it.

Danicia forked up buttery scrambled eggs. "You haven't done anything but work since Jenna left. That's not good, working all these double shifts."

Brenden fed Bear another bite, barely keeping the tips of his fingers intact. "I worked these shifts before she left. Jenna was always alone. Can I blame her for getting tired of waiting on me?"

"That's bullshit and you know it." Dani pointed her fork at

him. "Don't start guilt-tripping yourself. The least she could have done was faced you down. A letter on the table saying good-bye is the coward's way out. She couldn't even look you in the eyes. You know why? Because she was cheating, she was wrong, and she knew it."

Tucking one more bite of toast into his mouth, Brenden surrendered the rest of his plate to the dog. "Let's not talk about it anymore, okay? It's history." He rubbed his temples. The headache was building behind his eyes, a low throb warning that sleep would soon be imperative. Up since the morning before, the brief nap he'd snuck in with Líadán was wearing off.

Dani reached across the table, placing her hand on his arm. "I hope this woman is good for you. You need someone, Bren."

Brenden placed his hand on top of hers. Through this last year of turmoil, Danicia had been there, doing her best to shore up the walls he felt were crumbling around him. She'd helped him keep things together. "I think she will be. It doesn't feel like the light at the tunnel is the oncoming train anymore."

Dani laughed, tightening her grip. "If it is, get a ticket and ride it."

He nodded. "I plan to."

"I knew there was a woman out there just waiting for you to sweep her off her feet." She laughed, grinning. "Just needed a little of the old Dani magic to get things moving."

"Right . . . Dani magic . . . Well, give yourself a pat on the back, kiddo. It really worked." Shaking his head, Brenden sighed. Renewing its fight against the medicine, his headache was beginning to travel down his neck to the base of his spine. He needed to stretch out in a dark room, shut down the motor in his brain, and embrace oblivion for at least eight hours. "Think you can hold off from casting more spells until I've had a little sleep?"

Dani got up, gathering the dirty dishes. "Sure thing. Wouldn't want to overextend my powers all in one day." Placing the dishes in the sink, she ran hot water over the mess, preparing to clean up the kitchen.

Brenden rose, heading for bed and a few hours' rest. Bear got up, too, ready to go wherever his master went. The dog usually slept at the foot of his bed. "Thanks for breakfast."

Arms to elbows in suds, his sister glanced up. "I guess you forgot, but I didn't. Happy Birthday."

Brenden nodded, accepting her words. "Thirty-three now." Amazing how much his life had changed in the span of three hundred and sixty-five days. On his last birthday, he'd still been a married man, however unhappily. Fast-forward one year. He was now single, having sex in a hotel room with a strange woman who excited him more than getting his detective's shield and a promotion had. All of the sudden, his priorities had shifted from work to play. He wanted to play with Líadán. A lot.

Walking slowly up the stairs, Brenden rubbed a hand over his burning eyes, muttering. The day's exertions were all of a sudden crashing on top of him. Bear's ears perked up. "Not you boy," he soothed the big dog. "It's me."

Needing a shower, he headed into the bathroom. He reached out to flip on the light. As he stripped off his shirt, a blazing *red* brand stood out like a neon sign on his pale skin.

Líadán's bite.

Her exquisite bite.

Brenden turned his head, letting the light over the mirror shine onto his neck. Leaning closer to the mirror over the vanity, he could see a large bruise halfway between his ear and shoulder. The imprint of upper and lower teeth could be clearly discerned. Two punctures just missed penetrating his jugular vein. The holes were not small or neat, more ragged rips than a clean bite. The skin around the tears was prickled red and the punctures were puffy.

Brenden grimaced, pressing the tips of his fingers to his neck, touching the distinct holes.

The bite was surprisingly not painful, feeling more akin to an itchy rash. "Jesus Christ. She's got a hell of an overbite there." He hadn't just been bitten, he'd been mauled!

Brenden didn't exactly recall the pain. Thinking back, his memory was a little blurry. Only Líadán was in sharp focus in his mind, but what they'd done *after* she'd nipped him was out of focus, as if he'd acted as an observer and not a participant. Some of this he attributed to the whiskey, the rest to exhaustion; *in another few hours he'd pass the thirty-two-hour* mark with only a brief catnap in the hotel sustaining him. The last he attributed to the relief he'd gotten laid. A lot of pressures and tensions had dissolved like hot wax when he achieved orgasm.

Strangely, the idea of her taking a little taste and leaving one hell of a hickey didn't frighten or upset him.

It aroused him.

Closing his eyes, Brenden easily recalled how she'd mesmerized him. Thinking of her caused heat to creep through his veins, reigniting the desire he'd felt for her. He had to admit he was intrigued by what she'd done, more than a little turned on. Thoughts of Líadán fueled his craving, which had flared hot from the moment he'd first set eyes on her. Even now his jeans outlined his lean hips and the growing bulge in front. Closing his eyes, a low moan escaped his lips. He recalled the edgy sharpness whetted by climax as mesmerizing.

I've been tasted. Chosen.

Brenden swallowed thickly. The temperature was reaching an uncomfortable degree. He unzipped his jeans and let them drop to the floor. He kicked his soiled clothes out of his path in the general direction of the hamper.

Opening the shower door, he turned on the cold tap to full blast and stepped under the showerhead. Icy water pelted his skin. He welcomed the powerful sting on his pale skin, as though by punishing his flesh he could subdue his yearning for

Líadán. He quickly soaped his body, rinsed, then washed his hair.

Fifteen minutes later, dressed in sweatpants and a T-shirt, Brenden sat down on the bed. His bedroom, stripped bare of a woman's touch, was bland. Totally unromantic and unappealing.

He cast a critical eye over the blah, ratty bedspread coming apart at the seams, the lamp with its dented shade, the throw rug covered with dog hair. Definitely not a place for seduction. Ugh! He couldn't bring a woman in here even if he had one to entertain privately. His bedroom was the wreck of the *Titanic*, a definite bachelor's pad. He really needed to go shopping with Dani in tow.

Bear nosed his hand for attention. Brenden scratched the dog's ears. He didn't relish being single. He hated sleeping alone. Since the day Jenna left, he hadn't even bothered to turn down the comforter. Instead he slept on top with a blanket pulled over his body. He missed snuggling up to a woman, feeling a soft body against his.

He lay back on the mattress, closing his eyes. Without his willing it, his mind drifted toward Líadán's image, tucked so carefully in his secret box of mental treasures. He'd liked the way she'd looked at him when teasing him with her body, a wonderful spark in the depths of her glittering blue eyes. A hot, exhilarating surge filled his body. She was like a virus in his veins.

Without his willing it to, his hand moved to his crotch, cupping his penis. He began to rub his cock slowly, with subtle pressure. His heartbeat sped up. Tension shivered through him. A muscle jerked in his cheek. One corner of his mouth tilted up into a wry smile.

Eyes closed, Brenden savored the sensations that masturbation brought. In his mind's eye he imagined driving his hips between Líadán's thighs as she dug her fingernails deep into his back and cried out his name. He wanted to feel her nipples pressing against his chest, hear her ragged breath as she begged him to take her over the edge.

He wanted her so badly, wanted to open his eyes and drink in the sight of her naked flesh, see her face, alight with her need, feel the taut, fierce intensity of her creamy depths squeezing around his cock, experience again the exultation of going over the edge into a mind-shattering climax.

Her body . . . oh, God, what a temple of pleasure. She'd deigned to share it with him and he was profoundly grateful.

Brenden needed her as he'd never needed or wanted another woman. This brand of desire was new to him, unsettling, but possessing a strange urgency he couldn't put aside. The idea of pleasing Líadán excited him. Somehow she'd touched a place inside his soul more sensitive than any nerve endings on the surface of his skin.

I'll see her again. I'll have her again. A name. A phone number. All he needed to find her was at his disposal.

His hand stroked his cock harder, each pass of his palm sending vibrations of pleasure coursing though every nerve ending. His body clenched, tighter. Climax came in one long shudder. Release had never felt so good.

Sated, he invited visions of the raven-haired beauty to dance in his head. He wasn't even aware when the specter of sleep swooped in, spiriting him away to an erotic world where he pleasured her in every way imaginable—and a few that were not.

7

At the last moment, Auguste Maximilian opened his hand, letting Líadán fall. Dropped like a rock, her body crashed hard enough to knock the breath right out of her. Her head smacked the hardwood floor. A fierce bolt of pain jabbed through her temple, sending a blast of fuzzy lights through her brain. Her world spun.

Auguste knelt down, brushing her cheek with the tips of his fingers. She flinched physically and he smiled. Expression sharpening, he looked like a coiled cobra about to strike. A silent communication passed between them, master and slave. "You may play with your new toy, my pet." He chuckled and it rumbled deep in his chest. "But take care. Do not get too attached."

Líadán licked dry lips, fighting the urge to let her eyes drift closed. She nodded tightly, hand at her aching throat. "As you wish, my lord." *Thankfully, there would be no bruises.*

"Do not displease me again . . ." Auguste tilted his head and a vicious smile of glee stretched his lips. "Or I will have to set my leather belt against your tender little ass."

Líadán saw his hand rise and flinched, knowing he would

enjoy seeing her cringe under his dominance. Feeling the chill of his threat slide down her spine, she took a deep breath, fighting to keep her voice steady. In her mind she pictured knocking him down and scratching out those wicked eyes.

She did neither.

Some day . . .

Líadán whimpered, trapped between hate and her own miserable defeat. She wasn't strong enough. She knew it. Auguste certainly knew it. Stark despair washed over her. Dominated all her life by others stronger then herself, she hated her weakness and cursed her inability to escape. Even suicide hadn't been possible.

No longer wanting to face him, Líadán tucked her chin down as far as it would go in an attempt to hide, but he would not be wished away. A single tear spilled down her cheek. "Yes, master."

Having thoroughly disciplined her, Auguste rose to his full height. He made a dismissive gesture. With a shrug of his shoulders and a perverse arch of his brows, he prodded her with one booted foot, as if it were her own fault she was sprawled out on the floor.

Líadán rubbed her sore jaw and stood with as much grace as she could muster, struggling not to stumble.

"It has been a long night. Alas, the day sending us back into the shadows must have its time." A smirk stretched his lips taut. "Come. We will rest."

Líadán barely managed to suppress her shivers. She hated going into Auguste's private lair. He preferred to spend his day far away from the light that sapped strength and vitality from the vampyr.

Going down the stairs beside him propelled her into endless murk. Grayness curled around her, increasing her unease. The sound of her heels on the hard marble echoed in her ears, mocking her. Torches propped in high sconces lit the stone path. As though wading in a thick fog, walking along the extensive passages seemed to take an eternity. As they advanced deeper underground, the atmosphere grew frigid, its chill coiling around her.

A gray stone ceiling overlooking arched alcoves and beautifully paneled walls surrounded the heavy Victorian-style furnishings of his bedroom. Two of his thralls lay naked on the king-sized bed. The oils anointing their skin gave their flesh a luminous, otherworldly glow.

These were two of his favorite brides, an exotic set of Asian twins named Jai and Mai. Both were beautiful, with olive-tinged skin, almond eyes, and sensual mouths. Unblushing, they made no attempt to hide their nudity. Each woman was also marked with the strange brand and the hoop through their navels—Auguste's brand of ownership, marking them as his property.

Líadán didn't blink at the way the women nuzzled each other's bodies, making outright love in front of anyone who cared to watch. Even the sanctity of sex was defiled in Auguste's world.

Like the lion armored in the adoration of his pride, Auguste Maximilian ruled his jungle with an iron fist, a vibrant, commanding force. No matter how seemingly sophisticated and urbane Auguste appeared, there remained inside him a hedonistic, manipulating beast, never to be tamed. Brilliant, he possessed a keen knowledge of how society lived and worked. He would rarely do anything spontaneously. He would sit back and think and have the vision to see what was happening in the world and why.

Auguste's careful examination of events and objects made him a very perceptive man. If he didn't like the rules or laws of mankind, he bent them or out-and-out defied them in order to get his way. He had no love of the public masses, didn't want to deal with them, and absolutely refused to do so if he didn't have to. He deliberately remained as unavailable as possible in a modern world geared toward information and communication.

Since the beginning of time, a thriving and very active cultic subculture wound tightly around the fabric of everyday life. As much as it frightened some, others were drawn to the occult, harboring a dark fascination with the beasts of shadows. Such enthrallment served as a pathway for hellish entities desiring to inhabit the realm of flesh. God in his heaven had thrown down the challenge and the Devil had keenly accepted the bargain. To this day, angels and demons waged still a furious battle. Front and center in Satan's army, Auguste Maximilian was a thief of lives. His hunger for blood knew no limit. Nothing gave him greater pleasure than to suck away a man's mind and soul. In the twenty-first century, demons not only thrived, but prospered.

The chamber harbored a vault-like chill between its thick walls. This was chased temporarily to bay by the proliferation of candles burning in sconces and the fire cracking in a hearth gouged into the far wall. On the cobbled floor in front of it a woman sprawled, her pale skin drawing warmth from the fire— the sole concession to mercy Auguste would allow his unconscious victim.

Líadán gasped, pressing her hand to her stomach to still her nerves. The pulse of fear in her mouth tasted bitter. Hands chained to the cinderblock walls, the woman's feet were bound securely together by a length of rope. Bites and scratches riddled her pale skin, some viciously deep but none intended to be fatal—yet. Auguste and his brides had feasted well.

Bile rose in the back of Líadán's throat. Though she, too, had sated her unnatural hunger, she'd chosen a willing, if unknowing, victim. In a swift, half-conscious thought, it occurred to her she, too, was just as guilty as Auguste. She thrust the thought from her mind. Unlike him, she was no murderer. She didn't take the unwilling and she didn't kill them afterward.

A great sadness, of loss perhaps, tightened her chest.

Gazing down into the face of the woman she knew would not survive the night, Líadán felt a twinge of culpability, one eroding a channel through her very being. *I wish I could help you*. More jagged shards of guilt attacked.

As if sensing Líadán's mood, the flickering light around her took on an animation all its own, creating shadows that appeared to assume human shapes. Figures formed, proud and fierce, red eyes glaring over gaping mouths littered with sharp fangs. A wave of dizziness swayed her.

As though reading her mind, Auguste's voice, low and accented, broke into her contemplations. "She is not worthy to keep." In his view his victim's function was the same most humans thought of when considering cattle: bred for slaughter.

Hearing his words, Líadán grimaced, feeling a twinge deep in her gut. Turning her head away so that the others would not see, she squeezed her eyes shut. The woman's death would be long and painful.

Líadán willed herself to remain absolutely emotionless. She must keep discipline and self-control, watch her words, and reveal nothing. Gathering her courage, she reluctantly turned away from the victim on the floor.

There was nothing she could do, not even pray.

8

Brenden awoke with half a hangover and a hard-on. His hours of sleep had been restless. He'd tossed and turned endlessly, his thoughts plagued by Líadán. He wasn't sure exactly when he'd fallen into an exhausted slumber. When he was asleep, he'd dreamed of the woman with the dark, silky hair and even silkier lips.

Bundled up in his cocoon, he was loathe to leave its warmth and comfort. In his dream, she was a black widow spider, appearing out of mist, wrapping him in the embrace of her soft web before draining the life out of him. Why his mind should conjure her as such, he had no idea.

The sucking . . . Ah, yes. He relived his favorite fantasy over and over, masturbating himself to orgasm as he lay in the dreamy state between half awake and half asleep.

A swath of sun suddenly lanced through the blinds. He frowned. The light was on the wrong side of the room. Surely it wasn't going down? He glanced at his bedside clock, shocked to realize he'd slept almost the entire day away. Usually he was up by one or two in the afternoon, sometimes earlier. His regular trip to the gym would have to be cancelled. Though he was no longer a fresh-faced rookie with the regulation crew cut and desire to save the world, he wasn't content to let himself go to seed and get lazy. He liked keeping in top shape and exercised regularly. The gym was also a good place to ogle women in tight leotards. He'd been considering finding his future ex-wife there when he'd gotten run over by the sexy Mercedes that was Líadán.

I've been working too hard. Body aching from last night's acrobatics, which had tested muscles he'd forgotten he owned, he considered calling in sick.

He quickly nixed the idea. He was just twenty-four hours away from his much needed days off. He might as well go to work and tie up the loose ends in a few cases he and Monty were investigating.

To get his blood pumping, Brenden flipped on the television to listen to the evening news while he did two quick sets of sit-ups and push-ups. He stripped, then took his shower hot and steamy, enjoying the feel of the water on his skin.

As he ran his soapy hands over his body, he thought about Líadán. A bolt of anticipation caused his heart to skip a beat. She was the most fabulous woman he'd ever encountered. Excitement settled into resolve by time he turned off the taps. He knew without a doubt she would have a profound and disturbing influence on his life.

Toweled, but damp, he brushed his teeth, then took the time to shave off a couple of days' worth of whiskers. A vice cop could look like a dirty weasel, but today he felt like projecting an image more refined and civil.

Rather than dressing in his usual ensemble of faded jeans and a T-shirt with yet another obscene slogan printed across it, he chose casual khakis, a white shirt, and boots. The strange hickey Líadán etched into his throat was still very much in evidence, having turned into a purplish bruise. Because he didn't want to answer any questions, he needed to conceal it. A stiff-collared oxford shirt kept on hand for court appearances worked. Since he didn't want to overdo it, he refrained from wearing a tie.

Grabbing a cup of instant coffee and gobbling up the chocolate cupcakes Dani had left on the table in lieu of a birthday cake, Brenden headed out the door. Though he could afford better, he drove a late-model Oldsmobile. The sleek old sedan was fourteen years old, the tawny paint a bit chipped and faded in places, but the engine was reliable and gave him few problems. He always enjoyed the commute uptown. It gave him a chance to sit and just let the world go by through the thirty minutes it took to weave his way through traffic. Even nearing nine in the evening, Dordogne's streets were busy. Over two hundred thousand souls lived in the city, each restless, wanting to go somewhere, do something.

Dordogne's police station was located in an unbeautiful but functional two-story building, right beside City Hall and the Municipal Court building. Built new from the ground up about five years ago, it still had a neat and clean sheen, well maintained and well lighted.

The vice squad was located on the second floor. Brenden ambled through the station, ignoring the chaos of the front office, ears picking up bits and pieces as he passed dispatch. He stopped at the snack station for a cup of coffee, then headed for the elevator. Arriving in the squad room, he was in for a surprise.

Three men sat around their desks, perfectly engaged in their work. Sitting in his chair, however, was a woman of plastic proportions. With black hair and a gaping mouth, a scantily dressed blow-up sex doll was lashed down with a red scarf. Her legs were parted in a suggestive manner and a sign reading "HELP YOURSELF" covered her crotch.

Seeing the doll, Brenden felt heat rising in his cheeks, sure he was turning beet red. The men around him snickered, barely able to hide their glee. They weren't going to let him easily live down last night's fiasco. After Líadán had elegantly told him in so many words where he could put his badge, his partner and the others watching his clumsy seduction routine had given him one hell of a razzing. Though they'd gone on to bust two more working girls, Sy Simmons made a discovery that caused the cops to curse and Brenden to wipe his brow in relief. Somehow the video equipment malfunctioned. The tape with Líadán on it—all the evidence—was blank.

Brenden could only wonder what lucky star had spared him and thank his fates. He would never have been able to live that one down. He'd been sweating bullets over the thought of it being played over and over at the next Christmas party.

Stalking to his desk, he fumbled with the scarves holding the doll pinned in place. "Very fucking funny, assholes." As the newest man on the team, he was usually the butt of the veteran officers' pranks. Hazing was part of the ritual of becoming "one of the boys."

Such intense and stressful work needed an outlet to blow off steam and frustrations. He took their highjinks with a grain of salt and good nature. Working with these three men was many things, but dull was not one of them. As much as they annoyed, exasperated, and teased, he wouldn't have wanted to work with any other group. When the chips were down and backs were against the wall, he knew every single one would lay down their lives for him.

Ignoring the laughter, Brenden picked up the doll he'd freed, examining her. On any other day he'd have been amused the boys remembered his birthday.

"How do you like your present, Bren?" Sy asked, tagging himself as the guilty and acquiring party.

Brenden popped a lacy red bra strap on the doll's shoulder. "I'm mighty obliged to you guys for thinking so highly of me.

I'll get a lot of use out of her, since I don't suffer from—" He flicked the plug on the back of her head. The doll deflated with a fizz, going limp. He let the shriveling sex toy drop to the floor. She lay half-spent, looking every bit like most of them felt.

Chair freed, Brenden sat down. He reached for his mug. Like a gorilla beating its chest, he gave one last affirmation of his masculinity, saying smugly, "I'll have you know I got laid—quite nicely, I might add—last night."

Monty Blake nodded, eyeing his partner across his desk. "Ah. So that's why you're all dressed up nice today. Shaved, hair combed, reeking of stink-pretty. Can't mistake it, boys. Our youngster got himself a piece of ass." His crooked grin turned lascivious.

"You'd think none of you assholes ever got any tail," Brenden shot back.

Sy Simmons paused from stuffing a chocolate donut in his face. "You better check under the ponytail you're wearing. The only thing under a pony's tail is a horse's ass." He took another bite of his donut. "Throwing pussy in a man's face ain't kind, especially when the other dude ain't getting none." By the roll developing around Sy's middle, he wasn't missing any meals, and by the size of his giant appetite, he definitely wasn't getting any sex. "I'd give anything if my wife would give me a tumble."

"She would if she liked beached whales squashing the shit out of her," Roy Cho snickered.

Brenden motioned for silence. "Now that we've all had a moment to share our sexual adventures, can we please do some police work? Maybe we could get back to busting pimps, serving warrants, and slowing down the sin in the city."

"So let's get to it," Monty Blake agreed.

Brenden dug through the piles of papers on his desk, finding the yellow legal pad he kept his notes on. A business card was clipped to the top page. "So where are we with Exotic Jewels?"

Monty snorted. "Since that call girl made you for a cop, I don't know." He tapped his pen against the edge of his desk. "Aside from the phone number, there's no address or other contact information. My guess is they're working out of a central location, a home base. These girls aren't usually on the streets."

"It isn't illegal to run an escort service in the great state of Louisiana if it's legit," Brenden said, looking for justification to withdraw the heat. "Since there's no proof—yet—the ladies are trading sex for money, we can't just go in guns a-blazing. Their operation is only illegal if they're soliciting with the intention of promoting prostitution. Right now we can't even get them for operating without a business license because they're not in service at a specific location. We have to have the activity in a definite place and since they're working through a phone messaging service, there's no telling where the home base is located."

Monty nodded. "That one last night—she was pretty quick on the uptake." He snapped his fingers. "She knocked your dick in the dirt like that."

How very true. But she'd certainly made up for it afterward.

"I know," Brenden groused, not entirely sorry that events turned out the way they had. He wanted to see Líadán again. Soon. The question remained: how he was supposed to balance his desire to see her off-duty against the fact he was one of the cops investigating the business she worked for? "So how do we want to follow up on this?" His breath hung in his throat. "Arrange another bust?"

Monty grimaced like he felt a burn in his gut. Lines of worry puckered his forehead, whether he was worried or not. "Okay, so basically we're back to square one on this. So instead of trying to catch a girl live, I say we dig a little deeper. Find out some particulars, such as physical locations. Once we've got an address, we can tail a few girls, see where they go. Our best bet is to try to catch them in the act with an actual john."

Brenden shook his head. "Shit, it's only a misdemeanor for man to buy himself a piece of ass. The girl usually gets a slap on the wrist, fined a few hundred dollars, and turned loose to trick again. It feels like we're fighting a losing battle."

"What the hell do I say?" Monty Blake countered. "Swapping pussy for hard cash shouldn't be a crime. The girls should be given a health card, licensed, and taxed. The revenue would pay off the goddamned national debt." Monty Blake hated vice. To him, busting pimps, hassling whores, and shutting down dice games wasn't real police work.

Brenden raised his hands in appeasement to the liberal old fart. Between the two of them, they were well matched in their partnership of eleven months. Monty took the names, Brenden kicked the tails. Neither was opposed to applying necessary force a little harder than necessary. "I know, I know. Shit, sometimes I agree." But his position wasn't to judge. Monitor and control was his job.

Monty Blake sighed. "Right now, this is low priority stuff. We can let it sit a few weeks and then get back to it. As long as the ladies aren't peddling drugs, let them peddle their pussies a bit longer. You can't stop men from wanting sex, and you can't stop women from making a living on their backs. It's a fact of life. Hell, what's a wife, but a whore who's been bought and paid for?"

Sy Simmons and Roy Cho chuckled.

Brenden felt his stomach drop to his feet. He'd never hear the end of it if anyone present discovered the truth of how he'd spent last night and where. He swallowed, closing his eyes and squeezing the bridge of his nose. The idea he should never see Líadán a second time flashed through his skull.

He quickly shot that one down. It wasn't her glorious long legs, lush mouth, or tangle of black hair affecting him. Nor even those full breasts and tight cunt of hers. No, it was the way she'd taken him, claiming him with her erotic bite. He'd never experienced anything like it before. The idea it might not occur a second time was about to fracture him into a thousand shards. He wanted her to take him back to that pinnacle. He'd do anything in this world to experience those sensations a second time.

Even lie.

Voices that had faded away came back into focus.

"You know my wife would slug you for saying that," Simmons said, belly jiggling.

Monty Blake cleared his throat. "My wives just divorce me and take all I've got. They get the coal mine and I get the shaft, every time."

Brenden cut him off. "Yeah, yeah, you're preaching to the choir, Monty. We all know about those bitches you married."

Blake grunted. "Women are a pain. You gotta date them, feed them, and then hope you get some pussy." He leered like a perverted coyote. "Why can't you just hand them some money and get down to business? The world would be a whole lot better if sex was for sale, like groceries or a car."

Brenden was trying to come up with an argument when Ray Eddington walked into the office. Using his investigative talents, he immediately zeroed in on the half-deflated sex doll. Seeing her, Eddington rolled his eyes heavenward, looking put on, put out, and plain pissed. "God help the city." He gave all four men a not-so-subtle once-over. "Think you guys can look like you're working instead of standing around with your dicks in your hands?"

Everyone took what Ray Eddington said seriously. A hulk of a man, standing six foot four, Eddington looked more like a harried computer tech than a cop. But he was still a cop, and his willingness to keep the brass above his head from tossing Sy Simmons's ass off the force proved Ray Eddington would go to the wire for his men. At sixty-four years of age, he was nearing retirement. He'd spent his entire career in Dordogne and still had yet to draw his weapon in the line of duty. "Got a minute?" He could be forgiven for the slight note of irony in his voice.

"Sure," Sy Simmons burped, washing down his last bite of donut. "We're all here for your benefit."

Planting his butt on Roy Cho's desk, Eddington announced unceremoniously, "I got a little case I need you guys to look into." His bluntness ushered in silence. He wasn't here to waste time, or beat around the bush.

"We're all ears." Sliding open a drawer, Brenden found his cigarettes and half a pack of matches. Taking one out, he lit it, inhaled.

Ray Eddington opened the manila folder he was carrying. He picked through some papers. Finding what he wanted, he held up the picture of a striking, but not exactly pretty, young girl. "Anyone know her?" He passed the picture around so they could all get a good look. Everyone shook their heads.

Ray held up a second photo. The same girl, a few years older, but not her at all. The fresh-faced gamine had been re-placed by a stringy-haired, hollow-eyed addict. Her face was covered with bruises and cuts, and black circles ringed both her eyes. Her pupils were dead, empty holes. She looked like what she was, a strung-out addict.

All four men recognized her immediately.

"I know her. The Parker girl," Monty drawled through an exhalation of bluish smoke. "What's her name?"

"Janice," Brenden filled in. "We tagged her on the street a couple times for prostitution. She tricks up there on the drag strip." Though he had seen a lot of girls since joining Vice, he easily remembered the scrawny little whore with the hopeless eyes, stinking and filthy, wearing little more than rags from the Salvation Army. She was too damned young to be throwing her life away on the streets. He'd tried to get her some help, giving her addresses of a place to stay and people who could help her with her drug problem. He wondered if she'd bothered to seek aid. Probably not. Most likely she was laid up in some crack house, burning out the last of her brain cells.

"So what's up?" Blake wanted to know. "Did she claim we hassled her or something?"

Eddington shook his head. "Janice Parker's purse and a bag of groceries she was seen carrying when she left work early last night were found by garbage men this morning. No one's seen or heard from her since."

Blake shrugged, red-tracked eyeballs sliding back into his skull. "And we're supposed to what?"

"Find her," Eddington said, ignoring the chorus of groans. The policy of the department was the moment a person of any age was reported missing, an investigation was immediately opened. The sooner police were on the case, the better chance they had to locate clues that might lead them to the absent person. Sometimes it was as simple as someone's teenaged daughter sneaking off to spend the night with her boyfriend. Other times it was as complicated as some dude drowning his old lady in the bathtub before offing himself in the garage with carbon monoxide.

"Whores turn up missing every day. Why hand her to us? We've got enough going on as it is. Throw her over to missing persons." Montgomery Blake showed absolutely no interest in running down the whereabouts of yet another lost cause.

Eddington frowned. "I'm giving her to you guys because you're familiar with her looks, her territory, and you rousted her out during her last run-in with the cops."

Brenden cleared his throat to break the tension. "Maybe she just took off, left town. Why waste the time?"

Eddington laid a firm finger on the first photo. "Because this is who she was," he reminded them. "She has a mother who remembers her this way, a mother who says Janice is off drugs and has a real job at the Sunrise Diner on Granite and Second—

a job she didn't show up for this evening. Because there was money in her purse, I don't think robbery was the motive."

"You think some pimp or drug dealer came looking for her?"

Eddington tossed the folder on Brenden's desk. "Possible. Or maybe a john who thought she should give him a little good loving and she wasn't in the mood to oblige. No woman just walks off and leaves her food and purse unless she's forced to."

Monty Blake's eyebrows shot up. Both were very important in his world. "True."

Snatching the file away from Brenden, Roy Cho gave a brief wave, looking every bit like a kid about to piss his pants before the teacher gave permission for a bathroom break. "You think this has anything to do with the girl going missing last week, Captain? The convenience-store clerk . . . what's her name?"

Eddington filled in, "Kiki Olivarez."

"So what happened there?" Monty Blake asked, not really caring.

"Don't you assholes read the memos?" Roy Cho scolded, always anxious to prove he was on top of things the others let slide. Not a single one of the other detectives ever bothered to stop by the night-watch roll call, where the uniforms were briefed before heading out on patrol for the night.

The cops shook their heads. No, they tried to read as few of the circulars as possible.

Eddington kindly filled them in. "She's the one who disappeared at work last week, one of those all night Sak-N-Go stores. Went to throw out the trash, never came back. Poof. Gone without a trace."

"Those are thankless jobs," Sy Simmons said. "Jesus, if you want work more dangerous than being a cop, go work in one of those places. They get robbed like, what, every ten minutes?"

Brenden looked to Eddington. "You think they're related?"

Eddington gave his inner cheek a swipe with his tongue. Roy

Cho was putting two and two together when all they really had was one and one. "Don't think so," he finally said. "Kiki Olivarez was a grade-A college student, active in her church, and all the things that go along with being a good citizen. At this time I see no correlation or connection between the two. Later on, something might turn up, but for the moment we're treating them as two separate instances. From what her family has said, she had a bitter relationship with her ex-husband. We're looking at him as the prime suspect. They quarreled about custody matters over their infant daughter before she went to work. Mostly likely, he's our guy."

Brenden shrugged. "Okay, then. So we got one missing whore on our hands."

Eddington had one final thing to say. "Janice Parker's stuff is down in evidence if you want to go through it." He gave each man a pointed look, making sure each noted his serious expression. "I want some answers here."

9

Head tilted back, Líadán Niamh stood quietly at the window, watching the sun vanish behind the horizon. Standing near enough that her breath fogged the glass, she reached up and wiped away the condensation with her palm. She let her hand rest on the glass. She didn't move. Reflected back at her was a face looking bloodless, her eyes huge and strangely shadowed. She shivered a little. Even to her own eyes she looked vulnerable, unhappy. For four hundred and sixty-two years, she'd walked through time as one of the chosen, a vampyr.

Her mouth quirked up at one corner. It wasn't true that a vampyr had no reflection—just as the unschooled believed them to be undead, occupying a corpse. Her reflection was very much in place. She'd never died, never would die as long as she fed the jouyl, the demon living inside her. Created of the darkest magic, the jouyl was a gift from one vampyr to his or her chosen mate, a merging of blood, of hunger, of body.

If she looked into her eyes long and hard enough, she was sure she would see her lost innocence flickering like a monarch butterfly in their depths. Instead of innocence, though, all she could see was corruption, a slow decaying of her soul.

Innocence was a young girl, tending her family's flock of sheep in her small village. Innocence was hard work, from dusk to dawn, scrabbling to live, growing enough food to feed twelve mouths. How easily she remembered the picturesque landscape of Hungary, embracing a bucolic tapestry of verdant, meandering fields, winding stone walls, quaint cottages, a few satisfied brown cows, and goats with tinkling bells about their necks scampering amongst the chickens. Until her fifteenth year, her life was uneventful, the day before indistinguishable from the one to come tomorrow. Her future promised nothing more than eventual marriage, harder work, and birth after birth until she died of exhaustion, just as her own mother had.

And then the war commenced, a brutal affair. In 1541, the Turks occupied Buda and Hungary was split into three parts. The Habsburgs of Austrian descent governed the western part of the country, the central area was ruled by the Turks, and the southeast Transylvanian principality for a long time was the citadel of Hungarian culture.

"I lost my innocence. Lost it the day the Turks invaded our country, wiping my people from the face of the land as a man crushes an ant under his boot."

Unable to look in the glass any longer, she turned her eyes away. Even when she closed her eyes, all she saw were the faces of her family, as if their images were burned into her eyelids. Father, brothers, sisters . . . All were slaughtered under the trampling of horses' hooves and the unforgiving bite of steel from the soldiers' weapons.

Hands knotting into fists, she wanted to strike out at the windowpanes, shatter them into a thousand pieces. She felt a wild impulse to tear at herself with her long fingernails, beat herself bloody with her own fists, turn on and punish the unearthly loveliness that was, below the surface, so empty. She possessed a divine and pleasing woman's body, but to her mind it was little more than a shell holding nothing, not even a soul.

Líadán's head dipped. "Why? Why did they die while I lived?" A series of sobs shook her body. Even now, after all these years, the tragic events rose up from the murky pool deep inside her soul.

Swearing softly to herself, she scrubbed her hands across her face. Shedding precious tears for the dead was a waste of energy. They were out of this world. Safe. She was the one who had to live, to survive. How she wished she could forget, erase their memories from her brain. It hurt too much to remember she'd survived and her family hadn't.

I was spared because I was beautiful.

Shaking off the dazed feelings her past always delivered, Líadán tried to pull her mind from her unhappiness and the past haunting her. She could not change what Auguste had done. She could only accept it and go forward.

Her time on this earth had been too long. Weariness had set into her bones even as decay had set in behind her eyes and atrophy and apathy had settled in her soul. She no longer felt she was living. She wasn't even surviving. She was simply existing. Unchanging. Unending. Everlasting. Eternity's seductive kiss came straight from the foulest pit of hell.

Líadán let down the drape she'd tied aside. As she stepped back, the material slid through her fingers with a whisper. The feel of the cloth against their tips caused the fine hairs on the back of her neck to rise. She was acutely aware of her surroundings. Every physical sensation seemed magnified a thousand times past normal levels. Some days—and today was one—it felt as if she didn't belong in her own skin. In the silence of her chambers, even the sound of her breathing seemed too loud.

Parting her lips so she could take in air through her mouth, she tried to minimize the needs of her body, slowing the rise and fall of her chest to a minimal rhythm. Only the beating of her heart disturbed the deathlike silence she was desperate to attain within. She pressed the palms of her hands together, assuming the attitude of serene prayer. She lowered her eyelids, seeking soothing darkness. She could feel the pulsing of blood through her veins just beneath the surface of her skin. Though her body was still, her mind was racing. She wasn't yet ready for the night, that time when she was truly alive, to begin.

Surely, others like me must be more comfortable in the lives they've been reborn into.

Facing eternity, though, had never pleased her. The fountain Líadán been forced to drink from had granted her eternal youth. The gift—curse?—had come with a price, one she'd paid time and time again. Humanity stripped away to the bone, she feared she was losing every gentle emotion. She knew only hate, a dark seed festering deep inside her mind, nurtured by the absolute disgust she felt for Auguste Maximilian.

Overwhelming sadness washed over her like the consuming waves of an angry ocean. A moan escaped her lips, but it sounded like a scream to her sensitive ears. Perhaps she was screaming. Screaming, and no one heard. Or cared. Through her long centuries she'd always felt isolated, even from those who shared her secrets. Even the name she presently answered to wasn't her own.

She delved deeper into the refuge she'd created inside her mind. *I've never been what the others are. I've never been like . . . them.*

Líadán reluctantly opened her eyes, leaving the soothing void she'd created in her mind. Not so wise to retreat so deeply within. She sometimes feared she would dig down so far she would be unable to return. "I close my eyes and this evil world falls away. I don't want to come back to it, but I must. I must."

Footsteps, ever so subtle, sounded behind her.

Líadán's hands clenched tightly, so tightly her knuckles were white to the bone. She quickly tucked her agony back into the secret box inside her mind. She closed the lid with little regret. The past would always haunt her.

Auguste came, his hands settling on her shoulders, his lips brushing the back of her neck. "Another night." Breath humming across her ear, his accented voice stroked, yet cut directly through her. "The only time we are truly alive." His mouth came down on her neck, his lips hot and wet against the soft plane between ear and shoulder.

A soft gasp escaped when Auguste gently nipped her skin, his evil kiss seeming to drive all the air from her lungs. Líadán broke out in a trembling sweat, barely managing to suppress her shivers at his touch, one she had endured and cursed for centuries. She could no more escape Auguste's grip than she could tear out her heart and live. She belonged to his realm of the damned. Not by choice, nor by any design. She had simply been in the wrong place at the wrong time. Fate, she thought wryly, was as cruel as the Creator who'd knowingly unleashed evil upon mankind.

Líadán bit back on an escaping moan when Auguste pulled her closer, aligning their bodies so she could feel him, hard and full, throbbing against her. His cock was a searing steel rod pressed against her ass. Líadán whimpered when he swept a hand down her side, moving his palm across her belly, going lower to cup her intimately.

"I want you at my side for the hunt tonight." His fingers inched up the hem of her dress, sliding under the silky fabric. She felt her panties being pushed down. Hand braced over her Venus mound, Auguste's middle finger traced the slit between her legs. Behind her, his breath came in shallow gasps as he increased the pressure.

Líadán shut her eyes against the unwelcome sexual tension caused by Auguste's none-too-gentle touch on her hairless mound. She sucked in a ragged breath. Unbidden tears misted her vision. She blinked her eyes to hold them back. She knew what his words signified. Auguste was ready to choose another victim.

A tiny whimper escaped Líadán's throat when Auguste probed deeper between her legs, finding the tip of her tender clit. Her breath locked in her throat, unable to pass her lips. She had to struggle to spit out her words. "We have already taken two. Should we take another so soon?" She felt a wild impulse to scream or burst into hysterical, shattering shrieks. She did nothing. She'd successfully mastered the physical aspects; her body harnessed, brought into subjugation by strict disciplines. But her mind and—damn it!—her conscience still persisted in harrying her. Though she willed it otherwise, her soul, her sanity, would not entirely be broken down into madness.

Auguste mistook her uncertainty for passion. His probing grew heated, harder. "I've disposed of the others." A pause. "We need to hunt to keep our skills sharp." He ground his hips into hers so she could feel every inch of his erection, pinching and rolling one nipple with his free hand.

A hot flush rose to Líadán's cheeks. Inwardly cringing, she closed her eyes as a wave of dismay crested through her. She stayed immobile as stone, yet goosebumps pimpled her flesh and her heart slammed in her chest. Fearful rebellion quivered inside her, digging itself into the soft tissue of her brain.

Since arriving at this strange new place, it had taken root like a poisonous weed and started to grow. Her conscience gnawed the way a dog would worry a bone. A strange sort of prophetic dread lingered in the back of her mind, though she could not identify its source.

Líadán clenched her hands into fists at her sides, wordlessly seeking reassurance from a god long silent. She was actually afraid, as if the coming night would draw her into a tide pool of everlasting torment.

Another woman would be taken. Killed.

And there would be no mercy to spare the innocent.

10

The call came in just after midnight.

A body—reported dumped outside the perimeters of the city, in the Redwood Memorial Park, four thousand acres of forest land designated for camping, hiking, biking, and other recreational activities. Located six miles out of Dordogne, a tangle of trees and teeming wildlife, after hours the park was perfect for clandestine activities, a popular place for teenagers to go seeking privacy to have a few beers and smoke a joint or two.

Arriving at the scene, Brenden and Montgomery Blake found a beehive of activity. Flashing their badges toward the uniformed deputies guarding the perimeter, they parked their car and made their way by foot down a steep, rocky trail leading into a grassy knoll most people couldn't locate by day, much less by night. Discovered by a ranger following a trail of smoke for possible illegal campfire activity, the corpse was found by sheer luck.

The area Brenden and his partner walked into had already been roped off by the deputies with yellow tape. A line of high-powered perimeter lights illuminated the area. Sheriff Peter Mallerd, a crusty old fat fart, and Leland McCormack, Dordogne's coroner for nearly twenty-three years, were already present, pacing the scene the way bloodhounds sniffed the ground. By the look on his face, Peter Mallerd was a very frustrated man.

Seeing the outline of the body under the white plastic sheet, Brenden immediately tightened his grip on his flashlight. He felt some kind of primitive fear creep up his spine. He'd seen plenty of corpses in his nine years on the job, but each one always felt like the first. Death was never pretty, no matter how it happened. Death was ugly. Once the soul had departed, all that was left was an empty husk.

Brenden hated finding a body when it had passed its ripe stages, just like he hated seeing body parts scattered high and low. Every cop had one story about a happening so brutal the faces of the victims were etched into their memories as if with acid.

He had his own. More than one, in fact. And he didn't care to think of them. Instead, he blanked his mind.

As the recreational area was outside the city's limits, this case would go automatically to the county Sheriff's department. An interservice rivalry existed between the two branches of law enforcement. They hadn't always cooperated on cases, especially on narcotics and gambling raids. Often the two factions stepped on each other's toes, once to the point of blowing one entire investigation on a rogue biker gang suspected of running a methamphetamine lab. To make a long story short, an undercover Sheriff's deputy was arrested by two city vice cops, who then allowed the brains behind the highly illegal operation to skip off to safety across the state line, and, subsequently, across the Mexican border. Since that time, the concept of "combined forces" and sharing of information had resulted in more efficient law enforcement. At any crime crossing county lines or city boundaries, liaison officers from one agency were always present. As the corpse fit the general description of the missing prostitute, Brenden and Montgomery Blake were sent out to confirm the dead woman's identity, if possible. Neither man was happy about the turn of events.

Brenden shivered, pulling his jacket a little bit closer around his shoulders. He wasn't cold. He just didn't like visiting the departed at night, no matter how much light was around.

Peter Mallerd walked over and offered his hand. His face was wary under a thatch of messy white hair, brown eyes wide open and taking in everything over the rims of his plain black-framed glasses. "Fellas. Long time, no see."

"Peter." Brenden shook briefly, then let his hand drop.

Monty Blake fired up one of his disgusting cigarillos. "Looks like you got yourselves a little problem here."

"Uh-huh." Peter Mallerd reached into his back pocket, took out a dip of snuff, and stuck it in his bottom lip. "Big problem, actually. Naked, dead woman. No clothes, no identification, no tire tracks I can see in this grassy soil, and no reason I can think of why she should end up here." He grunted disgustedly. "Got the pictures, bagged and tagged what we could, which is fuckin' nothing."

"Got an ID yet?" Brenden asked, expecting something simple.

Mallerd shrugged and pulled a face, his upper lip dropping over his lower one as he sucked his chew. "She fits the gal you guys were supposed to be looking for." He shrugged. "Guess we found her first."

Monty Blake puffed. "Any idea what killed her?"

Another shrug from Mallerd. "She's like we found her, boys. Turn her over and take a look. It'll shock the shit out of you."

A classic understatement.

Brenden glanced to his partner. "You want to take it?"

Monty Blake shook his head. "Shit, no."

"Pussy," Brenden groused through a sigh. There was no way to budge the old cop into doing something he didn't want to. Might as well go and get it over with.

Not giving the Sheriff or his partner a second look, he walked over to the Jane Doe. She was well lit for all angles. Leland McCormack joined him. "Hate to do this to you, Brenden." He lifted the white sheet.

The victim lay facedown in the grass. She looked like a giant mannequin, waxy and unreal. Her skin was tinged an odd greenish shade.

Brenden scanned the naked body, taking a few mental notes. The deceased woman was Caucasian, a little over five feet tall, sandy brown hair cropped short. Her back, legs, and arms were perforated with deep scratches. Between the scratches the faded tattoo of an angel was imprinted on her left shoulder blade. He wondered where her guardian angel might have been when the woman was meeting the Grim Reaper.

Brenden drew in a breath. "She's torn up pretty bad."

McCormack indicated there was more. "That ain't the half of it. Turn her over."

Hunkering down on his haunches, Brenden put his flashlight aside. He slid his hands between the body and the ground and gave a hefty shove. Rigor mortis commenced with the muscles of mastication and progressed from the head down the body, affecting legs and feet last and generally manifesting in one to six hours. Rigor had already passed and the corpse was supple, an indication she'd been dead a good while. *Why the fuck did he leave her facedown?*

He soon found out. Her eyes were open, staring emptily. She'd died with her panic mask preserved, her features reflecting the traumatic terror she'd felt as death overtook her. Neck, arms, torso, almost every inch was ripped to shreds.

Brenden blinked and stared in horror, a mixture of fear and

loathing crossing his face. Panic and bitter bile singed his throat. He swung around and bolted, going down a few feet away on his hands and knees. His guts heaved. He vomited up the coffee he'd drank earlier, continuing to dry-heave for several minutes until there was nothing left in his stomach.

"You okay, Bren?" Montgomery Blake asked from the distance.

Brenden wiped his mouth on the sleeve of his coat. "Shit," he gasped though another gag. "I wasn't expecting that." His obscenity fairly well expressed how he felt about now.

Blake sucked his stogie. "Who we think it is?"

Brenden nodded. He easily recognized the girl in the photos Eddington had given them. "Yeah. Janice Parker." A once pretty girl who'd turned down the wrong road.

Janice Parker. Vanishing as if she'd never existed, only to turn up less than twenty-four hours later as a murder victim. Dead at twenty-two years of age.

"She looks pretty damn bad." Monty offered through an exhalation of blue cigar smoke.

Brenden grimaced. "No shit, Sherlock." Anger gusted up in his throat, pushing aside the revulsion. He looked back toward the corpse. His stomach made another lurch and he swallowed. His skin felt hot and taut, as if sewn too small to fit over his bones and stretched tightly to fit.

"Her throat's been torn out," McCormack said, clearly affected by the sight of the savage mutilations. No sensible person wanted to die in the buff, stripped of dignity and identity. "Look at the damage. She was literally shredded to death."

"Yesss . . ." Brenden echoed emptily. Needing to clear the nasty taste of vomit out of his mouth, he dug for his cigarettes and lit one. *Replace it with another nasty taste,* he thought dimly, almost grateful to feel the scorch of smoke on his lungs. He had no doubt they looked like a couple of pieces of charcoal.

Monty Blake pushed his porkpie hat up on his balding head, scratching his pate of thinning hair. "Wild dogs?"

Leland McCormack shook his head. "Wild dogs don't strip a person naked and dump them out in the middle of nowhere." He pointed at the grass, trampled by the heavy boots of investigators. "No blood or signs of struggle. She's too clean. She wasn't killed here but brought here from somewhere else."

Brenden closed his eyes. The hair at the nape of his neck prickled. Goddamn it. He had a feeling something huge had just fallen into their laps, something they weren't prepared to deal with. "Was she sexually abused?" His throat felt raw, raspy, when he asked the question.

McCormack shrugged. "Don't know yet. No bruising on her inner thighs, but it's too early to tell until I get her on the table for autopsy."

Blake shook his head. "I pass."

"I'll go," Brenden said, hardly aware he was saying the words. There wasn't really a need for him to be present, but something he couldn't quite identify was compelling him to attend. How was it the missing prostitute turned up a murder victim less than a day after vanishing? What had happened to her wasn't the most pressing question. The most pressing question was: would it happen again?

After a brief conference with Montgomery Blake, the cops decided they would split up. Brenden rode to the county morgue with Peter Mallerd, following the meat wagon transporting the body of Janice Parker. By this time, the airwaves were burning with news of the murder and the press was beginning to try and make contact. Between phone calls from Blake and Eddington, Brenden listened to Peter Mallerd attempt to fend off reporters looking to headline the morning editions of the newspapers.

An hour later, Brenden watched as the clean-up man swabbed down the enameled table and two more morgue attendants wrestled the body onto it. The smell of antiseptics and alcohol burned through his nostrils. If the smell of death was rot, the smell of the examination of death was just as stomach-turning.

Peter Mallerd stood beside him, sipping a cup of coffee spiked liberally with the bourbon Leland McCormack kept in the bottom of his desk drawer. No one could blame the old sheriff for having a nip. Brenden had considered a cup himself, but decided the tarry liquid was more than his stomach could stand. He didn't want to be hitting the toilet again for another round of vomiting.

Dressed in a white coat, Leland McCormack took his position in front of the table, dictating to his assistant as he noted the condition of the corpse. A few minutes into his examination, he lifted a bagged hand.

"Look here, boys—her wrists and ankles are bruised and raw, clear signs of binding. He put the limp hand back down. "She was tied up and tortured. By the scraping and rawness, I'd say she struggled pretty hard. She didn't die quickly—I think this took a couple of hours."

Both cops nodded, taking in the information. Mallerd took another gulp of his coffee and then decided to leave the coffee out of his second cup, going instead of a shot of straight booze. By his grimace the bourbon was burning its way through the pit of his stomach. "I need to retire," Mallerd whispered sotto voce. "I'm getting too damned old for this. Dead naked girls— I won't sleep a wink when I get home."

Brenden didn't think he would either.

McCormack continued his examination, measuring the deep bites. The teeth creating the marks were unusual. Almost every tooth making contact with Janice's skin was jagged and sharp.

"Human?" Brenden's hand rose to his neck, unconsciously rubbing at the mark under his stiff collar. He thought there might be a connection, but the idea left his brain as soon as it twinkled into existence. The bite mark of a passionate lover and those marring Janice Parker's flesh were too different when compared. There was no match. The idea flamed out, not entirely dying, but tucked away in the box where a cop kept useless information until it became useful or he forgot it.

Leland McCormack shook his head. "I don't know. There's a sign of at least two sets of lateral incisors on the top, lower jaw canines on the bottom, all abnormal in size. Dog's teeth aren't like this at all. What the hell can make these kind of bites? Well, your guess is as good as mine at this point. And look here—" He indicated a long set of scratches down the corpse's right thigh, setting his outstretched hand above the marks to mimic tearing. "See the shape? Clearly here we have fingernails, not claws."

Both cops agreed. As they mulled over his words, McCormack made a discovery. "You guys notice there's no dependent lividity on this body?" His even, neutral voice betrayed nothing. McCormack could be standing ass-deep in body parts and he wouldn't blink an eye. He'd been dealing with death since graduating from medical school. Death seemed to hold more fascination for him than living patients could. He could hold a corn dog in one hand and dig into bloody innards with the other and never spill a drop.

Both cops glanced at each other, then shrugged. "We're supposed to find the bad guys who committed the murder, Leland," Mallerd said, not a bit annoyed to be quizzed on something he should know by now, but didn't. "Not dissect the medical particulars."

Leland McCormack licked his lips. "It's the point where blood settles once the heart stops pumping. She was face down. There should be purplish skin throughout her lower extremities." He picked up a scalpel. "Let's take a look here." Hand unwavering, McCormack incised a deep Y from the edge of each shoulder to the bottom of Janice Parker's sternum before going all the way to the pelvic bone. He peeled back the chest flap. His assistant helped him pry open and spread the ribcage to expose Janice Parker's lungs and heart.

The corpse didn't bleed. There was not a drop of blood in her, nor so much as a single smear on her skin. At this point, they should have been siphoning off the pints of blood settled in the abdominal area.

"This is bad. She's sucked dry." McCormack looked over the body, pinning down each cop in turn. "Somehow, gentlemen, she's been very efficiently drained of every last drop."

"Aw, fuck." Mallerd shook his head and drank his bourbon. "We've got one sick puppy on our hands."

After conferring with the powers that be, a press blackout was decided on. Janice Parker's cause of death would be, "undetermined and under investigation." A later and more detailed report after the autopsy was completed would state Janice Parker didn't die from the throat wound. She'd died from the shock induced from massive loss of blood.

The "foul play" she'd encountered was, of course, murder.

II

Letting his keys slip from lax fingers, Brenden was barely aware of the muffled clatter they made when striking the carpeted floor under his feet. Lurching through the dimly lit living room like a man who'd just consumed a dozen beers with tequila chasers, he flopped down in the nearest chair. He was exhausted, utterly wasted.

Brenden didn't like coming home after seeing a dead body. It bothered him more than he cared to admit. True, he'd seen more than one in his career, but he never got used to the sight. Somehow a corpse existing after death was obscene, the onlookers left to pick up the remains violating something sacred, pure. *Bodies should just disintegrate after death. Just turn to ash and blow away.* It would be neater and a hell of a lot easier to handle.

Glad he was alone, Brenden buried his face in his hands, shuddering. He closed his eyes, seeking respite from the images burned into his corneas. No luck. Janice Parker's contorted face hung in the center of his mind's screen, a pale, waxy thing, hardly human. Her expression had been going past sheer horror into—

what? Terror? Her last few moments must have been filled with terror and terrible pain as her body was ripped under sharp claws and torn by even sharper teeth. How fragile the ties were to life. And how sad some beast would thoughtlessly—perhaps even with glee—snuff it out. Who was Janice Parker? Nobody. An ex-hooker with little hope. Still, she'd been a person. She'd walked, breathed, lived.

Janice Parker was dead and her memory persisted in running around in his head like a carousel set to run on an insane speed.

Brenden sighed, running his hands over his numb face. His mouth settled into a grim line. He hadn't eaten, but he wasn't hungry. Sometimes he couldn't eat for days after seeing a corpse. Protein shakes and lots of cigarettes sufficed. He already knew he definitely wouldn't be getting any sleep tonight.

It made him very damn glad he wasn't a homicide investigator. He doubted he could remain detached and keep a professional distance. For him, the search for killers would turn into a personal vendetta. He could easily understand why people were frustrated with the legal system and why some turned to vigilante justice to seek revenge. Sometimes it seemed like the cops were investigating blindfolded with both hands tied behind their backs.

At this time, police had no clues, no motive, and no suspects. The sad truth was Janice Parker would probably end up in the cold-case files.

Earlier in the evening, when cruising by the strips clubs, he'd winced. Strippers, too, were victims of Dordogne's sex trade. He settled in his mind he'd talk to Danicia again about quitting, finding herself decent daytime employment. He would much rather have her filing papers in some boring office than flashing her tits and ass to drooling half-drunken assholes. No matter how big the bouncers were, or how well lit the parking lots were after hours, it wasn't safe in this world.

Thoughts of Dani pushed him out of his chair.

As usual, she'd blown off calling him, leaving him to simmer in the juices of his own worry even as he and Monty had made yet another pass down the back alleys—a place always guaranteed to rouse a few cats and people ducking for a little illicit sexual activity. More than one whore had turned up beaten black and blue, lying unconscious amid the dumpsters.

His sister's little apartment was composed of a kitchenette-living room combo, a bedroom, and a bathroom, attached to a utility room sharing space with the water heater and the washer and dryer. Perfect for one, cramped for two, and crowded for three. Brenden's head was barely an inch away from the ceiling. He had to duck to pass under the doorframes, sometimes forgetting and earning himself a nice crack to the skull.

Dani loved her hole. Her place was as neat as a pin, everything where it belonged. The furniture was secondhand, but clean and decent. The windows, when the blinds weren't closed, gave a nice view of the driveway and the backyard grass, respectively. She decorated a bit on the wild side, with faux animal-skin prints, lava lamps, and other hallmarks of an unusual lifestyle.

Stripping was not the job Brenden wanted his little sister to work, but Dani was stubborn. She liked the power she had over men. She was drop-dead gorgeous and men drooled over her. And he was there to kick the shit out of any bastard who made her cry. The fact her brother was a vice cop meant she got treated with a little more respect and dignity than the average stripper. Thankfully total nudity wasn't allowed in the clubs; the girls had to cover their crotches and nipples. To Brenden pasties and a thong weren't enough cover.

All light blacked out, Dani was asleep, feet sticking out from under the covers, head under a pillow, a small fan blowing across her bundled body. Satisfied she was safe, Brenden crept upstairs.

Instead of a few beers, he decided on a shower. Heading toward the bathroom, he stripped and stepped into the stall. In the mirror a white, drawn face met his gaze. Dark circles ringed his eyes. Lack of sleep, lack of hope, and lack of caring had finally caught up with him.

Brenden turned on the cold tap full blast and braced himself under the showerhead. Icy cold water pelted his skin, immediately bringing him out of his bleary haze and back to full consciousness. He welcomed the powerful sting on his skin, as though by punishing his flesh he could subdue the memory of Janice Parker and her sad fate.

He switched the blast to hot, then lingered, soaking out the stiffness of sitting in a car for hours on end. Finally, feeling a bit more refreshed than when he'd first come home, he stepped out of the shower, toweled himself dry, and dressed in his usual sleeping ensemble: sweatpants and a T-shirt. His weariness was gone, but apprehension was still there, deep inside, feasting on his guts.

Flipping on the television to a twenty-four-hour news channel, he lay down on his bed, hands tucked behind his neck. He closed his eyes, lying quietly, simply resting. The night's trauma kept intruding and all he saw on the screens of his closed eyelids was a nude, torn body.

Eyes fluttering open, he found himself staring at the ceiling, caught in the grip of insomnia.

There was an old saying among cops: what went on at work stayed at work. The burdens of the job should never be brought home, especially to the wife and kids.

Well, he didn't have a wife anymore.

Divorce was a policeman's disease. So was alcoholism. The ultimate disease was suicide. He had only succumbed to one so far, was determined to skip the other two entirely.

He let out a breath, his mouth twisting. He was thirty-three years old and it felt like his life was falling apart. He felt too exhausted, too battered emotionally even to think about his lost marriage. All he wanted to do was to hide away from the world.

There had to be a happy medium between work and play.

Alone wasn't a good state to be in. Was this all there was going to be for him from now on? Coming home, going to bed, just to wake up and start the process of saving the city all over again. What would tomorrow bring? Would he be like Monty Blake, a four-time loser without a pot to piss in by time he neared twenty-five years on the job? The endless questions ran around inside his skull, refusing to be silenced.

It all boiled down to one thing. He simply didn't want to go to sleep in a solitary state.

So solve the problem.

Rolling over onto one elbow, Brenden reached over to his nightstand for the small pad he scribbled reminders and notes in. He'd copied down the phone number to the Exotic Jewels escort service on one of the pages, along with a few dashed-off notes only he could decipher. He didn't need to look at the number. He had it memorized. Seemed a little pathetic, even as he checked the digits to make sure all were in place in his head. Yes, they were.

Propping his pillows under his head, he lay back down, going over the case in his mind. Police had become aware of the service about two months ago when the business card went into circulation uptown through the bars, strip clubs, and no-tell motels. The information offered was straightforward. Simple. No-nonsense. It was one of the most frustrating cases he'd worked on, not least of all because he'd had a one-night stand with one of the Exotic Jewels in question. Their investigation was, at this point, still ongoing. There was no evidence to prove any sort of illicit activity was going on.

In a most enticing way Líadán had told him she was not what he believed her to be. A yank of his chain obviously. They'd gone on to have the hottest and kinkiest sex he'd experienced in his entire adult life.

Brenden closed his eyes. Yes, Líadán definitely rocked his world. He'd always heard the expression used, but it'd never applied to him. Given a taste, he wanted more. He let his mind drift again toward Líadán. He'd liked the way she'd looked at him when they'd met. No surprise there. Beautiful, hot, sexy, tempting—too many words tumbled through his mind to accurately describe her. In her presence, he felt special. Chosen.

Between pounding the pavement looking for clues into Janice Parker's disappearance, making the usual rounds of bars and adult bookstores, and busting a few illegal back-alley dice games, he'd barely had ten minutes to think about Exotic Jewels, though he'd taken plenty of private moments to think about Líadán. He thought about her in the shower—oh, glorious nakedness!—on the way to work, and during those long hours through the night when it seemed every whore but the one he wanted was on the strip.

He wondered where she was and if she were thinking about him. Probably not.

Brenden sighed. He knew only one way to get in touch with her. Thanks to the Exotic Jewels messaging service she was easy enough to leave a message for. Police had made initial contact via phone.

There was a little kink in their future romance, though.

Brenden was a cop and she was a suspected whore. He still had the sticky dilemma of investigating her background and the business she worked for. First solution was to admit his personal interest in Líadán to his superiors and ask to be taken off the case.

A vice cop dating a prostitute? Not unheard of, considering the scope of his work practically ensured he spent a goodly amount of time around such women. He'd never given a second thought to considering a call girl as more than an overworked, overused woman who made a living on her back. Certainly he wouldn't think about such a woman as girlfriend material. He'd never live it down if word got around he was seeing a hooker. And there was the little question of moral turpitude. He was supposed to be an upstanding, decent member of his community. Anything unseemly in his life could get him tossed right off the force without a by your leave or a chance to explain.

Suddenly, though, the two worlds had collided and he was giving serious consideration to the idea of pursuing Líadán. Even as a memory, her stunning loveliness was enough to steal his breath away. The recollections of their intimate moments, the sound of her accented voice, her warm hands on his skin, her welcoming depth drawing his erection deeper . . . were enough to send a shiver down his spine, along with a pure hundred percent shot of desire traveling straight to his groin.

Brenden groaned, rubbing a hand over his burning eyes. Blotting out Líadán's image was impossible. Deprived and abandoned were the only words he could think of to describe how he'd felt waking up in the motel room alone. He'd only known Líadán one brief evening, but it had felt like a lifetime, maybe more because she'd marked him in such in indelible way.

If he were to see her, the best thing to do would be to keep it on the QT. Say nothing to no one, give no information about his personal life unless asked.

He felt a ripple of inner pleasure. He'd met a woman who interested him.

"Damn." He muttered the curse, shaking his head. Reaching for his cigarettes, he lit one. He usually didn't smoke in bed, but since he was wide awake and had things keeping him from sleep, he might as well indulge.

Watching circles of smoke drift lazily toward the ceiling, he had to consider all angles. What did he really know about Líadán? Nothing. The not knowing made it too easy to let fanciful ideas of pursuing her run through his mind, spinning dreams around this beautiful woman who'd captured his attention and his heart—something he didn't give away easily or without thought. Even though he could count the number of women he'd slept with on two hands, Brenden's experience was pretty tame. Though his sexual adventures were not all mind–bendingly kinky, he was canny enough not to equate an earth-shattering experience between the sheets with any true emotion outside the bedroom.

Líadán, however, was far different from any woman he'd ever met. She'd gotten under his skin in a way that threatened to drive him quietly insane if he didn't see her again. Nothing could erase the feeling of her arms circling around his neck as their lips came together in a long kiss.

So what if she hadn't told him how to reach her privately? He was a cop. A smart man. One who happened to have at his fingertips every resource the city's law enforcement agencies had to offer. If he wanted to find her again, he could. Easily.

The ball was in his court. Part of the thrill of the hunt wasn't the conquest, but the chase. He knew he wanted another night in her bed. Several, if he could arrange it.

Moreover, he was truly interested in her, as more than a sex object. He wanted her to know he was serious about getting involved; he wanted to pursue more than a one-night stand.

But—and this was a huge one—just because he might locate her didn't necessarily mean she'd want a second go-round. If he were to see her again, then what? He didn't want to push her into anything neither of them was ready for.

Brenden took a long drag off his cigarette, exhaling smoke in a rush of aggravation. Usually a helpful tool in calming frayed nerves, the cigarette was doing him no good. The infusion of nicotine only served to hype him up even more.

He drew a deep shuddering breath. "You're a lonely, horny cop." Every time he hit the sheets or the shower, he ended up masturbating. An embarrassing habit, but a necessary release.

He'd much rather be having sex with a living, breathing woman than having his hand and dick form an ongoing relationship.

Fingering his plastic lighter, he let out a long-suffering sigh. He should simply turn off his mind, go to sleep, and just enjoy his time off.

The idea flew out the window because his urgent craving to see Líadán again was all encompassing. The blood in his veins seemed to surge every time he thought about her and the idea of letting her go simply would not leave him alone or allow him any peace. Everything about her appealed to him, from her magnetic allure to her absolute certainly in her ability to have men eating out of her hand like tame ponies. She'd walked into his life, performing the not-so-small miracle of making him feel not only alive, but like a man. His divorce had whacked him out, sucking away his confidence and self-worth as the lawyers hammered out each and every small detail.

So, here he was. Free. Single. Quite a bit over twenty-one. He could continue working, living the life of a half-alive zombie as he climbed up the professional ladder, taking the encounter as Líadán had probably intended—a one-shot affair. Or he could seize the bull by the horns and go after what he desired, what he most wanted.

Brenden snuffed out his cigarette, declining to light another. He was already chain smoking, killing two packs a day.

So call her.

The words were a whisper in the back of his mind, murmured by thousands of tiny little mouths. So far he'd managed to ignore them. Now, he had no reason to. He had a two-week vacation, some time to himself. Why spend the time alone if he didn't have to?

Brenden ran his hands though his hair. Was the idea of picking up the phone and dialing the escort service's number so harebrained?

He was close to reaching for the phone when he jerked his

hand back. Right . . . And what should he say? *"Hi, this is Brenden Wallace. I'm the cop some chick named Líadán had sex with the other night and I'd like to see her again."*

Uh-huh. Sounded downright ridiculous spoken aloud. He couldn't image actually saying the words. What would the ladies at the answering service think? He could picture some blue-haired old matron replaying his message to Líadán. After collapsing into gales of laughter, she probably would not be getting in touch.

The idea punched him right in the gut. Then he thought of Líadán's full red lips and the unexpectedly erotic bite she'd delivered just before he'd hit the height of climax.

A shaft of white-hot heat shot through him, hard and fast. The fever to see her—make love to her—was shredding him to pieces inside, a malady going past flesh and bone, straight to the center of his soul. There was no way he could mistake his body's reactions. Líadán had taken him to the edge of a sexual abyss he'd never known before to existed and then pushed him over. The fall was inescapably fatal.

He had to have her again.

Brenden picked up the phone, dialed the number.

12

Gay Paree was the swankiest restaurant in the city—the place to go to be seen not being seen, so to speak—sporting an intimately lit interior, private booths, and a dance floor the size of a postage stamp. Getting a booking was damn near impossible—the place was reserved months in advance.

Brenden had gotten his reservation with a single phone call. Not to the club itself, but to a friend who worked as a city health inspector—a lady who could shut the place down with a snap of her dainty little fingers. One call from Marianne Blackwood guaranteed a table in the best location. Brenden usually didn't use his pull to gain favors. Tonight, however, was a little bit different and warranted the use of brute force. He had a date.

Shaved, showered, brushed, and flossed within an inch of his life, he'd left his cigarettes at home. He hoped to cadge a few kisses from the lady—but not with ashtray breath. He was seriously considering quitting. More and more he hated the effects of nicotine on his body.

More than a little nervous, Brenden checked his watch. The

reservation was for eight, sharp. Líadán declined to let him pick her up, instead agreeing to meet him at the restaurant. He'd thought about waiting at the bar and having a quick drink, but the idea of being stood up in a crowd was more than he could take. He'd decided to wait outside. If she wasn't there by ten after, he could quietly slink off and nurse his wounded pride alone.

A far-off rumble caught his attention. Brenden cut a quick glance toward the sky and glowered at the menace. A storm was brewing in the north. Thick clouds were darkening, ominously gray. A heavy breeze winnowed the nearby river.

Líadán was five minutes early. Brenden saw her cab pull up to the curb. Inside, she dug out and lifted a compact. She rechecked her makeup, pursing her lips after quickly applying a fresh layer of lipstick. The parking valet hurried up to open the door, allowing a shapely pair of legs to slide out.

Brenden walked up, trying to keep his pace casual, unaffected. Inside his stomach performed a few back flips. He'd been expecting her to drive, imagining a lowslung, sleek sports car matching its owner in beauty. He reached for his wallet. "Let me."

She waved him back. "Not your responsibility." Líadán paid the cabbie, tipping the driver an extra five and a smile bright enough to melt steel.

Brenden let her have her way. This was obviously a woman who didn't beg favors. Not knowing whether to be flattered or offended, he decided on neither. She'd wanted to come, had gotten herself there. Arriving by cab opened two options. Either she'd be going home the same way—or she'd let him drive her. He hoped the evening would go well enough so she'd consider the latter. He really didn't want to go home alone if he could help it.

As Líadán grabbed her purse and got out to brush the folds of her dress into place, Brenden allowed his gaze to slide over her luscious body. Her clingy outfit, cut high around the neck and brushing her knees, bared her back in a daring plunge. She'd braided her long hair into a crown around her head, tucking in sprigs of faux jewels for a queenly effect. Her eyes were done up in a peacock shade matching her dress, a simple, stunning effect.

Brenden's heart lurched again. He swallowed, finding it hard to breathe. This woman definitely had an instant and deadly physical effect on him. *I'm glad she isn't a hunter. Caught in her sights, I'd freeze like a deer.*

There was a mischievous look in her gaze and a sexy grin on her face. "I hope I'm on time."

"On the dot."

Brenden offered his arm, gratified when Líadán slipped her hand into the crook of his arm, giving a slight squeeze of approval. Her fingers were long and slender, nails flawlessly manicured. Heads definitely turned when he guided her through the crowd. A few eyebrows shot up in annoyance when they went breezing through the velvet rope guarded on two sides by burly bouncers.

Líadán was clearly awed. "I've heard it takes months to get a table here."

Brenden shrugged as though he frequented the joint on a daily basis. "It's not what you know, it's who you know. I pulled a few strings to get a table."

She eyed the décor in admiration. "Impressive."

A formally dressed maitre d' guided them past other diners to their table, situated in a quiet corner, elegantly laid out with the best china, crystal, and flatware. The elaborate candlelit centerpiece offered a warm, cheery ambience without being intrusive. Across from the dining area on a raised platform, a small jazz band played low, bluesy music, perfect for hip-to-hip dancing.

"Something to drink?" their host asked when both were

seated. He offered a wine list. None of the vintages listed were less than two hundred dollars. Brenden knew the place would be expensive. In addition to a credit card, he'd tucked away a goodly amount of cash for tips. Tonight wasn't the time to come off like a tightfisted bastard. He wanted to impress the lady.

"Do you have a preference as to red or white?"

Líadán decided. "Red."

Brenden looked over the list, lost. Okay. Knowledge about wines wasn't one of his things. He chose a '94 Araujo Eisele Vineyard Cabernet Sauvignon, described as "a profoundly rich, silky-textured wine with an impressively saturated dark purple color."

The maitre d' was impressed. "Good choice, sir." He nodded in approval and sent the waiter to fetch the bottle. At two hundred-seventy-five dollars, it had better be good, damned good.

Their waiter returned a few moments later, bearing an appropriately dusty bottle, presumably retrieved from temperature-controlled vaults where it had been lovingly stored, awaiting its moment to be opened and enjoyed. Cork removed, two glasses were poured. Thank God the waiter didn't hand the cork over for sniffing. Brenden wouldn't have known what to sniff for.

Líadán lifted her glass, taking a sip. "Perfect." She graced him with a smile. "I find I enjoy red wine more than white. The heart and soul of the grape is in the color." She took another sip, her eyes pinning him down over the rim of the glass. "It's rich and full-bodied . . . like blood." Her eyes crinkled just a bit, mouth curving into a catty smile. Her eyes met his with a predatory intensity. "I find it is something I enjoy immensely.

Brenden didn't know if she meant the wine or the blood. Kinky. Very kinky. He loved it. Something about her made his instincts hum, like grabbing hold of a hot wire fence. A sense of danger hovered around her. But was it the danger of a devastatingly beautiful woman . . . or the fact she should be off-limits to a cop investigating her line of business?

To cool himself off, he took his own taste. The wine slid over his taste buds, wonderfully smooth with just a hint of tartness. "Excellent," he told the waiter. He secretly congratulated himself on his superior taste in women and wine.

The waiter handed over menus. "Let me know when you are ready," he said, discretely slipping off to attend to other patrons.

Líadán stiffened. She paused a minute before slowly opening her menu. Brow wrinkling, she perused it a moment, then set it aside. Nibbling her lip, she glanced around at other diners, as if taking in their individual selections. When her gaze found something familiar, she relaxed.

"Didn't see anything you like?"

Líadán laughed, not in the least bit embarrassed. "I know what I want."

Brenden rolled his eyes and made a *tsking* sound. He hadn't even had a chance to read the menu. He took a second look. In addition to exotic Creole favorites, the restaurant served a selection of popular down-home dishes. He bypassed the froufrou food, looking for the steak. Ah, good. Several nice cuts were offered. He made a mental selection, then hailed the waiter.

The waiter hustled over, pen in hand. "Ready to order, sir?"

Brenden deferred to his companion.

"Steak tartare," she said confidently.

The waiter scribbled.

Brenden didn't know what the hell steak tartare might be, but it sounded interesting. His own selection wasn't as exotic. "The eight-ounce rib-eye. Well done, no pink." A baked potato, salad, and bread completed his order.

"Very good, sir." The waiter bowed, snatched the menus, and melted back into the crowd.

Hating long silences, Brenden searched around in his mind for something interesting to talk about while they waited for the food. "So tell me about yourself." A lame opening. He had his reasons, though. He wanted to learn all he could about her.

Líadán blinked, obviously startled by his question. "Not much to tell."

He smiled. "There is something I am curious about."

An eyebrow wryly arched. Her heavy-lidded gaze burned right through him. "Oh?"

"Your accent—I can't place it."

Líadán hesitated. "Hungary. I'm Hungarian." Her eyes softened, perhaps seeing a distant memory. She leaned closer, elbows propped on the edge of the table as if she were going to offer a secret. "I am nothing more than a little peasant girl off the farm."

What an odd way to describe what he believed to be a woman of sophistication. "Born there?"

She nodded. "Yes. Many years ago. Too many, I often think. It sometimes seems like centuries have passed since I was a girl."

"Surely not. You speak English well. Have you lived in the United States long?"

Líadán paused, as if thinking out her answer, choosing her words with care. "I have lived mostly in Europe these last few years." She toyed with her wine, tracing the mouth of the glass with a single finger, a mesmerizing and sexy move. Brenden wished she'd trace her fingers along his skin the same way. "The majority of my, ah, education was mostly in England."

"Ah. And you studied?"

Faint color crept slowly across her pale cheeks. "Many things." She didn't elaborate.

Brenden tried again. "So what brought you here?"

Líadán sipped her wine, giving a slight shake of her head. A sadness came and went in the depths of her eyes, as though profoundly wounding regrets harried her thoughts. Her soft sigh seemed ripped from the very depths of her soul. "I needed a change—new scenery, fresh faces, younger blood."

Good answers, but vague and incomplete. The cop in Brenden was dissecting every word. She offered straightforward answers, giving no more information than necessary. She was being very careful, almost as though she suspected he'd planned the evening as more than personal entertainment.

Brenden wanted to dig deeper, but backed off. Sensing she was not ready to reveal a lot, he refrained from pushing her. First-date jitters were always a pain in the ass. Though they'd seen each other naked, shared the delights of each other's bodies, they were little more than strangers, barely acquainted, drawn together only by a mutual attraction.

The arrival of their food gave them a moment's respite from the delicate dance of getting to know each other. Their waiter served both with a deft hand, refilling their wine glasses before he departed. The food looked and smelled wonderful.

Brenden peeked at her selection, curious. Surrounded by butter lettuce, the fresh red, fine-chopped fillet was topped with a whole raw egg yolk. Individual small cups filled with chopped onions, pickles, and capers were sitting to be used on the greens. Additional condiments were set up on a separate smaller plate: mustard, virgin olive oil, Worcestershire sauce, cayenne, and regular pepper. His stomach turned. It looked perfectly disgusting. He wondered how anyone could eat it and not puke. He preferred his meat fully cooked. When he cut into the cow, he didn't want it to moo.

Líadán seemed pleased with her selection. She added little amounts of sauce and pepper to the meat, then used her fork to cut into the raw egg. A splash of olive oil smoothed the mixture, along with a teaspoonful of mustard. Toasted Italian sourdough with whole-grain mustard butter completed her order. Forking up a tiny bite of raw meat, she turned the spotlight on him. "So tell me about you."

It was Brenden's turn to grasp at straws and try to keep from wriggling in his seat. Since revealing details of his life might encourage her to open up, he decided to jump in with both feet and see what happened. To gather a little time to think, he gave his own food some attention, adding a dollop of butter and sour cream to his steaming hot potato.

"I'm afraid I'm not as well traveled as you. I've never been out of the United States. My four years in the Army kept me stateside."

Líadán's left eyebrow quirked up. A gleam lit her blue eyes. "Then you are a military man?" The edge in her voice was unmistakable. She was intrigued.

Brenden laughed, digging into his steak with knife and fork. The meat was tender, almost melting in his mouth. He swallowed, wiping his mouth on his napkin. "Not quite. I served my time and got out, still a snot-nosed punk." He forked up a bit of his salad, chewed, swallowed. "Got in a little trouble, disappointed the hell out of my parents, broke their hearts a little, I think."

Líadán tore off a tiny piece of her bread, tucking it into her mouth. "You don't seem to be the kind who would get in trouble." Crumbs escaped her. Brenden watched as her tongue swept her lower lip in an agile pink flick, feeling a familiar heat in his loins as he remembered her oral talents.

Brenden cleared his throat, trying to keep his mind on conversation. "Oh, yeah. I had my share of hell-raising. Even got busted and spent a few nights in jail." He paused for effect, letting out a mock sigh. "Since I decided I didn't want a career behind bars, I decided to go into law enforcement. Went to the police academy in Shreveport when I was twenty-four. After I graduated, Dordogne was hiring police officers, so I relocated here. I've been here ever since, nine years on the force. Made detective last year and transferred directly into vice."

Líadán gave a canny smile. "Which is how I met you." A neatly aimed poke at his aborted attempt to arrest her.

Brenden laughed. "Right. Which is how you met me."

A whisper of a smile touched her glossy lips. "And your investigation—," she started to say.

Brenden decided not to lie. What was the point? If he did and she found out the truth, she would feel he'd misled her. He wanted to be completely honest and open, especially at this very fragile crossroads in their relationship. He set down his utensils. "It's still ongoing."

Líadán stiffened in her chair. A brief blush stained her cheeks. Was she ashamed or embarrassed? Difficult to tell. She masked her emotions expertly, revealing little. "I see." She looked down at her food. For a moment Brenden thought she was going to say something, but she'd apparently decided to make no comment.

Instead, Líadán forked up a bit more of her raw steak; chewing slowly, swallowing carefully, as though she feared the food might choke her. She was eating, but with little enjoyment, focusing on the meat, ignoring the salad and bread. Her tiny bites wouldn't fill a bird. Like most women, she probably thought a big, piggish appetite was a turn-off.

Taking her silence as a cue, Brenden dug into his own food. Hungrier than he thought, he cleared his plate of every last morsel, then topped off his substantial meal with another glass of wine. Líadán barely took two more bites before laying her fork aside. She gave her attention to her own glass. She seemed relieved when the waiter arrived to claim their dishes.

"Dessert?"

Líadán shook her head. "Nothing more for me, thank you."

Brenden also passed. He would have liked to try one of the

rich confections Gay Paree was famous for, but decided it wouldn't be wise to make a pig of himself. The waiter refilled their glasses for a third time, emptying the bottle. In the mood to keep the evening going, Brenden ordered a second bottle. The waiter smiled and hustled away, mentally calculating his tip.

Conversation, which had sputtered to a stop, began again. Líadán made the first overture to get things going. "Tell me about your family."

Tension broken, Brenden relaxed. "My parents are dead," he said, feeling the rips he'd thought mended. "They were killed three years ago in a car accident. Drunk driver hit them head on."

Líadán's eyes dipped. "I'm sorry."

Brenden felt as if he'd just put his foot in his mouth. He was striking every wrong note. He'd answered without thinking about how the words would come out. "Don't be. Life happens. Not always what we want, but no one can control fate or what's going to come to pass."

A subtle tremor seemed to overtake her. "So you believe what is to be is already preordained?" Her question begged a reply.

Brenden licked dry lips. Even though he was raised a Catholic, he'd never formed a real opinion as to whether or not a supreme being existed. Some of the things he'd witnessed as a cop were things no human being should ever have to see, acts of violence so brutal it seemed no loving god could possibly exist in heaven above. If there was even such a being, was there a method in the madness of creating mankind?

"I'd like to think I control my fate. But I also believe we come to crossroads, where what we do will either see our lives continue or end. Whether we consciously make the choice or whether it's something we simply can't avoid because it's already carved in some celestial stone, I don't know."

Reaching across the table he opened his hand palm up, a

silent signal for Líadán to place her hand in his. "This is where I want to be right now. Here, with you. We both made a choice to be here tonight."

Líadán cocked her head to one side, glancing at his extended hand, hesitating. Seconds ticked by without her reacting, each one feeling to Brenden like the strike of a heavy eternal gong. Finally, she joined her hand with his. "I was . . . pleased . . . to get your message. I'd hoped you would call. I wanted you to, but I was afraid."

Her words speared his heart straight to the core. Brenden closed his hand, enjoying the sensation of her fingers tangling with his, her body's heat seeming to meld with his. Soft and smooth, her skin felt like silk. An image flashed through his mind of more body parts tangling together in a most erotic way. His pulse ratcheted into high gear, sending a delicious throb straight into his cock. "Why were you afraid?"

Líadán's gaze lifted. Shimmering like an ocean, her eyes lingered on his face with what felt like a heated, hungry caress. "Because of what I am . . . and of what you are." Her tone implied biting self-criticism.

Brenden nodded. Saying she was a call girl was not exactly great first-date conversation. He wasn't bothered. He knew what she did for a living. He'd made the decision to overlook it and pursue her. Once she learned he wouldn't judge her, perhaps she'd open up more and confide in him. He had the rest of the evening to win her faith . . . perhaps the entire night and beyond. But he had to take it slow, consider each move the way a chess player would carefully maneuver each piece toward the final objective of conquest. Trust was the best way to earn his way back into her bed.

"Doesn't matter to me. You're the one I'm interested in, not what you do for a living." He glanced down at her hand, so small and delicate against his own larger bear paw. Her fingernails were long, sharp. Visual sensations quickly translated into mental ones. All he could imagine were her nails raking down his back as he sheathed himself deep inside her.

Brenden drew a steadying breath, attempting to check his daydream. Good thing they were in a very public place or else he'd be clearing the table and lifting Líadán on top. A silent groan shuddered through him. His penis grew heavier inside his slacks as an erotic tug sent shockwaves deeper, lower . . . The need to take her was stronger than anything he'd ever experienced before. Líadán was definitely going to be worth the pursuit. Whatever world she inhabited, he wanted to be a part of it.

Líadán shook her head, drawing her hand away from his. Her hands dropped to her lap, toying with the napkin she'd earlier placed there. "You say so," she murmured. "But if you knew the truth about me, you would shun me."

13

Eyes fixed on her face, Brenden again detected her self-loathing. A quick feeling rose. He suspected the men in Líadán's past offered no respect, acceptance, or admiration. Like most women who used sex to make a living, she didn't seem to have any sense of her worth as a woman or a person. Men probably treated her like a pretty toy, to be used and sent away.

He shook his head. They needed to be a little closer to continue this conversation, Getting up, he rounded the table, took her hand, and drew her to her feet. "Dance with me."

Setting her empty glass aside, Líadán nodded. Her face was flushed and rosy from the wine she'd consumed. "As you wish."

Brenden guided her through the tables, toward the dance floor filled with other couples dancing to the low, throbbing strains of a mournful jazz standard.

"I haven't done this in a long time," he apologized, glad the music was slow and low. Dancing had never been his forte. He knew four decent steps, just enough to get by. Usually he was floundering about on two left feet. "Bear with me if I step on your toes."

Líadán shot him a teasing look. "I'll just step back." She parted her arms to welcome him into her embrace.

Brenden moved closer, savoring the anticipation of getting his hands on her lush body. He stepped into her embrace, basking in the moment. Líadán leaned into him, soft breasts pillowing against his chest. He could almost feel her need stirring under her skin, triggering his own lust. The fading bite on his neck seemed doubly sensitive under his collar. More than lust, more than sizzling desire, he felt a strange connection traveling between them, as though he could feel the pulse of his own blood under her skin.

Guiding her arms to his shoulders, Brenden slid his hands around her slender waist, feeling bare skin under his palms. She sucked in a startled breath at his unexpectedly intimate touch, shivering a little when he caressed the base of her spine. Her skin felt lusciously soft. His own seemed to heat when he touched her. Temptation surged in immediate response.

Another scent lingered under the sweet tease of her cologne, a headier, muskier odor hinting of carnal passions just waiting to be unleashed. The smell badgered his senses, setting his nerves on edge.

The wine must have helped loosen Brenden up. Their bodies glided together in perfect motion. They danced in silence through one dreamy blues standard, then a second, simply enjoying the caress of shadowy illumination and the gentle sway of other couples around them.

Drawing her as close as their bodies and public propriety would allow, Brenden enjoyed holding Líadán in his arms, guiding her to the gentle rhythms of the mellow notes. Her eyes closed in pleasure, lashes brushing her creamy skin. She was pliant in his embrace, snuggling close, her cheek pressed to his shoulder.

Brenden eased his hand up her bare back, enjoying her warmth. His hand found the nape of her neck, caressing the line where hair and skin met. "We all have things in our pasts we aren't proud of. Doesn't mean we have to let our past affect what happens tomorrow."

Líadán's head came up. When he gazed down into her face, he saw wonder mingling with disbelief. She tightened her grip. "I didn't think I could ever find a man who would accept me."

Her words made a direct strike to Brenden's psyche. Had she always felt like an outsider, a little girl standing on the outside of the window staring in? He knew the answer because he'd felt the same way for the longest time. Losing Jenna, watching her walk off to build a life with another man, tore him to shreds. He'd taken the vows of marriage, and he'd stuck by them one hundred percent. Things had gotten worse, gone sour. But instead of talking to him about her feelings, Jenna had decided their marriage was not worth saving. She'd gone on, leaving him stuck in neutral. Meeting Líadán had gotten him back in gear, restoring his interest in rebuilding his private life.

Brenden bent close to her ear. "You've found a man who thinks he's crazy about you."

Líadán's head dipped back, eyes glittering with happiness. "Tell me what you want, and I will willingly give it." Her words went straight to his cock, taking a short side trip to stitch up his heart.

Basking in her smile of pleasure, Brenden drew in an unsteady breath. "Everything." His gaze locked with hers. Sparkling in the depths of her blue eyes was absolute certainty mingling with a clear and unabashed desire. Her lips curved up in a soft, warm smile.

Before Líadán could change her mind, Brenden brushed a soft kiss over her mouth. Silky lips parted under his, welcoming the first eager thrust of his tongue. She tasted feral and wild, of rich red meat and exotic spices. The mix made him ravenous, causing his blood to boil with need.

With a moan, he eased his tongue deeper. Líadán parried

with a wet velvet stroke of her own. Her arms curled around him, fingers splaying across his back with an almost possessive urgency. Shifting on her high heels, she caught his lower lip gently between her teeth and suckled, causing an instant reaction below his belt. His cock heated and swelled. Oh, damn . . . He was losing the battle to resist the demands of his body.

He'd meant the kiss to be gentle, reassuring. Need escaped him, the fire of pure sexual heat flaring fast and without warning. His kiss grew harder, more demanding. Líadán surprised him by moving closer, her breasts pressing against his chest in a most enticing manner. There was no mistaking her reaction. Her moan of assent and her own lips—as hungry and searching as his—told him all he needed to know.

Brenden dragged her closer, the rhythm of the music lost to something more primeval between them. Every time she moved against him, he felt another wild blast of desire. Their bodies had developed their own motion. No one existed on the face of the earth except them.

He gripped her slender hips, eager to feel her heated skin against his. Even though they were both fully dressed, the tempest of desire swirling through them wouldn't be denied as their lower bodies collided, sending a shaft of searing heat straight through him, intense and sudden. The way Líadán could make his sexual senses react in response to a simple touch truly defied explanation. His cock rose inside his slacks, growing harder with each passing second. He had to regain control or he'd climax right then and there.

Ending their kiss before things got embarrassing, Brenden let out a slow low groan, trying not to alert the other people dancing nearby. The days gone by without feeling her body under his had been sheer hell. If this passion between them was happening too fast . . . well, he was willing to seize the reins and follow the trail to see where it might lead. "I think we need to move this someplace . . ."

Líadán immediately nodded in assent. "More private?"

"Mmmm . . . yes . . . Definitely."

Somehow, Brenden paid the bill, settling up with the maitre d', leaving a generous tip for the waiter, and claiming their unopened second bottle of wine. In all, dinner had ended up costing over six hundred dollars. He wondered if he could afford to keep Líadán in expensive wine.

The valet had his car waiting. This afternoon he'd washed and polished the Olds to a shine.

Above their heads, the churning, angry clouds advanced, rolling in over the city like a wet cloak. By the flashes of lightning and the chill in the air, it promised to be a furious storm. Droplets of rain were already splattering on the ground around them.

Brenden glanced to Líadán. Now would be the time to indicate she was going home the same way she'd arrived. Her decision was made when the valet opened the passenger door for her. She slipped inside without comment. He breathed a sigh of relief. They were leaving together. He wouldn't be going home alone tonight.

Tossing the keys, the valet winked. "Lucky you."

Brenden nodded as he opened the door. Yep, he certainly was. He slid in behind the steering wheel, tucking the bottle of wine under the driver's seat. "Your call," he said, voice huskier than intended. "Where would you like to go?" It went without saying he wanted her to invite him into her life . . . and into her bed.

She drilled him with a sultry look. "Your place."

All the encouragement he needed. Starting the engine, he guided the car out of the parking lot and into the street. Gripping the steering wheel, he glanced to his right. "You're sure? I can take you home if you like."

Taken by surprise, she met his gaze. Disbelief was etched into her features. It was as if she totally hadn't expected he'd be willing to give her time and space. Sure, he was eager to have her, but only if she wanted something to happen. If she needed to wait, he was willing. He wouldn't be happy, but there would be other nights—if she chose to grant them. His desire needed no mention. He'd let her decide what happened next.

Líadán laughed. "I'm sure." She reached over and slipped her hand into his. Her gesture was obviously meant to reassure him. At the same time it reinforced the electric current building between them through dinner, the one setting his nerves on edge and threatening to drive his entire nervous system to shorting out from the frustration of not being able to have his hands all over her luscious body. He was almost tempted to get out of the car and let the cold rain give him a good dousing.

As if to reinforce the vibes simmering between them, thunder rolled. Lightning blazed though the sky, mimicking the ebb and flow of raw sexual desire between a man and a woman. The violence and fury struck hard, stealing away his breath.

Brenden lifted her hand, giving it a light, quick kiss. "I'm glad." Damn, this woman was amazing. He almost regretted having to give his attention to the road, reluctantly letting her hand slip away. The storm wasn't letting up.

He tightened his grip on the steering wheel, reminding himself to concentrate on the slick pavement and not the woman sitting beside him. The crisp beat of rain hitting the windshield sounded around them. The drive through evening traffic in a fierce storm wasn't an enticing one. He eased the car down the wet streets.

Líadán remained silent during the drive. She looked out the window, watching the traffic pass and the tall buildings of the city merge and then melt down into comfortable, tree-lined suburbs.

Forty minutes later, Brenden pulled into his driveway. Líadán tensed. Drawing a deep breath, she lifted her hand to her head, pressing two fingers quickly to her temple. Her face went blank, eyes taking on a glassy stare.

Brenden slowed the car to a stop in the garage and killed the engine. "You okay?"

Líadán gave a little shake of her head, quickly recovering her cool self-possession. "The thunder seemed to go right through me. It was almost like I felt an electric shock."

Brenden frowned in concern, setting a gentle hand at the base of her neck, massaging her nape. "If you're not feeling well, I can take you home."

Her hand dropped. "I'm fine." She offered a reassuring smile. "Really."

"This is it. Home. Safe and sound from the rain." As if to punctuate his words, thunder boomed at a deafening decibel. The rain redoubled its attack, pelting the streets and sidewalks with furious force. Fingers of lightning scratched the earth below, plunging everything into instant gloom.

Brenden groaned, whether from frustration or providence he wasn't sure. Talk about a hint from the gods. Here he was alone with a sexy woman, an expensive bottle of wine, and very much in the convenient dark.

"I didn't quite plan that one." He leaned past her, digging in the glove compartment for a flashlight. A bight beam of light filled the interior. "But I think this will get us around." He claimed the wine, handing it over to Líadán. "Carry this."

She took the bottle without comment.

Brenden got out of the car and came around to her side to help her out. She held on to his hand, letting him lead. The house was deserted. The first thing he heard was Bear's yelps. The dog was trapped outside in the downpour. "One minute."

Flashlight in hand, Brenden opened the back door and rushed outside. The rain pelted relentlessly, instantly soaking him to the skin. He found Bear's lead. By the time the dog was freed, he was soaked to the bone, accompanied by a stinking, miserable, wet dog. *What a way to end a romantic evening.*

Líadán waited in the darkened kitchen. Seeing a stranger, Bear immediately went into a barking frenzy, ready to fight. Attacking at full speed, Bear could easily knock a grown man off his feet. Brenden made a swipe for the dog's collar and missed.

Pinned under the dog's fierce stare, Líadán froze. Then, very slowly, she held out a hand, kneeling down to the level of the animal. "Good dog," she said in a low, soft voice. "I won't hurt you."

Bear's barking fell into a long, low growl. Detecting no immediate threat, he inched up to the hand she offered, sniffing, and then licking, her fingers. A few minute later the hound was putty in her hands. Líadán laughed and patted his huge head. Bear rewarded her by sending his shaggy, wet body into a rolling shake, dousing her with water.

Brenden cringed. "Damn it, Bear!" he roared, half embarrassed, half amused. He grabbed the big dog by his collar and hauled him off toward the adjoining garage. "You big galoot! Get your ass out of here." Shutting the screen and penning Bear in the garage, he turned to Líadán. She was wiping water off her face. "I think he likes me."

Brenden rolled his eyes. "I am so damn sorry." He snagged a dish towel hanging by the stove, offering it to her.

Líadán daubed at her face. "He's just doing his job." A smile tugged at her lips. "No harm."

"You're wet."

"I think you're the one who's all wet." Líadán reached up, swiping at his forehead and cheeks. Her simple gesture was all it took to bring out her alluring femininity and his reaction to it cascading back. She was drenched, her makeup ruined. Brenden hadn't thought she could look any sexier. He was wrong.

Líadán's compelling gaze met his, offering what felt like a

heated caress. "You're soaked to the bone," she prompted, bringing him out of his daze.

Brenden swallowed thickly. He didn't feel a bit of the cold or wet. He just felt desire, a desire where he imagined her body's heat melding with his as he lowered her to the bed and parted her thighs with his. The sound of the rain swept against the house, the rolling of thunder matching the intensity of his heart. "Guess I should do something about this."

She smiled. "Yes. You should get out of those wet clothes."

Brenden needed no more encouragement.

14

Wine bottle and two glasses in hand, Líadán followed Brenden into the den. He knelt down before the fireplace, throwing in a few pieces of wood, then packing it with wadded newspapers. Digging a lighter out of his pocket, he set the paper aflame. In a few minutes a warm fire crackled enticingly.

"Well, we have the light and the heat." Brenden wriggled out of his wet jacket and draped it over a nearby chair. "Let's get more comfortable." He retrieved a throw blanket from the back of the sofa, spreading it out on the floor in front of the fireplace.

Watching him move, Líadán's hand tightened on the neck of the bottle. His wet shirt clung to his broad shoulders, revealing every ripple of his muscles as he spread out the blanket. Her breath caught in her throat. Heavy awareness pulsed through her, a delicious accompaniment to the beat of the rain against the windows. She'd promised herself only a single night, then she would leave, never to see him again.

One night hadn't been enough.

Líadán narrowed her eyes, letting her gaze take in every inch of him. Knowing the inevitable conclusion to their affair, the truth chilled her soul. Auguste had sensed his strength and allure—wanted Brenden Wallace for his brethren.

Much to her dismay, Líadán found herself entranced by the idea. Centuries had passed since she'd found herself drawn to any man, both sexually and emotionally. Were Brenden to join them, she felt her life would be almost bearable.

For a moment she considered turning around, walking away. She could vanish . . . But, no . . . for her betrayal, Auguste wouldn't hesitate to execute Brenden Wallace. A shard of pain pierced her heart, a mingling of guilt and regret. *I've damned him, but I can't let him go.*

Yet . . . the strength he wielded so casually, along with the simmering passions he kept so carefully controlled, would make Brenden a formidable threat should he choose to unleash it. She believed his fury would be enough to make him a very dangerous man if challenged.

Oblivious to her thoughts, Brenden settled down on the blanket. He patted the floor beside him. "May not be the classiest way you've ever spent an evening, but it's warm now." He unbuttoned his wet shirt, fanning it away from his body, giving a tantalizing glimpse of his six-pack abs and sinewy arms. He was perfect in every way, right down to the bulge in his slacks.

Líadán laughed. Kicking off her heels, she padded over to sit down beside him. The glasses she carried clinked together. "It is the best way I can think of to spend an evening." Settling close to him, she could smell the scent coming off his skin—fresh rainwater mingling with the musky scent of his aftershave—and the sharp tang of burning wood. The primitive mix reminded her of the days when she inhabited a world lit only by fire, where people lived only from sunrise to sunset, trembling with superstitious fear when shadows settled across the land.

She'd learned the hard way the demons that mankind feared were all too real.

Brenden took the wine bottle from her. "Well, I think we can make it even better." He popped the cork, pouring a healthy amount into the two glasses. He set the bottle aside, then touched his glass to hers. His intriguing gaze bore into hers. "Here's to good wine and the beautiful woman I have the pleasure of sharing it with." He reached out, stroking a hand softly down her cheek.

Líadán felt a fierce blush heat her skin. His touch was sensual, intimate, and seduction was his goal. She already knew she would give in to his needs and her own. She closed her eyes against the tremor of awareness racing through her. What she felt for him went deeper than the pleasure they'd shared. Brenden Wallace inspired confidence, and, despite her reservations, she trusted him. The notion scared her as much as it intrigued.

She drew a deep breath, then took a quick drink of her wine. Its enticing blend slid down her throat, a soothing sense of warmth uncoiling throughout her body. The snapping of the fire and the fury of the storm outside compared little to the fierce carnal heat this man set off inside her soul. For the first time in her life she wanted to experience real love, pure and special, to give her heart away. "You flatter me."

He grinned. "I've heard flattery will get you everywhere."

She laughed. "You're right. It will."

This was nothing compared to the emotions roiling inside her mind. Coming home with Brenden, she'd found not only a haven for the night, but was gaining a look inside his life.

The den was unfailingly masculine. The fire highlighted an eclectic mix of battered but comfortable furniture; a leather sofa and a few heavy lounge chairs were arranged to take advantage not only of the wide-screen television set, but also of the cozy hearth built out of natural stone. This was clearly a man's haven, a place no woman would dare to intrude unless invited.

Brenden caught her glancing around, taking in the details. "Not the fanciest place in town. But it's where I hang my hat."

"I think it's perfect. It suits you."

"Thanks." He stretched out, giving her a full view of his long, lanky frame. He was as close to perfect as he could get without being naked. With his long hair matted by the rain, he looked like a sleek wild animal. "It seems too big for two people sometimes. I've thought about selling it, but never can bring myself." The snapping flames threw shadows, casting his face half in shadow, half in light, giving his tangle of golden blond hair and strange multicolored eyes an almost angelic glow.

Líadán drew a small breath to steady desire. Soon, she would allow herself to indulge. "Two people?"

Brenden nodded. "My sister, Danicia, lives with me. She's a trip, a real brat sometimes." He laughed. "She fancies herself a witch."

His words sent a prickle of recognition down Líadán's spine. Now she understood the harsh, painful electric shock invading her system when he'd driven into the garage. She'd had to bite down on her tongue to keep from crying out. As the pain had ebbed, she'd wondered if Auguste had sent the spark, a little punishment to remind her freedom was a limited thing. But the invisible force she'd encountered hadn't originated from Auguste. It had radiated from another source—one dwelling inside the house. When Brenden allowed her to cross his threshold, his invitation granted her entry into his sanctuary, breaking the barrier's invisible grip on her.

"A witch?" Líadán tried to keep her tone light and her voice neutral. Inside she was quivering like a willow in a windstorm. Had she been able to use all the gifts her jouyl granted her, she would have been able to sense these things without asking. Auguste's sigil and spells kept her abilities leashed, allowing her only a minimum. "Fascinating. Tell me about her."

Brenden rolled his eyes. "Not much to tell." He shrugged.

"Since she was a little girl, Danicia's been attracted to the occult, to all things mystical and Irish. I suppose it has to do with
our Scotch-Irish heritage. The other half has to do with all
those stories our grandmother fed her about the blood of the
mythical heroes supposedly in our veins."

"Do you believe?" she asked, half in jest, half in seriousness.
Had she found a man strong enough to topple Auguste from
his seat of power?

Brenden shyly shook his head. His expression revealed he'd
said more than intended. "Oh, no, I don't take those stories seriously at all. They're just old Irish tales my grandmother spun
to entertain. For myself, I prefer to stick to being a lapsed Catholic. I haven't set foot in a church since my wedding day."

Líadán cocked her head, angling a look his way. "Perhaps you
dismiss your grandmother's stories too easily. Think about it.
You're a police officer. A man who serves and protects people.
Makes you a hero of sorts, doesn't it?"

Brenden snorted, releasing a short, wry laugh. "A hero?
No . . . I don't know if you'd call me one." He turned his head,
meeting her gaze. "Crazy, maybe. I work bad hours for crummy
pay and put my life on the line every time I go out onto those
streets. It's not heroic. It's suicidal."

"It's admirable. Someone has to step up and protect the
weak."

Brenden sighed. "Let's not go into the psychology of what
makes a man heroic. Work is the last thing I want to talk about
on my days off." He rolled over onto his side and reached out,
tracing her bare arm. "What about you? Any brothers or sisters?"

Líadán blinked, startled by his question. Emotions warred
inside her. She couldn't reveal the truth. She found herself at a
loss. She didn't like lying to him, yet she couldn't bring herself
to given even a condensed version of her unhappy past. "I am
all alone."

"That's sad." His hand curled around hers. "You shouldn't be all by yourself."

Stunned, Líadán glanced down at their entangled fingers. There was nothing sexual in his touch, just one person offering another comfort. Brenden's simple gesture breached her well-erected defenses. Her heart, if she gave it, would not be abused by this man. True love was a real and startling emotion for her, but she welcomed the bulldozing of her high emotional barriers. It felt good to savor these extraordinary new feelings.

A smile caught hold, despite the negative thoughts whirling through her mind. Líadán looked up at him and a strange sensation passed between them, the same force that drew them together the night they met—his touch so much more real to her than the air she breathed. To distract herself a bit, she swirled the last of the wine in her glass, drinking it down. "Some of us are meant to walk alone," she murmured when her glass was empty.

He lifted her fingertips gently to his lips. "I want to do something about that." The arousal blooming so softly when they'd danced body to body suddenly exploded into roaring flames. His eyes found her face, studying her, waiting for her reaction. Sensual awareness pulsed thickly between them.

Brenden sat up, taking the glass from her hand, setting it aside. He leaned forward, bringing his face within inches of hers.

Without thinking, Líadán tipped her head toward his. Their mouths brushed together, gentle, slow, and ever so exquisite, tasting each other in a kiss made all the more erotic because of its stealth in arriving. Neither planned it. It just happened. Beneath the gentleness was a longing neither could ignore. As a ribbon of desire curled through her breasts down to her nether regions, the need to make love to him overtook her.

"Wow," he breathed, when their kiss had ended. "I've never felt anything like this before."

Líadán drew in her own breath. In that instant she knew without doubt Brenden Wallace would follow her though hell and back, even if it meant he was destroyed himself. A man like; Brenden didn't come along often. She would hold on to him; this lifeline unexpectedly had been tossed into the dark void of her life.

Silence followed, a silence in which nothing but the rain came between them. No more words were needed.

Climbing to his feet, Brenden pulled her to hers. Slipping off his shirt, he let it drop to the floor. Just as she reached up to undo the thin chain across her neck keeping the backless halter in place, he caught her hands. "Let me," he rumbled in a husky voice.

Líadán nodded. His hands slipped behind, expertly loosening the clasp. Freed, the silky folds drifted over her breasts, down her hips, falling around her feet in a soft hush. Dressed only in panties, garter, and hose, her bare breasts were proudly erect, the tips of her nipples hard little beads. At the sight of her, Brenden groaned, an earnest and besieged sound escaping his throat. When he reached for her, his hands trembled.

She watched as his eyes betrayed the effect her almost nude body was taking on him. While many men had gazed upon her body with admiration and desire, she had in turn despised them, knowing they were weak and could be manipulated by their sexual needs.

"You're so beautiful," he murmured. "So perfect."

The humbling, marveling tone in his voice almost brought tears of emotion to her eyes. Her mind screamed a volley of warnings and objections, but her senses screened them out. They were not what she wanted to hear. Instead she wanted to hear the sounds of love, the erotic sounds of his breathing, the soft feel of his hands as they moved over her skin. Mesmerized, she waited. Only when he drew her into his arms did she relax. She could feel his whole body trembling with anticipation, the fierce hardening of his erection under his slacks. She aroused him and he wanted her. Her heart fluttered with a ray of hope. He so clearly demonstrated physically what she was feeling.

"It's crazy, I know, but I need you so much." Brenden's hands touched her face, his fingertips skimming her cheeks before sliding to the nape of her neck. His head dipped and his mouth captured hers.

Líadán opened her mouth to allow the invasion of his tongue. She pressed herself closer to him, sliding her arms around his shoulders. Brenden nipped at her lower lip, tracing it with his own tongue before sucking it gently. His hand found her breast, cupping its weight and squeezing lightly. His fingers began to tease, making slow circles. Her nipple came to instant attention under his fingers, the pebble-hard nubbin acutely sensitive. She sucked in a breath, her body arching against his. A small moan escaped her lips. "That feels so good."

His exploring tongue traveled the delicate whorl of one ear, tracing a warm wet path along the delicate shell-like curve. Catching her dangling earring between his teeth, he gave it a gentle, teasing tug. "Only the beginning of what you're going to feel tonight." Kissing the soft pulse at the soft base of her throat, he worked his way lower, each teasing lap of his tongue setting goose pimples of excitement into action across her exposed skin. Her breath caught in her throat, hovering like a tiny hummingbird in flight, anxious, oh so anxious when he flicked at one pink peak.

Stifling a cry of pleasure, Líadán curled her fingers through Brenden's thick hair. He seemed to take her anxious tugs as a sign she was enjoying the sensations. Tongue swirling in clever delicious ways that aimed blazing little darts straight at her vibrating core, his teeth raked the sensitive nub. His free hand covered her right breast, rolling the little pink nubbin between thumb and forefinger.

"That feels so good." A shiver ran through Líadán's body.

Lust heated, then sizzled. The throb between her legs made it impossible to think about anything but gratifying this aching need.

"I want to please you this time." Brenden kissed the softness between her breasts. "Taste you . . ." His hand slid down to her flat belly, then between her legs to gently caress her softness. The feel of his fingers sliding against silky panties wet with her cream created a mesmerizing sensation. He slipped a finger between the elastic of her panties, maddening her with an erotic flick against her little button.

Tilting back her head, Líadán gasped aloud. Her body shuddered with tiny tremors when his finger found and stroked the slick softness between her labia. He added a second finger, searching for her depth. Finding her slit, he slid in, to work his magic.

"Oh, wow!" Jerking in surprise, she sagged against him. She needed to get a grip, control and pace herself or she'd lose herself to orgasm too quickly. She didn't want to. She wanted to wait, enjoy the moment just as he came to climax with her. *Steady . . . Take it slow.*

Brenden, however, wasn't giving her that chance.

15

Brenden dropped to his knees. Holding her hips, he trailed soft warm kisses across the smooth plane of her belly. Unsnapping her garters, he slid his fingers into the waistband of her panties, guiding them down her legs. One hand swept over her bare thigh.

Settling a hand on his shoulder for balance, Líadán lifted first one foot, and then the other, as he freed her from the undergarment. The tiny scrap of material covering her shaved mound was no more. The straps of her garter dangled, brushing her hips in a most sensual manner. She was clad in only hose, a sight he seemed to enjoy. His gaze glided over her body, heated by his caresses. From the need alive in his eyes, he wouldn't be holding off from his own pleasure much longer.

She let out the breath she had been holding. The way Brenden could make her body react with a simple look defied all logic. He leaned forward and slipped his tongue through her slit. All rational thought vanished at the warm feel of his tongue invading her most private space. The moist glide on her sensitive skin sent white hot darts of fire straight into a core already molten with longing.

Her hand tightened into a fist at the back of his head when he slid his hands around to cup her ass cheeks, delicately tracing her sensitive crack and the tender patch where butt joined with leg. At the same time, he guided his tongue between her swollen lips, stabbing at her clit with a stroke guaranteed to drive her insane. He was drawing out the torture, making sure he provoked every sensation a woman's body could experience. He was doing a damn good job of it, too.

Líadán tilted her head back and closed her eyes. "Don't stop."

Brenden guided one of her legs onto his shoulder, giving him better access to her peachy delights. "I want some more." More probing licks teased her sensitive core, ushering in a pleasure both fiery and breathtaking in its intensity. All chances of keeping her cool vanished. Wriggling her hips, Líadán moaned. His tongue felt like wet silk across her lightly furred sex. Oral was so much more exciting when skin slid against skin.

"You like?" His voice was muffled, but understandable.

She grinned. "Oh, I like." Another moan escaped her when he nibbled at the folds of her labia. Without her consent, her hips jerked wildly. Brenden held on, licking and kissing until she was almost insane with the fury building inside her with fierce intensity. No use in holding on, denying herself. Her tremors began in small waves, continuing until they engulfed her in blazing convulsions.

Still shaking for the aftermath, she let Brenden guide her down onto the soft blanket. The fire warmed her skin. She stretched out, enjoying its heat, feeling liquid, luxurious and absolutely spoiled.

Somehow Brenden wriggled out of the rest of his clothes. As he lay down beside her, she knew she was responsible for what was about to happen, but she was helpless to stop it. After all, she'd invited him to play first.

"Are you sure you want this?"

"Absolutely." He kissed her long and hard, like a man who had been denied too long. By the time he ended the second kiss, Líadán was caught up in a daze of fierce desire and soaring expectation.

Taking control, Brenden kissed the hollow of her throat, then between her breasts. His tongue stroked her bare skin, and then the slope of her left breast. She could feel him against her hip, and the height of his arousal was intensifying her own. She shifted, feeling herself grow wetter when he brushed his tongue around the sensitive tip. He suckled softly on the hard pebble until a thickening haze of pleasure blurred her senses.

Líadán rolled her head against the soft blanket and closed her eyes, feeling Brenden's tongue, lips, and fingers delving across every inch of her needy skin. He explored with the experience of a man who knew how to prolong a woman's pleasure until it bordered on torture.

She molded herself to him, relishing the hardness of his body, the surging erection straining for release. She hadn't expected a lot of foreplay. Usually the average man got down to the business of their own pleasure. Not so with this man. She was but a prisoner of his ministrations, a prisoner so desperate for release she would willingly give him her soul.

Brenden moved lower, pausing to swirl his tongue around her navel. When he tongued the depth inside her belly button, she felt an odd stirring between her legs. Positioning his shoulders between her legs, his eyes moved over her body before settling on her most private parts. He spread her legs further apart, murmuring under his breath.

"What you did to me the other night was incredible." He smiled wickedly. "I want to return the favor." He spread her legs wider.

Líadán propped herself up on her elbows. "What I did, I do not do often." Her confession was totally honest.

"I'm glad you chose me." Brenden kissed inside one thigh and then the other, making small wet circles over her skin with the tip of his tongue. Líadán shifted a little and he kissed the top of her mound, then gave one labia a gently taunting tug with his teeth. The next thing she knew, his warm wet mouth covered her clit, sending a delicious tingling sensation rippling throughout her entire body. She could feel him licking, poking, and flicking all over her sensitive little nubbin; stirring her lightly in one spot and then nudging at her in another new place. Bolts of electricity crackled through all her senses. Her clit pulsed with carnal delight. She shuddered under his unrelenting onslaught, dazed and overwhelmed by the sensations of his oral genius.

"Brenden . . ." Líadán gasped, lifting her arms over her head and arching her body against the floor. "I don't think I can take much more . . ." She released a soft needy sound and her hips ratcheted up and down with wild abandon.

A smile lit up his face. "I've only just gotten started, Lía. You haven't been fucked 'till you've been fucked by me." He moved back up to face her, propping his head on one hand. Hot and rigid, his cock swelled against her bare thigh. Grinning, he leaned down and kissed her.

Líadán's hands lifted, tangling in his hair, pulling him down so she could savor every flavor completely. Her tongue swept into his mouth, drinking in the honey of wine and cream he'd consumed. When he pulled back, his gaze delved into hers. "I want you," he stated tersely. "I want to be the last man who'll ever have you."

Her eyelids fluttered shut. "I cannot promise . . ." she started to say.

He hushed her. "You can. You feel it as much as I do."

Opening her eyes, she pressed two fingers against his mouth to silence him. "No, you don't understand. I'm not what you think I am."

Brenden misunderstood her words. "I don't care. I only care that I've found you."

"Please . . ." She tried to shimmy away from him. What had she been thinking, letting him come this far? She should be the one in control. He should be the one begging for release, not the other way around.

Brenden wouldn't let her get away so easily. "I want you." Pinning her down, he settled his body on top of hers, positioning the head of his cock between her thighs. "After tonight, you'll be mine."

Líadán felt his shaft rubbing against her clit in the most melting way. Moving his hips a little more, he thrust, sheathing himself to the root. Hands on either side of her body, he lifted up so Líadán could look down, see their joining. "You belong to me." He started to move his hips, slowly pulling his cock out, almost to the end, then plunging back in. Her juices oiled his shaft, aiding his glide into her depths.

Líadán lifted her arms, fingers curling around the back of his head. As he lowered himself to kiss her, she wrapped her legs around his hips, pulling him down. She bit his lip as she arched into him. A quick well of blood dripped. "As you belong to me." She tightened her legs, thrusting up her hips. His blood trickled down her throat, feeding more than her body.

Brenden moaned into her mouth. "More." He thrust harder. "Take all of me."

Líadán wasn't sure if he meant his cock or his blood. Her hands clenched across his broad shoulders, scratching, tearing skin as she pulled him in. Wet and tight, her sex clasped, contracting around his erection. Spine-tingling sensations drenched her as his shaft slid deeper, his hips undulating against hers. Líadán closed her eyes, bracing herself for the pounding.

Without warning, Brenden suddenly pulled back, leaving only the tip inside.

Líadán's eyes shot open. "Damn." She writhed, feeling her senses whirling away. Engulfed in heat, fierce spirals of pleasure electrified her senses. "Don't stop now." Her fingernails dug in hard.

Brenden drew in a sharp breath at the pain she delivered, but refused to relent. Instead of a thrust, he gave her a lazy smile, one infuriating her even as it wrapped around her heart. "You wild little vixen." He slicked his tongue over his swollen lip, smiling as he tasted blood. "You like it, the pain."

"As much as you seek it," Líadán countered, hardly recognizing her own voice. She struggled to pull him back in but couldn't. He was controlling her, using his size and weight to manipulate their bodies. She whimpered helplessly, drawing her nails down his arms. She had never expected to experience such passion. So intense . . . so wonderful.

Obviously near to reaching the edge himself, Brenden chuckled and it rumbled deep in his chest. "You little hellcat . . . I'll fix those claws of yours."

"Try it!" She squealed in delight, squirming under him.

Eyes fixed on her face, Brenden expertly grabbed her hands, pinning them above her head. Years of police training and self-defense techniques armed him with an advantage the average man simply didn't possess. He was lightning fast, moving with grace and skill. He had her blinking in wonder before she was aware she'd been captured.

Líadán reared in reaction as a gasping cry of surprise escaped her lips. Realizing he had the upper hand now, she writhed under his hard body, not out of displeasure but surprise. She was actually enjoying his dominance! The musk of her excitement scented the air around them. Unable to free her hands, she released a soft moan of defeat.

Brenden smiled down at her, holding her firmly in his grip. He was strong, physically powerful. Almost unnaturally so. The two colors battling for dominance in his eyes danced, flecks of amber and green awhirl. "Looks like my kitten has been declawed." Chuckling, he proceeded to illustrate his point with brutally deep thrusts followed by slow arousing withdrawals. He moaned and Líadán felt his body begin to tense. His grip on her wrists grew harder, fingers bruising her delicate skin. She felt every inch of his merciless possession, his jutting cock filling her to create an exquisite torment. Her eager gasps filled the air.

He pulled back to the tip, holding her at the edge. "I want you to climax again." His voice was taut with sheer lust. He was in control and wasn't going to let her off easily.

Lost in the sensations, Líadán closed her eyes, listening to the sounds of their sex. An incredibly sensual moment, made all the more sensual because she could feel the beat of his heart still echoing in the blood she had consumed. Hands locked above her head, her only recourse was to fight back with her body, arching under his weight, meeting his every thrust with gyrating hips.

"Let yourself go." Voice rough and demanding, his words almost an order. Without pause, he shifted into a fast and unforgiving rhythm.

Reeling on the circumference of an earth-shattering meltdown, Líadán whimpered more. Like a mallet striking a spike, Brenden hammered into her slick heat until the fragile grip on his own control snapped. Veins popping, muscles corded, he speared deep, his final thrust clawing an orgasm out of his magnificent masculine body. Submerged in her slick sweet sex, a spurt of blazing semen jetted.

Her own precarious control cracked. Líadán's crash and burn into ecstasy arrived with brutal and explosive force. Fighting to overcome the thrill, she shrieked, simultaneously shattering into a million tiny molten pieces, agonizing and dazzling at the same beautiful moment.

Time froze. Minutes ticked away uncounted. Líadán panted

and closed her eyes, shuddering with delicious aftershocks. In the aftermath, both lay stunned by the intensity of their fierce joining.

When he finally collapsed in a heap beside her, Líadán pressed herself against him. Running her fingers over the sweat slick ridges of his abdomen, she couldn't stop trembling.

They held each other close, panting hard, enjoying the feeling of their heartbeats slowing as they basked in the warm glow of the nearby fire. The rain outside slowed to a gentle patter, mimicking the spent energy of their passion.

Brenden swept damp clinging tendrils of hair away from her face, kissing her brow, then her eyelids, working his way down to her lips. The kiss was gentle and full of delicate feelings. "Fabulous." He rubbed his swollen lip with a fingertip. "Even if you do suck me dry."

Líadán looked at this mortal who had captured her heart. A bittersweet pang filled her. The vein throbbed in his neck, still bruised from her first taste. She touched it with her fingertips, counting the furious beat. A new need filled her. Tasting his blood had only ignited it. She lowered her hand to his chest. His skin felt warm and damp.

Líadán lowered her head, tracing his vulnerable jugular with her tongue. Mmmm. He tasted wonderful. She nuzzled harder, like a kitten seeking a teat. He shuddered and stiffened, almost as if expecting her bite. She nipped gently, but didn't break the skin. Brenden murmured sleepily, palm tracing down the smooth plane of her back. She was tempted, oh, so tempted to take him a second time, savor the sweet taste of his life's force pouring into her, strengthening her.

The knowledge of his impending initiation opened a wound in her heart. *Let him have his innocence a little longer.* Suppressing a soft sigh of regret, she left his neck alone.

Brenden pulled her back, wrapping her in his warm embrace. The fire was dying, burning down to embers. "It's getting cold in here. Let's move this to the bedroom."

Pleased to be asked, Líadán nodded, her assent catching in her throat. After the incredible intimacy they had shared, now was not the time to get dressed and run off. As Brenden gathered her up in his embrace, blanket and all, she glanced across the den toward the window. She could play until the dawn broke. Then, the harsh light of day would drive her from his arms.

Líadán closed her eyes, laying her head against his shoulder as he carried her upstairs. His easy strength surprised and delighted her; he'd swept her up as if she weighed no more than a rag doll. "Hold me, please," she murmured, anticipating his touch all over again.

16

The sky was overcast, the storm refusing to release its grip on the city. Clouds, already low to the earth, sank, mingling with translucent fog appearing from no apparent source. It seemed to flow and change, light and shadow waltzing together. An all but invisible pulsation of power brightened and then darkened to expel a creature from a more sinister side of existence.

Auguste Maximilian emerged from the mist, hovering in the heart of a vast empty space. The haze around him shimmered like rime, but the odd, filtered light cast no shadows. His lean body held no human form, instead assuming a canine's shape, a huge gray wolf. Grass withering under his massive paws, strings of yellow saliva dripped from his canines. Realigning his senses into the brain of a stalker, he tilted his head toward the sky.

Dawn was close, too close.

He cursed the coming of the day, the unblinking eye of the all-seeing sun. He hated the orb that sent his kind skulking back into the crevasses and corners sheltering them from the shafts of illumination so eager to devour unholy elements. What the day revealed, the night concealed. Since the dawning of mankind, humans had huddled around flame for safety, fearful of beasts stalking the midnight hours.

Despite the coming threat, he would not be deterred from his hunt.

The wind laughed, knowing firsthand the secrets of his kind. Cold fingers reached to caress his elongated snout. Birds were silent, other predators still, as if afraid of the demonic being walking among them. Dark, wet city streets lay deserted, neatly paved avenues showing no signs of early morning traffic.

Lithe body springing into motion, Auguste set into an easy lope. He didn't know the lay of this land, had never been to this place. Given time, though, he would know it like the back of his hand; know its weaknesses, foibles and follies.

He laughed, the sound emanating from his wolfish throat as a low growl of menace. As he searched the streets, he felt a rush of expanding outward consciousness, a heightened awareness of his surroundings. The third-eye of his jouyl took flight. It would see what he could not; it could perceive where others would be blind.

Paws coming down hard and fast on soil and concrete alike, Auguste penetrated the boundaries of manicured gardens, running up sidewalks and alleys. He was looking, searching, pausing only to sniff the air, take in the odors, sorting through them to discard what was meaningless. When he found the scent he wanted, he set into motion again, following the trail he'd so easily picked up.

Líadán was close. Very close.

Quickening his pace he ran with a speed that blurred his form to all eyes. The miles fell away under his swift feet. He ran until his gaze fell upon the dwelling he sought.

This was the home of Líadán's lover; the man branded with her bite. The house was silent, the windows unlit.

To Auguste's immortal gaze, the house was far from dark. Seeing beyond the human plane of existence, he easily detected the iridescent lines of a magical force. Pink pulses of shimmering light swirled and eddied in sparking trails, emanating outward in a force shield around the house. The meaning of the pulsing lines was very clear.

Prickles rose along the back of his furry head. *This place is guarded by the hand of a witch.* He knew by the colors the conjurer was female. Had the creator of the spell been male, the colors would have been darker.

Auguste didn't like this unexpected development. This was something he hadn't anticipated. Someone residing within those walls was wise to the ways of magic, knew how to use it for protective purposes.

The great beast, twice the size of any earth-bound wolf, pawed the ground, clawing long trenches into the damp soil, marking his territory, a warning to others he would tolerate no trespasses. He could feel Líadán as much as smell her. Beyond joining their bodies, they'd shared the blood of the same victims. Any prey she took, Auguste felt their soul energies coursing through his veins—could discern their DNA down to the tiniest atom.

He remembered tasting the blood of the first victim she'd taken after her long suicidal fast. Beneath the taste of the blood lingering on her lips was a powerful force, something old, something magnificent—but untapped.

Curious, he'd focused his heightened psychic awareness, delving down into the molecular level and beyond, feeling the pulse of an awesome energy. For an instant his mind merged with the force and he was rushed headlong into the core of an entity so glorious he could only draw back in terror—a blaze of light so stunning it eradicated in a broad sweep every shadow lurking, burning away the wicked darkness the way a flame cleansed the flesh of the damned. He'd had to retreat or face being purged by the terrible radiance.

Auguste immediately felt a cold shudder of fear gnaw into

his belly. A low rumble broke from his throat. *He possesses the roshtyn . . . the power of the ancient Wyr sentinels*—the Wyr belonged to an ancient clan called the Gwyd'llyr, or seekers of purity. Guardians against darker forces seeking to bastardize legitimate magic into twisted and foul things, the Wyr were bearers of the legendary flaming swords that could pierce a vampyr's heart, sending the demon spawned jouyl spinning back to the pit of evil giving it foul birth.

The power of the Gwyd'llyr extended back even further than his own, tracing its origins to the days when the hours were uncounted and the earth's mountains and valleys were still covered by mists, a time when magic was a real and palpable force among mankind.

Wanting to know more, Auguste tentatively sent a mental thrust into the force field around the house, exploring the waves of emanating energy. There was a short bright flare of light and a fusion. He was immediately struck a blinding mental blow. "Sorcery." His words emerged more as a low rumble than actual human speech. *The witch practices the pishagys of the elder times with a skill only a true inborn druiaghtey can use.*

He forced himself to calm, absorbing the strike then discharging it with a few muttered spell words. Before he had been thrust away, he'd caught a hint of a young woman's face and form. This, he knew without doubt, was the sister of Líadán's lover.

Lips curling back, he glided stealthily forward, coming closer to the house. With each soft step in the damp grass, his awareness of Líadán's presence developed into sensations so acute he could almost see her in his mind's eye.

Because of the protection spell circling its walls, he could approach the house, but could not enter, nor do harm. He could see the ancient symbols burned into the sills of the windows, placed where untrained eyes would not notice. He knew without searching further these symbols would be carved around all doors and other entrances. One such as himself had to be willingly invited to set foot under the threshold.

A wraith in shadow, he inched closer. His breath fogged the glass when he pressed his snout against it. The scent of raw lusty sex lingered heavily in the air, soaking his senses with the caresses of desires recently shared.

Auguste settled down on his haunches, resting in the night-cooled grass. Breathing deeply, he lapped his long pink tongue out as if he could taste the mingling juices of two bodies so recently joined. Aroused by the lust, a low territorial growl emanated from his thick throat.

He could not get into the house, but he could bring what was inside outside by focusing on the connection he had through blood with Líadán. Traveling psychic paths was a dangerous move to make when out in the open and exposed. Should anyone disturb him while he was in his trance, the link could be severed, stranding him in a void of nothingness.

Centering his energies, Auguste slowed his body's rhythms to a standstill. He sensed rather than felt the relaxing of his muscles as his body went insensible. For an instant nothing existed but a yawning void and he was aware of nothing, not his own breath nor even the beating of his heart. In his mind's eye, he pictured Líadán, activating the psi-link between himself and his bound servant.

His concentration deepened as the connection focused and became clearer, images slammed into his brain, ricocheting off the walls of his skull They were fully connected now, allowing him to share the tempest of passions.

Auguste's third eye could see Líadán was in her lover's bed, naked flesh pressed to naked flesh. His ears picked up the echoes of her moans. With a sound mingling between a growl and a moan, Brenden Wallace kissed his way down her neck, dipping his head so his tongue swirled around her soft pink nipple.

Líadán threw her head back and gasped in delight, enjoying the skilled lips teasing and caressing her. She reached down to stroke the hard muscles of his shoulders, letting her fingers dig into his flesh until her nails left marks pressed into his skin.

Brenden lifted his head, giving her a wild look through the tangle of blond hair brushing his face. His cock bobbed when he lifted himself, moving up to ease his weight on top of her.

Auguste inwardly grimaced when Líadán welcomed the sleek naked body conquering hers, sighing in submission when Brenden pressed his hips between her spread thighs. He drove into her in one hard stunning thrust. She moaned as he pumped his body against hers, jarring her hips with long steady strokes. Releasing a drawn out moan of pure bliss, the sensations of pleasure had her arching to meet every thrust.

In a smooth movement, Brenden rolled over onto his back, bringing Líadán into the superior position above him. As though driven by her own racing need and instinct, she captured his arms above his head, pinning his wrists together. Impaled on his cock, she in turn dipped low. Her lips brushed the soft pulse of his exposed neck seconds before her fangs extended, coming out to their full length. Biting hard, she sank her teeth deep, drawing both blood and semen from his body and into hers until her lover collapsed, limp and delightfully sated by the force of his climax.

Suddenly, with unimaginable violence the fragile mesh of their connection shattered. Auguste's mind spun dizzily, a blaze of pain and crimson lights rocketing through his head. For a moment he teetered on the brink of losing consciousness.

Auguste abruptly closed his eyes, quickly severing the psychic link. His mind, once freed of the grip of their connection, felt numbed, empty.

Reentry into his body was accompanied by a jolting thud of dismay. There was a buzzing pain in his skull. Agony lanced through him, an icy pain squeezing his head in a vise-lock grip.

He gasped, painfully. Somehow Líadán's bite, the drawing of Brenden Wallace's blood into her body during the peak of his arousal, had triggered the dormant psi-forces of Brenden's ancient heritage. This in turn had sensed a natural enemy in Auguste's invasion and instinctively attacked.

Head and heart pounding, he was caught in the terrible depletion taking place through his nervous system when he utilized his telepathic abilities. His eyes were aching. A wave of nausea rippled through him, vaguely reminding him he needed to replenish his sustenance.

Jealously wasted no time in joining the fray, thrusting through his heart like a hot iron poker. He could not shake from his mind the sight of Líadán conquered by another man's body—a mortal man's body.

Auguste's lips drew back in a frosty glower of fangs. He ignored the impulse of sanity, giving himself to the ravening beast controlling his soul. His furry head came up with the intent to shatter the glass, bound inside and rip out the throat of the man who dared to enjoy his slave's delights.

The storm unexpectedly kicked up again, pelting him with rain. Lightning cracked afresh and the wind tore at his lungs. He felt an enormous wave of energy, a great blow setting his head to reeling. He struggled inside boiling darkness as a strange vision flashed through his mind, one filling him with a cold black terror even more frightening than gazing into the face of the devil.

The darkness was illuminated by a dazzling glare as an image of Brenden Wallace appeared shifting into the body of a great cat and lunging!

Another savage peal of thunder boomed. Lightning lit up the sky and the darkness receded into a great screaming wind.

An omen. A warning of danger not to be ignored.

Auguste stumbled away from the window, steadying himself as he remembered he had four paws, not two booted feet.

He clamped his eyes shut, willing the vision away. It was blinding. It was crippling. It was mutilation. His death at the hands of the empowered warrior.

Now that Líadán had twice tasted Brenden and awakened his slumbering power, the unknowing Wyr would not be allowed to walk away unscathed. Yes, he definitely wanted to get his hands on this one.

A rumble in his guts begged attention. He would have to feed doubly well to replace his depleted energies.

Auguste growled. The sound broke the night into a thousand shards. Massive head dipping back toward the sky, he howled. Other hounds joined in, their mournful baying filling the silence of the night with a music stimulating his primeval senses. The air around him clouded and thickened. Swirling lines of force eddying around him formed a circle ever larger, ever faster until the fibers between the dimensions loosened, pulling him back into the fabric between heaven and hell.

The wolf vanished, but not for long.

17

Brenden woke in a darkened room, blinds thankfully shuttered against the late afternoon sun. Turning his head, he glanced over to Líadán's side of the bed. Empty. There was no note. Nothing. She was gone, getting up and creeping away as he'd slept.

He pushed aside the bed covers. Blackness blurred his vision when he started to rise. He sat still, resting his head in his hands. His limbs felt leaden and heavy. Despite his hours of sleep he felt sluggish, as if weighed down by some strange force of gravity. With an inner strength he didn't know existed, he clung to alertness. His chest rose and fell as he struggled to breathe. Chilly sweat drenched his body.

He moaned. "Oh, shit. What the hell is going on with me?" Sick inside, his nervous system was knotted and cramped. Spears of pain shot through his belly. He felt alternately hot, then cold as his body convulsed with the frantic shudders of his strange illness. His throat felt swollen, sore and scratchy.

His memories of the last hours were blurry, distorted. Closing his eyes, fighting against the dizziness, he struggled to bring the last hours of the night to the surface of his addled brain. After he and Líadán had moved their lovemaking to the bedroom, his mind went blurry. He knew they'd had sex, several times. But it had seemed to take place through a strange filter of half-waking dreams.

"God . . . feels like the fucking flu . . ." he gasped, gagging when his stomach rolled. Knowing he was going to be ill, he forced himself to stand, stagger into the bathroom. He barely made it to the sink before he threw up. Only bitter yellow bile came up, burning his throat and scalding its nasty taste on his tongue. Chest heaving, he gagged, but nothing came up.

Turning the cold-water tap on full blast, he rinsed out the sink before splashing icy water on his face to soothe his burning skin. Unbearably thirsty, he cupped his hand near the faucet and drank until his need for water was sated.

Feeling a bit better since his body had purged the toxins from his system, he reached out to flip on the light. Shards of light stabbed. He covered his eyes, waiting for the acute sensitivity to pass.

When he was able to see again, Brenden hardly recognized the sharp, drawn face in the mirror. Cheeks covered with stubble, weariness was etched into his eyes. His face was lined and ashen, as if he'd aged overnight. Jaw hanging slack, dark circles ringed his eyes. His pupils were huge, dilated. His flesh was dead white. Bloodless. He looked like a junkie who'd been smoking crack for a week.

He swallowed, feeling a sharp twinge in his neck. He turned his head. A huge purple bruise surrounded two fresh ragged punctures in his neck.

Swallowing again, he felt the pain of deeply injured tissue. He grimaced and lifted a shaking hand to his neck, pressing the tips of his fingers to his irritated skin, touching the small holes. This bite had left more of a distinct imprint than the last, almost as if Líadán had intended for him to permanently bear her strange mark.

Beneath his fingers his pulse was racing out of control. He shivered with the violent cold crawling around his body. He didn't feel dangerously ill, just drowsily delirious. Though he hadn't planned to wake up alone, he was almost grateful Líadán had decided to slip away. He didn't want her to see him a shivering wreck of sickness. He was tempted to go lay back down. His limbs were weak, sapped, and he was forced to stand still for several minutes, holding on to the bathroom vanity as he gathered his strength. He wanted to sit, but was determined not to.

"First day of vacation and I get sick as a dog."

Chilled, he needed warmth, heat, a total, all-over body soak. He had two choices: the sunken porcelain tub or the glass-tiled walk-in shower. Both were absurdly large, the height of luxury. Since he needed to wash his hair and shave, he decided on the shower. Getting into hot water would warm his bones. Maybe the hot steam would help put this terrible bug in its place.

He reached in and turned on both taps, adjusting the temperature to a comfortable level. Steam filled the air as he eased under the water. For a long while he stood beneath the stream, relaxed by the pleasurable massage of the water on his abused skin. After a few moments of breathing the heat, he felt better, less shaky. He might survive after all.

Picking up a bar of soap, he began to wash, enjoying the feel of the creamy cocoa butter lather. Dani did the shopping, so he used what she chose. His hands brushed lightly against his chest, under his arms, around his flaccid penis, washing secret places. An unbidden rush of sexual warmth filled him. His body still tingled in the places Líadán had touched. He wanted more than a woman for his bed, but one for his heart and the hungry gaping loneliness inside.

A heavy knock at the door bought him out of his reverie. "Bren?"

"Yeah?"

The door cracked open. "You up?"

He rinsed soap out of his eyes. "No, I always shower in my sleep."

"Funny guy. Ha-ha. You almost done?"

"Ten minutes, tops." A pause. "Why are you bothering me?"

"Got a message from your lady friend." Dani's voice held a note of annoyance.

His senses pricked up. So Líadán hadn't left without leaving a message. "Oh?"

Curious as to what Líadán might have said, he hurried to conclude his shower. Toweling off, he shrugged into his robe, belting it around his waist. Amazing how a cleansing wash could bring out the best in a body. Already he was feeling less shaky. Get a little food into his stomach and he would be fine.

Towel around his neck, he padded into his bedroom. Dani, bless her, was making the bed. She was good about keeping his piggish ways from turning the house into a disaster zone.

Dressed in a pair of too-tight, fashionably faded jeans and a baby T-shirt emblazoned with BITCH GODDESS IN TRAINING, she showed entirely too much tanned skin as she smoothed the wrinkles out of the new comforter she'd helped him choose, a masculine-hued blend of browns and blues.

"Hey. Thanks for cleaning up. I owe you one."

"You owe me more than that," she said, nodding her head toward his dresser. "Coffee's over there." She slid the pillows into their shams and plumping them into place at the head of the bed.

"Thanks."

Brenden retrieved the mug, savoring the aroma of strong, black, hundred-percent Columbian. Dani made coffee thicker and blacker than tar, just the way their mother had. The hot liquid was welcome on his empty stomach, instantly filling him with the jolt he was so dependent on to wake up. Gulping down half a cup in one swallow, he felt almost human again. He glanced out the blinds Dani had drawn open. To his dismay the sun was slowly sinking into the west, beginning to vanish as the day waned. "What time is it?"

Dani glanced at the digital. "A bit after six."

He shook his head. "I didn't mean to snooze all day." He barely recalled going to sleep. The last thing he remembered was Líadán's body curling into his under the covers, and murmuring a sated "good night." The rain pattering against the windows had created a steady, soothing beat, a perfect end to the evening.

"Uh-huh." Her tone was noncommittal. "I suppose you were up late last night."

He nodded. Every move he made only served to remind him of his strenuous evening with Líadán. The coffee was chasing away the nausea and Brenden had to admit he was feeling pretty good. "So what did you think of her?" He felt a bit like a kid presenting a new toy.

Dani smiled at him, but there was no joy behind the gesture. "She's a real babe, Bren," she said in a thin, indifferent voice. "Very pretty."

Brenden knew his sister. Something was on her mind. "And?"

Finished with the bed, Dani turned. Her hands immediately settled on her hips, striking a pose. The move signaled that Danicia was getting ready to jump on her high horse and air her opinion. "You want the truth?" she asked, then answered without giving him a chance to reply. "She gives me a hinky feeling."

He shot her a look over the rim of his cup. "Is that an official witch term, Dani? Hinky?"

Frowning, she sat down on the edge of the bed. "Don't tease

me. That woman you were with last night gives me the creeps. She's weird."

Regret swelled inside him. He had hoped Dani would hit it off with Líadán. Of course, they'd only just met. It might take a little time to ease Dani into the idea of a new woman in his life.

"Weird?" He let out a long-suffering sigh. "How so?"

Dani shook her head and shrugged. "Just weird. Like she's walking in a different world than the one we're in, you know."

He blew out a puff of air in disgust. "Oh, shit, that's stupid as all get-out. You're not making one bit of sense. You said she left a message." His stomach lurched in anxiety, but he got the words out anyway. "Care to tell me what it is?"

"She said she enjoyed the evening and you had her number if you wanted to call."

"That's it?" Getting answers was like pulling teeth.

She picked at a piece of imaginary lint, ho-humming around in an infuriating way. "Pretty much."

He nodded. "I see." He certainly couldn't accuse Líadán of being a clingy woman. She definitely wasn't the kind who hung around a man's neck like a millstone. Independent. Had her own thing to do, didn't count on a man to fill her every waking hour. Her stock rose a hundred percent. There might be hope for a relationship after all.

Finishing his coffee, he set his mug down. He thought about calling Líadán, then decided not to. Space. Go slow. Give her some time and breathing space to think about him. Good. A day's respite would show he wasn't desperate, had things to do, too.

Since the day was almost gone, he'd have a little jog on the back trails behind the house, order some takeout, and maybe rent a couple of movies. Just enjoy his time off. Relax. Unwind and leave the pressures of work behind. The last week had definitely been a downer.

Flipping his towel off his shoulders, he rubbed his dripping hair. He wanted to get dressed and get on with his evening, not stand around and debate his girlfriend's worthiness. If the two women didn't get along, fine. They would just have to ignore each other. He and Dani each had their own space, their own lives. They could come and go without seeing each other. If push came to shove, he'd have to put his foot down. He couldn't make Dani like Líadán, but he would insist Dani respect her and treat her civilly when Líadán was a guest in their home.

Dani grew pale beneath her tan. "Oh, shit!"

Her strangled gasp of surprise stopped his movements. He studied her face, concerned. "What?"

Face dead white, eyes wide as saucers, Dani's hand flew to her mouth. "My spell," she mumbled from behind her fingers. "I think it worked."

"The love spell?" He laughed and winked. "Sex spell is more like it."

She shook her head adamantly. "No. I cast another . . . a destiny spell." She walked over to him, arms extended in front of her, hands splayed out in a protective manner as if she expected to ward off blows. "The first time I saw it, I should have known. But I didn't pay enough attention to the warning signs."

Brenden tapped his index finger against his forehead. "The first time—what?" He deliberately bent the word. "Speak English, please."

Dani reached out, holding him by the arms. Her grip was tight, unrelenting. "Bren—don't freak, but I think a demon has latched on to you."

Looking at her in astonishment, Brenden barely managed to suppress an incongruous ripple of disbelieving laughter. He met her horrified gaze with his best rational-cop stare, the one employed for hysterical people and the mentally disturbed.

"A demon has latched on to me?" He struggled to keep from rolling his eyes to the ceiling. "And how, in your crafty wisdom, have you come to such a conclusion?" Good God, he hoped Dani hadn't said something like that to Líadán. The woman would be afraid of his psychologically infirm sibling and probably never want to see him again.

Dani's hands were trembling with fear. Something was upsetting her, badly. Her gaze settled on the telling bruise on his throat. "Your neck . . ." she stammered. "Look at your neck, Bren. You've been bitten again. Marked."

Brenden felt the vague throb and twinge in his neck. Reaching up, he again explored the injury with the tips of his fingers, feeling the steady beat of his pulse. "I know it's there. No big deal."

"No big deal! It is a big deal." She speared him with a questioning look. "Do you even remember it happening?"

Her question brought him up short.

"Of course I do," he started, then went abruptly silent when he realized he didn't have a clue. He searched his memory, trying to bring to mind the instant of Líadán's second bite into his flesh. He couldn't. "Not really. I mean, things got pretty wild last night. I probably had my mind on other things . . . if you know what I mean."

"You can't remember because she's bespelled you to hide her evil deed." Dani's expression was calm, but he could see the fear taking root deep in her eyes. "We've got to break her hold—destroy her enchantment." She shook her head, more mumbling to herself than speaking to him. "The first time . . . I knew . . . I should have said something. Shit . . . they've gotten a good start on me. . . ."

Brenden followed her words—a smattering of English mixed with some Gaelic words their grandmother had taught her—with some difficulty. It sounded like Danicia had lost her everloving mind and gone right 'round the bend to loony town.

Brenden broke away from his sister's grasp, his brow knitting with irritation as he raked his damp hair away from his face. What went on between Líadán and him was none of Dani's business. She was butting in where she was not welcome. He turned on her, his fury escaping before he knew what he was saying. "Don't start more witchcraft shit on me just this minute, Dani. I'm in no mood to listen to your stupid beliefs. It's all a bunch of bullshit, nothing but fucking nonsense!"

Flinching as if physically lashed, Dani let her hands drop. "It's not nonsense," she said sharply. "That's what demons do, Bren. They blind you to the truth, take away your abilities to perceive when something's wrong. You're seeing, but you can't comprehend because your rational mind is telling you vampyrs do not exist."

Vampyrs?

He snorted. "Bullshit!"

Their eyes locked in hostility.

Brenden grasped for patience, finding very little to hold him in good stead. "She got a little excited, Dani, and bit a little hard." He tried to find the humor in the situation, lacing his words with a little dry sarcasm. "Hey, ever think I might be a good lay? Ever think I could rock a woman's world?"

Dani dropped her eyes. "I'm not saying you can't. That's not what this conversation is about. You have to listen to me. You have to deal with this. It's time."

Patience evaporated. "Deal with what? A bunch of stupid Irish legends Grandma told you about beasties and demons and whatever else she made up? Please! This is the year 2007, not the Middle Ages."

"Why can't you listen to me?" Dani still sounded angry. She clutched at his arm, pulling him a few steps forward, her strength contradicting her diminutive stature. She was dead damn determined to get her way. "Just come with me. I have to show you something."

Shaking off her grip, he cut her short. "Forget it."

She begged. "Please."

He shook his head, refusing. "I'm not interested."

"But—"

Brenden raised a hand in warning to silence her when she moved to interrupt. It was time to give her the plain, honest facts. "You know I don't condone your practices anyway, Dani. I have to live and work in this city. Having you working in a strip club and running around declaring yourself a witch hurts my reputation on the force." His head throbbed, beating time with the headache building behind his eyes. The evening wasn't getting off to a good start after all.

They glared at each other like two rams about to begin battering heads.

"I know you don't like my lifestyle," she shot back, firing the first stubborn volley. "But it's my life and my decisions are my own to make."

Forcibly, he calmed his irrational surge of anger. But he also had to admit he was tired of all things supernatural and magical in her life. None of it made sense and because she was younger and because she was so precocious he'd allowed her to perpetuate the fantasy their grandmother had fixed in her head. Dani, however, was no longer a child. She needed to put away her fantasy life and come into the real world.

Brenden countered with the second shot, aiming to wound. "It's getting out of hand and it's going to have to stop—the dancing and the witchcraft. It's time you grow up and get a grip on your life. You're not twelve. Grandma's stories about us being descended from some ancient Celtic clan of Druids are just stories. Just like your stupid love spells."

As he'd spoken, her face crumbled in disbelief. Head bowing down, she wiped away a tear trekking down her cheek. His words had punctured her like a dart would burst a balloon. When her head rose, there was a wounded look in her eyes.

Then her chin came up. Determination sparked in the depths of her gaze. Standing her ground, she clenched her fists, unwilling to be cowed. She was going to persist at gnawing at him the way a dog worried a bone. He could tell by the look on her face that she felt what she had to say was important.

"Just let me show you."

Brenden shook his head. His head was really banging now and he could say with certainty it was stress. "I just said—"

Dani broke in, saying, "If—once you see it—you don't believe it, then I won't say another word." For the first time she didn't sound so certain, so confident. "I promise."

He could clearly see the conflict in her face. Softening a bit, Brenden released a long-suffering sigh. "I'm going to get dressed and have a quick jog." He thought her words over a moment. "When I get back, we'll talk. Okay? I need to get out a bit, clear my head."

Sighing, Dani reached out her hand, laying it on his arm. "Bren?" Her smile wavered, but at least she was smiling again.

"What?" Holding a grudge would do neither of them any good. She was trying to make peace. He should at least accept it. Later, they would sort through things. He'd talk to Dani, try to discover what lay beneath her sudden, irrational outburst about Líadán.

"Don't be mad," she whispered, tightening her clasp to an almost painful degree. "Whether you choose to accept it or not, we are what we are."

He frowned and sighed doubtfully. "We'll talk about it when I get back. I need some time just to think. A good run will clear my head."

Letting her hand fall away, Dani looked unhappy. "Just be careful." She shivered faintly. "You haven't seen the newspaper yet. Another girl's gone missing, just last night. Three in less than a week." Her lips pulled down into a worried frown. "Something wicked has come to town. I feel it in my bones."

Brenden turned away, unable to answer. A slow prickle of dread filled him. The weight of the world was suddenly crushing, seeming to bear down on his shoulders without relenting.

Damn.

18

The sun was angling toward the horizon when Brenden hit the jogging trail behind his house. The advantage to living in a city virtually dropped into the middle of a forest was he only had to pass the fence in his back yard to encounter nature at its best. The land around Dordogne consisted of rolling uplands and interconnected ravines and valleys, with a mix of pine and other hardwood trees covering most of the region. The woodland was thick and breathtaking. Freshened by last night's rain, the air was crisp with the bite of autumn's coming chill. Graded and well-hedged trails were wet but not too muddy to run on.

Dressed in a jogging suit and sneakers neither expensive nor designer, he clipped along at a steady pace, not going too fast, but keeping enough speed to get the benefits of the workout. Happy to be out with his master, Bear kept up the beat, his four paws coming down in perfect synchronization. The big dog loved to run and would go at a moment's notice.

They ran, a man and his dog, enjoying the freedom and beauty of nature.

Taking a sharp right, he veered off the established paths and took a rabbit's trail through the brush—less smooth, definitely not as well established. People had gotten lost taking these back pathways, but he wasn't worried. He'd been running these tracks for nearly nine years. He believed he knew the ins and outs like the back of his hand.

Not really paying attention to the deepening shadows, he let his feet carry him where they would. The pounding of his heart, the rush of blood through veins, was like an anesthetic. He could understand why people got addicted to the rush of endorphins through the body during physical exertion. Lost in the zone of physical activity, he was aware of little more than the earth under his feet and his lungs taking in and then exhaling oxygen.

Brenden stepped up his pace. His feet hit the ground with solid regularity. A mile passed, then two. He had a motion going, a rhythm. Breathe, in and out. He ducked under a low-hanging limb. Almost didn't see it. Was it getting darker? He wasn't ready to turn around. He wanted to keep running.

He didn't want to think about Dani's words. Not yet.

He was entering thick brush now. Keeping the trail in sight was getting harder as the sun sank lower. He'd need to turn around in a few minutes, head back. He didn't want to be lost at night. It might be hours before he could make his way home. Should he have grabbed a flashlight? No, he'd be fine. He'd turn around and head back as soon as he'd covered another mile.

Legs feeling the heat, sweat beading his brow, Brenden could barely breathe, but he kept pushing himself. His heart hammered harder in his chest, breath coming a little harder, lungs burning from the effort. He was thirty-three, not nineteen, but he could still go the distance. Head down, Bear sped beside him, never losing the pace. The old dog was panting heavily, too, mouth hanging open.

Bren—don't freak, but I think a demon had latched on to you.

Latched on to?

He panted. "Fucker couldn't even catch me." Brittle sticks cracked under his shoes. He was invincible. He couldn't be stopped. He was Super-duper-man.

Without warning, the ground veered sharply down. There was no time to stop or try to avoid the fall. He'd have to take it and hope for the best.

Brenden stumbled over the edge of the ravine, hitting the ground a few feet below with a body-shuddering thud. The air left his lungs in a rush, leaving him breathless and gasping. That hurt. Badly.

He lay, stunned.

Opening his eyes, he found himself staring up at the dense ceiling of branches. The clustered, thick foliage was tangled, almost impenetrable. No wonder he hadn't seen the drop until the last moment. The ground beneath his body was spongy with the loam of fallen leaves and pine needles. Stirred from its shelter, a wild hare skittered off. Bear looked down from his perch above, head cocked at an angle seeming to say, "Whatcha doin' down there, bud?"

Terrific. Bear would be absolutely no use in a rescue situation. Pretty bad when your own dog thought you were an idiot.

Okay. So now he was flat on his back. He supposed the day couldn't get any worse. He lay for a moment, just breathing, letting his body recover.

Taking a mental assessment from the tip of his toes to his head, he wriggled each limb in its turn. His left ankle had taken a bit of a turn, but it didn't seem to be broken. The swelling of injured tissue warned him the sprain was bad.

Brenden sat up, brushing bits of twigs and leaves out of his hair. Seeing his master rise, Bear loped down into the gully a little more gracefully. The big dog automatically circled the perimeter of the unfamiliar area. Hearing a sound in the bushes, the shepherd chuffed a warning, nostrils flaring as he sniffed the air. A low growl emanated from his thick throat.

"Bear, get over here."

Bear trotted up, butting Brenden with his head, giving him a whiff of doggie breath in between a big, sopping lick.

Brenden glanced around at the unfamiliar area. He'd never gone this far off the trails. "Looks like I went and got us lost." He wasn't worried. Almost any direction would eventually lead to civilization. This area was full of camping and hiking facilities—and, for Christ's sake, right behind his own house. *Too bad Dani isn't here right now,* he thought wryly. Maybe she could conjure him a map.

Damn their stupid argument.

"You hear that, Bear? A demon has got me." Dani's words seemed senseless. "Who in their right mind would believe in vampyrs?"

Apparently his sister did. He remembered the look on her face. She'd been genuinely scared when she'd seen . . . *the bite.*

Brenden felt as though a brick had been dropped on his head. A key had just been handed to him and he was too stupid to realize it. "Last night . . . It happened again . . . But I don't remember . . ."

Going back to the previous evening, he searched all the way through his skull, peeking into dark corners and darker recesses to dig out the pieces of the hours he'd spent with Líadán. Dinner? Yes. Well-remembered. Her taste in food was a little strange. Raw meat. Ugh! Dancing? Definitely yes. The feel of her body pressed against his was unforgettable. The storm, driving home, more wine . . .

Things got sketchy and faded into black.

Brenden closed his eyes. Recollection blurred by the wine he'd consumed, some parts of the night were a little fragmented after he and Líadán had gone upstairs. Bodies aflame with need, their sexual heat had ignited all over again once they'd hit the sheets.

Brow wrinkling, he dug deeper, parting murky veils to recall their lovemaking. He found a few memories, arranging them like the pieces of a jigsaw puzzle until he'd put together a coherent set of images.

What he saw chilled him.

He remembered the feel of the mattress under his back when he'd rolled their bodies, allowing Líadán to assume the superior position. Smiling down on him, her enigmatic eyes had seemed to crackle and spark in time with the lightning flashing outside. The little ribbons of fire in their depths almost mesmerized him with the display of sheer energy embracing and filling her body when she'd locked his arms above his head. Her strength and speed were amazing, but he was too gone at the peak of orgasm to notice or care.

And then she'd bent and he'd caught a glimpse of her strange canines—seeming longer, more extended as she'd rolled back her lips, baring those sharp, sharp teeth.

Somehow he'd known she would bite. The erotic assault on his body and senses had made it impossible for him to resist her intent. Something deep inside his soul said to accept . . . to enjoy.

Her fangs sinking into his flesh had unleashed a battalion of fireworks in his mind, a massive explosion of exquisitely carnal sparks sending him pinwheeling into the abyss of sheer orgasmic ecstasy. Somehow the pain made their joining sweeter, more sacred.

Brenden sucked in a breath, body heating all over again at the thought of what Líadán's touch could usher in. The memory alone was enough to stir his cock, send a tingling, tightening thrill straight to the tip. She'd swallowed his blood, creating a spiritual union between them almost holy in its intensity.

Without conscious thought his palm came down flat on his

wounded neck. "Oh, Christ." He felt his guts tighten. *I'm the victim of a vampyr.* "This can't be happening. It doesn't make sense."

That it didn't make sense didn't necessarily make it untrue. The proof—so to speak—was in the bite.

Dani was right. Líadán had marked him. Twice.

As for the sense part, well, Dani had said he was bespelled into blindness.

What part of bitten don't you understand, Brenden? Another bitter twist aggravated his innards. He'd accepted Líadán's first nibble without question—almost as if he'd known the truth but was afraid to acknowledge the genuine meaning. He'd been chosen. Question was: what exactly had Líadán chosen him for?

A mate?

Something else, perhaps?

A victim.

The image of Janice Parker's torn flesh flashed across his mind. The bite on his throat matched almost exactly a few of those on the corpse. He hadn't made the connection because her bites were larger, deeper, located in different places on her body. And where he had one single, small, non-fatal nip, Janice Parker was riddled with dozens, her body mauled almost beyond recognition, close to consumed by some terrible hunger— a hunger draining her of every last drop of blood.

Uneasiness gripped his heart with cold hands and squeezed until he thought he'd lose all ability to breathe. "How could I have been so clueless?" He was a trained investigator, educated to recognize what civilian eyes could not. Logical minds would question exactly how he'd missed the obvious.

The answer was simple, and he cringed. He'd been so enamored with the good feeling between his legs that he'd totally overlooked Líadán's fangs in his neck. Bespelled? *Pussy-whipped* was more like it.

One woman was dead.

Two more were missing.

And Brenden held the sole connection to a woman who was shaping up to be the only logical suspect thus far. A woman whose last name and address he didn't even know. *Way to go, Sherlock. Talk about idiocy in action.*

"You're useless, Bren." Talk about setting oneself up for the fall. He'd done a fine job. He might as well go all out and leap off the cliff. When this got around, the only thing he'd be doing as an officer would be driving a golf cart and writing parking tickets.

He didn't have to think very hard to imagine the reaction he'd meet if he walked into the station talking about vampyrs as suspects in a recent murder.

Just thinking of the words coming out of his mouth made him cringe. People, especially people who were supposed to be the sane entities of law and order, simply didn't go around flinging out theories about vampyrs attacking citizens—even if said cop had the proof right on his own tender little neck.

They'd theorize stress had gotten him, maybe put him on administrative leave for an undetermined amount of time. A laughingstock—his career would be toast.

Brenden glanced toward the sky, lost in the tangle of thick branches above his head. Now he knew how Chicken Little felt. The sky was falling.

And no one would believe him.

19

Bear's low and menacing growl dragged Brenden's attention back to his surroundings. A rustling noise cutting through the heavy brush made him turn his head. As he climbed to his feet, the fine hairs at the nape of his neck prickled. His left ankle gave a twinge of protest, but held his weight.

Hackles up, Bear set to barking wildly, baring his teeth at some unseen predator. The shepherd had heard what Brenden could not—the soft brushing of paws against the ground, the stiff crackle of displaced branches seconds before the threat emerged.

Brenden saw the huge gray shadow spring out of the brush. As it hit the ground with a thud, a low growl emanated from the wolf's throat. A chill crawled straight up his backbone at the sight of the massive animal. The wrench gripping his bowels was no longer anxiety, but fear. He'd heard talk of wolves in the wildlife preserve, but had never heard of any venturing this close to the city. How far off was he from the established trails? A mile? Surely no more than two.

Paws splayed in a defensive stance, the wolf obviously felt

its territory had been invaded. The beast was huge, twice the size of Bear. Head down, the wolf stood stiff legged and tall. Under angry eyes, sharp incisors were displayed in a snarl. Ears erect and forward, its hackles bristled and its tail was vertical and curled toward the back, as if to show its rank as the dominant male to all others in the pack. In the low light sinking over the edge of the horizon, its gray figure glowed with a strange bluish illumination.

A cold spasm of fear squeezed his heart. *This fucker means business.*

Bear barked and kicked at the ground with his hind legs. The big dog was ready and willing to fight without question.

Now was not the time to test Bear's courage or stupidity.

Thinking fast, Brenden lunged for the shepherd, slipping his fingers under the thick leather collar. Bear was big, aggressive, and protective of his master. But the domestic dog was no match for a wild wolf twice his size. The animal's head was massive, almost unnaturally so, and its body was lean and sleek. Huge and bull-throated, the wolf was larger than any he'd ever seen. The beast was too large to be a female, or he would have thought pups were nearby and the bitch was protecting her offspring. One thing was clear. He'd accidentally stumbled into what this animal considered to be its territory and the wolf was pissed.

Scarcely daring to breathe, placing his steps as quietly as possible, Brenden struggled to keep the straining dog at bay. He wasn't carrying his off-duty weapon—something his superiors encouraged, but he didn't subscribe to. He was reconsidering the decision as unwise. Not that hindsight would do him a whole hell of a lot of good just this minute.

"Good boy." Eyes fixed on the wolf, he took a step back, dragging Bear with him. The shepherd refused to relent. *Damn it, Bear. Let's not do anything stupid.* "Stop it," he hissed. "Stop it. This is one you won't win."

Bear wasn't in the mood to listen.

Instantly, the dog broke free, leaping forward to attack the crouching wolf. The wolf's huge head shot up, a blur of fangs, right before Bear barreled in with the drive of his full weight.

Brenden yelled a warning, ran blindly toward the dogs, then drew back when a snapping mouth turned his way. Unarmed, he didn't stand a chance.

Neither did Bear.

The wolf's fangs closed around Bear's throat. Teeth clamped tightly, the wolf flipped Bear over onto his back. Four paws flailing, body writhing, Bear fought to free himself from the deadly grip, but was too easily overpowered by the larger predator. The flash of limbs, the clashing of teeth, happened too quickly to comprehend. Giving no mercy, the wolf ripped out the soft flesh under Bear's neck. The death-bite was quick and hard. Bear squealed in agony. Blood formed an ever-widening pool when the dog's body dropped to the ground, a mangled heap of bone and fur.

Brenden barely had time to react, watching in horror as Bear's great body trembled through the throes of his dying agony. Eyes staring vacantly, he died with a small incoherent whimper.

"Oh, no!" His words broke through numb lips. Hardly able to accept what had happened, Brenden felt oddly dizzy. He was swaying a little, but his feet were rooted to the ground. He couldn't move, couldn't react. It felt like some strange magnetic force held him in place. For an instant, he wavered between panic and sheer terror.

Massive head lifting, the wolf's muzzle was gory with blood. Eyes narrowing, it drew back its lips, showing stained teeth. There was a gleeful, almost intelligent gleam of vulgar merriment in its features, as if it had taken pleasure in killing. The otherworld glow surrounding its body grew brighter, piercing the darkness with an aura seeming to radiate from the deepest pit of hell. Smoke seemed to gush from its nostrils and flames danced in the depths of its wicked, unblinking stare.

The wolf winked and Brenden would have sworn the accursed beast was smiling. The wolf had killed Bear. Now it would kill him.

Run or fight. His mind hung, undecided, not knowing what to do. Try to escape and the wolf would surely run him down within seconds. His strength and speed were simply no match for the massive canine. To fight was the only other option he had.

"You fucking bastard!" Eyes blinded with tears, Brenden felt rage and frustration surge up, giving him a fresh strength he'd believed his depleted body incapable of finding. Hate filtered through him. Before his mind could even catch up or comprehend, his body was instinctively swinging into motion. Stooping, he swooped up the nearest weapon he could find, a good-sized rock. His intent was clear: to dash the wolf's brains out of its head.

Seeing his move, the wolf immediately hunched down, snarling defensively. It barked and there was a great roar like an avalanche through his skull.

Lunging forward, Brenden raised his weapon, bringing it down hard against the wolf's temple. The rock thudded solidly, meeting its mark. The wolf yelped in surprise. Massive jaws snapped toward his hand.

Gasping in anguish, Brenden rocked back, just missing losing his fingers. The blow staggered the animal, but didn't do enough to completely incapacitate it.

Snarling, the wolf quickly regained its senses and lunged again.

Brenden stumbled out of reach of the gnashing jaws. There was no time to find another rock. All his defiance seemed like a child's bravado. He'd given it his best shot and he was probably going to die for his ineffective effort.

Releasing an ear-splitting growl, the wolf attacked.

Struck with its full weight, Brenden tumbled backward, landing heavily on his back. His head struck the ground, the blow nearly blinding him with a dazzling display of streaking white lights. A heavy weight came down on his shoulders, feeling like two thousand-pound anvils had landed.

As though shocked by an electric fence, Brenden felt an invasive tension and force pouring through his body, a focused energy so overwhelming he couldn't even lift his arms to push the great beast away. Felled by the crushing blow, normal reflective response deserted him, all physical control of his body abandoning him as his strength and ability to defend himself dissolved. He could only lie limp, unable to move.

Opening his eyes, he found himself staring straight into the wolf's face. Its matted fur stank of musk and urine and something worse. Decay. His sister's warning was true. This cold-blooded brute was his demon.

Stomach knotting, Brenden retched from the awful stink. He tried to turn his head, gag, but something seemed to be holding him immobile. He was absolutely paralysed. Standing over him, the great beast had him securely pinned. Sharp claws poked through his sweatshirt, digging into his flesh in a most painful way. More painful was the way the wolf had fixed one of its hind legs squarely atop his crotch. The lupine brute weighed a ton. One rake of those deadly claws against his tender privates and he would be a eunuch.

The beast snorted, nostrils flaring. Cold, rigid dignity in its stance, the wolf glared down at him through savage eyes that blazed like the lava at the center of a volcano. A hostile, strange intelligence shimmered. Ominous sparks of energy crackled through their depths as if seeking to make a connection through the web weaving them securely together.

Brenden felt the assault on his consciousness, as though his mind were swimming with a thick viscous fluid, which drained through his body to fill his limbs. Snared like a rabbit in a trap, he fought to keep control, but not even fear could give him the strength to fight. *Oh, God, no . . .* His words echoed tonelessly through his skull. He opened his mouth, but no sound passed his lips. He couldn't even scream.

Through the channels of psychic upheaval, Brenden clearly felt the wolf's contempt for his kind, for humanity. The beast felt no sorrow for humans, gave them little regard. Humans were merely prey. Sick to his very toes, Brenden felt its maddening urge to tear, to bite, to shred flesh. He focused his mind, trying to stay calm. If he wasn't about to be killed, he would probably end up very badly mutilated. Hardly cheering or desirable.

Blood tingling with the awareness of danger, he was looking mortality in the face and his Reaper had arrived in the shape of a wolf. Not true a man's life flashed before his eyes at the instant of death—Brenden would have been glad to watch something less terrifying than the menace hovering over him.

The wolf shifted its weight, reminding Brenden his cock was in danger of being gouged off at the root. Tipping its head to one side in something akin to amusement, it released a deep, booming bark.

Brenden flinched. "Oh, yeah, you're still here," he wheezed under the crushing weight.

Lowering its snout toward his cheek, the wolf bared its huge teeth. Its fangs gleamed, glowing from inside with an energy not belonging to anything on earth. The foul stench of its hot breath scorched his nostrils.

Brenden clenched his eyes shut, sickened. He gagged, morbidly picturing how the gnash of those deadly teeth would tear through his skin like it was tissue paper. A low moan of dread broke from his throat. So this is how it felt to die. Not the way he'd imagined his death at all. All his life he'd been a protector, the man to charge to the rescue when others failed to answer the call. The irony that he was unable to protect himself was not missed.

Through his fog of panic and dread, the wolf's bloody muzzle lowered toward his ear. He clenched his teeth, holding on to the last tiny pieces of his fading self-control. Steeling himself to meet his end, he waited through long seconds for the penetration of teeth into his soft skin.

"You're all mine," the wolf chuckled in a very human way, using very human words. The voice was passionless, cruel. It ground its foot hard, digging its big paw into his penis.

The words barely reached through the agonizing grip on his groin. Hardly believing his ears, Brenden didn't have time to contemplate his sanity or the fact the wolf was speaking to him. He lost hold on his last shred of defiance. What followed would always be a blur in his mind.

"I will enjoy claiming you as my pet," the wolf continued in its unbelievable voice. Head flinging back, the great beast lifted its furry head toward the sky. Mouth opening wide, a great, space-filling howl shattered the darkness. The wolf's cry of triumph hit like a sonic boom, a paralysing emission chilling his blood and searing Brenden's heart. The lusty sound seemed to echo on forever, bouncing off the walls of his skull, easing, then dying, leaving for a moment abject silence in its wake.

When the wolf's head came back down, ripples of rolling illumination filled the air. Brenden's world exploded. The next thing he saw was the wide, blue flash, coming out of nowhere, blinding him. A great palpable vortex sucked him into a void of disjointing luminosity. A painful, dazzling electric shock suddenly short-circuited his synaptic functions, plunging him instantly into an abyss of unconsciousness.

20

Cradled inside an unresponsive husk, Brenden Wallace hung suspended in an endless void. Lost in his strange, nightmarish dreamscape, he entertained no real logical thought or image. He was alive, he knew, but trapped in total darkness. Where, he didn't know. Through the darkness he experienced the sensation of rising and falling. Unable to open his eyes or move a finger, he felt as if he was situated on his back, sprawled out, at one point dropped so hard that his body had become embedded into the ground. Briefly, through the pulsating nothingness he felt a chill, the sensation of being shucked to the bone.

Brenden fought the veil smothering his consciousness, fighting to find his way out of the dark, airless void and back into the light. His body seemed to be ignoring him, the rebellious beat of his heart refusing to follow any sane synchronization of normality. His blood pulsed rapidly through his veins, seeming too thick and too hot for the flimsy pathways to contain. Full to overfilling, he felt that he'd explode soon from the incredible pressure.

Knowing he would die if he didn't find the light, he struggled harder toward the faint cracks in the endless ceiling of his mind. Body aching painfully, he gasped. Then abruptly, without the ease of any transition, he was awake, but not fully aware.

Brenden stayed still until the swaying sickness inside his body receded a little. The physical sensations roaring simultaneously through his mind and guts were like the side-effects of a suicidal and sustained alcoholic binge. Nothing, it seemed, save death, could offer any relief.

Tiny black specks floated in front of his eyes. Disoriented, bathed in sweat, his body was battered and swollen, bruised in a dozen places. Where was he?

When he attempted to rise, a fierce bolt of lightning-like pain flashed through his skull, receding a moment later and leaving a dull ache behind his temples. Feeling as if he'd been cold-cocked with a thousand-pound steel hammer, he braced himself with a shaking arm to keep from falling over. Every bone in his body ached. His skin felt tight. Suffocating.

A fresh wave of nausea rippled through him. His head was spinning. He squeezed his eyes shut, fighting the surge of fresh sickness, but the flickering light around him crawled through his eyelids. He moaned aloud. The sound broke into fragments in his ears.

Brenden lifted a hand to rub his eyes. His arm seemed to weigh a ton. Something was weighing his hand down. Why couldn't he move? Dimly he recognized the scrape of chains rattling against hard stone. The ominous sound echoed, shattering the unnerving wake of empty silence.

Forcing himself to open his eyes again, he blinked to clear away the film of fatigue. His vision was blurry, his breathing a heavy rasp. He struggled to drag his weary body into a sitting position. Rough steel cuffs bit into his wrists.

Confused, his gaze followed the cuffs from his wrists to the wall. Fear sparked like a flint struck to stone. He felt his heart-beat leap, then pressed it down, forcing himself to remain calm.

"This can't be." The instinct to flee prompted him to tug at his bonds. The ends of the chains were firmly affixed to bolts in the concrete wall. He wasn't going anywhere. "What the hell?" Alarm seized his bowels, squeezing with a merciless grip. In his unconscious state, he'd been taken and chained up like a dog.

Feeling the nip of the cold against bare skin, he glanced down. His tracksuit was gone. While he was unconscious, foreign hands had stripped him. He'd been redressed in a long, loose-fitting robe woven of shimmering blue silk—and nothing else. Heat creeping into his cheeks, he drew the folds of the robe together to cover his nudity. The feeling of being violated cut a deep track in his psyche.

He sat quiet for a moment, resting. He tried to tell himself he was dreaming, that the dungeon was not real. Somehow he'd tumbled into the ravine and knocked himself unconscious. Yeah. Sounded more logical. Bear would soon lick his face with his great, sopping-wet tongue and he would wake up.

Uh-huh. Tell yourself another story.

Brenden lifted one cuffed hand. The heavy chain rattled. He twisted his wrist, testing the strength of the cuffs. The rippling pain grew greater as he struggled, chafing his skin. "This is no dream." A sense of total helplessness, almost complete resignation, washed over him.

His shackles were heavy and barely long enough for him to stretch out his arms more than a few feet in any direction. Slipping his wrists out of the thick cuffs was out of the question. They fit tightly and appeared to need a key to be reopened. His wrists were raw and sore. In his unconscious state he'd obviously fought against his bonds.

"Shit. This is unbelievable." His mouth was dry, his tongue feeling as though it had been Scotch-taped to the roof of his mouth. It didn't take an expert to know the chains were designed to hold more than mere men captive. Even if he had possessed the strength of a diesel engine, he couldn't break free. Someone intended to keep him.

With a gasp of mingled agony and relief, he settled down with his back against the wall and gazed around his prison. The space around him was windowless and dimly lit by a slew of candles burning on a low table just a few feet away from where he had been sleeping. The sticky-sweet scent spicing the air was almost too overpowering in the confined space.

The walls were covered in thick velvet, and the floor swathed with a rich, deep shag carpet. A heavy drape of some dark material obscured half the prison from his view. A luxurious cell, but a jail nevertheless. A thick blanket and a few pillows were thoughtfully placed under him to stay the chill creeping along the edges of the walls, but he'd apparently kicked them away in his sleep.

Brenden felt deeply disquieted. No one knew where he was, not even Dani. It might be hours before she knew he was missing. Where would searchers begin to look? How could they follow a beast with the magical ability to swoop him up and deposit him . . . Where? He didn't have a clue of where he might be. How long had he been here? He had no idea.

Drawing his legs up, he leaned forward, resting his head on his knees. Tiny ignitions sparked off his nerve endings. His brain hurt as if it had grossly swollen and was pinched by the confines of his skull. Trembling and streaming sweat, he breathed in ragged, heaving gasps. He shivered. If only his blood didn't feel so hot and his skin as cold as ice. When he tried to swallow, his throat hurt.

He lifted a shaking hand to his neck, acutely conscious of the clank of chains. His throat was still tender, the glands swollen. The tips of his fingers felt damp and cold, as though something had drained the warmth out of his body. He could feel a fresh bite on his neck, opposite those Líadán had inflicted. He opened his robe, glancing down at his body. His skin was riddled with bite marks covering chest, abdomen and thighs, the piercings into his flesh red and swollen.

His nightmare instantly clarified.

"Jesus, this is unreal." He'd been served as the main course at the buffet, feeding more than one mouth. The idea of such a curiously intimate moment of fusion chilled and disturbed him. Stark despair clawed at his psyche. He half wondered if he'd died and gone to hell. He took a deep breath. No, he was still very much alive. And as long as life remained, there was hope he could somehow get out of this place.

Brenden closed his eyes. Slowly, as though through a thick veil, he saw shadowy forms, strange and hardly human, begin to emerge. Strange, luminous figures came to the forefront as images of not just one, but several demon wolves filled his brain space, crowding in from impossible angles. It seemed as if the beasts were standing over him again, bitterly cold air ruffling their fur, a dozen sets of eyes sparking and gleaming with unnatural intelligence. It seemed the wolves spoke, though he knew—knew, damn it!—in a logical world wolves could not talk.

Brenden's mouth pressed into a thin, tight line. "What the fuck is going on?"

The sounds of a door scraping back on its hinges caught his attention, making his spine crawl with fears imagined and unimagined. He swallowed, fighting the rise of bitter acid. Muffled whispers accompanied soft footsteps. A moment later, the heavy drape cutting off half the area was lifted aside. A man stepped in. Líadán followed behind, carrying a small tray of food.

Brenden's gaze settled on the most obvious threat. Standing

well over six feet tall, the stranger was a solid tower of muscle, stunningly handsome. His eyes gleamed with an unnatural chatoyancy, the undulating luster adding an eerie effect. Ice and frost, steel and iron bracketed his gaze. Strange and unsmiling, these were the eyes of a beast harboring no human soul. His face brooded with a detached and inhuman composure. He was immaculately groomed in a white linen suit, a cascade of burnished rust sweeping his shoulders. When he smiled, his eyes narrowed, and the pull of his lips showed unnaturally sharp and long canines.

Bleariness instantly dissipating, Brenden recognized the demon-wolf in the man's fierce and cruel stare. This brute had killed Bear right before his eyes. Wild fury rose up inside, pulsing through his being with renewed strength. A calming wave of reason negated action, telling him, logically, he was unarmed and chained and could do no harm except to himself. He sat back, clenching his teeth against his impotency to dash up and slam the smirking stranger in the face with his fists. His murderous rage would have to wait. *If I ever get the chance, I'll kill him.*

Eyes flicking over him, the man snapped his fingers and made a brief motion with his hand. "Serve him."

Líadán knelt and set the tray within Brenden's reach. Without a word, she settled her hands in her lap, lowering her head. The strong, confident woman who'd attracted him seemed only a pale shadow of her former self. She wore a leather push-up bra, leather and chain g-string, and sharp black stiletto heels; her neck was ringed with a black leather studded collar. Locked wrist and ankle restraints were also firmly in place. Her skin, normally pale and unblemished, was laced with thin red welts and dark purple bruises. Seeing her as a submissive reminded him of an ox roped to the yoke. She was just as much a prisoner.

An invisible hand tore sharply down Brenden's spine, all but ripping his heart from his chest. Tongue tracing his dry lips, he let out his breath and cleared his throat. "Who are you?"

Legs braced wide apart, his captor didn't answer right away, but amused himself with smoothing the wrinkles in his sleeve over one muscled shoulder before folding his arms across his chest. Standing stiff-legged and radiating absolute control, the stranger gave him a disdainful stare, assessing his captive from the top of his head to the tip of toes. The wicked smile turned up one corner of his mouth. "I am Auguste Maximilian." The chill of nobility marked his voice. His accent was thick, but his words were easily understood. A significant pause. Then, as if to push the thorn deeper, his smile widened when he added, "Your new master." There was a ripple of mockery in his words. His eyes radiated with strange, curling fires, seeming almost as if his skull were boiling with energies too fierce to contain.

Master, my ass, Brenden thought spitefully, fighting to keep himself from spitting out the words aloud. Somehow he had a feeling Auguste Maximilian wouldn't take kindly to uppity back talk.

Brenden shifted, wondering how he could retain a shred of dignity when he was shackled, nearly naked, and unable to stand. "What do you want with me?" He let his gaze skim the tray Líadán carried. He could see a large ceramic mug, a plate with some sandwiches, cigarettes, a pack of matches, and an ashtray. With food so near, hunger gnawed at his backbone. He ignored it, even though some part of his mind warned he would need strength to remain alert. If they were feeding him, they were planning to keep him alive.

For the moment.

Auguste Maximilian took a step closer, and then another, planting one of his expensive leather boots squarely between Brenden's legs. The tip of his boot was less than a crushing inch from Brenden's crotch. A fierce, swift smile stole across his face, then vanished without a trace as he regarded his prisoner.

"Whoa—careful there!" The words came out before Brenden could check them. "That's the family jewels you're threatening."

As he knelt down, Auguste's knee planted Brenden firmly back against the wall. Cold washed over Brenden, a chilly breeze on an already glacial day. Then the smell of closed, musty chambers, dry and stale with age. Auguste's breath . . . the reeking stink of the carnivore consuming decaying flesh and brittle bones. Evil had a face, a name. He knew because he was looking into a stare holding no mercy and a shell with no soul inside.

Auguste's hand snaked down, finding and fondling Brenden's cock through the thin robe. Sharp fingernails dug into vulnerable flesh. "Oh, you are a jewel, indeed."

"What the—!" Too shocked to speak coherently, Brenden felt his face heat under the intimate grip. Beads of sweat broke out on his brow, and he bit his lip to keep from crying out. Flesh crawling with revulsion, he raised his chin, refusing to be cowed. Auguste's fingers were like iron bands. He was definitely the rabid type, on edge and just looking for an excuse to cross the line from maniac into full-blown psycho.

The unwelcome grip tightened, giving a not-so-gentle squeeze. A calculated move of control, of emasculation. Auguste was showing that *he* was the dominant alpha male in the pack. "I have had the pleasure of tasting you this evening. You are indeed a rare prize. The blood of the *Wyr* runs strong in your veins."

Every nerve in his body igniting with loathing, Brenden winced, giving the reaction he knew was desired. This was a man who knew his way around torture and it wasn't wise to test the knowledge while his dick was on the line. "Wyr?" Everything was happening too fast to make sense of and he surely couldn't think clearly with another man's hand wrapped around his dick. He didn't find the touch erotic at all. "I don't know . . ."

Brows rising, acrid humor waltzed in Auguste's kaleidoscope eyes. His grip relented a tiny bit. He glanced to Líadán, sitting so still as to be a statue. "It is a pity—or perhaps a joke—the sentinels against darkness have no idea of their origins."

A strange disquiet, a sickening unease flooded Brenden's veins. The battle for self-control was one he was close to losing. He struggled to keep from trying to strangle the son of a bitch with his chains.

As if reading his intent, Auguste's fingers tightened on his tender penis. Searing pain choked a gasp from Brenden's throat. He muttered a vile curse, involving a move physically impossible but entirely imaginable.

Spearing his victim with icy amusement, Auguste leaned forward until the shadows deepened the razor-like lines of his face to an inhuman degree. "No wonder humans don't have a chance. Those who were born to protect them don't even know what they are."

Brenden stifled his moan, finding the closeness unnerving. Drawn to, yet repulsed by the power Auguste radiated, fear and fascination tumbled together in his skull. Facing down a cobra and trying not to flinch with a deadly bite looming just inches away was almost impossible. Crumble now and he would be lost.

Auguste opened his mouth, lips curling back, fangs seeming to extend to a longer, deadlier length. His gaze remained steady, and the fire heated in its depths. An iniquitous smile twitched over those fangs, as though a most pleasant thought had just occurred to him. "You belong to me. I will take much pleasure in the penetration of your flesh, filling you with the gift of the jouyl."

Swallowing back fear, Brenden set his lips into a tight, thin line and glared back with all the fury in his aching bones. The invasion on his psyche and physical self, being maliciously fondled and threatened, was a little more than he was willing to swallow all in one day. He wrenched at his restraints, feeling the burn of the cuffs against his wrists. "I'll belong to you when hell freezes over," he snapped, flicked raw by the taunting. "I'll fight it every step of the way."

Instead of taking offense, Auguste drew back, laughing mirthlessly in a chuckle laced with malevolence. A sly look sidled in. "Oh, I want you to fight, precious one." A hint of glee seemed to linger on his arid lips a moment longer than necessary. "I'll enjoy breaking your spirit even more."

Something in his words made Brenden tremble with the anger he could not unleash, an anger giving him a welcome surge of fresh strength, of unrelenting will and sheer inner determination. He would not willingly make sacrifice to the beast. Single-minded resolve tightened his muscles, strengthened them. Brenden hissed and bared his own teeth. "You'd better not ever turn your back on me, close your eyes, or let down your guard. The minute—the second—you do, your ass will be mine." Conveyed with slow deliberation, his words had the desired effect.

Auguste's expression abruptly lost its humor. Grin sliding off, his grip on Brenden's cock fell away. "The blasphemy you speak will not be ignored. I take no threats carelessly, for I know mine enemy well."

Brenden flexed his hands, creating a brazen clamor of his chains, as though those alone would not be enough to hold him much longer. "Good. Then we understand each other perfectly."

Something flickered in the depths of Auguste's unblinking stare. Fear?

Brenden couldn't be sure, but he liked the effect. He hoped to see it again. Soon. Closer and without relent.

Mastering the unease he'd unintentionally revealed, Auguste abruptly straightened, slipping back behind his mask of unshakable calm. "Stay with your lover until it is time for the ritual." The purr of confidence was missing from his tone. "Your chosen, my lady, is going to be the first I take tonight."

Without a backward glance, Auguste slipped away, a silent, fuming wraith.

21

Left alone with Líadán, Brenden turned to the woman who had entangled him in this hellish mess. His first instinct was to hate her. Deeply and to the core of his soul. Hate, however, was an emotion he could not quite bring to the forefront when she raised her head. The desolation in her eyes was agonizing to witness. He detected the slightest tremble in her shoulders. She was trying to hold on to her control and losing the battle.

"I'm sorry." Numb, spiritless, her head dropped heavily to her chest, and she sighed. "Forgive me for what I have done."

Brenden wanted to reach out to her, but his shackles prevented free movement. He felt like a deflated balloon. Beyond weary, he was ready to cave in. His head hurt. He rubbed his fingers through his badly tangled hair, feeling filthy, violated, and impotent. Usually on the other side of the fence, he now knew why victims of violent crime crumbled once danger had passed.

"What's going on?"

As she lifted her head, a single tear tracked down Líadán's cheek. She quickly swiped it away. "You've been chosen by

Auguste as one of his brethren. In a few hours . . ." she paused, gulping. "You will join us, become what we are."

"What are you?"

She indicated her bondage apparel. "A slave."

A slave? Oh, shit. This was not shaping up to be a pleasant conversation. A small, quiet voice in the back of his mind warned him Líadán wasn't lying. One look at her pale face and the damages on her skin told him she was absolutely serious.

"Then it's true he's a—" the word hung in his throat.

"A vampyr." She lowered her eyes, continuing in a low voice. "As I am, as all of us who perform for him are."

Brenden shook his head, trying to orient himself. He was cynical enough to jeer a little in his mind. "This doesn't make sense. Things like this can't exist."

A flicker of faint amusement passed over Líadán's face, then her gaze grew sadder. "You have seen with your own eyes what Auguste can do."

The wolf's brutal attack leapt immediately to mind. "I saw it, but believing it . . ." Brenden tugged at his chains. His fingers shook around the metal. His entire arm shook. His stomach lurched at their cold solidity. He wasn't hallucinating, nor lying unconscious in the ravine he'd accidentally tumbled into. Simple logic said everything was real. The proof, the appalling truth, was in the seeing. With reality arrived the inevitability of acceptance, no matter how farfetched or implausible. "If I see, it has to be real."

Líadán watched his struggle. "It's hard, I know. I've been in your place."

He tugged again. Nope. The chains wouldn't give. He gave up. A few minutes passed, then several more. Finally, he had to ask. "Why me?"

She moistened her lips, the sexy little tip of her pink tongue flicking out for a second. Watching her compose her answer, he almost forget the question. Every move she made was sexy, reminding him all over again why he'd been so eager to get involved with her. She oozed sex appeal without even intending to. "You harbor the strength of the ancient slayers in your lineage."

First Dani, then some supernatural psychopath with a god complex. Thoughts of what those luscious lips could do to a man's body were tossed out the window. "I'm not what he thinks I am. I'm just a cop and—"

He wasn't even able to finish his own sentence, so completely overwhelming was the recognition sweeping over him. Pulse pounding in his temples, the image of Janice Parker's poor mutilated body suddenly jumped into his mind, hammering his own words home. As an officer of the law, his fundamental duty was to serve and to protect the innocent against deception, the weak against oppression or intimidation.

Brenden's heart beat harder, faster. He felt as if the oxygen had been sucked out of his lungs. "It's true, isn't it?" His voice was curiously calm. "What did he call me? That word he said."

"Wyr." The unfamiliar word sounded much like *where* to his ears. "Even though your power is untrained, Auguste feels you are a threat to our kind."

A beat of silence. Brenden had only a vague notion of what this all meant, but instinct told him to go with it, learn as much as he could. There was no other choice. "He fears me?"

Face lighting up, Líadán didn't hesitate to answer. "Yes." Satisfaction rang in the word. She clearly liked the idea of Auguste being afraid.

Brenden leaned back against the wall and drew a deep breath to steady his nerves. He pulled a leg up and tried to settle himself more comfortably within his limited space of movement. A rumble in his stomach reminded him of hunger. He glanced toward the tray. "Then why is he even bothering to keep me alive? He could just kill me and get it over with."

Her answer was immediate and chilling. "You are more valuable alive. Yours is a strength Auguste believes he can use."

He scowled. "What makes him think I'd cooperate?"

"What makes you think you can refuse?"

Brenden considered. Good point. Right now they had the advantage of being the home team.

Sighing, Líadán pushed the tray toward him. "You have not eaten. Come, take some food. You will need your strength."

Brenden glanced at the food. He reached for the mug. "I hope that's a fuckin' cup of coffee with a shot of whiskey. I could sure use a drink about now."

Líadán's unblinking gaze followed his movements when he lifted the mug to his lips and drank. "Milk."

"Milk is for baby cows. Not grown men." In desperate need of caffeine to clear his head, he would have rather had a cup of coffee. He sipped. The milk was icy cold and tasted pretty good on an empty stomach. He took another long drink and eyed the food. "Is this safe to eat or is it loaded with some kind of poison?"

A distant smile sidled into the depths of her crystal-flecked eyes. She burst into harsh, pained laughter. "If it was, I would eat it."

"Ah. Gotcha." He admired her answer. If push came to shove, he supposed suicide could be an option. "Well, I guess Auguste isn't going to let me go since I'm something he wants." He reached for a sandwich, gave it a suspicious sniff, then tore off a bite and stuffed it into his mouth. Roast beef and Swiss cheese on rye with mayonnaise. Not his favorite, but not bad either. He devoured the sandwich in a few gulping bites. The meal barely took the edge off his hunger, only whetted it.

As he ate, Líadán watched him. A grimace twisted her lips.

"Not to your taste, I suppose." He washed down his last bite with milk. Food in his belly put him on more solid ground mentally. He wondered what he would have done if he'd just been left chained up to starve to death.

"I am no longer . . . bound . . . by the need," she answered, honestly as though a diet of blood should be the most natural thing in the world. "I can eat if I wish, but I no longer enjoy it."

He pushed the empty plate away and reached for the cigarettes, lit one. "Thanks for the small things."

She nodded.

Brenden blew out smoke. "You still need to feed yourself?"

"It is the hunger of the jouyl."

"Jouyl?" He pronounced the word as he heard it. Jewel. No wonder the bastard had found his earlier use of the word so amusing.

Her face paled when a vein in her temple throbbed. She touched it with her fingertips. "My demon." Her voice was a curious monotone. "The companion sharing my body."

"Interesting way of putting things."

"It's true."

As if looking for some sign of abnormality, his gaze moved down her body, over her breasts, which were tugged and bound by the leather bra. He could clearly see the outline of the taut, erect points of her nipples. He felt an involuntary sense of warmth and stirring in his crotch as his penis quivered. Given the chance, he would be willing to make love to her right then and there. Just looking at her made his heart flip. If he closed his eyes, he could imagine he felt her hot breath against his bare skin, the way those hard little points had peaked under his exploring tongue, the way she'd arched in pleasure when he slid his cock deep into her slick, clenching depth.

She regarded him steadily. "Yes. It shares our bodies and grants us its gifts."

Brenden's hand trembled as he put out his cigarette. Unconsciously, his fingers traveled to his bruised neck. He tried to keep his voice neutral, uncommitted. "And you feed its hunger?"

Her eyes grew shadowed, her body tense. "If the jouyl is fed, it is content."

Brenden got the gist, but felt there were some parts she wasn't eager to explain. He decided to give her the nudge. "But sometimes it gets too hungry—"

An unsmiling expression crossed her face. Her struggle to keep the truth locked up disintegrated. "No! That is Auguste. We do not have to kill to feed. I—I don't." Filled with an angry intensity all her own, Líadán's hands clenched tightly, an unconscious and automatic gesture as she spoke. "Only Auguste does . . . The imperfection of humans disgusts him. He will not allow an inferior one to live. I beg him to spare them, but he never does."

Brenden closed his eyes, refusing to let the corpse of Janice Parker cross his mind's screen a second time. Nobody deserved to die such a torturous, undeserved death. Not even a former whore.

The chamber became oppressive, the walls closing in around him and triggering a pang of claustrophobia. On a deeper level he forced his fear back into its corner, where it crouched, hovering, waiting to strike again.

Reluctantly, he opened his eyes, returning to the ugly reality of his own situation. "Then you never wanted to be the way you are?"

Líadán shook her head. In the flickering light he could see the dark circles under her eyes, the hollowing of gaunt cheeks. Defeat was etched into every line of her body. "No. Like you, I was kidnapped."

Brenden's hands clenched. He pressed them into his lap, fighting to control the new surge of anger her words riled. "Tell me what happened."

Mouth drawing into a tight line, she squeezed her eyes shut.

Opening them a moment later, she lifted her chin and told her story.

"When I first encountered him, Count Auguste Maximilian was an emissary of Emperor Ferdinand I of the Habsburg line and brother of Charles the Fifth. He took me from my village when I just fifteen summers, not as his wife, but as his unwilling mistress." She paused, frowning with distaste. Her expression was calm, but something haunting lingered in her gaze, embedded there as though the things she'd been through were never far from her thoughts. "On my first night in his bed, he introduced me to the pleasures of flagellation."

Her words made his guts twist. Jesus. The evidence of truth, however, was in her bondage apparel and the lash marks maiming her flesh. As if feeling his probing stare on her bare skin, she nodded in silent affirmation. Her throat worked as she gave voice to previously remote and unshared memories. "Equipped with his leather belt, Auguste generously indulged himself on my rear before raping me. The louder I screamed, the more exquisite and orgasmic his amusement became." She touched her left thigh, tracing the freshly inflicted wide red welt. "I soon learned not to beg, but to endure. It's what I have done ever since. Endured."

Brenden grimaced, remembering the jolt through his senses when Auguste had attacked. How had it felt for Líadán, then barely out of her childhood, a young woman not yet in the full bloom of sexuality? Maybe he was weak, but he didn't want to think about her pinned beneath Auguste's heavy frame, forced to undergo something she so clearly despised.

"Was he a vampyr when he took you?"

"No. That came later. Auguste has always entertained a fascination with the occult. He gathered into his court persons of peculiar and sinister arts. Welcoming them into his presence, he gave each of them lavish attention—as long as they could sustain his most unusual needs and interests. If not, they were tortured and killed in out-of-the-ordinary and particularly painful ways."

"Sounds like a real nice fellow to spend an evening with." His voice was brittle with disgust.

Líadán offered a tight, humorless smile. "If nothing else, Auguste is a master sadist of the highest order. Among his admirers were those who professed to be witches, sorcerers, and alchemists, who practiced the most degenerate and corrupted deeds. They taught Auguste their crafts in intimate detail and he was enthralled."

"How so?"

Líadán leaned closer, her words coming out a low whisper. "Auguste fears death. He does not want to grow old, suffer the ravages of old age. Maintaining his youth and vigor is his sole obsession. Those teaching him the ways of dark magick gave him the key." No sooner had she finished speaking than she drew back. Hand going to her mouth, she glanced over her shoulder as if expecting immediate retribution for her traitorous revelations.

Pondering her words, Brenden leaned back against the stone wall, massaging burning eyes with the tips of his fingers. What men so easily spilled, what martyrs shed in the glory of God, and what demons hungered to consume was the thing preserving Auguste through the centuries. "Blood."

Líadán gave another nod. "I was the first he made—a thing I despise."

There was another period of silence. It fell over them with a palpable weight, bringing with it a wave of hopelessness. "There's no way to get out of this, is there?"

Líadán's mouth tightened at the edges. A hostile laugh escaped her lips. "See here why I can not escape him." Her hand went down the plane of her abdomen, stopping just above the hoop ensnared in her navel. The ring seemed to glow with a light all its own, little ribbons of fire crawling within its circle. "Auguste practices the darkest of witchery. This sigil binds me to him. There is no place I can go that he cannot find me. It will be the same for you."

Her words did not inspire confidence. The idea of belonging to Auguste wasn't cheering in the slightest.

22

Brenden sagged back against the wall, his muscles aching, his stomach rolling. He felt dizzy. Nothing was good about this situation at all. Nothing. He shoved the heels of his hands into his eyes and rubbed, as if trying to obliterate everything in his mind. The effects of his captivity gnawed at his nerves, throwing him off his normal manner of thinking. Calm was close to deserting him. He forced it to stay in place. He wasn't one to panic. Auguste Maximilian wasn't getting under his skin. He wouldn't let that happen. He dropped his hands, then lifted his shoulders in a world weary shrug. "Talk about shit happening. I think I need my hip waders here."

Clearly exhausted by her hellish ordeal, Líadán blurted out, "Forgive me." Her blue eyes grew distant, unreadable. "I have damned you." The words had no more fallen from her lips than she turned her head, looking away as if a fierce battle were being waged within her soul, a despair made doubly worse by her attempts to conceal it.

Brenden's reaction to her pain was instantaneous and overpowering, a mix of desire, frustration, and a touch of fear. His overriding instinct was to soothe her, hold her. He reached out, tentatively offering his hand. His emotions had been in a tumultuous whirl since he'd first set eyes on her, and he hadn't gotten a firm hold on them until this moment. His stomach knotted at the thought of her belonging to Auguste. What was between them was powerful and needed to be acknowledged. She had to know he was going to stand by her, come hell or high water.

"You don't have to ask for my forgiveness." He swallowed, hearing his own voice grow roughened and hoarse. "You're unlike any woman I've ever met before. The way you make me feel . . . You've affected me in ways no other woman has. If ever there was a case of love at first sight, I think I've just experienced it."

Líadán's expression was one of shock and pleasant surprise. A delicate color fluctuated under her skin. Her hand, trembling a little, slipped into his. "I—I've felt the same way."

He grinned in relief. "Good. I'm glad." He patted the space beside him. "Now do you think you could get your ass over here so I can have a few minutes to hold you before that asshole comes back?"

Líadán moved closer. Her fingers tightened around his, as though she wanted to hold on and never let go. Her hands were cold, unnaturally so. Cleansed of makeup, she looked very young, and he thought she must be no older than his own sister, if even near the age of twenty-one.

Brenden's hand curled around hers in an attempt to offer feeble warmth and some comfort. Her touch roused in him a sharp intense physical awareness of her body—lovely and full, clad in a sexy leather bra and barely-there g-string.

She snuggled against him. "You feel so good. I wish I could go to sleep in your arms and wake up far away from this life."

He kissed the top of her head, stroking his fingers over her cheekbone and jaw. "Me, too."

Silence crept between them as they enjoyed the simple pleasure of each other's bodies, locked together, rocking softly. He could sense her fears as she pressed against him, her head resting on his shoulder, staring into the soft candlelight. Cradling her close, Brenden drew the blanket over their bodies. He was careful to move slowly so the rattle of his chains wouldn't disturb Líadán.

His head dropped forward, brooding. His muscles felt tight and he lifted a hand, pinching at the tight tendons in one shoulder, trying to relieve some of the tension. Conflicting emotions bombarded him. Lust was definitely part of the equation, tearing at his insides, making his guts cramp. But there was also an unexpected streak of tenderness piercing his heart, tightening his chest in a squeeze threatening to cut off his air. His love for Líadán would bind him irrevocably to Auguste, Auguste would bind him to vampirism.

Sighing with regret, Brenden broke the companionable quiet so comfortably enveloping them. He needed some answers. "What's going to happen to me?"

Líadán stiffened in his arms, then pushed off against his chest. Shifting her head, she blinked up at him. "Perhaps it is better . . ."

Mouth dry as parchment, he swallowed against the looming unknown. His jaw tightened. An invisible fist squeezed his heart. "Tell me. I want to know what happens."

Her expression changed. Brenden saw the sadness hidden beneath the layer of longing in her gaze. He reminded himself to be strong, for both of them.

"I have to ask."

The joy, so brief, faded. She lowered her eyes, dark lashes sweeping her pale cheeks. Her face turned as if he had slapped her.

Brenden put a little more force in his tone. "I want to know."

Líadán's eyes threatened to turn liquid. She blinked back her tears. "The rite is intensely sexual." Her lips came together slowly, her cheeks reddening with a blush. "You will be taken—tasted— by many mouths. When you are at the height of arousal, Auguste will guide the jouyl's entry into your body." Her matter-of-fact words punched like a fist.

Brenden drew in a deep breath, barely daring to let it out. "I've already been tasted by more than one, haven't I?"

"Yes." She answered quietly, almost impassively.

Brenden, about to speak in a way that would deeply wound her, decided not to, swallowing his words back into silence. His heart swelled painfully in his chest. This wasn't the way he'd imagined their happily ever after would end.

Gently, with a desire he wasn't aware he possessed, he reached up to caress her hair, her soft neck, her ripe breasts. He indulged his need to touch her, filling himself with the smells and textures of her body. Amazing how danger was proving to be an unexpectedly intoxicating aphrodisiac, dredging up ancient primal instincts. Without any conscious decision, their shared undercurrent of desperation unexpectedly began to spin into something deeper, lustier.

"Then arouse me." A rasp of raw hunger tinged his voice. All his frustrations and fears were suddenly channeled into sexual desire when he pulled her into his embrace.

Without quite knowing what he was doing, he tipped back his head and covered her lips with his. Her lush mouth softened and warmed under his. She made a small sound of confusion, then desire, as her lips parted, welcoming the sweep of his tongue, needing everything he was willing to give. Her mouth was hot, incredibly hungry and eager, returning a kiss laced with an all-consuming carnality.

Arching her into his body, he could feel her curves flexing against his solid sinew. Insides burning with raw desire, he nipped at her, wanting to taste every inch. The low moan of assent escaping her told him she wanted it, too.

The sound of her unrestrained pleasure elicited a low, husky, vibrating groan in response. Brenden hadn't meant to let his libido get out of hand, but fear and adrenaline had triggered something deeper in his body—the need to survive at any cost.

Kiss ending, he drew in an unsteady breath. "I want to make love to you one more time."

Their eyes locked and Brenden tumbled headfirst into desire. He tugged the strap of the tight leather bra off her shoulder, finding and teasing the erect nipple beneath. The chains were damn inconvenient to have to wear, but at least he could move his hands.

Líadán's assent came like a contented purr. High cheekbones slashed with aroused color, her blue eyes were enticing pools of shimmering lust. She wriggled out of the bra, her breasts gloriously naked.

His gaze burned over her, lingering in places he wanted to explore with his mouth and tongue. He felt his muscles tightening, savoring the spiral of delicious heat radiating in his groin. Shaking hard, body trembling, he was aching to take her. He sucked in air and tried to think coherently. "You're so beautiful. So perfect."

Since he was chained, sex was going to have to be accomplished sitting up. He drew her into his lap, her spread legs bridging the erection barely covered by his robe. Dipping his head, he captured one of the teasing nipples. His hand traced her thigh, stroking silken skin. His mouth moved in slow, hot circles on her breast. Switching sides, he circled the forgotten nipple, using the rough tip of his tongue to torment her.

Líadán's response was immediate and passionate. "Brenden," she whispered between a vibrating moan.

"I need this. I need to feel your touch on my skin."

"As I have needed yours." Parting the silky folds of his robe, she slid her palms over his chest, going toward his thighs before finding his erection. She gripped his shaft and he felt the unmistakable urgency of sex radiate from her. Their passion seemed laced with some deeper need to make more than a physical connection.

She moaned aloud with pleasure when he slipped a hand between her thighs. Wriggling his fingers through the slit in her split front leather g-string, he could feel the dampness dewing her swollen flesh. She was wet and ready.

Brenden fondled the lips of her vagina, softly and slowly, just the way he imagined his tongue would if he were allowed to taste her essences. Her hips moved with his fingers, seeking more of his touch. The place could have collapsed on top of him and he wouldn't have noticed. He was only aware of the feel of her and her musky female scent, stronger when aroused.

Slipping a finger into her depth, he could feel the pull of her creamy, pulsing warmth. His body quickened with desire when he remembered the sounds she'd made in her throat when he'd mounted her the night before, opening her wide to take his cock deep. He wanted to hear those sounds again.

Líadán pressed down against his hand, moving her hips in a slow, rhythmic motion. Her face was an exquisite picture of pleasure, eyes closed, mouth slightly parted, nostrils flaring. Brenden closed his eyes, letting mental images fill his brain, images of him gripping her hips while she rode him, taking him inside her until he exploded. His mouth went dry. His cock was so hard he ached. His breath came harder, his stomach clenching in anticipation. *Slow. Take it slow.*

When he opened his eyes again, Líadán's glittering gaze locked with his, revealing without words that his touch was finding all the right places. Hands tangling in his hair, she pulled his head back, covering his lips with slow, hot kisses. His mind shut down on everything except the wild, savage way she made him feel.

Sliding two fingers inside her weeping cunt, Brenden pumped steadily, wantonly soaking up the currents of sensation as they gathered and undulated around his fingers. "I want to see you come. Hard."

Her eyes were cloudy, unfocused in her concentration to reach for and attain her pleasure. Her lips parted as she panted for breath, her intake growing shallower as her inner tension increased.

Brenden's fingers moved more insistently, stroking harder, sliding smoothly between her slick flesh. His thumb worked her swollen clitoris with a light, rhythmic touch. Her skin flushed, and her lush mouth trembled. As a pulse thrummed in her throat, her fingers bit into his shoulders. She was perilously close to the edge. Watching her take her pleasure, his erection strained against his lean abdomen, thick veins cording its length. Wet drops of pre-come glittered like diamonds on the rosy tip. His balls throbbed like a water balloon overfilled to bursting. If he didn't get inside her soon he would explode from sheer frustration. He was so stiff a mere touch would have shattered him. In a rasp totally unlike his normal tone, he ordered, "Come on, honey. Let it go."

She obeyed.

Chest heaving, her throat arched back, Líadán bit her bottom lip, moaning low. Her entire body shuddered against his hand when she welcomed the powerful surge of her climax. A moment later her shoulders went limp. Eyelids fluttering, she looked at him, slightly dazed. Her skin was dewy with perspiration, lit with a soft glow from the nearby candlelight. A sated look filled her eyes.

Brenden met her gaze and held it. He lifted his fingers to her mouth, tracing her full lips with her own cream. He followed it with a long kiss of lingering need. She tasted pure and sweet and delicious. Despite their circumstances, he could never regret giving her pleasure. He smoothed her hair away from her face with trembling hands. "That was beautiful." His voice was husky, affected by more than his sexual need for her.

She glanced down at his very raging erection. "But unfinished."

He groaned aloud, "Oh, yeah."

Grinning like a naughty little imp, her hands searched for and then stroked his flat male nipples. Her hungry mouth nipped lightly at his chest. The erotic nibbles felt like small electrical charges on his skin.

"I don't want to share you," he gasped. "I want you all to myself."

Líadán laughed, soft and low. "Someday . . . perhaps . . ." She tipped a smile up at him, causing his heart to brim over.

Brenden felt as though his brain were melting. A delicious lassitude crept over him, dulling his wits. All he could think about was her lithe body hovering so tantalizingly over his. He reached out, letting his fingers trail over her pale shoulders, a touch saying secret words only for her. He traced one swollen welt and then another, watching her shiver as sensitive skin electrified. He wanted to stroke those ugly lash marks away, chase away the pain. It upset him to think of her cruelly tied down and whipped.

She had survived. So would he.

He didn't want to think of that now.

Brenden's hands moved lower, finding and cupping her breasts. His thumbs circled her pink areolae, the tips of her nipples coming back to hard attention under his touch.

Leaning forward, she accepted his kiss, her tongue darting out to tangle with his. His hands roamed her body, slender and strong. She quivered with tension. Though she was no virgin, he was delighted to watch her discover the pleasure of his touch when he ran his hands over her hips, then her firm ass.

She let out a small, breathy moan. "Take me now."

Cock throbbing, Brenden guided her lower until the tip was positioned snugly between her petal-soft labia. She growled, trying to push down, take him inside her sheath.

Resisting the need to impale her with one hard thrust, he

slowly steered her lower, savoring the way her tight, wet flesh welcomed his shaft. Oh, heavens . . . she was so wet, warm, and snug. Her soft breasts nestled into his chest as he slid his hands down her sweetly curved ass to cup her full buttocks. His body pulsed, erection throbbing painfully.

Her eyes widened in fulfilled pleasure. "I can feel every inch of you." She whimpered when he guided her up again, bringing her clit in contact with the tip of his cock before abruptly pushing her back down to take his full length.

"I'll give you that and more." Gazing into her flushed face, he watched her pleasure build with every slow thrust.

Líadán's hands slid up to his shoulders and she gyrated her hips, driving him to the edge with a motion born more of instinct than practice. Like a wild animal, she writhed and twisted and cried out, leading him to give everything.

Brenden concentrated on holding on for one more second. Teeth gritted, his growl through his haze of lust was feral. "Oh, damn, honey. I can't hold off much longer."

With a groan of effort, Brenden captured two handfuls of her hair and, straining upward, drove himself to the hilt for one last fantastic jab. His cock lurched brutally, releasing a warm jet of semen into her clenching womb.

Even as he reached his pinnacle of pleasure, strange hands were grabbing, drawing them away from each other with a brutal fierceness. They struggled to hold on for one last sweet moment, but it was too late.

Brenden was about to meet his destiny in the most vicious of rituals.

23

Three men appeared without warning, sliding out of the shadows. Lost in the brief pinnacle of orgasm, Brenden hadn't heard their approach. Even if he had been on his guard and fully alert he doubted he would have heard them. He certainly couldn't have done anything to stop their assault.

Without a word, one knelt, unbolting Brenden's wrist cuffs. His long dark hair was drawn back from his face, revealing high cheekbones and deeply tanned skin. His left ear was ringed with a gold hoop. Inscribed into his neck between ear and shoulder was the strange brand also etched into Líadán's skin. Auguste apparently took great care to bag and tag his subordinates. Lips going back to reveal a nice set of sharp incisors, Brenden's captor gave him a fierce prod. "Stand." A gleam of delighted cruelty lit his gaze.

Unwilling to wait on him, two other larger men bent, hauling him to his feet. Picking Brenden up as though he weighed only ounces, they set him on unsteady feet. They, too, were similarly ringed and marked. All three were strong, well-built males—each could have easily graced the cover of a magazine, such were their model-perfect looks. Líadán's words came back to his mind: Auguste didn't allow those he considered inferior to survive.

Head still reeling from the shock of having his pleasure so rudely interrupted, Brenden scrambled to regain his dignity. His first instinct was to cover his nudity. Then he decided not to. Realizing he hadn't a shred of poise to hold onto, he gave up the attempt. His robe hung open.

"Please!" Líadán begged. "I will go with him."

She was immediately silenced with a hard slap. Her head rocked back.

"Keep your place, whore," one of the males hissed.

Líadán ceased struggling. She looked helplessly at Brenden. Their eyes locked briefly, hers moist with tears. Brenden gave a brief nod of his head, indicating he understood her silent message. He rubbed his sore wrists. Those cuffs had bitten deep and done some damage. There would be scars.

Arms pinned painfully behind him, Brenden was forced past the dark curtain in his cell. Oblivious to his resistance, the men propelled him down a short hallway, into a deeper endless gloom. The place was pitch dead dark, yet they walked as if in broad daylight, obviously able to see where they were going. Nerves screaming to resist, he willed himself to make no sudden moves. Locked in grips as steely as the cuffs, his strength was no match for theirs and he knew it.

The hall abruptly came to an end. A sharp turn ushered them into a vaulted chamber of vast proportions, one easily recognized.

Shit! I know this place. It's the old abbey. A shiver crawling down his spine chilled him. A brotherhood of a different kind had taken up residence, defacing and defaming hallowed ground with unholy intent. Brenden didn't miss the irony. He cast a glance around, giving no indication he recognized his surroundings. It had changed so much. Not in the best of ways, either.

Walled with tall columns supporting an arched ceiling, the multilevel sepulchere was lit only by fire. Hundreds of candles flickered, spilling their light across walls intricately worked in natural stone. An oval mirror hung high, reflecting back the pulsing flames, bestowing an elusive, unreal quality on the platform beneath it. Unmistakable, the remnant of the many stained-glass windows, shattered, the gaping holes plastered over with thick slabs of plywood.

Raised off the ground to the level of about three feet, a thick set of stone steps led up to the altar's surface. Altered to suit a darker, forbidden form of worship, the pure white marble was darkly stained with layers of blood and wine from the brutal sacrifices offered. A circle with a pentacle star in its heart—a symbol of forbidden magic—was carved into its face. Several more obscure symbols were engraved on the inner and outer edges of the circle, their meaning going back to a time when heaven and earth were a single entity. The pentagram itself was fashioned upside down so the horns pointed northward.

Embraced between the horns, Auguste Maximilian was seated beneath a wolf of carven stone. His frosty features seemed unreal, illusive. He dressed now in black robes edged with fine crimson braiding. Four braziers positioned around his chair snapped with charcoal-fueled flames. The pitiless light gave his face the imprint of cruelty, of something hard and vicious lurking behind his demeanor. He gave a long, silent look of assessment. If he liked what he saw, or didn't, his face revealed nothing.

With Líadán beside him, Brenden was cast down at the foot of the platform. He immediately pushed himself up, climbing to his feet. The robe he wore hung off his shoulders, open, revealing his otherwise nude body. Chin leveling a notch, he looked at Auguste. Between them the air was heavy and oppressive—subjugator and slave, conqueror and conquered.

Auguste inclined his head in acknowledgement. His calm,

unfeeling eyes were like a cobra's, ready to strike. Judging by the set of his mouth, he was pleased. "Tonight you become mine, one of the brethren of Au-ayl, demon god of the vampyr. It is to his glory you will be expected to serve." He spoke English well enough, but at vital moments his emphasis hit the wrong syllables, making the words thick and harder to understand.

The meaning was still crystal clear.

Swaying on his feet, Brenden struggled to keep his balance. "I won't serve any demon god as a slave."

Auguste raised an arched brow, spearing Brenden with a look of wry amusement, as if he thought the man standing before him too witless to detect the mockery behind his sneer. His stillness, as though he were made of stone, was unnerving. "You will serve."

Feeling physically struck by the glint of steel in Auguste's gaze, Brenden refused to let fear overwhelm him. One blink and he was a goner. Hardening his resolve, he popped off before considering the consequences, "I won't."

Auguste's lips curved higher, smile becoming a scowl still more vacantly brutal. "If you think goading me will deliver you unto the hands of death, you are wrong. Death will offer you no safe shelter."

Brenden snorted in derision. His steady stare didn't waver one inch. "Do what you think you have to. I will not willingly serve you or your false god." Somehow his words didn't sound very convincing, but he'd said them with all the conviction he held in his soul.

Auguste's smile, the show of his brilliant canines, never wavered. "I see." Behind his smile his gaze narrowed, anger chilling ominously in the depths of his brilliant icicle stare. "Perhaps this will help change your stubborn mind." The vampyr master's hand came up, his gesture assured and perfect. Palm turning outward, his hand pressed forward, as if against some invisible object. The words of a spell slipped from his lips in a low rumble, the sweep of his tyrant power fierce and terrible to behold.

Arriving out of thin air, a vibrant force throbbed in the air, a pulsing power brightening as it gathered strength and speed before striking Brenden squarely in the chest. His body arched backward and he stumbled, feeling his feet leave solid ground.

Brenden hit the floor with a bone-jarring thud. Breath knocked out of his lungs, he shut his eyes, hearing a groan slide out of his throat. His battered and bruised body didn't appreciate the blow. He was aware of Líadán kneeling down beside him. "Defiance will only bring pain," she warned. "I will ask him to spare you the agony."

Brenden shook his head. "Don't beg for me," he grated. "Just be there." Before he could regain his senses, two of the men seized him with ungentle hands and dragged him back into his place before Auguste's throne.

Barely repressing his snort of glee, Auguste's hand lowered. "Did that hurt, precious?" Tone dripping with false politeness, his expression reflected little of his annoyance.

Brenden wheezed. "Nope. Didn't hurt at all. I could do it again with no problems." He drew a deep breath to steady his senses and draw on his self-discipline. Wasting his strength with resentment would do him no favors. The process of breaking down and rebuilding a psyche was no mystery. Auguste was carving him apart like a piece of meat, slice by slice—soon there would be nothing left but bone.

The smile faded from Auguste's features. He rose, gliding on bare feet. Cowl thrown back from his head, his rust-shaded hair seemed to attract shafts of light, soaking the illumination in and emitting a strange reddish glow. Tall and deeply pallid, there was but one word to describe him: stunning.

An unbidden wave of revulsion rolled through Brenden's gut. Fighting the urge to rub his chills away, he kept his arms at his sides, balling his hands into tight fists.

Auguste slipped behind him like a wraith. His hand came up, gliding through Brenden's hair. The feel of cold fingertips on Brenden's skin caused the fine hair on the back of his neck to rise. His mouth went bone dry. Acutely aware of Auguste's presence, his every physical sensation was magnified a thousand times past normal.

Auguste's fingers dug into the back of Brenden's neck, his grip tight and unrelenting. "You reek of human stink. Your weaknesses, your fear—the odor offends."

Gasping, Brenden bit back the pain. "Being chained up like a dog didn't exactly give me time to use the facilities." A vein in his temple set to throbbing and a shard of agony lanced through his head. Blazing steel talons squeezed his brain until a heavy layer of sweat beaded his forehead. He couldn't swallow, trembling so hard his legs would barely hold his weight.

Just as a black pool was beginning to swim before his eyes, threatening to plunge him into welcome darkness, Auguste released his grip. Brenden immediately pressed his hands to his bruised neck, cursing under his breath.

"Let me give you a taste of what defiance will earn you." Raising a hand, Auguste snapped his fingers at Líadán. "Fetch me the strap."

Líadán hesitated . . . then obeyed. A large armoire stood in one corner, silent and forbidding. Inside, it held a variety of items designed to bring great pleasure—or pain, depending on how they were employed by the user. A strap was chosen, long and thin.

Auguste claimed it. He began to circle Brenden, going around his body thrice. "Take off the robe." Grinning like the god he believed himself to be, he flicked his wrist. The leather strap cut air with a menacing hiss.

Brenden flinched, growing warm with embarrassment. The thought wasn't appealing. He drew in a sharp breath. Hot rebellion flowed through his veins. "No."

Auguste kept up his pace. His hand jerked. The strap snapped sharply, releasing a crackling hiss. "You can take the robe off yourself, my pet, or it will be taken off you." He motioned to two silent guards. They moved Brenden's way.

Brenden tightened his jaw. "I'll take it off myself." Shrugging off the robe, he slid it down his arms. Bunching it into a ball, he tossed it to the floor. Drawing back his shoulders and raising his chin, he stood, naked and erect.

Smoldering eyes took inventory. A nod of approval followed. "I will enjoy breaking you." As a warning, Auguste smacked the strap against his palm. The slap of leather cut through the tension like a gunshot. All pretenses vanished.

Brenden felt the tension deepen, felt his skin prickle. He heard the sound of leather cutting the air before he felt the sting across his bare ass. The crisp snap of leather on soft flesh startled him. Red-hot fire lashed out with lightning force, sending a blazing agony blossoming though his entire body. He hissed, resisting the urge to run his hands across the burn. *Holy shit!* He hadn't had a strap laid across his rear end since he was twelve years old, the year his parents determined corporal punishment was useless.

Without warning the strap cracked a second time, scorching Brenden's buttocks all over again. He cursed and twisted under the intense sting.

"Enjoying your punishment, my pet?" From behind, Auguste's words fell like stones. The leather cracked a third time. Snap . . . Sizzle . . .

Another hiss escaped through Brenden's clenched teeth. "Only a goddamned masochist would enjoy this," he retorted. "I don't happen to be one."

The strap bit again with ruthless intent. Four strikes. Crimson welts threaded his skin. A cry ripped up his throat, vibrating the bones of his skull as if to shred his brain into shattering atoms. Strength seemed to evaporate.

Stumbling forward, Brenden struggled to keep his balance, lest he pitch to the floor face down. He bit down hard, letting only a muffled moan slide through his clamped lips. He wasn't willingly submitting, but being forced to submit. This was not his choice.

"You seem to be enjoying it, beloved," Auguste mocked. "All you have to do is ask me to cease, and I shall. Can you do that, pet? Beg?" Cruel laughter rippled.

Brenden's mouth tightened in grim concentration. He could feel the breeze of displaced air before it made contact, giving him time to mentally and physically steel himself to take the strike. *I won't beg,* was his firm and silent resolution. This sadistic bastard could beat him until doomsday, but he wouldn't crumble. Hate clutched at his core, an intense and unrelenting ogre. Bad as the pain was, it still pissed him off. "I'll kill you for this."

The strap answered three more times, each strike falling harder than the last. "I can't hear you."

Brenden staggered. Thinking through the haze of pain was difficult. Rivulets of sweat mingled with the burn, intensifying the sting tenfold. Despite the chill in the air, he was sweltering. "I said fuck off and die!"

Displeased by his answer, Auguste sent the strap into motion, rising and falling with nightmarish regularity. Sizzling lines of fire erupted across Brenden's back, ass, and legs. Driven to his knees, he arched painfully under the intense barrage of blistering slaps. He felt as though he'd been dropped into a vat of pure acid. "Stop," he moaned brokenly, gasping for breath, shivering uncontrollably.

Silence fell with startling abruptness as the strap stilled. The only sound filling his ears was the sibilance of his own harsh breathing.

"What did you say, pet?" Auguste's voice dripped with gloating.

Dropping forward, shaking arms barely able to support his trembling weight, Brenden half gasped, half moaned, shocked by the intensity of the pain. "Stop," he breathed, trying to find the strength to make his utterance heard. The single word quivered, and a prickling of shame crawled across his exposed skin.

In no mood to be merciful, Auguste went into motion again. A fresh array of blistering welts spread over the surface of Brenden's exposed back with expert meticulousness and breathtaking speed.

An anguished cry from Líadán brought the lash to an immediate halt. "Enough. He has suffered too much."

Brenden cringed against the wailing undertone in her voice. He shut his eyes, relieved she had saved him from having to beg; he couldn't have endured another strike of the leather.

Silence.

"Will you let a woman beg for you?" Auguste prodded;

Feeling bitter acid rise in the back of his throat, Brenden winced as he shifted, his feverish skin acutely tender, fiery red, and pulsing with heat. His body might have betrayed him with a human's weakness, but his deep-seated spirit wasn't quite ready to surrender. The hate seeding his heart grew rather than lessened. "I ask for nothing."

Auguste snapped the strap toward Líadán, striking her exposed skin. She cried out in surprise. "Perhaps you will plead for your lover instead?"

Worse than the physical pain engendered on his own body was the spiritual pain of seeing Líadán flogged. With a fatalistic impulse, Brenden spat out, "You sadistic fuck."

Auguste paused, lash poised mid-strike. "You wish me to stop?"

A long pause ensued.

"Well?"

Brenden's shoulders sagged in defeat. "Don't hit her any more."

Just when he thought no more strikes would fall, the leather strap nipped again, catching him around the thigh, before falling back and burning three more quick slashes across his exposed cheeks. "Wrong answer." Auguste prodded, his words hanging. "Stop—what?"

Brenden struggled to spit out the hateful word. "Master."

"Good boy. You learn fast." Nodding with dark satisfaction, August knelt beside him. He seemed to exist in every corner of the chamber, immovable and dangerous. His close presence ushered in the scent of musk and exotic spices. His hand came down on naked skin. "Amazing, is it not, how pain heightens the senses?" he murmured as if sharing a delicious secret.

Head brought up sharply by the unexpectedly erotic touch, Brenden winced. "Don't." His single word was little more than a hoarse whisper.

Auguste persisted, sliding his palm along the curve of his spine in an intimate touch. "I know your mind . . . what you think of at night . . . alone . . . in the dark . . . The longing . . . the hunger . . ." His caress continued sliding lower. He squeezed one stinging buttock with suggestive intent.

Anger dissolving with astonishing ease, Brenden closed his eyes. Pain faded into a pleasant faraway haze. Other sensations, deeper, more primal, rose to assume dominance. He felt a warm tingle as the blood rushed to his cock. Sexual impulse rose and throbbed with unexpected appetite, the spark of enticement too concentrated to withstand.

Auguste's palm cupped and claimed Brenden's throbbing ass with domineering satisfaction. "You have always denied what you believed to be forbidden." His caress was sending away the pain, replacing it with something else, something much more pleasurable, seductive. "Embrace the sins of the flesh; welcome them."

Brenden gasped as fluid fire, molten heat, and voracious

yearning poured into him as though he were an empty vessel being filled with a dark, rich glaze. *Oh, damn . . . that feels so good.* He shook his head, trying to clear the fog in his mind. Drowning, he was going under for the third and final time. "I can't . . ."

Another stroke crossed his abused skin, more intimate. Tension melted. "You want this."

"No . . ." Despite his denial, carnal delight fisted tight and hard in his belly before cutting a blazing swath straight down to his cock.

Auguste leaned forward, giving his shoulder a light nip. His warm lips traced the curve, his body pressing up from behind. He breathed heat and menace. "Everything you've ever dreamt of is within your reach. I can give you so much more." Probing fingers slipped deeper.

Brenden sucked in a sharp breath. Feral heat blazed through his senses, delivering another violent throb of anticipation. Rebellion was fading even as a new passion was blooming, one secretly wishing to embrace bondage and domination. "Please. I—I can't."

Lips drawing back to bare his long canines, the vampyr master dipped closer, grazing his jugular. "Follow me and your reward shall come tenfold throughout eternity. You will be a god among men, worshipped, revered. Stand at the right hand of your liege and lord and I shall lay the world at your feet."

Echoing Auguste's prophecy, a gust of wind seemed to emanate throughout the chamber, bringing a faint chant of faraway voices.

Brenden tried to bite back his moan and failed. Despair and temptation bracketed his soul even as conflict tore through his brain, the passion of dark desires warring with the control of denial. The apple the serpent was offering was a tempting one. Even as the sexual violence and degradations repelled, they also attracted, lighting a fire in his soul not ever to be entirely

quenched. Líadán had unleashed his repression. He'd hungered—
and eaten—from the forbidden fruit.

And wanted more.

The realization left him a little uneasy.

Head swimming, heart hammering a staccato against his ribs,
he blinked against the sweat dripping into his eyes. Through the
wet film, a strange scene began to illuminate and take shape, the
clarity coming as though a black veil were being ripped away.
He could see himself, centuries into the future, lazy and indo-
lent, surrounded by riches beyond imagine, indulging in the
blood of young and beautiful men and women, bringing them
across a threshold into a realm envisioned as heaven on earth.

Age would not touch him, nor would his youth melt away.
He would walk unscathed through time, untouched by mortality's scythe—yet embraced in the grip of the darkest, most de-
praved evil . . .

24

B renden closed his eyes, shaking his head, willing the vision to leave his feverish brain. This wasn't what he wanted. He wanted to choose to submit, not be beaten into submission. Force went against his own inner desires to control, to dominate.

He dug his nails into his palms. A gasping cry broke from his throat. Twisting out of Auguste's hold, he climbed to his feet. Spell broken, he could again feel each merciless stripe tattooed into his flesh. The burning sting stole away his breath all over again with its intensity.

Hands clutched at his sides, he stood, half swaying, yet somehow managing to draw his flaming body utterly erect. "I don't accept your temptations, demon."

Auguste stood squarely, frowning, his countenance grotesquely twisted in shadows falling across his face.

"Defiance will be your downfall." The frown turned into a small chuckle of withering contempt. "You are a strong one—it will take much to break your stubborn will." A hint of dark menace colored his voice. "But time is on my side."

Brenden glared back with quiet malice. The lines around his

mouth tightened. Body aching to the bone, exhaustion was his biggest enemy. Inch by grinding inch, Auguste was wearing him down, whittling away pieces of his psyche. "You forget revenge is a dish best served cold. And time will soon be no enemy to me, either." He drew back his shoulders, making himself stand straighter. "I have a long memory and this day will not be forgotten or forgiven."

Thick brows narrowed over a frigid smile. "A threat, beloved?"

Brenden's own gaze chilled in challenge. "It's a promise."

"Never make a threat you can't carry through." Auguste gestured toward two of his largest guards. "Take him—prepare him."

Dark figures came down, descending suddenly from all sides. A slow, soft chant could be heard, more a murmur than actual raised voices.

Determined not to be taken without a fight, Brenden lashed out, throwing all his strength behind a lightning-fast punch at the man closing in on him from the left.

The vampyr ducked with smooth precision. "Don't fight it."

Brenden cursed and swung again. He was a solidly built and powerful man, but his attempt was ineffective, embarrassingly puny. His attacker simply caught his flying fist in a single hand.

Auguste laughed, cocking an eyebrow. "You're no match for him—too human, too weak." His eyes mocked and his smile curled upward, showed his long, sharp canines.

Brenden swore and wrenched free. Seized again from behind, his arms were twisted up behind him, the grip none too gentle. He was lifted off the floor, his feet going out from under him. Squeezed uncomfortably between Auguste's guards, his twisting and writhing failed to bring freedom. The men bore him up onto the platform as if he weighed only ounces.

Plunked uncomfortably on his ass, he tried to roll away. The move earned him a sound clout. His head spun. The crushing weight of two men pushed him down, forced him onto his back. His wrists and ankles were seized and securely cuffed. The grinding sound of ratchets zipping into place was chilling. The bite into his wrists widened his eyes.

The smooth surface of the altar was icy against the warmth of his skin. Positioned in the center of the pentagram, spread-eagled, an unbidden shiver crawled down his spine. Naked and helpless. His gut warned worse things were ahead. His brain seconded the motion. Time to do some serious worrying. Like a trapped animal throwing itself against the bars of the cage, he began yanking against the cuffs. His whole body trembled with his attempts to pull free.

He wasn't going anywhere.

Auguste glided over. In his hand was something long and thin, an ominous object Brenden immediately recognized: a branding iron.

Struggle immediately ceased. *Where the hell did that come from?* He stared up at the branding iron in panic.

With a deliberate move, Auguste plunged the brand into one of the nearby braziers. The minutes dragged on as the iron thoroughly absorbed the heat. When lifted from the fire, the end glowed like a single little evil eye, unblinking and blazing red.

Brenden blinked, feeling the blood drain from his face. Goddamn, surely he wasn't going to . . .

Auguste lowered the iron. The ominous sizzle, the pulse and ebb of the heat hovered barely an inch from his cheek. The temptation to shut his eyes and cringe was great, but he resisted. He was determined to show no fear. No cracks in the armor. Pressing his lips together, he refused to flinch or let a sound escape. He was going to be branded whether he wanted it or not.

Auguste jabbed the brand closer. "All who belong to me wear the mark of the master."

A harsh breath escaped his lips. This asshole had the power and he knew it. Auguste was playing, the way a coyote would run a rabbit to exhaustion before making the fatal bite.

"I don't—I never will—belong to you." He turned his head, baring his injured neck. The other men wore their marks there. Well, it was better than wearing the burn on his face.

Brows lifting, Auguste's frigid eyes lightened. The tip lifted the tiniest fraction. "Very observant, pet."

Brenden pressed his lips together. He was giving in. No other choice. He stared straight ahead, unblinking. "Just get it over with." Inwardly, he steeled himself to take the burn. How bad could it be? It would be quicker than traditional needle work, faster and bloodless. He had a tattoo—just a one, on his right bicep, a combination of Celtic knotwork and barbed-wire ringing his arm, his only formal recognition of his Anglo-Irish heritage. He'd been too drunk to recall if it hurt or not. He'd never gone back for another.

No hope. No pride. Auguste was slowly stripping everything away.

Conquer the demon. Show no fear.

The brand pressed into his naked skin. The chamber exploded into blinding whiteness, then blazing scarlet. A raspy, wounded-animal sound tore from his throat. The odor of cauterized flesh attacked his nostrils at the same time the searing pain punched against the back of his chest, stealing the air from his lungs. The burn was like the Devil's own pitchfork digging into sinew and spearing his soul.

Veins bulging in his temples, his head whipped back and forth. He could see nothing beyond the crazed, brilliant pain, think of nothing but the scream locked tightly in his throat. Dimly, through the agony, he realized Auguste hadn't laid the hot iron against his neck. He'd been marked, all right, but on his chest, between his shoulder and left nipple.

"What do you think, beloved?" Auguste purred, his liquid eyes brewing unnatural light. Like a fox, his eyes were on his prey, watching every reaction.

Chilled to the bone with perspiration, Brenden was tired of shaking. He felt strength return as anger rose. "I think," Brenden gasped, swallowing hard, "you've made your point clear."

Tossing the used brand aside, Auguste spread his arms, beckoning. Líadán obediently glided up. "Let your lover pleasure you. She will prepare you for your rebirth."

Líadán stretched out, giving him a sad smile. "I will make it as easy as I can." A moment later, her wet mouth was dancing over him, licking, sucking, exploring every inch of him. Firm fingers wrapped around his cock, beginning a slow, sensual hand job.

Brenden quickly forgot the cold and discomfort. All he could think about was Líadán's hands on his body, as he made the unsettling discovery his will could be so easily surrendered through sexual persuasion. To his horror, he was getting a taste of real bondage—and he liked it. A lot. If he allowed himself to let go of his inhibitions, he could easily imagine himself stepping into the vampyr's society of debauchery and depravity. To stalk, feed, and fuck was the basic instinct of the animalistic nature of the beast.

The chant filling the air grew longer, louder. The words rolled and reverberated around him, stretching his emotions to the point of snapping.

Licking his left nipple, Líadán nipped the tender tip with her teeth. The burn in his skin tingled when her soft fingers traced the tender path etched into his flesh. Oddly the pain of the burn had gone, leaving only a strange numbness in its wake, as though a shot of novocaine had been administered to the affected area.

Kissing down his stomach, her tongue snaked out, gliding smoothly over the glans, tasting the pre-come seeping from the tip of his cock. She moved her lips down his length, slowly taking him in to the very root. Coming back up the same route, her lips tightened, holding just the head in her mouth, lashing at the swollen purple corona with her tongue.

Brenden moaned, straining against his cuffs, unable to resist lifting his hips to get her to take more of him into her hot, wet mouth. She pulled back and the lascivious pleasure ebbed, only to return when she sucked him down again. To fight, to resist the urges of his body was impossible. He was as lost as any soul, damned. Like a drowning man, he was sinking for the third and final time. His eager gasps and long, drawn-out moans filled the chamber. There would be no rescue, no chance of salvation against the haze of excruciating carnal pressure building in his loins.

His reason died a shuddering pitiful death.

Teetering on the brink of total breakdown, he felt raw need plundering him with an unstoppable, forceful craving. Engorged to fullness, his penis was solid and weighty, pulsing as his seducer took him down her throat. When Líadán pulled back, her sharp teeth grazed over his silk-encased shaft before her soft tongue flicked the underside.

Brenden arched ferociously under the tide of molten heat rising from the depths of his loins. Her tongue waltzed on him to the rhythm of thunderous rolls of ruthless delight. Small, helpless sounds escaped his throat. Lost in the sensual dance of skin on skin, he could hardly keep up with the sensations threatening to overwhelm him like the waves of an all-consuming ocean. Just as he was about to peak and explode, the ride to the mountaintop abruptly ended.

"No climax for you yet, beloved." Casually flicking long hair off his shoulders, Auguste knelt between his shackled legs, spread wide open. "You wear the mark of Au-ayl, so must you be bound to serve."

Fantasy shattered, Brenden was instantly furious, but couldn't tell if it was from yet another strike of humiliation or from the unappeased sexual frustration. He craned his neck, straining to look at the man positioned between his legs.

Opening his hand, Auguste lifted something from his palm, balancing it between thumb and forefinger. Brenden caught the gleam of metal, a thin, short length of what appeared to be a stick of solid gold about two inches in length. "What are you going to do?"

Auguste reached out and wrapped his fingers around Brenden's erect penis. His touch jolted, settling into a tingle that raced from head to toes. He smiled with malicious intent. "I'm going to pierce this nice hard cock of yours." He slowly jacked his hand up, then down, the length of Brenden's shaft. His long, cool fingers felt like bands of pure steel.

Brenden almost choked on his own shock. He flushed, feeling heat flood his body. He remembered the hoop in Líadán's navel, the ones the subservient males wore in their ears. Terrible understanding dawned in his mind. Surely Auguste didn't mean for him to wear his sigil . . . down there . . . on the tip of his shaft. Oh, shit . . . He gulped hard. Tiny beads of sweat dotted his upper lip. His tongue snaked out, tasting salt and heat, the taste of fear . . . or excitement. He didn't know which.

His mind flew back to the first night he'd spent with Líadán, recalling the anticipation he'd harbored at being bound and sexually dominated. He'd enjoyed it. The pressure of having to act as the aggressor was nonexistent, allowing him to relax and enjoy sex in a way he never had before.

Being dominated by another male—an entirely different story. He didn't like being bullied, made to feel weak and helpless. Humiliation didn't sit well at all. His body's betrayal rankled. He didn't relish the idea of another man pawing at him.

His penis apparently had a mind of its own. Revulsion was giving way to a need threatening to steal away his very sanity as his cock surged, the purple veins cording his long, thick erection. Hunger and desperation for release were quickly beating down embarrassment.

Auguste's firm fingers continued the slow, long strokes up and down Brenden's willing flesh, giving precise pressure with an expert's hand. His gaze of cool assessment was intimate, as though measuring every inch he fondled. He was taking exquisite care, bringing Brenden to the edge before letting him back away from the precipice of climax.

With every long stroke against his aroused flesh, tension rose and pressure unexpectedly built to the point of explosion. Being jacked off by another man was usually not Brenden's idea of a good time. Yet his cock surged, strained. He was pumped up by fear . . . and maybe a little excitement. The need for release was driving him insane, even as he loathed himself for being aroused all over again.

Teeth bared in a snarl, Brenden pinned Auguste under a beam of malicious loathing. "Can't you put that somewhere else?" He nearly strangled himself spitting out the words. His voice was embarrassingly hoarse with strain. After all, who could be calm when shackled to the floor, branded like a steer, and facing a hoop through his cock. Every scrap of dignity and confidence was quickly flooding away. Even more painful than the beatings was the unwelcome realization he was somehow taking perverse pleasure in his own torture. Confusion beat through his mind with heavy, dark wings, but there was no time to examine the psychological aspects.

Auguste gave Brenden's penis a light squeeze. A smile curved his lips. "In your current state of arousal, I can assure you the pain of entry will be minimal." He murmured a few dark words of an ancient spell.

Brenden didn't hear a thing. Heart thudding a deafening beat in his ears, he could only wait and see what would happen. For no particular reason, his mind pulled out an old vice cop's expression *Anything can be fucked.*

He had a feeling he was the one about to be screwed. Painfully.

25

Chuckling, Auguste lowered his hand, holding the gold stick to Brenden's exposed head. The gold wriggled, animated with the power awakened inside its metal heart.

Brenden's breath caught. Sweat trickled down his armpits. His palms grew clammy, wrists and ankles straining against the cuffs, brain barely acknowledging the chafing of tender skin. "You're one seriously sick fuck."

Releasing his tiny golden snake, Auguste grinned. "Something I enjoy immensely."

As if sniffing, the gold poked around the engorged head of Brenden's penis like a worm. Finding entry, the molten metal began burrowing. As much as he wanted to look away, keep from witnessing the unnatural assault on his body, Brenden couldn't tear his eyes away from the grotesque show. "You bastard."

Eyelids half lowering, Auguste made a low, pleased sound in his throat. "That—and so much more."

Brenden grunted, gritting his teeth when he felt the invasive metal digging down inside his penis. The thing was alive and its penetration sent fresh spikes of red-hot agony straight to his toes. There was something else clawing at his senses . . . a perverse sense of pleasure lacing the intense boundaries of pain. His body's sexual response staggered him.

The metal unexpectedly twisted, drawing a yelp when it tore through vulnerable flesh. Brenden felt skin break, raising his head just in time to see the tip of the gold appear. The single stab blazed, but the sudden hot tingle immediately following in its aftermath as the blood spilled from the tiny hole delivered an unexpectedly erotic rush. A sweet cocktail of potent hormones poured through him. Instead of going soft, his shaft leaped with renewed vigor.

Pleased by his response, Auguste accelerated the rhythm of his strokes. "Almost there."

Heat rising, Brenden shuddered, his growl of pleasure turning into a choked gasp. Driving arousal tightened his balls, bringing him dangerously to the edge. Had he been able to string two words together, they would have been gibberish. There were no words to express what was happening to him at the moment.

Breath exploding out of his lungs, the pain pierced his panicked arousal, bringing him a sense of clarity he couldn't have otherwise attained. Stomach clenching with knotted tension, he breathed in, calmed himself, then exhaled. Losing control of the delicate line between danger and need, between reason and desire, Brenden disengaged his mind from processing the sensations and simply let himself feel, savor, and welcome. Along with the carnal throb came the realization his pain was a wave, to be ridden and crested by sheer force of will. He didn't want it to stop.

Still wriggling, the head of the gold stick came around, merging with its tail to form a perfect gold hoop around the tip. Shock sizzled up his spine as the two ends heated and melded together; its end or beginning could no longer be discerned to the inquiring eye. As the hoop completed itself, a blinding surge of pure electric power thrummed through his penis.

Coming softly at first, the concentrated quiver washed through him—brutal, delicious, heated, a tempo throbbing with intensity. Then, with mounting energy, the sensations lifted him into the stratosphere of near insensibility, stealing away heart and mind and returning a ravishing rapture of pure orgiastic bliss.

Hands clenching, fingers grasping only air, Brenden felt as though his skin were melting away from his bones. He gasped, feeling the jolt rise and surge anew, the unrelenting appetite of lust sweeping through his system. His body shuddered under the assault.

He barely had time to catch his breath before a final wave of intense pleasure claimed him, and then another, and another . . . All thought fled but for the ache in his loins. His cock arched over his lean abdomen, seconds from release. Balls drew tight, muscles strained and corded with tension; his chest rose and fell with hard, panting breaths.

Half maddened from need, he writhed against his shackles, straining harder. In an iridescent burst of flame, his penis flexed, surged . . . Hot semen spurted over the rippling ridges of his stomach.

A rocket blazing and then disintegrating into ashes, he collapsed, weak and shaking, utterly spent. Mouth bone-dry, he swallowed down an escaping moan. The stone beneath him was damp with sweat. Climax painfully achieved, his cock twitched for a moment, then went still.

His normally impassive face taut with admiration, Auguste murmured, "You enjoyed the pain. Few men can climax through the merging."

Dazed but sated, Brenden managed to look up through blurry eyes. Gathering his brain cells and senses, he grunted. "It ain't exactly easy when a piece of metal is crawling up the end of your dick." Releasing a long, slow moan, he pressed his head back against the hard floor, struggling to control the heart hammering in his chest. He'd never experienced an orgasm so intense. Weak and shaking, he was no stronger than a newly born kitten. Every ounce of energy vanished. If released this second, he doubted he could rise, much less walk.

Drawn by the blood, Líadán leaned forward, opening her mouth. "Blood is life." She ravaged his cock with hungry lips. Her wicked tongue flicked at the gold hoop, bringing a spill of sensation both painful and pleasurable.

Brought to attention by her exquisite tongue working along the abused tip, Brenden instantly forgot pain. His first urgency was over, but the desire was not completely gone, simmering in the background like an angry swarm of bees. The combination of the throbbing ache, the hard metal, and Líadán's soft lips sent him into the stratosphere all over again. The delicious sensation of her mouth lapping up the line of blood was delivering another devastating jolt straight into the center of his libido.

Pure lust came to life all over again, a blazing wildfire threatening to consume everything in its path. Scorching heat, rigid fullness, and a seductively delicious friction . . . the sensations were both extraordinary and awful, a dream and a nightmare. His strength to resist was fast fading.

Lost, he was barely aware of more naked women closing in. "Taste him, my darlings," Auguste urged. "His blood will be sweet."

Through horrified eyes, Brenden saw their features begin to change, distort, evolving into what he could only describe as demonic. Deep ridges formed along their foreheads, down the bridges of their puggish noses as their faces assumed animalistic characteristics. Ears morphed into points, and the canines in their mouths became longer and sharper, completing their unholy transformation.

Brenden tried to draw back from the hideous visions. The pounding of his heart caused a deafening racket in his chest, sending a surge of adrenaline through his veins. His mouth opened. He tried to cry out for help, but no sound could escape the cavity of his throat. The women attacked without hesitation, biting deeply into his flesh, eagerly sucking the blood seeping from the savage wounds. An orgy of drinking ensued.

Head flailing side to side, Brenden forced his eyes shut. "Please, God, please..." All his shock and horror was betrayed by his voice.

God was not listening.

The women seemed to take pleasure in his useless straining, his pitiable cries for mercy. He was panting, his fear almost smothering him. The sounds of sucking filled his ears, blackness flowing across his vision like ink over a sloping surface. He could vaguely hear Auguste crooning strange words, gibberish to his ears. The voice sounded farther and farther away until stark silence raged in his ears.

The coldness of death washed through his body. Moments later, he felt buoyant, as if floating outside of his physical shell. The hurts inflicted by the savage bites were beginning to fade as a strange numbness overtook the pain.

His heart thumped, raced, then grew sluggish again. Gasping for breath, he could feel his blood draining away and coldness ebbing in more quickly with each passing second. His jaws clenched with anguish. Unable to endure any more, but still pinned down, he was helpless to save himself.

Suddenly the vampyr women crept away like silent shadows.

Brenden's head lolled weakly to one side. He was limp, pliant, too weak to resist. He lay in a misery of cold and terror. His world was fading. In every direction he looked he saw horribly demonic faces, felt the threat of their gnashing fangs.

Fingers limp, his body twitched, feverish, pained. He could not get warm. He could not free his mind of this damnable nightmare. He was whimpering like an animal, begging for death. Through terror-filled eyes, he could see Auguste sliding off his black robes. Gloriously naked, his flesh seemed to glow with an unearthly radiance.

A smile curved Auguste's lips. His lean physique was flawless, impressive even to the eyes of another man. Beautifully sculpted and muscular, his broad shoulders suggested strength enough to set the whole world under his foot and crush until it bowed under his grinding heel.

Brenden's breath lodged in his throat. Floundering in the nightmare, the search for logic was abandoned when Auguste straddled his exposed body, hard male hips and buttocks pressing into his abdomen.

One of the men glided up, pressing a dagger into the master's grip. When Auguste lifted the blade, the etched silver reflected the excited glitter in the depths of his strangely radiant eyes. He murmured softly, "Obey my words of power, watchers at the gate, unbar the guarded door, hear this command, servant of power . . ."

Pressing the tip to Brenden's heart, Auguste carved out a circle of strange symbols. Brenden felt no pain, only the pressure of the blade moving across his skin. Strangely, little blood came to the surface.

When Auguste had completed the mysterious runes, he lifted the blade and cut quickly into his own palm. Crimson pooled into his upturned hand as he spoke. "Earth to ashes, I bid thee, let this spirit come to me. I evoke and conjure thee, O spirit Au-ayl, the true god who grants the gifts of our eternity, to show your true shape to thine eyes."

Auguste's blood began to rise and writhe as the demon sharing his body immediately started to assume its foul shape. A misty vapor at first, it gradually assumed the figure of a grotesquely twisted imp. No more than three inches high in full form, its tiny face, ridged brow, and sharp fangs promised menace.

The evil creature screeched, its horrendous, ear-shattering

wail swirling around him with the force of a tornado. The vision took on the reality of a mirage. Hazy, slow, rippling . . .

A single cry of terror escaped Brenden's lips. Fear locked his throat and no words could cross his numb lips. There was no escape, only a hellish fate waiting for him. *He felt like a man clinging to sanity with tenuous fingertips.*

Auguste smiled. Lowering his hand, he bid the demon to step into the bloody circle he had carved. "Two hearts to beat as one. Two souls to become as one. I share with thee thy gift of the jouyl, forever to guide thee in the life of night."

The demon's tiny body burst into flames that seared through Brenden's flesh, following the circumference of the magical circle carved in his skin. He felt an enormous thrust of power, a great blow sending his body into shock. Pure terror leaped into his throat, skimming icily up his spine. His eyes rolled backward in their sockets. His chest stretched and bulged to accommodate the jouyl's penetration. His body arched painfully as heat and pressure blazed through every fiber. Within seconds he could feel the thing crawling beneath his skin, insinuating itself into his veins.

The more excruciating the invasion became, the harder Brenden fought the demon's presence. He winced, clenching his fists and pulling against the cuffs ringing his wrists and ankles. In his mind he willed the metal to snap. The cuffs held, solid against the strength of a mere mortal.

His flesh crawled. A terrible stab of pain came and went near his heart. As the demon latched onto his lungs, he felt himself losing breath . . . weakening . . . dying. His heart slowed; his pulse disappeared. Nothing existed but a void of darkness, a maelstrom seething with menacing shapes and half-formed faces.

Brenden Wallace, human being and mortal man, ceased to exist. Though he didn't die in the physical sense, he was reborn into a life promising to span ages.

Auguste finished the rite. "Join with thy chosen and return to your sphere of origin, o spirit, Au-ayl. By the authority of the true god, I command thee do no harm to him."

Wracked by intense discomfort, feeling as though his very soul had just been raped, Brenden ground his teeth together. His mind and tongue struggled to produce words and failed. Behind the barrier of clamped jaws and pinched eyes, he prayed fiercely, *Please, God, kill me now.*

His silent plea carried the substance of a man whirling into a vortex from which there was no return. His mind, his heart, his soul were in revolt, all of his senses shattering into a million tiny pieces, never to come back together into any coherent shape.

All of a sudden, leathery wings swooped through Brenden's mind. His eyes were glazed and unblinking as a low wheeze of air escaped his lips. He was barely aware when merciful unconsciousness claimed him.

26

Waking up in strange places was getting to be a habit.

Lifting his head, Brenden groggily rubbed his eyes and tried to focus. He felt a little dizzy, a bit weak and headachy, like he'd had just a bit too much to drink the previous night. He rolled his shoulders to relax the aching tension in his neck, feeling the remnant of last night's beating. His back was tender, swollen. He was in a bed, soft, warm and comfortable.

Jerking into an upright position, he moved too quickly. Dizziness washed over him. His guts contracted and he fought to swallow back the rise of bitter vomit. Head cradled between his hands, he sat still, taking long, deep breaths. For a few minutes it was touch and go, then his stomach settled down, the sickness receding.

Never having experienced such a brutal ordeal before, he felt shaky, sick. He was used to dealing with sex crimes, but from the detached point of view of the investigator—not the victim. He now understood what it felt like to be weak, defenseless, and unable to stop the attack of stronger predators. He'd gotten a look at the other side of violence, up close and personal, and it frightened him.

With each passing moment more of what had happened came back, scattered bits and pieces of memory weaving back into a coherent tapestry and drawing him back to full recognition of his predicament. Brief, elusive flashes solidified into full pictures, living and breathing color. He could still smell the stench of burning skin, mingling with the sour odor of sweat and blood. Skin layered in grime and reeking of his own fear, he felt filthy, abused, and defiled.

Then he remembered the demon. How could he have forgotten it for even a second? Stomach lurching, a hiss escaped his lips. *That thing Auguste conjured . . . it's inside me.*

Hand flying to his heart, his head dipped down. The mark branded over his left nipple was raw and tender, skin blistered. He expected to see the circle Auguste had carved into his flesh marring his chest. Not even the slightest hint of a scar lingered.

The demon was there.

He could feel it.

Maybe that was why his mind had shut down at the close of the ceremony, granting him a merciful cessation of the knowledge his body had been invaded. Hairs at the back of his neck prickling, he looked himself over. Hands going to his chest, he felt a strange surge under his skin. Voracious tingles were rushing through his veins, making a direct line for his brain before widening out in icy ripples to penetrate flesh and bone.

Alarmed, Brenden lifted his bare arm, digging the fingers of his free hand into his flesh as though trying to scratch away the peculiar sensation. He could feel the demon walking around under his skin, trying to settle down in a comfortable spot. A moan slid over numb lips. The horror, the really overpowering horror, was that part of him was enjoying the sensations it delivered. The demon was a seductive bastard. "Fucking cocksucker . . ."

Throwing aside the quilt, he quickly scanned his body. At least a dozen sets of bites lingered, the areas around the small tears in his skin puffy and bruised, more than a little sore. Swallowing thickly, mouth paper-dry, he dared a glance down toward his groin. Sure enough, a little gold eye at the tip of his penis winked up. The hoop was firmly in its place.

"Shit. It's really there." The tip was swollen and tender. Handling his abused penis with the gentlest of hands, he examined the damages. Aside from a little discomfort, there seemed to be no sign of infection or other ill side effects. The hoop wasn't in a place where it would interfere with normal bodily functions.

Shaking his head to clear away fear and phantoms, he felt an urge in his bladder that reminded him he needed to use the facilities. He looked around. Heavy drapes, four-poster bed, rich paneling, and an ocean of plush carpeting surrounded him. Very dark, austere, and every bit the style of a Victorian whorehouse. The bed was comfortable. Apparently vampyrs liked their luxury like everyone else. There were two closed doors to choose from. Hopefully one of those was a bathroom.

At the foot of the bed was a large cedar chest. His tracksuit, or what was left of it, was folded on top. At least he'd have something to wear. He had no idea how many hours passed since he'd been snatched.

Brenden swung his legs over the edge of the bed and stood up. Wooziness blanketed his mind. He felt consciousness draining away and willed himself back to clarity. Summoning what strength he had, he took a deep breath and let go of the bedpost, hoping he wouldn't collapse. His legs held. He wobbled toward the nearest door. Pushing it open, he stumbled inside.

Much to his relief, he'd chosen correctly. Someone had prepared the bathroom, lighting the oil lamps perched on sconces, adding the amenities of soap and a few other bathroom items. Thick towels, a robe, and slippers were hung on racks.

"Well, at least someone's trying to make me comfortable." He suspected Líadán had a hand in the arrangements.

Shutting and locking the door, he wobbled over to the vanity basin. The old-fashioned porcelain sink and faucets were heavily ringed with chalky layers of mineral build-up caused by years of unfiltered water passing through the pipes.

Hoping for water, Brenden turned the left handle. A brackish brown liquid spurted out, pumped directly from natural reservoirs. Not fit for drinking, but suitable for washing.

Breath reeking, tongue tasting like shoe leather, he rinsed out his mouth, careful not to swallow. He didn't need a raging case of dysentery from drinking unfiltered groundwater. Wetting the tip of a washcloth, he scrubbed his teeth. Not exactly a toothbrush, but at least it got the film off.

Face washed, he attended to the needs of his bladder. He eyed the deep claw-footed bathtub, wondering if a bath were possible. The thing was the size of an Olympic pool. He could probably do laps. He flipped on the left tap, full blast, and was rewarded with a steady trickle of water. Not blazing hot, but comfortably warm.

While the tub was filling, he turned his back to the mirror. Craning his neck around to look over his shoulder, he saw a series of black and blue marks crisscrossing his back. How many times had Auguste hit? He couldn't even recall how many times the strap whizzed across his skin. Thirty? Fifty? Enough to take him to his knees, make him plead for cessation. That was the worst part, the part he wanted to cringe away from and refuse to acknowledge.

Brenden didn't want to think about it. If he did, it would become a perverse repetitive drill; he'd go over and over it to the point of obsession. Revenge would take awhile, but the craving for it would drive him insane.

Unwrapping a fresh bar of soap, he slid into the tub. He sighed, relishing the feel of the water lapping on his abused skin. He lathered up. Washing away the grime had a cathartic effect. He felt a thousand times better. He hoped some food would be arriving soon. Nausea fading, he was starving. A cup of coffee and a cigarette would also be welcome. A shot of caffeine and nicotine would pull his mind together a little better.

He took extra care when washing his privates. "Who in their right mind would want their cock pierced?" Working vice, he knew body piercing was common and popular, especially among the Goth crowd. He'd never wanted to experiment with something he considered to be a vital body part.

He held his penis, examining his new piece of jewelry. Pierced straight through and ringed, there wasn't a single seam to be found in the metal. In the back of his mind Brenden had to admit it looked pretty damn cool—definitely an eye catcher. He could imagine whipping out his penis and showing the hoop.

It might have been acceptable if he'd chosen to put it there.

Since someone else *forced* him into the mutilation against his will, he wasn't precisely happy to be wearing it. Especially since it now bound him to the vampyr master.

Anger poured in. He wasn't about to wear Auguste's slavery sigil. "This thing is coming off." Question was, how? Unless he yanked it off and tore through skin, there didn't appear to be a way to remove it.

He reached down, slipping the tip of his index finger through the hoop. He gritted his teeth. "Gonna hurt like hell, but it's gotta come off." He shut his eyes and pulled. A sizzle of fire whizzed straight up his arm. To his dismay, he couldn't move his hand a fraction of an inch.

"What the fuck? This ain't right." Grunting, Brenden pulled again. Same dull sizzle, like a nudge from a cattle prod. Frozen solid, his hand would not obey the order from his brain.

His shoulders sagged. "Shit." He slid his finger out of the hoop. His hand obeyed perfectly. Switching hands, he tried the operation again. Same result. Any time he attempted to tug at the hoop, his arm locked into place as if in the grip of an invisible force field.

Brenden didn't know a lot about magic, but Auguste had apparently bespelled his sigil to prevent any sort of removal. The hoop was intended to stay in place and was going to do so despite every effort to the contrary.

Shit. Shit. Shit.

He finished his bath, wringing the water out of the washcloth and hanging it on the edge of the tub to dry. There was no telling how long his stay was going to be. Might as well make the best of it until he could figure out a way to escape.

Dressed in the robe, he emerged ten minutes later. Crossing to the window, he pulled aside the drapes. Late afternoon sun flooded over his skin. A vein in his temple began to throb. A shard of agony lanced through his head. Icy pain squeezed his brain. He gasped, then gritted his teeth. A heavy layer of sweat broke out on his forehead. His mouth went dry. He could not swallow. His breathing was heavy and painful. He was all of a sudden nauseous, trembling so hard his legs barely held his weight.

He placed a hand to his clammy forehead, trying to will away the sensations incapacitating him. Grimacing, he felt a twinge deep in his gut. How could he not know what it was? Not nervous tension, but hunger. Not for food. Shutting his eyes for a moment, he inwardly recoiled with dread. The voice whispering though his skull wanted something richer, warmer, thicker.

Blood.

Brenden shook his head, trying to ignore it, turn a deaf ear to the primeval cries of the demon inside, the disease living under his skin, infecting his body. He realized its need would soon be his. The craving for blood was worming its way through his system, weaving its fine but perceptible roots through his mind.

He didn't want to think about it. Not yet.

Instead, he blanked his mind, staring into the blurry reflection in the windowpane. His face was pale, haggard. Dark smudges of nervous fright lined his eyes, lips pressed into a tight line. His gaze was remote, his mood bleak. What he was to become was frightening.

A vampyr.

A shiver ran up his spine. Knowing he wasn't quite alone in his own head was a frightening sensation. He was no longer the master of his own body.

Lost in his thoughts, Brenden didn't hear the door open. A silent presence slipped in. A man's voice filled the silence. "I see you have awakened."

Brenden glanced over his shoulder. Auguste stood at the edge of the room, well away from the light flooding in. Immaculately groomed in one of his Fantasy Island knockoffs, he looked as fresh and unwrinkled as a daisy. Líadán stood behind him, pale, washed out. Her features were taut, inexplicably thin, as though loss of hope had depleted her.

Brenden narrowed his eyes. "I thought vampyrs couldn't walk in daylight," he grunted.

Auguste smiled broadly. "It is always a new day somewhere in the world. In the day, our powers wane, but we are able to get around. We need only stay out of direct sunlight."

Curiosity filled him. To know the enemy was to know one's own weaknesses. "What happens when the sun touches your skin?"

Auguste reached for Líadán, propelling her into the sun's light emanating through the window. Her skin immediately reddened. Within a minute a series of large, nasty pustules erupted and the smell of putrefaction rose. Grimacing in pain, Líadán stumbled out of the light, rubbing the injured area. Relief filled her face as her skin returned to normal.

"We die," Auguste said simply.

"You bastard! You didn't have to do that to her."

Auguste shrugged. "You needed to know." Stalking closer, his careful appraisal made Brenden acutely aware of his near nakedness. He felt his stomach knot when Auguste suddenly tugged open the thin robe with a familiar hand. Curious fingers brushed bare skin, tracing the brand burned above his nipple. Brenden winced. The burn was still tender.

Meeting Auguste's gaze, he tensed throughout his body, heart striking mallet blows against his ribcage. *Here we go again*, he thought, steeling himself for another battle of the wills. He inhaled. Exhaled. Waited. He wasn't going to back down. He couldn't lose face again.

Eyes never wavering, Auguste's hand slid lower, cupping his flaccid penis. "You belong to me, pet. I will take good care of you. When I put you out on the streets, you'll bring me many customers."

Brenden stood, motionless. He refused to flinch. Beads of sweat broke out on his forehead, but he didn't move, not even to wipe them away.

Auguste squeezed his tender penis a little harder. In the blink of an eye his face changed ominously. His grin turned downward, his features mutating into something forbidding and frightening, brow ridging and canines lengthening into long, deadly points. "Soon you will know the hunger, beloved. I shall enjoy watching your fall from grace, Wyr. Then you will no longer be of noble heritage, but a tainted, foul thing."

Stomach lurching, churning bitter acid, Brenden brushed Auguste's hand away. Anger welling up inside, he snapped, "Do you fucking mind?" Turning away, he belted the robe to cover his nudity. "I don't belong to you. I never will. You can't hold me hostage here forever."

Silence.

Jesus. Brenden felt as if a laser beam was burning straight through his skull. When he couldn't take another single second, he sighed, drawing his shoulders back, and turned to gaze once more on the hateful apparition.

Auguste's features returned to normal. His teeth were still

unnaturally long and pointed. A shit-eating grin crossed his face a second time. He was clearly amused by Brenden's display of ineffective foot-stamping.

"You are free to leave as you wish, beloved. I will always know where to find you through your sigil." His insidious grin grew wider. "And when your hunger comes, you will need help with your crossing. You will come back of your own will."

Looking into Auguste's eyes, Brenden felt the inexorable pull of an invisible vortex sucking him into a dark place he didn't want to go. He bared his own teeth. "I won't."

Auguste met his defiant gaze without flinching. "You will accept the hunger or you will die. Your choice, pet." He gave a slow nod. "Accept and you belong to me. Refuse and you go to your grave. It is that simple."

"It seems to me the dice are loaded when the only other choice is death." His tone was cold, rejecting.

Atavistic savagery came to life across Auguste's features. "Pass the time to take first blood and you will be consumed from inside. It is not a pleasant way to die."

As if he couldn't have guessed it himself.

The idea was a bitter one, almost intolerable. Anger washed over him, a chill saturating every nerve. Turning his back to Auguste, Brenden cloaked himself in soothing light. For a moment, the sun was the only ally he possessed. By the rumblings of the creature inside, that would soon be stripped away, too. "Get out." His voice was so strained it sounded harsh to his ears. "I can't stand the sight of you."

27

Líadán stood quietly, studying every nuance of the man standing at the window. She understood what Brenden was experiencing, what he was feeling. Confusion. Shock. Dismay. She'd struggled with each. Now it was his turn.

Sensing the battle within him, her heart ached. Strangely, it wasn't with sorrow, but lust. She had no reasonable excuses for her feelings. She didn't need Brenden Wallace. He was a complication in her life. A mistake. Making love to him that first night had been stupid, even if she couldn't bring herself to regret it. Not for one second—no matter how hard she tried.

The heart wanted what the heart wanted. Despite—or perhaps because of—the punishments Auguste had rained down, she refused to go back mentally and replay their first night to a different conclusion. She wanted Brenden. And because of that she could harbor no regrets.

Traveling every inch of him with an unblinking stare, she caught her breath. Haloed in the sun's rays like a defiant angel, Brenden's shoulder-length blond hair was damp and mussed around his shoulders. The sight of him, dressed only in a thin robe hugging his broad shoulders and narrow waist, made her knees tremble.

Heat rushed into her face when she remembered how his powerful body had felt pressed against hers, the feel of her lips spreading around his ... that cock, oh that magnificent tool. He had a beautiful one and, unlike most men, knew how to use it. Remembering how he'd explored her, slipping into her crevasses and slickness until she panted for release, Líadán wished he would draw her into his embrace and make passionate love to her right then and there.

Gritting her teeth, she struggled to pull her brain and her libido apart. "How do you feel?" Breath hovered in her throat. She'd rather die than lose him now.

Brenden swung around. Far from looking like he was in a loving mood, his expression said he was more than a little upset. Eyes hooded with betrayal settled like a laser beam, his mouth a thin, compressed line. Distrust hung between them, tangible and heavy. Was he recalling her part in Auguste's ritual, hating her for arousing his body? "Considering I've just been soundly fucked and not even kissed good night, I'm a little pissed." His tone was controlled, but his eyes were not. He jabbed an angry finger toward his groin. "And I'm really not happy about this goddamn earring on my dick."

Her gaze automatically moved lower, curious. She already knew what he had attempted. "You tried to pull it off, didn't you?"

A hint of his uneasiness tugged at the edges of his mouth. "How did you know?"

She shrugged. "I have tried, too."

He frowned. "Every time my hands go near the damn thing they freeze up. I can't move them."

She nodded. "It's the spell."

He snorted. "How is it shit I didn't believe in a few days ago has suddenly come around and bitten me on the ass?"

"Karma." She shrugged.

The easy feeling between them vanished. He shot her a glare. "Don't be a smart-ass." Restless, he prowled the room, a magnificent beast unwillingly caged. He stopped after a moment, turning an accusing face on her. "What did Auguste mean when he said he'd put me to work?"

No use in lying. Might as well tell him the truth. "You will go on to the streets like the rest of us."

A harsh laugh escaped his lips. "Selling my body?"

She shook her head. "You don't understand. We don't sell ourselves sexually. Humans buy the pleasure of our bite."

His brow wrinkled. "I don't get it."

"They pay us to take their blood—let them experience the thrill of being taken by a vampyr." She smiled ruefully. "We call them *suck junkies.*"

Frowning as her words sank in, Brenden ran his hands over his stubbly face. "Jesus, that's twisted."

Líadán had no argument. "Some will pay thousands for the bite of a vampyr. Not all are here unwillingly."

Brenden's eyebrow cocked in defiance. "And if I refuse?"

"You will be beaten. Auguste allows no deviation. His plans are to regain the strength he lost."

Brenden leapt on her telling words. "Then he isn't all-powerful?"

Líadán expelled a ragged sigh. Meeting his gaze, she decided to tell the truth. "The Wyr are why we left England."

Satisfaction crossed his face. "So there are others of my kind hunting him?"

"Oh, yes. The battle never ends. Perhaps it is why Auguste wanted you so badly. To show the watchers they are weak."

Making another disgusted sound deep in his throat, Brenden returned to the window. Arms bracketing the panes, he dipped his head back, basking in the warm rays of sunshine. "There has to be a way out of this."

Looking at him enjoying the light, the heat, envy poured into Líadán's skull. She could barely recall what it had been like to feel the sun on her skin. She had often thought of going into the light for the final time, but the death was too painful. She wasn't strong enough.

He glanced over his shoulder, a strange look haunting his face. "You know, it's funny, but I have the feeling a second set of eyes is looking out behind my own." His voice was flat, detached from what he was saying, as if he didn't want to admit the words belonged to him. He turned back to the tangle of gardens outside. "Curious eyes. Eyes that have never viewed a sunlit day. Everything feels so different. It's like I am seeing the world through a fresh perspective."

Líadán tried to find a smile and failed. Reading his body language, she could tell he was struggling to come to terms with what had been done. In a single night his whole life, his whole human identity, was snatched away. His life would never be the same from this day forth. A daunting thing to face. Even more so to accept it. "In a way, you are seeing the world through new eyes."

"A faraway voice is whispering from the shadows of my brain. It tells me my time in the sun will not last."

She nodded. "Soon the darkness will come and you will lose the ability to walk in the light. You never know what it is to lose it until it is taken from you."

"Damn it! It isn't fair." Without warning, one fist shot out, punching the thick pane. The sound of shattering glass tinkled. Cursing under his breath, Brenden drew back, staggered by his impulse. Blood dripped from the cuts he'd inflicted.

Líadán gasped at his violence. His anger was there, simmering, waiting to explode. A deep carnal hunger stirred and she felt herself going moist in private places. She had to get a grip before her own desires flamed out of control. The quick jumble of emotions made her chest tighten. Amazing how he could send her to the sexual edge with such a move.

He saw the look in her gaze, but misinterpreted sexual need for physical appetite. It mirrored his, hungry and feral, the craving of the carnivore. "You want it . . ." He paused, licking his lips. "I feel it in you because I feel it in myself now—the need to feast. Damn! It disgusts me, but I want it, too. I can almost taste it." He lifted his bleeding hand to his mouth.

Entranced by his movement, almost able to taste his blood on her lips again, Líadán stood immobilized by his anguish. His hand hovered less than an inch from his mouth, his face twisted with the fierce inner battle. His arm trembled with the effort not to complete the move. To taste, or not to taste. He wanted it, but was resisting.

"Your hunger has already begun?"

For an answer his hand fisted, sending a splatter of droplets onto the carpet around his bare feet. Clamping his lips together, he turned his head. "The need is driving me crazy. I can feel it tempting me, leading me. I see how easy it is to be drawn into the web. But I'm not ready. Not yet." His knuckles grew whiter from the intense pressure. More blood flowed, a river of crimson across his pale skin.

Quickly drawing the drapes across the window to shut out the deadly light, Líadán went into the bathroom, returning a few moments later. She gently took his hand in hers and wiped the blood away. His cuts were already beginning to mend. A moment later, they were little more than fading scars.

"It's setting in," she said, almost relieved. "Your first gift—to heal without scarring."

Brenden flexed his hand. "I didn't even feel it." He looked at her, eyes alight with amazement. "What else?"

She smiled, relieved. His tension was lessening. "We do not all get the same gifts. To heal, yes. To shapeshift, each of us gets something unique."

"Then you don't turn into a wolf?"

She laughed, shaking her head. "I have never been able to attain wolf form."

His look grew curious. "Then what are you?"

Creeping heat stained her cheeks. "A cat. A little black cat."

He smiled at her obvious frustration, looking her over from heat to foot. "Seems very appropriate, my lady." A wicked little gleam came into his eyes and his mouth hiked up in a smile. Yes, the wild side of him was definitely there, just waiting to be let loose. "You're certainly a pussy I love petting."

Líadán's heart kicked into a double-time beat. Just standing next to him could set her pulse to racing. "At least you haven't lost your sense of humor."

Brenden's smile disappeared and he sighed. "God, I will be sunk if I get something puny."

She exhaled, letting out a rush of air past her lips. She put her hands on his chest, enjoying the feel of his masculine solidity. Going up on tiptoes, she put her lips as close to his ear as she could. "You will be something amazing—feline, I hope"

His hands caught hers, head dipping down so he could answer back. "Why?"

She lightly traced her fingers down his exposed chest. As she touched his skin, she felt a sharp tug of anticipation from her belly to her toes. "Because we would be of the same species, able to mate."

Brenden looked at her for a full minute without saying anything. He must have seen the anxiousness in her eyes, because he didn't laugh. His fingers laced with hers. His touch was warm, confident. "Guess there's no telling what I'll get this early." He paused, struck by a thought. "How long does it take for this thing to activate?"

Líadán held his gaze for a long moment. The silence grew. "It's different for each of us," she admitted softly. "Sometimes a few days, other times as long as a week."

"Then I have a little time?"

"Considering you are facing immortality . . . you have more than a little time . . . if you accept the jouyl."

Lips turning down, Brenden expelled a ragged sigh. "I know. I'm going to have to make the choice: to live or to die." He gave her a small, tight smile. "Accept this thing and I'll be damned to a life of walking the nights. Deny it and I'll be dust, plain and simple."

Her throat again thickened painfully. She searched his face, probing for the answer. "How will you choose?"

Brenden pressed his lips together, breathing deeply through his nose. His clear eyes with their strange half green, half amber hue were calm. "I'm not ready to be dust." He pressed a sudden kiss into her palm, a silent signal of his acquiescence. "I'll accept it. For you—for us—I will. Promise me you will stay with me through the change."

Líadán's hands tightened in his. "I will not leave you."

"Even through eternity?" He cocked a sexy brow, mouth curving at one corner. His simple gesture was all it took to bring his masculinity and her reaction to it flooding back.

Freeing a hand, Líadán reached up to stroke his cheek, jaw rough with sexy stubble. The distinct scent of soap mingling with his male aroma was instantly arousing. "Yes." The pressure wasn't lifting, but was receding to a tolerable degree. There was hope as long as there was life. And love. He wasn't the kind of man in a rush to give his heart away. He'd chosen her because he loved her.

Brenden reached for her, gripping her waist in his hands. His hands slid down to cup her ass cheeks, pulling her close. "I should get the hell out of here while the going is good, but I don't want to."

She tilted back her head, gazing up at him. Sensation swamped her. The feathery tingling at the nape of her neck was followed by a demanding throb from other areas in her body.

The tips of her nipples suddenly seemed extra sensitive when he drew her closer. Emotions she'd believed long ago lost were unexpectedly at the forefront of her brain, dizzying her. She felt her throat growing thick with a massive lump and swallowed. "You can go home if you like. Your sister . . ."

He winced. "I wasn't even thinking about Dani!" His perceptive gaze suddenly lit. Líadán could see his brain going to work, ticking at double speed. Just like her heart. "Quick, tell me—if a spell can be done, it can be undone, right?"

Warily, she nodded. "As far as I am aware, all spells can be undone." Where was he heading with this?

Brenden's brow furrowed, as if he were trying to draw some forgotten knowledge from the depths of his brain. "And he's gotten them written down, right? In a book of spells, a . . . a . . . oh, what do they call those things?"

Líadán stammered her answer. "Grimoire. Yes. Auguste has one."

Clamping down on his excitement, Brenden gave her a direct look. "Can you get your hands on it?"

His question sent a spike of ice right through her heart. Auguste kept his sacred book in a chest locked in his private chambers. She'd only seen it a few times. A dreadful, evil tome, holding unspeakable secrets not meant for the eyes of any sane man. She'd witnessed Auguste working from his book, the cryptic writing on the yellowed parchment seeming to dance, each letter wrapping around the other in a sensual mating. "Why would you want it?"

Brenden didn't miss a beat in answering. "Dani's always talking about spells and counterspelling. Perhaps if she had the book Auguste uses, she could break the spell of these sigils."

Líadán gasped, immediately raising her lips to her fingers in warning. "Don't speak so clearly." She glanced around the room. Auguste's powers weakened during the daylight hours. There was a chance he would not hear, not be aware of their plotting.

FLESH AND THE DEVIL / 241

She pressed trembling fingers over her mouth. If there was a chance . . . the slimmest chance . . . that they could get the spell, freedom might be within reach. A *daring* idea, one she'd never entertained before.

Heeding her warning, Brenden went silent. He knew how to interpret and work off the signals of his partner.

Placing her hands on his chest, she rose on the tips of her toes, bringing her mouth close to his ear. "It's possible. Very possible. But a single mistake could cost us our lives." She could barely choke the words out.

Brenden nodded. Pulling back, he looked into her eyes. His eyes were unflinching in their intensity, lingering like a passionate embrace. "I'm willing to try if you are." His grip on her hands grew tighter, more possessive. His strong face betrayed an emotion so pure it almost hurt to look at him. "Isn't our freedom worth the chance?"

His words were like a ray of light down a dark, impenetrable shaft.

Líadán couldn't bring herself to glance away. Just looking at Brenden, so calm and able to keep his wits about him, awed her. His strength sent butterflies into flight in her stomach, started a delicious throbbing need between her thighs. Except for holding her hands, he hadn't touched any part of her body. She hoped he would. Soon.

Heart pumping fast and furiously in her chest, she was almost trembling with unrestrained desire; a desire so strong it both stoked her carnal needs and unnerved her. "I'll try to get the pages we need. Tonight." Her throat closed up all over again. Her vision blurred as a single tear slipped down her cheek. She bowed her head. She hadn't cried true tears with any emotion behind them for centuries. The release, the pain, felt wonderful. "I want to be with you."

Brenden slid his fingers under her chin, tilting her head back. "The chance will be worth it if you say you love me."

Rich, warm, and tender, his voice caressed, a translucent veil of quiet confidence. His trembling hands and irregular breathing gave her a sense of reassurance. He wasn't deceiving her.

Líadán blinked, sending another tear rolling down her cheek. "I do love you." She paused to gather courage, then went on in hesitant words. "I knew you had great strength in your heart, but also gentleness."

Brenden drew her closer. Their bodies were only inches apart. His voice was a low huff of air in her ear. "I'm going to find a way to get us out of this, so help me God. And when we're free, we can fight back, destroy him."

A tremor shook her. Auguste Maximilian cast a long, menacing shadow. Many men, mortal and not, had tried to topple him. All had failed.

"Do you think that's possible?" Conspiracy was entangling them in an intimacy closer and more binding than sex.

Brenden took a breath, released it, waited another moment. Then he nodded. "Yes, I do." His gaze never wavered, not even to blink. He believed every word he was saying. His conviction, in turn, gave her courage.

28

If words could be an aphrodisiac then those three, uttered with unshakable conviction, melted any resistance to cooperating in the crazy plan they'd hatched. The idea was so insane it just might work. Líadán knew where the book was hidden.

In the middle of her thoughts, Brenden suddenly reeled her in, capturing her mouth the way a starving man would bite into his last meal. The kiss didn't start out slowly. With last night's desire rudely interrupted, his need was now too urgent to contain. His lips were soft and warm, and hers parted eagerly for the invasion of his tongue. He swept inside and she tasted ecstasy.

As if caught in the bonds of a dream, Líadán gave herself willingly to his embrace. A shudder of sensation shot downward, tightening deliciously in her belly. Something about this man's impassioned assault made her quake. More than sensual, his kiss was a claiming, a branding, as if he were trying to imprint himself on her in a way no other man could. Her fingers parted the folds of his robe, finding the muscular body beneath. She was fascinated by the hardness and heat of him, grazing her fingers along his bare skin. Her own body coiled and heated, creating a wonderful torture. The thunder of her heartbeat—or perhaps it was his—threatened to deafen her. He was so close. She wanted—she needed—Brenden inside her.

There wasn't time . . . She should let him go.

They stood, simply looking at each other. Something held them together like magnets. In a brief battle of wills, their bodies made the decision for them.

Body shuddering, Brenden drew back. Unsure of what was going on in her mind, he said, "Whatever you're planning, don't tell me. You know where I will be."

Líadán brought her palm up and placed it on his rough cheek. She gazed into his intoxicating eyes, so mysteriously halved with different hues. "I will do this. For us."

"I know." Shrugging off his robe, Brenden's hand drifted toward his penis, but he didn't touch himself. He simply stood, posed, letting her visually examine every inch. His eyes never strayed from her face as he watched her swallow, gulping down air in nervousness. His intense gaze held a strange frustration and a simmering, potent need. An amused smile drifted across his generous mouth. "It's changed a little."

"It's different." Eyes drawn to his erect cock, her senses tightened like a bowstring. She felt hot, her blood burning in her veins. Her body had a lot of unfulfilled needs. She longed to feel his hands on her hips, guiding their motion as he plunged his shaft into her waiting depths.

He reached out, drawing her into his arms. "Hopefully it won't be there much longer."

Leaning into his embrace, Líadán slid her hands up his chest and tilted back her head. Her thighs were touching his and her breasts pushed against his chest, her nipples rigid and tingling, aching to be suckled. Closing her eyes, she savored his strong hold, the warmth emanating from his muscular frame. Brenden closed the narrow gap, not giving her time to think or draw back. Hand slipping down her back, he dipped his head and captured her lips with his.

Líadán moaned deep in her throat, trying to draw his hips into hers. She couldn't because he was holding back, torturing her. She felt dizzy from her awareness of him, from her over-responsiveness to him. Even now she was completely unable to control her body's physical compulsion for intimacy, unable to control the soft melting sensations within her soul.

Breaking their kiss, he drew back, gazing into her eyes. "I want you." He was so close. "All of you." With steady fingers, he undressed her, unbuttoning her blouse then guiding it down her shoulders. Skirt and bra followed, leaving her clad in panties and heels.

His mouth covered hers, hot, wet, and hungry, and all Líadán could do was moan. Burning with an infuriating, arousing anticipation, the intensity of his need left her a little breathless from what they were about to do. Her hand pressed between them, curling around his hard-on.

Brenden groaned as the feel of her hands stroking his length. "Every time I look at you, I get horny as hell." He grinned shamelessly with the confession. Desire flared in the depth of his eyes, deeper and more intense than anything she'd ever seen before.

Líadán tightened her grip, giving him her slowest, most agonizing hand stroke. "What are you going to do about it?" she teased.

Brenden swept her up into his arms. "This is what I'm going to do."

With quick steps, he bore her down onto the bed. Eyes glowing with anticipation, he stretched out, all hard, tense muscles, trembling with need. Light blond hair covered his arms and his chest was sleek, solid, deliciously rippled. His cock jutted against her bare thigh, straining. The gold hoop at the tip winked in secret amusement. One of his large hands settled over her breast, softly teasing her nipple. "This may be our last time together for a while. I'll have to go soon."

Rolling onto her side, Líadán kissed his chest, running her hands over his hard abdomen. His huge frame shuddered under her touch. "When Auguste is away," she murmured, "I will get what we need. If I do not come . . ."

His jaw tightened. "I understand."

"If he finds out—"

Brenden cut her off. "Once you leave here, you're never coming back. Just get to my house tonight. I'll take care of the rest."

Circling a dusky nipple, she nodded. Her hand moved lower, her exploring fingers finding and wrapping around his rigid erection.

Brenden's breathing grew ragged. His cock pulsed in her hand, all heat and velvet-encased steel. A tiny drop of semen leaked from its head, glistening in the firelight.

Pleased that he was letting her take control, Líadán dipped her head, flicking her tongue across the swollen purplish head. The salty taste of pre-come hinted of a richer, thicker ambrosia. Using the perfect pressure, she stroked his penis with a steady motion. Her tongue flicked out, gently tracing and teasing the hoop. Brenden moaned. Fingers delving into her tangled hair, he guided her lower. His breathing grew harsh, labored. Strange words tumbled from his lips.

Líadán welcomed his slick penis. Giving him her best service, she worked her mouth and tongue over every inch of him. His cock pulsed, the friction of his erection heating. He was getting harder, bigger, hotter.

"You'd better stop," he warned between gritted teeth.

She lifted up long enough to flash a teasing smile. "Or what?" Her tongue manipulated the little gold hoop with an expert's touch.

"Or this—" Brenden caught her arms and pulled her body against his. Rolling her over onto her back, he came up on his knees between her spread legs. As he held her wriggling hips with both hands, his erection arched and strained just inches away from her panty-clad crotch. He rubbed his length along the silky material covering her, giving her a sample of delights to come.

"You think that's a threat?" Giggling, Líadán planted her heels firmly into the mattress and lifted her ass.

He grinned. "It would be assault with a friendly weapon. But I'm not quite ready to use force yet."

Líadán pulled a mock pout. "What are you going to do to me, officer?"

Brenden's strong hands came to rest at the vee on the insides of her thighs. Using his thumbs, he traced the line where the elastic of her panties met the insides of her legs. He grinned like a kid anticipating a rich, creamy dessert. "Oh, I think I'm going to have a little snack."

A series of hot kisses glided over her abdomen. Giving a little payback, Brenden nibbled his way down her rib cage and belly, his every touch bringing a new surge of excitement. He paused to tongue the little gold hoop snared in her navel, manipulating it in a way that sent fiery darts straight to her molten core. Creamy honey drenched the crotch of her panties. "Yummy. Can't wait to taste this."

Líadán shivered at the delightful thrill the thought delivered. Bracing her heels into the mattress, she opened wider for him, a hint to put that mouth of his into action.

Giving her a sexy grin, Brenden moved lower. Bracing one of her legs over his shoulder, he stroked his tongue over the silky material covering her sex.

Líadán squirmed. Her throbbing clit made it impossible to think of anything more than her own satisfaction. "More," she moaned.

Brenden winked, stroking the tender bud through wet silk. "I'm here to please."

Lust sizzled through every cell. Her clit was swollen, sensitive, and she had to control herself from coming right on the spot. "I'm about to die of frustration . . ." She shifted her left leg and tapped his back with the long spike of her heel. "Giddy-up, horse. I want to ride."

He laughed, bringing a low rumble into his voice. "Oh, you're not the one who's going to be holding the reins." Easing the elastic aside, he delved in, tasting, exploring, delighting. He circled his lips around her protruding button. His tongue circled her most sensitive spot, rewarding her with a long, slow suckle, as though he were drinking in the purest of nectar. He added two fingers, sliding into her depth to plunder her with unrelenting strokes.

Líadán slid her hands under the bed's frame. Her back arched and her thighs quivered as she ground her hips harder, needing to take as much as he could give. Her whole body trembled alarmingly, racing toward a shattering climax. Before she knew it, a startling and swift pinnacle of pleasure saturated every atom with a flood of sweet ecstasy.

Skin covered in a slick film of perspiration, she lay, waiting for her heart to settle down in her chest. She pressed a palm across her chest to steady her breathing. Her damp panties disintegrated when he wrapped his fingers in the thin elastic and tugged, tearing them off her body. She was naked, dressed only in heels.

Brenden stretched out beside her. His erection rested against the soft nest of her warm belly. He grinned down from above. "Good?" Líadán sucked in a breath as his thumb circled her pink areolae in a persuasive manner. "Better than good," she gasped. "Excellent."

He shaped a nipple with his fingers. The tip hardened under his touch, growing instantly erect. "Should I make you beg for it?" He bent to trace the taut, straining peak with the tip of his tongue. When his mouth covered the nipple and suckled, she almost exploded from the pleasure. Against her sensitive nipple, his tongue felt like warm satin, sucking gently then harder. After a moment, he moved to her other breast and slicked the tip of his tongue over it. He took it greedily, brazenly, into his mouth, suckling hard.

Líadán felt the ache between her legs intensify. Her desire was as much of a bond if he had tied her down. Desire coiled tight in her belly, hot little spirals searing her blood with scorching intensity. She bit her lip, body trembling uncontrollably. A fresh and incredibly fierce pleasure shot through her surrendering senses, an uncontrollable tide sweeping her into a depth from which there was no return.

Rising to his knees, Brenden palmed his penis, stroking, bringing his fist up to the large purple head, then back down. The gold hoop at the tip gave his cock a tantalizing allure. The wanting, the needing, was driving Líadán wild, yet he was holding back, making her wait. His heavy-lidded eyes cast a spell, holding hers captive. "I need you." His whisper was raw, rasping.

Even as he was preparing her body to receive him, Líadán wondered how she would accommodate his new piece of jewelry. His very control was nearly her undoing. She was almost willing to beg, plead even, to get him to take her. "I can't wait much longer."

As a tease, Brenden rubbed the tip of his cock against her swollen lips but didn't enter her. The hoop, hard against her softness, created an out-of-this-world friction.

Líadán clenched her teeth. "You're being a rat bastard."

"Only a rat bastard would do this." He dove in with one single, stunning thrust, penetrating clear to his balls.

Stretched to the max, Líadán moaned. She rippled her inner muscles, enjoying the feel of her tight, slick sex closing around his length. The fit was perfect. She could feel every inch of him, and more.

Brenden gasped in wide-eyed surprise. "Oh, Jesus." He moaned. "I felt that one." Giving her a smile both wild and wicked, he teased her with a slow, delicious withdrawal. His eyes mirrored every melting emotion she felt.

Missing the sensation of being so ruthlessly speared, Líadán gasped in mock outrage. "Give it back."

Brenden shifted his hips in a most enticing way that allowed her to feel the hoop caressing her soft outer lips. "You asked for it, baby." Grin taking on a feral cast, he spiked in hard, making sure she felt the impact. Mouth crashing down over hers, he ground hard between her spread legs. He wasn't going to spare her a single sensation. "There it is, every damn inch."

"Yes," Líadán grated breathlessly. "And . . . you're so hard."

He speared again, impaling her like a fly on a pin. His hips rolled. "What else?"

"Big." She gasped, delighted.

His gaze sparked with carnal animation. "Payback is hell," he breathed. "Don't think I've forgotten about last night." He drew back, slammed again, impaled.

Last night . . .

Prickly heat blazed up her spine. "Don't you dare," she squealed, hoping he would do just that.

Brenden dared. Beyond words, a growl rumbled deep in his throat as his cock shuttled in and out, the hoop dancing on the tip of his shaft doing exquisite things.

Líadán's fragile grip on control snapped. Circling his hips with her legs, she locked her ankles together and let him ride. Every time he struck, the sear of his shaft flung her higher into the stratosphere of shooting stars and blazing rockets. Scented with the musk of unbridled passion, the air was as scorching as the heat generated between two bodies in furious motion.

Sensing her need to speed things up, Brenden braced his weight, pumping harder. His shuttling cock jarred her body with long, steady strokes. He wanted her fast and hard, not giving a bit of mercy.

Líadán clamped her hands across his back, fingers curling into claws. The bite of her nails grew deeper each time his massive cock took another deep dive into her slick depth. With every thrust, his pelvis rocked against her sensitive clit, delivering sizzling thrills of sheer delight from the top of her head to the tips of her toes.

Líadán bared her teeth and welcomed the tension. Another orgasm was within her reach.

"How does it feel with the ring?"

Dazed and dizzied by the sensations, she barely heard his question. "Huge," she gasped, searching for more words. The ability to put her thoughts into coherent speech seemed to have vanished. "Good. Don't stop."

"Not planning to." Eyes focused on her face, Brenden slowed, letting the tension between them ebb a bit. He moved a hand to her breast, squeezing, teasing the dusky nipple into an erect peak. His head dipped, teasing the sensitive little tip.

Líadán shuddered violently, her lips pressing together. She moved her hips in rhythm with his, her breath coming in quick feverish gasps underlain with a continuous pleading moan of sheer pleasure. Before she could control the impulse, she bared her fangs. Wrapping her fingers in his long hair, she pulled his throat to her waiting mouth.

Realizing her intention, Brenden rolled onto his back, letting her assume the superior position. Fingers digging into her hips, he turned his head to clear the way. "Hard. I need the pain."

Líadán bit. Deep. Seated to the root, she felt his shaft pulse the same moment that rich, thick, warm blood caressed her tongue. They were thoroughly joined, both feeding their hungers.

"Damn, that feels good." Gasping in delight over her penetration, Brenden writhed beneath her weight, forcing his cock in even deeper than she'd thought possible. The angle he lay at made him feel larger and harder than a length of steel pipe.

Mouth full of liquid heat, Líadán rode him like a wild stallion to be mastered and gentled. The experience of taking a human soon to be a vampyr had never been so intense.

Hips locked together, their bodies became one. Details didn't matter at that point, who penetrated or was penetrated. They shared a connection so intense their consciousnesses merged into a single entity. Bodies pulsing in multiple rhythms of awareness and excitement, they floated, submerged in a rapture blended from the sharing of intense love and passion.

Giving one final thrust, Brenden's hard frame stiffened. He threw back his head and roared, bursting with the dazzling sparks of his own molten climax.

Líadán's final orgasm rose and crested without warning, her cry stifled because her fangs were still buried in his neck. She screamed into his throat as a tidal wave of shimmering pleasure washed over her senses, taking her to a pinnacle of sheer delight that no mortal could ever hope to attain. Beast and burden were finally joined in her soul, a lush, erotic merging cementing her bond with her mate.

29

Brenden arrived home to the sight of seven naked women sitting on his living room floor. Privacy and modesty shattered, they all shrieked and grabbed for their clothing, including Danicia, who'd been enclosed inside their circle. Feeling like a fox in the hen house, he quickly pivoted on his heel to stare at the door he'd just stepped through. "Good God! What the hell's going on here?"

Danicia answered. "We were doing an astral search for you."

Interest perked. "Naked? If I'd have known about this aspect of witchery sooner, I might have shown a lot more interest.

"Don't be a smartass," Dani shot dryly. "This is serious business."

Naked women sitting in a circle certainly sounded serious. Brenden heard giggling and wiggling, the shift of clothing skimming over skin. Amazing. He'd never been so aware how telling simple sounds could be. Of course, the women weren't exactly being quiet. They argued over which piece of clothing belonged to—and looked better on—whom. He was halfway tempted to turn around and offer his two cents. He refrained, but just barely. It would be rude to ogle his sister's girlfriends.

"We're not naked now," Dani chided.

Another girl chimed in with a giggle, "We're decent."

Tongue lodged in cheek, Brenden slowly turned around. A cornucopia of beautiful women clad in tight breast-clinging T-shirts and tighter hip-hugging jeans met his eyes. Dani's coven-mates were also strippers. Considering the company she kept, it made sense.

Brenden shook his head, lifting his eyebrows to show disapproval. "You're going to have to explain to me what an astral search is."

Dani sighed as if he were a blooming idiot. "Meditating sky-clad—nude—allows for a clearer psychic channel between the physical and non-physical planes of existence." The other women nodded, backing up her words as the gospel truth.

"And this is useful how?"

She huffed. "When you didn't come home last night, you big jerk, the fastest way for a witch to search is to enter the astral plane and seek out the vibrations every living thing gives off. I know your aura and psychic patterns. I got as far as the woods when your trail vanished. It was like you were sucked off the face of the earth."

I literally was. Brenden sighed, suddenly weary. But there was no time for sleep. He had other concerns to deal with—and without a gawking crowd of strippers. "I'm sorry. I've been through a lot."

Relief written across her pale face, Dani burst into tears. "I'm so glad you're okay. When you didn't come back, I knew something bad had happened." She broke away from the group, rushing to embrace him. Her arms circled his neck in a smothering hold. Her body trembled with an intensity that revealed her fear.

Her hug, pressing her smaller body against his, put Brenden

almost unendurably in touch with her mind and emotions: her exhaustion, her fear, and her concern. Deeper were her own doubts and terror about her abilities as a witch to fight a menace she knew to be a very real and dangerous thing—a thing no one in their right mind would believe existed outside of films and fiction.

Confused and dismayed by his new awareness of a previously invisible realm, the intensity was like a blinding flash of bulbs going off in his skull. He shivered at the new knowledge, coming too much, too soon. The prospect of being so sensitized to other people's emotions dismayed him.

Not for the first time he was aware of a second consciousness thriving within his head. Apprehension cut a deep channel in his psyche. He wasn't sure he liked the sensation. But he wasn't sure he disliked it, either. Once again, two dual natures were at war within him. Which would win? He was almost afraid to find out. And he was even more afraid to admit which side of this new nature he wanted to prevail. Wholly untaught and untrained in the ways of the Wyr—his own fault, he realized—he was going to have to take a quick crash course in witchcraft.

Step back nonbelievers. The shit was about to hit the fan.

Sensing their need for privacy, the rest of the women quietly gathered their belongings and departed. Their work was done.

Feeling a little guilty, Brenden disengaged from his sister's clinging grasp. "I know—" He reached out, cupping her cheek in his hand. "I wish I had listened to you last night. You were so right."

Dani's astonishment was huge, but quickly suppressed. "I didn't want to be." A single tear slipped down her cheek. She swiped it away.

Brenden offered a stiff smile. "I'm in deep shit. In spades and up past my knees. There's no time to fuck around." Time was ticking away. Each second he lost, Auguste gained the advantage.

Drawing on inner reserves, Dani put away away fear and focused. "I understand."

Brenden leaned forward, briefly pressing his lips to her cold forehead. "I'm glad you do. I need you to teach me now. I need to know how to fight these things."

Dani concealed her astonishment well, hope lighting her delicate gamine features. "Then you believe?"

Brenden's jaw tightened. "In the Wyr?" He nodded. "Yes. I do. Wherever these things walk, I'm going to find them and kill them."

The stubbornness of a mule set into her small frame. A cloud of anger passed over her face. Her voice held unexpected force. "Not without me."

"Not without you, Dani." *And not without Líadán.*

She looked him over from head to foot. Her gaze settled fondly on his face. Without warning her eyes widened in alarm. Her relieved smile evaporated. "Oh, no!"

Confused, he reached for her. She stumbled back. "What?"

Dani lifted a hand, pointing a shaking finger at his mouth. "Your face—it's changing right before my eyes. Bren, you've got fucking fangs!"

Brenden immediately ran his tongue over his teeth. The tip stabbed against one sharp incisor, then a second. "When did this happen?"

He hurried down the hall into the spare bathroom. Looking in the mirror, he cringed at the shocking changes. His forehead was ridged, rippling in an unnatural way. Under the heavy brow, his eyes had changed as well; the pupils were slit up and down, like a cat's. He peeled back his lips, seeing two well-formed canines. The demon inside was coming to the surface.

As the tip of his tongue explored the tip of his tooth, the demon inside lifted its head. He felt a strange, tentative outreach of contact, like a light coming on in a dark corner of his skull. His mind merged with that of his jouyl. Something deep inside his gut stirred. He felt the prickle of tension, of need. Hunger. A strong swirl of desire rushed through him and he knew blood—life's precious nectar—would taste wonderful. He could almost feel the gush of thick warmth in his mouth.

The desire rose up, sickening him. Feeling as if he'd choke, his mind skittered away from the idea like a frightened animal. But his soul was curious. The time was near. Too uncomfortably close for his liking.

He closed his eyes, concentrating savagely on not letting the beast emerge. He forced the jouyl back, mental whip and chair in hands. *No. Not yet.* The shadowy beast wavered and flickered, sliding reluctantly back into its hole.

With a long sigh, Brenden looked into the mirror again. His eyes and face were normal. Only the burgeoning canines remained.

Dani came up behind him. Her expression was grim and gloomy. "Welcome to the dark side, Bren. I think you'd better tell me what happened."

30

Líadán moved cautiously down the long, dimly lit hall. Candles gave off an odd illumination, casting flickering, distorted shadows on the walls. The air was stale and hot and her eyes burned from the smoky soot clogging the closed atmosphere. Her white teeth showed in what might have been a smile but wasn't. Her lips were drawn back in a silent but determined growl she dare not let issue from her throat.

Once Auguste and his brethren had departed for the night's hunt for a fresh victim, her main pursuit was to penetrate the heart of her master's sanctuary, the place where he hid his most valuable treasure. Not money or jewels, but the grimoire containing all his forbidden spells.

Her expression was desperate; but the look was a calm, controlled desperation. She'd never ventured this deep into Auguste's chambers—the idea being the further away, the safer. That she was daring to penetrate this far into the vampyr master's lair took more than courage. It took nerves of steel. If she faltered, it could cost her and Brenden their lives.

The little demons of doubt circling her throughout the long

day suddenly went free in her skull, gnawing at her mind. Their sharp teeth and claws tore deep into the soft tissue of her brain, and their bellies grew fat as they glutted themselves on her self-doubt and fear. They never quite closed in for the kill, for then the hunt would be over. No, oh no. They wanted to torment her some more, stalk her.

A spasm of grief washed over her. She felt caged, locked in and shut out all at the same time. The doubts inside her head would not relent. When Auguste had taken her, she'd no choice as to her destiny and how she would use her unholy power. Auguste had decided for her.

Punished. She would be punished if she failed. The idea pained her, but not enough to turn back.

Remembering his ways of torture was weakening her resolve to be strong and brave. She could not stay the terrible fear manifesting itself in her churning stomach.

Líadán shook her head. The struggle inside was so intense that perspiration dotted her forehead. Her mouth felt dry, her head bursting. Feeling as though she were being ripped in half, she attempted to cast the treacherous memories out of her mind.

Close to sobbing, yet knowing it would be the worst thing she could do, she kept her own cries stifled behind her hand. Her whole body trembled with silent, unreleased agony.

One tear and then another trickled down her cheeks. Confused, bewildered, her skull felt as though it would crack and shatter into a thousand shards. The palms of her hands felt damp and cold, as though something had reached out of the darkness to touch her.

A skittering sound startled her.

She turned her head.

There was nothing there.

Breath catching in spasms, a little sob broke from her lips. "I can't give in." After four hundred years, she wanted to be free.

And to be free meant taking a stand for herself and her lover. There was no more time to be afraid.

The underground maze was a mystery forbidden to most. In the flickering illumination of the ever-burning candles, the walls were embellished with ancient symbols, cryptic in their arrangement. Only Auguste used these tunnels—no one else knew the full extent of these caverns and where they led. Her anxiety was understandable. Danger of discovery was very real—almost close enough to taste. Sometimes it seemed the shadows on the walls were playing with her mind.

Her walk continued. She picked up her pace. She could almost imagine something mysterious was moving around her, like a magnetic field guiding her every move. Reaching the end of the tunnels, Líadán moved into an antechamber that branched off into several warren-like rooms.

A silent wraith, she ghosted under the threshold of the sacred area where no one was allowed to set foot. She felt as if her heart were squeezing inward, threatening to suffocate her. Her nerves were tightly strung, almost to the point of breaking. Once it seemed this hour would not arrive fast enough. Now, she wasn't sure she was prepared to steal the book. The idea flashed through her mind that she should bolt, run until she found a small, dark corner to hide in. Only Brenden's image in her mind steadied her resolve. Of course, she could not run away.

It's just nerves. Soon it'll be over.

The smaller chamber was lit by no natural or manmade illumination. A single wooden chest was placed on a low stone altar. A blue-tinged ring of light emanated from no apparent source— bright, pulsing, powerful. The grimoire was well guarded even when its master was away.

A chill lingered around the edges of the small stone cell, but Líadán didn't allow herself to think of the discomfort of the cold seeping into her bones and provoking goose bumps on her pale skin. In a trembling voice, she whispered the words of the spell Auguste used to disable the circle's energy. Right or wrong, she had to try. If she missed a single cue, the guardian light would blast her to pieces.

Líadán hesitated, gathering courage. It was now or never. She took a step into the light. Nothing. No invisible hands reached out to tear her apart. She breathed a sigh of relief.

Once she was safely through, the atmosphere grew frigid, seeming to curl around her. She shivered with a chill not altogether born of the damp cold, as though wading in a thick fog. The fear of failure again clutched at her throat, but she could not give in to something as small as dread. The knowledge that she would be committing sacrilege was a sharper knife slicing through her mind.

She opened the lid, reaching inside to lift the damnable tome from its bed of soft linen. She had the book, actually in her hands. She was now the possessor of the heart of Auguste's power! She could feel the vibrations of the demonic forces locked within its pages.

Líadán thought she heard a strange, low, rhythmic chanting, as though the book were speaking to her. The throb of blood through her veins sounded strong in her ears, a muffled throbbing seeming to entwine with the mystical words filling the atmosphere.

She swayed and her vision blurred. For a moment, she felt as though she were rising, expanding toward the ceiling, passing through it to touch the far-flung moon. Her soul fluttered in an invisible breeze, a wraith of energy shimmering as lightly as a snowflake in chilly air.

Suddenly, her senses shifted. Light and sound seemed to fuse, twisting and contorting into an indescribable blending of her pulse and the hot darkness of the jouyl alive in her heart. The power she held was a vast one ... endless ... eternal.

Hers for the taking.

Her spirit slipped back into its shell of flesh, leaving her almost insensible. Líadán held onto consciousness with what she was sure must be the last wisps of her strength. She stood twitching as if blasted by an intense jolt of energy. She wasn't sure. She felt as though she'd lost all control of her mind and body.

Líadán felt an unbidden prick of the skin, followed by a slow sense of unease. Blood going cold, her heart thudded dully in her chest. A lump began to grow in her throat, threatening to steal away her breath. She tried to speak, but her command of the language seemed to have deserted her. A low, primordial groan rose up from her throat, creeping past her parted lips. "I'll not be tempted by the lure of demons."

Guts twisting, Líadán clenched her jaws and swallowed back the bitter bile rising to her mouth. Hatred, fear and disgust ricocheted through her brain, stabbing deep and hard, a mocking entity that would never let her forget she, too, was tempted by dark magic.

31

"And then the bastard ringed my, uh . . ." Brenden stumbled to a halt, unable to finish the rest of his story.

Dani raised her eyebrows, questioning the pause. "What?"

Brenden felt his face flame. Freshly showered and dressed in comfortable jeans, boots and a T-shirt, he'd slugged down several shots of straight tequila as he recounted his terrifying experience, sparing no details. Instead of getting drunk, or even feeling comfortably numb, his senses were still on edge. He wanted to get drunk, blot out everything. His system seemed to be immune to the alcohol. He might as well be drinking water.

Since he usually didn't make it a habit of discussing his private parts with his sister, telling her about his abuse was hard enough without having to go into graphic detail. She needed to know, though. She was the only one who could help get the hoop off.

Brenden winced, remembering what he'd been through. He swore under his breath, then blurted out, "He put a hoop at the end of my cock."

Dani's wide-eyed stare immediately shot toward his crotch. Catching herself, she giggled in embarrassment. "Oh, shit."

Brenden huffed, sulking, "It isn't funny." It felt strange to be sitting in the den, trying to get drunk and discussing an experience more on a par with alien abduction. Unbelievable. Fucking surreal. He wanted to pinch himself, make sure he was awake.

Dani's gaze dropped again. He could see the gears in her head working, trying to put together a mental picture. Finally, she asked, "Can I see it?"

Hand tightening around his shot glass, Brenden speared her with a lethal glare. "Christ, no! I'm not showing you my willie." He downed his tequila, relishing the burn all the way down to his gut. He needed something to wash away the bad taste in his mouth. Alcohol was not what his jouyl demanded. *Piss on the little fucker. Maybe I can drown it.*

Dani's brow furrowed. "It does sound funny, but I'm not laughing at you."

Brenden reached for the half-empty tequila bottle, refilling his glass. "I need to get this thing off. Auguste knows exactly where I am as long as it's there. There's no getting away from him unless it comes off."

"I know about the properties of a sigil." Dani shrugged helplessly. "My hands are tied unless I know the spell I am trying to reverse."

"Líadán's going to try and get it." Brenden shifted a glance toward the window. The night shadowed the sky and she still hadn't arrived. A thousand scenarios—all of them bad—fast-forwarded through his mind. What if something had happened to her? Forcing the bad thoughts back into darkness, he clamped down on his worry. He must believe Líadán would get the spell and get out safely.

Raking her hands through her hair, Dani sagged back against the cushions. "That bitch is the whole cause of this," she spat.

Shaking his head, Brenden held up a hand. "Part of this is your own fault. You cast two spells, a *love* spell and a *destiny* spell. The answer just arrived in one package."

His sister's eyes narrowed over her disapproving frown. "Oh, please. Don't tell me you love her?" She slapped her forehead. "Oh, damn. What have I done?"

He smiled ruefully. "You meddled, little sister. And if you have to ask, yes, I love her."

Drawing her knees up to her chest, Dani moaned in misery. "A vampyr in the family. We can't have this. We're slayers, Bren. We kill them."

Brenden bared his fangs. "I'm about to be one. Remember? What are you going to do? Have me killed?"

Dani nibbled her lip. "I suppose this makes you some kind of an oxymoron—a slayer who is also a vampyr. Don't know how we'll get around the Wyr council with this one."

"What do you mean, the Wyr council?"

Unfolding her body, she sat up and explained. "Everyone has a boss, Bren. The council monitors cultic activity, identifies threats, and sends out agents to get the job done."

Frustrated, but knowing perfectly well she was right, Brenden simmered with impotent rage. "I'm not waiting for someone give me the okay to go in and kill these things. Every day we wait, more women will die. As a police officer, I can't sit on my knowledge and do nothing."

Of course, he also couldn't go to the police with his knowledge. A rock and a hard place. Such a terrific position to be in. He hadn't felt this much frustration since he discovered his ex-wife cheating on him.

Dani held up her hands in appeasement. "I know . . . I'm not saying we don't have council sanction to act. I'm just saying we have to be careful, take it slow, and let them adjust to the idea you've been infected."

Fury filled him. He flung his glass away. It shattered against the far wall, spraying tequila and shards every which way. "Infected? You say it like I've got a goddamned cold." Rising off the sofa, he kicked the coffee table out of his way. The room was suddenly too small, too confining, as he stalked around its circumference. "I was taken, beaten within an inch of my life, practically raped, and there's now a hoop in my dick. Not only that, I've got some little fucker lurking in the back of my brain whispering in my ear that your neck looks awfully tasty and I ought to take a nibble." He stopped, pounding his hands against the wall in frustration.

Fear flickering in her eyes, Dani stood up. By the look on her face, it was clear she wasn't exactly sure what she was dealing with. Brenden couldn't blame her. How often in a lifetime does one encounter a vampyr? "Calm down. We'll handle this."

Bowels coiling into tight knots, he growled deep in his throat. Scarcely aware of it, Brenden whirled on her. "Calm down? Do you know how scared I am? Not because it's disgusting—and it is—but because I want to do what it tells me."

"I'm not the enemy here," she soothed. "I'm doing what I can to help, remember?"

Head falling, his shoulders slumped. "I know. I'm sorry."

Dani's face mirrored the agony he felt inside. She walked over to him, planting her hands on his shoulders. "I'll do the best I can to reverse the spell," she whispered.

Brenden sighed and nodded. "Thank you." Turning away, he walked to the window, raising the blinds and peering out into the street. *Where is she?*

The answer came in the form of a little black cat. Thudding against the screen, the cat hung, peering in at him.

"What the hell?" Dani exclaimed from behind him.

Relief filled him. "It's Líadán. She's made it."

Safely inside, Líadán shifted back into human form. Brenden's eyes widened in wonder, his sister's in envy. Líadán chuckled, remembering this was the first time he'd seen her change from animal to human. Anxious as to how her lover was holding up, her gaze slid over his figure. She gasped in pleasure, feeling a familiar thrill. Broad shoulders, narrow waist and long legs, he was a wonderful sight for sore eyes. Beams of illumination from the light overhead touched his shaggy hair, turning it from dark blond to a richer golden shade, almost a halo.

Brenden's husky voice, half gravel, half whiskey, snapped her out of her contemplations. "I was so worried you wouldn't make it, honey." He folded her in his strong embrace, pulling her close. His touch shot through her like a jolt of electricity. He was holding her with an intensity that set her heart to beating double-time. She knew her feelings for this man ran much deeper than simple sexual attraction. The connection was so strong that it felt like a magnetic force was drawing them together. His strength seemed to pour over her like a warm shower on a cold winter's day. Even though they were both facing grave danger, she felt secure in his presence.

Líadán tilted her head, looking up into eyes shadowed with concern. Fortunately, she was not discovered with the book in her hands. She'd known better than to take it away. She smiled. "I'm fine."

Brenden caressed her cheek. Then his fingers slipped under her thick fall of hair to stroke her nape. "It's been hell not having you with me." He lowered his mouth to hers, his lips warm and demanding, tongue pressing for deeper entry.

Closing her eyes, Líadán willingly opened to him, tasting the faint hint of salt and tequila. Pressing her hands against his shoulders, the tips of her fingers dug into his T-shirt. She wanted to pull him closer, never let him out of her sight again. His hand closed over her breast, squeezed gently at the full flesh. Their embrace grew progressively hotter, rich sensations radiating through her body. No man had ever filled her cold, empty heart with such passion.

A rough "ahem" cut into her pleasant haze. "I'm about to puke here. Can we save the kissy-face shit for a more appropriate time?" Dani's brisk tone cut the romantic mood like fingernails raking a blackboard. Her laserlike stare mirrored her disapproval.

Brenden reluctantly released his hold. "I hope there is a more appropriate time," he whispered, looking intensely frustrated.

Dani scowled and rolled her eyes. By the look on her face, she wasn't happy with her brother's choice. "I heard that."

Líadán swiped at her damp mouth with the tips of her fingers. Danicia didn't like her and didn't want her around. A tight knot of worry formed in Líadán's stomach. "I'm sorry," she started to say, eager not to offend her hostess. She understood Brenden and his sister were very close. She didn't want to intrude on their relationship. Rather she wanted to join their comfortable circumference, settle into a domesticity where she truly belonged. A nagging in the back of her mind told her this was going to be easier said than accomplished.

Eyes brewing jealous thunderstorms, Dani launched at her, ready to tear ass. "You bitch! You seduced him into this sick shit!"

Líadán steeled herself to take the slap she fully deserved. Yes, she had used her body as a lure. Guilty as charged.

Brenden grabbed his sister's arm, dragging her back. "Stop that, Dani! You're being stupid. She didn't do anything I didn't want her to."

Dani glared daggers. "You expect me to accept this . . . this thing into our home!"

Brenden nodded. He stepped toward Líadán, arm protectively circling her waist. "I expect you to show a little respect for the woman I intend to marry. Like it or lump it, she's going to be around awhile."

Líadán was as startled by his words as Danicia was. A shower of sparks exploded in her veins. She stood, stunned, her breath laboring, her nipples tightening. Their glances met and held, his probing hers as if seeking some sign of reassurance. A feeling greater than happiness rose in her heart. Anticipation. Her body leaped into throbbing readiness when his fingers skimmed the corner of her mouth. The intimacy of the moment hugged them, seeming so right and feeling so good.

"You will marry me, won't you, sweetheart?" His voice near her ear warmed her. He spoke in a tender way, both frightening and exciting her.

Dani let out a choked exclamation. "You're proposing?"

Líadán looked up, locking gazes with Brenden. By the expression on his face, he was absolutely serious. His eyes were so hot she felt scalded by their intensity. "Brenden?" She released his name as a breathy moan.

His fine mouth parted in a sexy smile. "I'm serious," he said. "I love you." His voice held promises spoken and unspoken.

Oh.

"Say yes," he prodded in the wake of her silence.

Too overwhelmed to speak, Líadán nodded. Hardly able to believe he'd proposed, she fought to breathe against the lump building in her throat. Her knees were suddenly so weak she thought the bones in her legs had melted. Vision blurring, she was having trouble standing. The tension between them rose another notch as she fought to give her reply.

Brenden gripped her hands, folding his strong fingers over her trembling ones. His grip was strong, sure. There was no hesitation in his manner, no doubts or regrets in the depths of his eyes. "You're going to piss me off if you say no," he warned.

Tears blurred her vision, She rubbed them away, sniffing and gulping like a child. "Y—yes," she finally stammered. "I will." She bit her quivering lower lip, not sure if she wanted to laugh or cry. Maybe both. The bliss of this moment almost made her forget the difficulties they faced.

Brenden smiled with satisfaction. "Well, at least that part's settled."

Líadán gasped, fanning herself with a hand. She was burning

up. She let her breath out slowly, waiting for another explosion from Dani.

A cat-eating-the-canary smile creased Danicia's face. "Looks like my love spell worked after all," she said with satisfaction. Warming to the idea, she was willing to take credit for a successful love match. Brenden was right. Her future sister-in-law was a brat with a capital B. They might get along just fine after all.

Tension broken, all three laughed.

A familiar lazy grin curved Brenden's mouth when he drew his little sister into a bear hug and ruffled her hair with one big hand. "Yes," he agreed. "It worked."

Líadán couldn't help but laugh when he drew her into the fray and tipped her head back for a welcome kiss.

32

Smoking his way through two packs of cigarettes, Brenden hovered anxiously over the two women bent over the yellow legal tablet. Crumpled pages littered the floor; more scrawls from their pens covered line after line. They were working their way though Auguste's spell. From what he could see, they were not succeeding. He sighed in frustration, adding yet another butt to his overflowing ashtray. "Anything?"

Dani looked from the single page of frayed parchment to the pad to the many books on spell-casting she had opened at her elbow for reference. "Slow going, Bren. You have to remember this is written in a language I'm not familiar with. Even with Líadán translating, I have to find the correct key or the counter-spell is not going to work."

Hope plummeted. "You think there's any chance?"

Líadán answered. "I have known none to get free of Auguste's hold."

Brenden could tell she was fighting to hold on to her calm—and losing. "We're going to do this. It's going to work." He glanced at the pages, unable to decipher his sister's illegible scrawl. Even if he had been able to read her handwriting, he couldn't have made out the words. She was working the way her grandmother had trained her, in the old language of the Celts of their clan.

Dani ran her hand through her hair, further mussing the long tangle around her face. Dark circles ringing her eyes and the fatigue set into her face made her look older than her actual years. "I think I have a solid base down. I can't be sure until we try it, but it's worth a shot."

Brenden was suddenly curious. "You do a lot of this stuff . . . spellcasting?"

Dani looked at him as though he'd grown a second head. "You know I do. You just never paid attention, Bren. You think it's easy to operate when your own brother thinks you are a crazy freak?"

He automatically started to defend himself. "Damn it, I didn't mean—"

Dani made a gesture for silence. "Yes, you did. I remember how you treated Grandma, like she was some kind of loony old lady."

He shrugged helplessly. "Mom and Dad . . ."

"Didn't believe either," she finished. "But at least they didn't roll their eyes or run her down."

Brenden flexed his jaw and told himself in the silence of his own mind to just shut up. This was a battle he simply could not win. He was already in over his head. Why make it worse? "I'm sorry. I've been a jerk. It's hard to toss out thirty-three years of disbelief in one night. But I'm trying. I want to know all of it."

Dani relaxed. "You just need to know the fighting, Bren. I'll handle the witchcraft."

At last. Action. Better than sitting around, waiting. While they'd worked, he'd paced through the house, looking out windows . . . expecting what? He wasn't sure. Instead of taking the whole book, Líadán had taken only the single page. If it was even the right page, he had no clue. He'd had to rely on her knowledge. How long would it be before Auguste discovered her treachery and came after her, seeking revenge?

He was ready. And, for once, he didn't feel helpless. Líadán had clued him in that it didn't take stakes and holy water to kill a vampyr. No, it turned out these complex creatures were just as susceptible to head and heart wounds as any other being. If the shooter's aim was good, a well-placed bullet designed to rip and tear flesh would do the job just fine. If the shooter's aim was bad, a shotgun would do better. And Brenden was well armed.

"So what do we need to do?" he asked.

Dani's answer was immediate. "I need a quiet room, totally blacked out."

Brenden nodded. "Go on."

Dani tapped her pencil against her pad. "There's nothing else except for you two being prepared to do exactly what I say."

Brenden glanced to Líadán. She gave a brief silent nod. "We can do that," Brenden said.

Dani took a deep breath. "Okay. Let's do this."

Twenty minutes later, all three stood in her basement apartment. The small living room was now cleared of furniture so they could work from the center of the area. Nine white candles, anointed with spicy, fragrant oils smelling like cinnamon and sandalwood, were set in a perfect circle.

"A circle of safety," Dani explained, "to keep malignant forces from interfering with the energies you are trying to generate."

Her explanation sounded foreign and seemed a bit ludicrous, but now wasn't the time to mock things he didn't understand. He'd already been smacked down hard for being a nonbeliever. "Go on."

274 / *Devyn Quinn*

"When you step inside the circle, I need you to say '*Nine times 'round, the circle's bound. Send all evil to the ground.*' Those words clear the channels of negative energy you've picked up through the hoops."

More stupid stuff. He bit his tongue to keep from saying so. "Makes sense to me."

Líadán agreed. "Me, too."

Dani went on with the rest of her plan. "Now, when you're inside the circle and the candles are lit, say the reversal spell. Don't pull on the sigil while you say the words. Just let the energy you are concentrating on generating flow into it. Hopefully this will be enough to counteract what Auguste's done and break his hold. The hoop should come off."

Brenden rubbed his hands together, eager to get on with the game. "Let's get this done." He started to step into the circle of wax.

Dani pulled him back. "Naked. You have to be naked. Energy's stronger when you aren't wearing clothes."

He gave her a look of alarm. "You're not going to be in here, are you?"

She shook her head. "No. You and Líadán have to do this. I've told her the spell. After she lights the candles for you, she will tell you the words to say." She laid a reassuring hand on his arm. "Believe what you are saying, Bren. It's half the battle."

Brenden had never been a big believer in blind faith, preferring the backup of Smith and Wesson to that of angels and saints. "Okay."

"You have no choice." Dani went over to the wall, plugging in a black-light strip dating back to the seventies. She extinguished the other lights, plunging them into a strange, purplish gloom. "Good luck," she said, heading up the stairs.

Brenden looked at Líadán. He couldn't resist flashing a shit-eating grin. "I'll show you mine if you show me yours." He lifted his T-shirt over his head and tossed it aside. He kicked off his boots, and his jeans followed, landing in a heap. He stood, naked and proud, muscles in his thighs and chest quivering as he breathed. His primal appetite was ready to feast.

Giving him a playful smile, Líadán doffed her own clothes, a simple skirt and blouse. Bra and panties followed.

His eyes drank in every luscious inch. She was magnificent, a woman with a body made for sin: breasts firm and lush, belly flat, hips gently flaring, and her legs . . . miles long and sleekly muscled. Like a jungle cat poised to attack, there was a heated stillness around her. A ghostly, graceful figure in the strange illumination, she looked unreal in the flickering light, almost as though her flesh were made of stone and not skin. Tension hovered between them.

Brenden felt a thrill race through his veins. Anticipation shortened his breath. A feathery prickle brushed across the back of his neck. All he had at the moment was an erection and a smile. "Damn, every time I see you, I want you." Without her, he was alone, locked in a cold, airless void. With her, he was complete.

Líadán flicked long lashes. "What's stopping you?" A sexy smile curved her soft-as-sin lips. Her chest, bare to his eyes, rose and fell with quick pants. She looked enticing and tempting and Brenden wanted to bury his cock inside her until they both screamed out from the pleasure.

He raised a single eyebrow. "Not a damn thing."

They came together without hesitation, bodies entwining. Whispering her name, he lowered his mouth to hers and kissed her in a soft, gentle way. Making no apologies for his erection, Brenden rubbed against her. The ache for her fueled his body and his heart. He wanted this moment to be more than sex—he wanted it to be the binding of two souls who belonged together. Forever. No roses or champagne or even a soft bed under her back, but that was something he'd make up to her later.

Her mouth, her throat, her breasts . . . not an inch was ignored. Brenden bent, sucking one pebbled nipple deep into his mouth. The feel of his tongue on the pink bead made her gasp. Encouraged by her response, he slid his hand between her legs, fingers tracing her inner thigh to touch her intimately. He caressed the soft petals of her labia, drenched with the evidence of her arousal.

Líadán trembled under the sensual assault of his hand and mouth. Her inner muscles gripped like a silken glove when he sank a finger into her moist channel. He withdrew a little, then thrust again. She rewarded him with a low, throaty moan.

Switching sides, he flicked his tongue against the tip of her other nipple, bringing the little nubbin to rigid alertness. "I love the way you taste." He nipped lightly, then sucked the tip into his mouth.

Her sigh low and intimate, Líadán pressed harder against him, tangling her fingers in his hair. A tremor ran though her. Thick lashes fluttered down, fanning across her cheeks. White teeth flashing, she drew his head back. "Take me," she commanded. "I'm all yours."

Brenden pressed her back against the wall. "This one won't last long," he murmured. "But I need you." Sliding his hands under her ass, he lifted her up, settling her neatly on his erect cock. Crushed against him, she sank down to the hilt until he could penetrate no further. Thighs tensed, he did all he could to keep from losing control.

Control didn't last.

Face flushing, Líadán curled her long legs around his waist. Sharp nails dug into his shoulders, rending his skin with delicious scratches. He held her hips and lunged upward. Her face clouded with pleasure. Her inner muscles clenched, tearing a groan out of his throat.

Fingers burrowed into her hips, Brenden plunged and withdrew, then plunged again. Lost in the throes of passion, his hips thrust upward with reckless abandon, forcing her to take every last inch. Creamy core rippling, she grasped him in a grip so powerful it stole his breath away. He jerked as if prodded in the ass with a hot poker, banging her against the wall so fiercely she gasped.

Brenden captured her mouth with his. When her lips parted, he slipped his tongue inside, caressing one of her sharp canines. Her tongue explored back, tasting, feeling, enjoying. She bit down gently and their kiss deepened. Fire pulsed through his veins, settling all over again in his throbbing erection. His cock strained and throbbed in response, his voracious need to come clawing its way down his spine and gripping his balls.

Hips pummeling, he stroked her deeper and faster, pushing her toward climax with all the energy he possessed. Muscles bunching in his thighs and ass, orgasm roared out of him with the ferocity of a beast. Balls drawn tighter than bowstrings, the release of his seed brought with it a delicious lassitude, loosening tight knots in overly wound tendons. He took a deep breath, cursing, "Damn. I wasn't ready."

Taking everything he could give, Líadán clung to him. Skin slick with perspiration, her body melted against his. By the glow of the black light over her head, he watched her features first grow taut when her pleasure peaked, then relax when the sensations ebbed.

Intimately joined, they clung to each other, lulled by the twin heartbeat sharing a single rhythm between them. A few minutes later Líadán lifted her head off his shoulder, giving him a smile conveying satisfaction. "That was wonderful, my love."

He groaned. "I came too quickly. I wanted it to last longer."

She pressed a quick kiss onto his lips. "Next time." She kissed him again, the touch of her lips filling him with renewed desire. With a reluctant groan, he parted their bodies, setting her on her own feet. "I guess we'd better get on to trying Dani's spell."

Líadán reached for his arm. "I'm a little afraid. What if it doesn't work?"

He put a single finger across her full lips. "It's going to work. I know it."

She gazed up at him through trusting eyes. "It will work," she said, as if reinforcing good karma.

Drawing a breath, Brenden turned toward the circle Dani had created out of the white candles. "You want to go first?"

She hesitated. "You try it."

"Okay." He stepped into the circle of candles, sat cross-legged, and said the words as Dani had instructed. Líadán lit each candle as he spoke. Nine little eyes winked around him, offering an incredible warmth and comfort. He felt . . . walled . . . as though nothing outside the circle could touch him. The sense of safety was amazing.

"Now what do I say?"

Líadán told him the words of the spell.

The words sounded a little stupid. A long shot—if the spell even worked at all. Cock in one hand, two fingers lightly gripping the hoop, he said the words. "Dark souls who haunt the night, those who would destroy light, loosen your bond upon my body, take no more of soul or self for thou are not master of me. To myself, I shall be free." As he spoke, the hoop assumed an otherworldly glow, the gold turning iridescent to the eyes. Seconds later the first magical rush poured through his fingers, seizing and directing the hoop to change its shape. As if coming to life, the metal turned molten between his fingers. The two ends opened, parted . . .

Barely daring to breathe, Brenden slid the thing off. The metal wriggled like an earthworm between his fingers. "It worked."

Líadán clasped her hands together. "I don't believe it."

Brenden stood up, urging her to take his place. Candles extinguished and relit, Líadán sat in the circle and performed the spell. A moment later, the hateful sigil binding her slid out of her navel. "I'm free," she murmured, half in wonder, half in relief.

Hearing their cries of joy, Dani called down, "What happened?"

Brenden reached for his jeans, tugging them up his legs and over his bare ass. Watching Líadán wriggle into her clothes made him want to take them off all over again. He reluctantly tucked his lust away. That would have to wait. "It worked," he called. "Your spell worked."

Dani hurried down the stairs. "Let me see."

Líadán handed over hers, glad to give it away.

Dani poked at the piece of metal, still strangely animated by the energies in its cold core. Deep inside its heart, ribbons of fire moved like blood flowing through veins. "I've never seen anything like this. It's like it has a mind of its own." Her brow knitted, as if she were trying to be very exact in her words. "It still feels warm, like a thing alive."

Brenden pulled on his boots. "Just get rid of the fucking things."

Dani continued staring at the writhing metal, less than two inches in length. "This is fascinating. Look! It's crawling." Taking on a corkscrewing motion, the metal snaked toward her third finger. Before she could react, it firmly circled the digit. Panic crossed her face as two ends fused together and solidified. "Oh, shit . . ." She tugged at the ring, trying to pull it off. *"The damn thing's got me."*

Fighting back the crawl of nausea, Brenden felt a perceptible surge of terror. "Get the fucking thing off!" Standing up, he felt a sickening sensation, as if the floor were shifting under his feet. *What now?*

"There's no time!" Appearing from nowhere, a strange bluish illumination emanated around Dani. Embraced by the surging electrical force field resonating around her, she twisted painfully in its grasp. "No! There's a shield of safety around this house. This cannot enter." Evidently something had managed to penetrate her invisible wall.

A flash, followed by a dazzling electric shock, sizzled through every nerve and cell. Brenden gritted his teeth as the pulsing blue light grasped his body with invasive fingers. Just as Dani was held captive in the center of the light, so was he rooted to his spot. He could not lift a foot or move an arm. His body seemed to weigh a ton. A great and palpable fear clutched his innards. His very blood tingled with awareness of his helplessness to give Dani any aid.

Swirling and eddying around Dani, fading a bit before regaining its brilliance, the light seemed to be gaining strength and intensity. Dani's feet lifted off the floor, her body pulled toward the ceiling. She hung, suspended, snared like a fly in a web. Then a short, bright flare of light. Abruptly, without any transition, Dani vanished.

Brenden stared in shock at the vacant space. The emptiness lay blank and terrible before him. He blinked, as if opening and closing his eyes would return Dani to her place. His astonishment was a raw wound. He sagged, sick and drained. That bastard had stolen his sister! "She's gone."

He turned his gaze on Líadán, to a menace he'd invited in. Suspicion slammed into his skull. Did she have something to do with Dani's abduction? Was she really the victim she pretended to be? "What happened?"

Líadán swallowed deeply, shaking her head. Her mouth opened slightly, as if in shock. "I—I don't know."

Brenden grabbed her shoulders, shaking her in sudden fury. "You set me up, you bitch!"

Líadán's delicate features contorted with fear. "No." She flinched when his hand rose. "Brenden, please!" She twisted out of his hold, stumbling back.

The sound of his name falling from her lips pulled Brenden out of the blind and baseless anger engulfing him. Shaking, he realized he'd been about to slap her, scream at her with anger for jeopardizing Dani's safety.

Remorse filled him. His tongue grew thick and dry. His jaw clamped shut. He was laying blame on an innocent head.

On one level he had been checked. And Auguste had moved the game between them into mate. His heart clenched so tightly in his chest his hands shook. The gauntlet had been thrown at his feet and he had no choice but to accept the challenge. "Auguste's gotten even with me. I took you. Now he's taken Dani." He choked back a surge of sickness. *If that bastard lays a finger on her . . .*

Sitting down on the edge of the coffee table, Brenden buried his face in his hands. From the moment he'd come face to face with Auguste Maximilian, he'd known his task would be to take the vampyr master down. If any vampyr deserved slaying, Auguste did.

Brenden just didn't know how he was supposed to do that. Yet.

33

Deep inside the heart of the forbidden-to-outsiders estate, a stealthy figure was a barely discernible blur in the pale wash of moonlight filtering through a strange, almost luminescent mist.

Close to the ground, Brenden's fingers splayed and pressed hard against the gravelly soil in the classically frozen position of the hunter on the prowl. A man with a mission, he was clad in black jeans, boots, and a dark jacket over a T-shirt. Around his waist was a dagger in its sheath. A second, similar weapon was strapped to his left thigh within easy reach of his hand. Across his back was a heavy double-barreled shotgun, also at the ready. His long hair was tied away from his face with a piece of leather thong. His lips were drawn back in a silent but determined growl.

Nostrils distending, his face mirrored the seething thoughts alive in his skull. His was the face of a man with demons riding on his shoulders. The knowledge his hand would soon bring an end to other men bothered him not a whit. The rules of his world had suddenly changed and the law of the supernatural realm was to kill or be killed.

Brenden clenched harder at the ground. The late summer humidity brought out the damp, earthy smell of the woods. Body taut with anxiety, knees aching from his prolonged crouch, palms riddled and raw from the grind of sharp stones, he held his position. Pain was easy enough to put aside when one's mind was focused. At the top of his physical resources, some primeval drive had taken over and his own thoughts were no longer his body's sole master.

Breath coming to a stop, his eyes raked the landscape again, memorizing every detail. The subtlest of all cues ratcheted up his sense of heightened alertness. Words could not express how his newly burgeoning abilities functioned. His jouyl's instincts were jacking into his neural circuits. Sight, hearing, taste, smell—all his senses went way beyond any human capabilities. He heard every leaf turn, every twig snap, saw through the darkness as clearly as daylight.

The old abbey was in ruins. Abandoned about ten years ago it was falling into quiet decay. Located twelve miles outside Dordogne, bracketed by the wildlife preserve, and plastered with NO TRESPASSING signs, the abbey was the perfect place to be if one wished to remain undisturbed.

Arriving at the midnight hour, Brenden had slowly made his way closer to Auguste's lair. A predator on the prowl, he knew entering forbidden territory could cost more than his life. It could cost him his soul. For his sister, he was willing to take the risk. He was a man who had everything to gain and nothing to lose.

Dipping lower to the ground, he slithered forward, using elbows and knees to propel his body closer to the targeted area. More sharp rocks bit into his flesh. He maneuvered fast but with stealth, well-practiced in the art of moving under an enemy's eyes. He had to get closer. Auguste's guards patrolled this perimeter heavily, cloaked in the shapes of wolves and other wild animals. Two lurking hyenas seemed to be unaware of his nearness. The crunch of their footfalls said they weren't paying attention to stealth. Unaware of his presence, they paced the perimeter in a careless, easy manner. He could strike when he wanted.

Plans, he thought. *Got something special for you two.* Oh, yeah. Payback. For sure. In spades.

There was silence. Not even the night animals made a sound.

Brenden hoped the strange lull would break soon. It unsettled him more than he cared to admit. His anxiety was understandable. Danger of discovery was very real—almost close enough to taste. The wait for action seemed endless. Sometimes it seemed the mist was playing with his mind, and Auguste's guards were a figment of a mind stretched too tightly.

Though the night was cool, his body was drenched in sweat. Nerves. Going out on patrol always meant there was a chance he wouldn't be coming home at the end of his shift. Same danger. Different shit.

Forehead ridging with determination, he drew a breath to steady himself, trying to control the beating of his heart. The rush of blood through his veins threatened to deafen him. He'd never quite learned to conquer his nerves before engaging in the fight. He needed the adrenaline rush to give him the extra burst of strength he might not otherwise have. He needed to taste bitter fear in his mouth—maybe a little proof he was human and liked being that way. Fear was a tool to be used and respected. A man who knew no fear was a fool. A man who knew no fear wanted to die.

Gathering his wits, Brenden blinked, screwing his eyes shut to clear his blurred vision. Opening them, he tensed, ready to spring into action. Nothing was happening. The two guards he shadowed simply moved on with their patrol, trotting away unscathed, low growls becoming indiscernible as they disappeared into the brush.

Brenden released the tense breath he had been holding so

long it felt his lungs were going to burst. The only thing worse than the actual action was waiting for the action to happen. He didn't want to move too fast. He was one man and he didn't know exactly how many men Auguste might have patrolling. Better to be safe than sorry, to take things slowly. Being stupid and rushing in wouldn't accomplish anything. He wasn't the kind of man to linger over speculations serving no immediate purpose. He was a realist. Failure was a more certain outcome of this invasion than success.

There was more silence, which was just as well. Brenden heard the all but imperceptible sound of a fractionally dislodged piece of rock. The sound saved his life.

He whirled, hand reaching for the blade strapped to his thigh. He'd been right about one thing. It wasn't going to be easy to get through Auguste's defenses. Not one, but two more men were frozen in a crouch very like his own not ten feet away.

Stupid! They had been waiting for him, he realized, or someone like him. He wondered if the guards had been keeping tabs on him since he and Líadán had entered Auguste's territories.

To show he wasn't afraid, Brenden slowly uncurled from his crouch. He held his head high, his long-limbed, statuesque body defiantly erect.

The two men also stood, ready to fight.

Never one to hesitate, Brenden attacked first. A man outnumbered couldn't afford to give in to fear. He had to get the upper hand and even the odds. Two on one was unfair, especially when the two could call more backup.

The first man instinctively drew back, lifting his own weapon high in self-defense. Brenden didn't complete the follow-through on his first target. Instead, he turned almost mid-step and hurled his dagger toward the second man. His aim was true, the blade well crafted and balanced. The sharp point slid through the soft tissue of the man's exposed throat like a hawk through the air. The man didn't even have time to lift his hands to his neck before he pitched forward. He died, a sick gurgle escaping his slack lips.

One down.

Giving the second man no time to react or recover, Brenden reached over his left shoulder and unsheathed his shotgun. With a harsh cry, he wheeled around and swung the heavy weapon with all his might. This time his prey was faster, ducking to avoid the stock whistling above his head.

Carried forward by the momentum of his attack, Brenden felt his foot twist under him when his boot hit a protruding stone. The second man saw his chance. Instantly shifting into the shape of a spotted hyena, his jaws opened wide.

Brenden felt searing pain when sharp canines closed around his upper arm, taking the heavy weapon right out of his hand. His guts clenched. A determined animal with sharp teeth was an uninviting prospect to face.

Mind awhirl, Brenden reacted instinctively, grabbing the hyena's scruff more by good luck than skill. Both tumbled heavily to the ground. Brenden twisted the hyena's thick neck, but it seemed to be overlaid with steel cording. Damn, this beast was strong! He could feel his hold begin to falter as the oddly shaped carnivore writhed out of his grasp. Lose his grip now and a bite of those teeth could come down across his jugular. He had to kill the vampiric hyena before more guards were alerted.

Brenden steeled his nerves, preparing to renew his savage efforts. Snarling fiercely, the huge hyena advanced. Throwing himself forward in a suicidal lunge, he hit the hyena square in the chest. Straightening in a convulsive jerk, Brenden lifted the huge animal clean off all four paws before body slamming it to the ground.

An outrush of air escaped the hyena's gaping mouth, a half

growl, half snarl of confusion. It barely had a moment to draw more oxygen into its lungs before Brenden snatched his second dagger and neatly plunged it into the creature's belly. In a blindingly quick reverse, he ripped the long blade upward, carving open the stomach the way one would gut a fish. The noxious brute died with a soft sound, body shuddering briefly, and then going still.

Brenden climbed to his feet, wiping sweat from his eyes, trying to steady his uneven breath. The sweeping pound of swift paws turned his head in alarm. His mouth went bone dry and his hands turned cold and clammy when a sleek black panther leaped into view, shifting into the shape of a woman before all four paws hit the ground.

He relaxed. This was not the enemy.

Líadán rose from her crouch, standing like a warrior goddess amid the slain. She looked at the dead hyena, wrinkling her nose in disdain. Dressed in a pair of Dani's jeans and a denim jacket, she was a brave and beautiful savage, coming into her own strength. Splattered with the gore of her own kills, her black hair was a careless tangle around her face.

Bending over Brenden's first victim, she tugged the dagger out of his throat. "Head and heart," she murmured. "Destroy both. It's the surest way to kill a vampyr." Features locked in a hard grimace, she hacked off the man's head, then buried the blade in his chest. She was fluid and graceful, striking with an impressive and deadly accuracy—and the ice-cold calm of a professional killer. She'd learned from the master and didn't waver an inch. "We don't want them rising as nosferatu."

He wiped stinging sweat out of his eyes. "They can do that?"

Beheading the second man with her own blade, Líadán fixed him under a penetrating gaze. "Yes." Her cheeks were ashen and there were deep circles under her eyes. She looked just as ragged as he felt. She offered a grim smile. "But you did well. Getting them down is half the battle."

Brenden shook his head in wonder at this sexy beast who was his lover. They shared had a bond deeper than anything he'd ever had with another woman. Freed from Auguste's hold, the little black cat had metamorphosed into one giant feline. He hadn't wanted her to come witness such terrible carnage, but she'd insisted. Only the two of them stood against Auguste's brethren. They had no plan. They were simply working their way forward, downing any who crossed their path.

Swallowing a ragged lump building in his throat, he suddenly found the idea of surviving without Líadán unendurable. "Where do you think he's keeping Dani?"

Líadán lifted her eyes, giving him a fierce stare. "Auguste would have her down in his private chambers." The sharp urgency in her voice hammered home. Each second passing was another Dani had to endure as a hostage.

Anger in his actions, Brenden reclaimed his shotgun. Swept by a wave of determination, he'd never felt stronger, leaner, or meaner. *Accept the gifts this thing is giving you*, he told himself. "You take care of the others. It's a lot, I know. If you have to, stay ahead of them, scatter them out."

Líadán immediately shook her head. She wasn't going to be left behind so easily. She fixed him with a level gaze. "I'll create a diversion." She spat out the words as if challenging him to stop her. "I can keep them running for hours."

Brenden nodded. "All right." He grabbed her arm before she could shift again. "Be careful, honey. I don't want to lose you now."

Undeterred, Líadán hardened her jaw. She smiled thinly, her blue eye sparking with righteous fury. "We have to do this." Her mouth quirked up at one corner in a fatalistic half-smile. "I have waited a very long time for my revenge."

Brenden stiffened his spine. The defensive edge in her tone bit hard. "Don't do anything stupid. If they outnumber you, run." Hand trembling, he briefly touched Líadán's cheek. The air sizzled between them, solidifying their connection. "I can't stand the idea of losing you. That would kill me." As he spoke, cold awareness filled him. Walking away alive tonight might not be his destiny.

There was no question about not going.

He had to.

Dani's life depended on it.

34

The stage in Auguste's private chambers was carefully set. A heady mix of sandalwood and musk incense hazed the air amid flickering candlelight and waltzing shadows. Swathed in silky white sheets dotted with a scattering of dark red rose petals, the huge four-poster bed seemed more an oasis of eroticism than one of danger.

Looks were deceiving.

Bound hand and foot, Danicia lay pinned beneath Auguste. Face deathly pallid, eyelids half lowered, her lips slack, Dani seemed to be in a trance. A small sound, a kind of moan, escaped her lips. The ring that had trapped her was still on her finger, winking with malice.

Horror poured through Brenden's veins. This was unthinkable. Obscene. His stomach heaved with nausea. Trembling, he raised his shotgun, but didn't pull the trigger. His shot wasn't clear enough and Dani could be injured in the scattering blast. "Get the hell off her!"

Head jerking up, Auguste snarled, revealing his true face—deeply ridged forehead, glowing red eyes narrow over a snout-like nose, sharp fangs extended to their fullest, most deadly length. Blood stained his mouth. His feed interrupted, a long, low snarl broke from his throat.

Evil hovered, burning indelibly into Brenden's skull. A shiver clawed its way down his spine. His gaze cut to Dani's unconscious figure. His mouth tensed. She wasn't moving. Was she still alive? He was close to losing control between danger and anger, reason and action.

"Get away from her, you bastard." Mouth set into a hard line, Brenden stalked closer to the bed. He kept the barrel level with Auguste's head. If the fucker made one false move, he'd risk the shot. Not a choice he wanted to make, but if push came to shove, he'd pull the trigger and hope for the best.

Auguste rose to his knees. Body stiffening, his skin rippled, arms and chest cording with effort as he forced his will over that of the beast inside. Taking a deep breath, he lifted his head. His features were normal—a chill in his eyes and a smirk on his lips. His shirt was unbuttoned to the waist, but his slacks were—thankfully—zipped. Had he been exposed, Brenden held the notion of blasting his dangling dick to kingdom come.

"You are too late," Auguste said with sarcastic emphasis. He slid his palms along Dani's hips, up to her belly, then her breasts. "She belongs to me. She will be my queen, rule at my side as Líadán never could."

Clothes bloody and torn, Dani had obviously fought hard against her captivity. A thin trickle of blood seeped from the punctures gouged in her neck, staining the silken material beneath her head. Had she been infected with the jouyl?

The hair at the back of his neck immediately prickled in alarm. "That'll never happen." Brenden searched his sister's pale flesh for the hateful brand. The sight sent a wave of righteous hatred and rage coursing through his blood. He could barely tolerate the thought of his little sister locked beneath

Auguste's weight, blood draining away to feed the hunger of this despicable beast.

Brenden's jaw tightened. Auguste had gotten his talons deep into his psyche and would never release his hold as long as he walked this earth. He could take it. He doubted Danicia could. He wouldn't let her suffer the agonies infecting his soul. The craving for blood had already wound its roots deep.

If Dani is . . . A violent shiver shook him, left his muscles quivering. This was no time to crumble. He had to be strong. "Is she—?" He fought to push back the nausea rising in the back of his throat.

Auguste arched an eyebrow. "Dead? Oh, no. She is very much alive. I would not kill the one I truly wanted."

Brenden tensed, heart striking jackhammer blows against his ribcage. In an instant everything fell into place and it all made sense.

Auguste smiled. "You think you were clever to get the sigils off? I knew your intent before you even thought through the plan. I only let you believe you were the one I wanted."

Shrugging his shoulders in a gesture of disdain and contempt, he reached out to stroke his palm along Dani's flat belly. "She is the one of true power. The magic she so capably wields will be an awesome force under my guidance. Imagine the possibilities of vampyr and sorceress merged." He chuckled. A sly look sidled into his eyes. "Our two bloodlines will create a species unique unto itself."

Brenden's hand tightened on his gun. He pictured himself squeezing the trigger and smiling as he did so. "You're not fucking her!"

Auguste's gaze flicked, eyeing the weapon. "And you intend to stop me? How noble." His lips curled in distaste. "Stupid, but noble." Gaze unwavering, he slid off the bed the way a spider would leave its web when a new victim was caught in its strands. Flames flickered, stirred by some mysterious breeze he silently summoned. Shadows aped his movements, a dark army ready to act. When he stood to his full height, the chamber seemed suddenly smaller.

Brenden stood motionless. Tendrils of fear writhing in his stomach became coiling spirals winding around his lungs, making it hard for him to breathe. Rivulets of sweat poured down his brow. "One of us has to die tonight. You know it and I know it."

"Indeed, I do." Auguste's hand raked the air. The door behind Brenden slammed shut. There was no other way out. "No one shall disturb us as we settle our differences."

There was a long uneasy silence, each regarding the other across the narrow space.

Ignoring his refusal to be baited, Auguste said, "You think you are strong enough to stop me? I am ready anytime you care to try." The hint of a smile seemed to linger across his arid lips longer than necessary. He was toying with his prey the way a cat would a wounded bird. He knew he had the advantage. He knew he had the time. He certainly knew he had the intent to kill.

Forcing down another surge of panic, Brenden retorted with derision, "I'm more than you think I am."

Auguste raised a hand for silence, inclining his head in a condescending manner. "You haven't even fully crossed yet. Your strengths are not even developed."

Brenden snorted. Hot rebellion began to flow through his veins, further strengthening him. "I don't need some voodoo demonic power to know I'm about to blast your ass back to hell." No more hesitation. Time to put this fucker in the ground.

He pulled the trigger.

Nothing.

Auguste's smile grew wider. A lean man with jutting cheekbones and devious eyes, his steady stare didn't waver, nor did the line of his jaw lose its insolence. "Your weapon will not work."

Brenden pressed his finger down a second time. "Goddamn it!" A double-barreled shotgun should be practically foolproof. He'd had visions of Auguste's head and chest exploding under the onslaught of double-ought buckshot.

His frustration appeared to amuse Auguste.

With a jerk of his left arm, the vampyr master spat out a string of vicious words. A sudden force gathered strength and volume. Pulses of energy radiated from the top of his head to the tip of his toes. His figure glowed, a shimmering aura of energy enveloping him. His hand shot out, as if shoving the power away.

The weight of the stillness before the strike was crushing. Brenden knew what was coming. He was aware of the pressure building against him with a tangible weight. He felt rather than saw the air around him quiver, sensed some faint distortion gaining strength and speed, but he couldn't get out of the way. His feet were locked to the ground. Not a single limb would lift or obey his mental command.

Here we go again . . .

Knocked off balance by an invisible wallop, Brenden slammed into the far wall. The impact was shocking, a sonic vibration seeming to beat on his body with bone-breaking reiteration. Air whooshed from his lungs and a black veil settled over his eyes. Grip on his weapon lost, the shotgun clattered uselessly. He reached for backup. There wasn't any. The dagger strapped at his hip faded away before his hand could even make contact. He didn't bother going for the blade strapped to his leg. Logic told him it wouldn't be there.

Panic escalated several notches. Brenden gulped. He was totally unarmed. Not good. Not good at all. He couldn't stop to think about how Auguste might have made his weapons vanish.

Auguste smirked with contempt. "My world, my rules."

Eyebrow cocked at a mocking angle, he lifted his hand. "You give me no choice but to defend myself." He made another quick gesture, pulling out of shadows and thin air a sword of some size and length.

Gaining his balance and rising, Brenden could only stare, thunderstruck. His situation was getting worse. He suddenly didn't feel so big, brave or strong. His gaze flickered between Auguste and his sword. *Oh, shit . . .*

Striding over to the downed cop, Auguste kicked the shotgun across the room, far out of reach. He thrust his sharp blade under Brenden's neck. "I could take your head now."

Brenden drew a long breath, raising himself up, climbing to his feet. The fight was about to commence. A vampyr with a sword was an uninviting prospect to face, especially when use of his weapon was as natural as breathing. "You won't do it." Voice strained and taut, he was in no mood to be taunted. "It'd hardly be a victory to kill an enemy so easily."

Face rigid and unyielding, Auguste regarded him steadily. He was no longer smiling. His mood had taken an abrupt downturn. By the malignant glint in his eyes, he was ready to put his weapon to lethal use without conscience or compunction. "Very well. You may stand up before I gut you like a chicken."

That didn't sound promising at all.

35

Climbing to his feet, Brenden perceived Auguste's intention—insolent, narrow eyes peering through slits told him everything. There was murder in them, plain and simple.

The vampyr master set into motion, circling his prey like a rabid hound locked in a death-cage. A large man, his height and brawny strength threatened serious damage; he was literally a mass of flesh.

The big cop had never been one to back away from a brawl.

Not that Auguste was offering that option. "Your death will be painful."

How kind of him to say. The prick. Hardly amused, Brenden bared his teeth, showing his own fangs. "I'm not planning to die."

His words seemed to amuse.

"You plan prematurely." Auguste swiped his blade to cut the air, a teasing move to test his opponent's reflexes.

Brenden instinctively flinched. He considered how to stop Auguste from carving him up alive, then decided there was nothing he could do to prevent serious injury to himself. Unarmed, he'd have to go for broke and hope he was the better fighter.

Setting the blade into motion, Auguste turned the tip loose. The first nick sizzled.

Brenden had no more turned his head before the second scorched down his cheek. His body shook, trembled, and for a moment he lost sight of Auguste, the sword in the vampyr's hand dimming to a faint shaft of blue. The glow of the tip filled his eyes—he was smothering in the light it projected. Blinded, he staggered back. A series of tiny cuts scored his face.

Another flick struck above his left eye. "The beginning of a thousand cuts," he heard Auguste say.

Another whiz of the sharp blade caught Brenden under his jaw. A thin trickle of blood warmed his skin. He clamped his palm to his damaged neck, sucking in a breath just as the blade brushed the tip of his nose, but didn't cut.

Lips curling, Auguste's gaze glimmered with glee. "I could drag your death out for hours," he taunted through an exaggerated yawn. "Imagine feeling your skin drop away inch by inch as I carve you apart."

That was exactly what Brenden didn't want to imagine . . . or experience.

As he struggled to find focus, to maintain consciousness over a gulf of nothingness, a new bolt of exquisite pain offered a focal point when the blade sizzled along his upper arm. Blood steaming thickly from a punishing slice dripped down his elbow. "Damn!"

"You didn't even see it coming." Voice calm and unbothered by angst, Auguste set to carving. Steel whipped across Brenden's chest. A glimmering spark of red fire followed the give of his skin. He felt warm blood, felt his knees weaken a little.

Brenden was barely aware when another thin welt of blood opened beneath the first. Three, four, five more slices . . . Unable to react fast enough, fear and frustration tied his bowels into knots.

Face a quivering mask of vengeful mirth, Auguste's breath gushed from distended nostrils. "You can't even step out of the way." Smile mutating into something horrible and forbidding, his face mirrored the sadistic intent alive in his skull. "You're too slow, too weak. You might as well be standing still." Intending to drive the blade home, Auguste attacked.

Brenden ducked sideways, twisting to avoid the sharp tip. It missed his eye by inches, striking the stone where his head had been only seconds ago.

Auguste cursed and drew his weapon back. He lunged to deliver another strike. At the same instant Brenden cocked his leg and kicked it speedily upward. He felt his foot slam against the vampyr master's abdomen, saw him lurch backward. He followed through with a second snap kick to the solar plexus.

Auguste was quick to regain his balance. Silver blade flashing with menace, he swung with a blind lunge.

Brenden dodged. He ducked low, hitting Auguste in the center of his chest in a bullish rush, as unorthodox as it was surprising.

Auguste hit the floor with a bone-crunching impact. Weapon jarred from his grip, he cursed in anger and surprise.

Without losing momentum Brenden kicked out, driving his booted foot squarely into Auguste's crotch. The crunch was sickening.

Auguste howled.

With the sound of blood pounding in his ears, Brenden piled his full weight behind another punt. "I'll kick your fucking nuts to the moon and back." He delivered more blows, fast and furious.

Rolling away from the ruthless barrage, Auguste scrambled to his feet with amazing agility. Brenden could feel the power gathering around him. The vampyr smiled and thrust out his hands.

Strength draining from his legs, Brenden saw no way to dodge the energy bolt. Aimed straight at him, the blow rammed his body sledgehammer hard. In his head a dizzying black cloud mushroomed. He hovered, weightless. Then he dropped.

Landing flat on his back, Brenden couldn't skitter aside fast enough to avoid the crushing impact of Auguste's knee into his chest. Wave after wave of pain rushed outward from the contact point. He barely had time to think as another hard slam stole his breath. Ribcage cracking, searing fire raced down his spine.

Struggling to regain the winning position, Brenden's knee came up hard across Auguste's back. The solid jolt had little effect; and even as he hit a second time, Auguste swung his fist and delivered a full facial blow. A show of stars sparkled, a dazzling display of red and blue.

Breathing hard, Brenden knocked Auguste aside. Lunging up, he angled to the left, jamming his elbow into Auguste's stomach.

Locked together, they came face to face. Brenden looked into a visage contorted by hate; eyes bulging, Auguste's lips curled away from a bloodstained mouth. Struggling to break Brenden's pythonlike grip, Auguste's flesh rippled and changed, body twisting in sudden transformation. In the blink of an eye a massive gray wolf had taken the place of the man.

Brenden's guts spasmed. Savage menace glowed in the wolf's eyes, backed by insanity. Auguste's intent to mutilate was a hurricane, sucking Brenden into the gaping maw of his hate.

The huge wolf pounced, taking him down hard. More strange lights whipped across Brenden's vision. Another few inches lower and he would have lost consciousness. Breath a shallow whistle in his throat, the haze around his vision darkened and solidified.

Eyes like twin pools of lava blazed with malicious intent. "I will enjoy draining you dry." The words were little more than a snarl.

Giant jaws latched around Brenden's shoulder. Sharp teeth ripped through his denim jacket. He felt the give of skin, followed by glimmering shards of agony. The rush of blood through his veins was maddening and painful. His strength was draining away.

Auguste's jaws tightened. Brenden had the sensation of free-falling, as if he'd been pushed from an airplane without a parachute. He ceased to feel anything when the wolf shook him like a rag doll.

A swirling mass of images overtook him without warning. Everything disintegrated, a gale wind of power unleashing roared through his skull. The next moments were chaotic. A surge of unholy energy poured through him, two ancient forces merging and coalescing into a single entity. Brenden fought to hold on to human perception, but his mind was no longer occupied by anything remotely so. Everything was a blur as his beast took over his mind, shoving his thoughts aside and assuming control.

Caught between man and feline, one shape battled the other for dominance, a strange new energy zapping every nerve with raw voltage. Head snapping back, his transformation set in motion; thick ridges furrowing his brow, ears elongating into long points, the terrible pain of teeth growing longer and sharper. Muscles cording, his body shifted into an alien shape with stunning force and speed. Skin melted away, replaced by a pelt of silky fur.

Brenden caught a glimpse of stocky forelimbs covered by brownish-yellow fur. Hands became paws, fingers flexing claws. The realization of what happened was instantaneous. He was no longer a man. The gift of his jouyl was the body of a sleek and powerful jaguar.

Brenden roared, actually roared! His lithe body twisted, breaking the wolf's suffocating grip. He came up on four solid paws. Towering in majesty and menace, he glared down at the wolf. Opening his mouth, a second great, ear-shattering growl rolled up from his chest.

The wolf blinked stupidly at the great cat, rooted in place by the change in the enemy. Cat and wolf locked gazes. The wolf's eyes widened with the realization that his victim was no longer helpless.

Launching his new supercharged shape into action, there was no limitation in Brenden's movement and balance. Streaking forward in fury, he charged straight at the wolf, wheeled into a semicircle, and struck with punishing force. Swiping out with a massive paw, he caught the wolf squarely in the chest.

Reeling back, Auguste hit hard, knocked nearly insensible. Snorting in anger and surprise, the wolf scrambled to its feet. Teeth bared, a ravening, wild look contorted his features. Behind the mask of the wolf was the soul of a demon determined to destroy.

Not wasting a moment, Brenden lunged. Maddened by the hunger to tear, bite, feel flesh rend under his fangs, his massive jaws latched around the wolf's neck, trembling with bloodlust. The sharp, sleek edges of his canines met the warm, soft flesh of the wolf's throat. Great jaws closed and fastened, his nostrils filling with wolf stink. He bit. Hard.

The wolf released a high howl of anguish. Body bucking and writhing, Auguste couldn't shake off the bigger, stronger cat. Hot blood spurted from the wounds, crimson rivulets cascading.

Brenden swallowed.

Body shuddering, the wolf produced a little bleat of pain and fear as its paws helplessly kicked in the air. As his life drained away, Auguste's metamorphosis reversed itself, the wolf again becoming a man.

Brenden drank deeply, reveling in the coppery liquid flowing down his throat. Its taste was sweet, like sun-warm honey fresh from the bee's hive. The symbiosis was completed. He and his jouyl were joined as one, a complete entity.

Forever.

Instinct kicked in, warning him not to take too much. To get lost in feeding on a dying victim could be fatal.

Sated, Brenden drew a long breath and raised himself, his mind clearing as the beasts inside receded back to their own dark corners. Time and space refocused. Like surfacing from a pit of tar, he came back to separate awareness.

Brenden noticed that his paws were again human hands. Auguste was semiconscious beneath Brenden's palms. A trickle of scarlet oozed from the ragged bite in his neck.

The deed was done. He'd taken first blood. Shaking and drained, he retched at the taste lingering on his lips, clogging his throat. He sank to the floor, moaning with shock and dread.

Auguste's head rolled to the right. He placed a trembling hand on his neck. Touching his torn throat, he lifted stained fingers above his face. A fleeting smile crossed his lips, an unexpected sigh rising like a gentle summer zephyr. A convulsive shiver tore through his body. "I didn't believe you could beat me." His words were a wheeze, barely audible.

The sound of heavy footsteps brought Brenden's head up. Fearing new danger, he twisted around. Seeing Líadán's dark silhouette, he relaxed.

Without a word, she knelt. Picking up Auguste's sword, she laid it near his hand. Their gazes locked. "Finish him."

Through his haze of shock, Brenden responded to the urgency in her voice. His hand slipped out, fingers curling around the jeweled hilt. Their eyes met. Nodding her chin slightly, Líadán give him a strained smile. "End his life and we will be free."

Rising to his knees, Brenden grasped the sword in both hands. Without stopping to think, he leveled the blade above

Auguste's chest. He was about to commit murder—wanted to with ever fiber of his being. He gritted his teeth against the cold spasm of realization squeezing his heart, ignoring conscience and favoring instinct. Auguste was no man. He was a dangerous, rabid animal.

Brenden thrust, twisting the sharp steel viciously so it would penetrate the ribs and destroy the heart.

Fatally struck, Auguste arched painfully. Screamed. Skin withered and veins bulged through his body as his head whipped back and forth. Skin peeled away from the bone as Auguste thrashed convulsively. His arms and legs pounded with jerky violence, his jaws snapping open and shut as his fangs shredded his lips to bits. Eyes, ears, nose, and mouth released a fountain of brackish black liquid. Then he lay still. The beautifully engraved sword, a relic from his own time, protruded starkly, the marker of his doom.

Candlelight and silence ruled the chamber. It finally felt safe, peaceful.

Brenden climbed to his feet, wiping sweat from his eyes. Líadán's hand found his shoulder, squeezing. Face pale, her eyes were wide with shock, disbelief, and relief. She offered a weary smile. "We're really free."

Brenden pulled her into his embrace. Holding her with fierce protectiveness, he said a silent prayer of thanks. She was solid, real, and safe. His gaze found the bed. Behind them, Dani stirred, mumbling incoherently.

Líadán didn't seem to hear. Limp and worn in the aftermath, she swayed for a moment, as though she might faint. The last remnants of her self-control suddenly shattered. Her whole body shook with unreleased sobs of relief.

Throat contracting painfully, Brenden kissed her temple. His arm tightened around her waist. "It's all right. He's gone." There was no need to say more. Their bond as survivors spoke for them.

Recovering a bit of her composure, Líadán shook her head. "Not yet." Her voice trembled.

"What else—"

"Let me." Breaking free, Líadán stepped forward. She needed to be the one to strike the last blow, to bring closure to the nightmare engulfing them. Lifting the heavy blade with an ease belying her sex, her steel blue gaze suddenly held the flare of righteous lightning.

Brenden fixed his eyes on Auguste's withered body. He silently swore he would remember this sight as long as he lived.

Líadán swung the heavy weapon. Her delicate features contorted with anger. "May God have no mercy on your soul."

Auguste's head rolled.

Líadán began to laugh deliriously until her laughter became racking sobs of relief. Blade slipping from her grip, she crumpled to the floor in a heap.

Kneeling, Brenden scooped her up in a bear hug. He closed his eyes, pressing a fresh kiss onto her cold forehead. She shivered and held on tight.

The nightmare was over.

Exhausted, Brenden drew a calming breath. The woman he loved was safe in his arms. He hadn't known until tonight how deeply he loved her. Whatever happened, he could protect her now. Thanks to—oh shit.

As if on cue, Dani's voice piped up. "Hey, bro, a little help here."

He'd been wrong about his baby sister. Because of Dani, his life had changed forever. In a big way.

"On my way, kiddo," he answered.

Epilogue

Brenden awoke, stiff and sore. He lay still for a moment, tempted to groan. The night before had wrung out every ounce of strength he possessed. He still couldn't believe he'd survived.

Feeling the shift of a body beside his, he rolled over onto his side. Líadán lay beside him, sleeping peacefully. The sight of her was enough to make his heart tip over—and his blood heat.

A thousand little wildfires ignited beneath his skin, a blaze of need winding though every vein until the heat settled in his cock. His instincts about her had been right. From the first time he'd set eyes on her, he'd known this was the woman he wanted to spend the rest of his life with.

Leaning forward, Brenden nuzzled her warm cheek. "Wake up, sleepyhead."

Líadán opened her eyes, yawned, and then sat up. Silk sheets pooled around her hips, revealing her bare breasts. Black hair spilling around her face and shoulders, her nipples stiffened under the erotic brush. "Good morning, husband."

Feeling an intense mix of desire and contentment, Brenden drew a deep breath. They were two days into their honeymoon and he couldn't imagine waking up without her. "I still can't believe you're here with me." He brushed her long hair back from her face, touching the soft skin of her cheek before cupping the back of her head with his hand and pulling her mouth to his. Their kiss was deep and hungry, tongues tangling deliciously. His heart beat furiously as the tenor changed, the slow, gentle pressure of her mouth turning into something else, something more demanding, more emotionally charged. It needed no translations, no clarification, and its message was as clear as the one given by the ache deep in his loins.

"So this is what eternity will be like." He nuzzled her fragrant skin, inhaling her scent of fresh melons and sexual musk. He licked one rosy nipple. "I think I'm going to like it." *Especially in the bedroom.*

Líadán tipped her head down to meet his gaze, her blue eyes crinkling around the edges when she smiled. "There's only one drawback. We can only live our lives fully by night." Releasing a delighted giggle, her hand drifted under the covers. Her first stroke had his erection blooming in a fierce sweep of heat. "I'm afraid we'll be spending our days in bed."

Pulse jumping to his mouth, Brenden groaned and squeezed his eyes shut. Swollen, thick and achingly hard, lust tugged with urgent insistency. "I don't think I'll mind very much," he breathed, settling back onto his pillows and letting his wife work her magic. "I never could get my shit together in the morning anyway."

Supersexy. Superhot. That's Jami Alden's
A TASTE OF HONEY,
available now from Aphrodisia . . .

Though she hated to admit it, Kit only cared about holding the attention of one pair of gleaming green eyes. Keeping her lids lowered, she snuck another glance at the bar, her rhythm faltering when she found the space formerly occupied by Jake's broad shoulders now filled by two nearly identical bleached blondes.

Suddenly a large, proprietary hand slid around her hip to flatten across her stomach. She didn't even have to turn around to know it was Jake. Even in the crowded dance club, she could pick up his scent, soapy clean with a hint of his own special musk. Without a word he pulled her back against him. The rigid length of his erection grinding rhythmically against her ass let her know her dance floor antics had been effective.

What she hadn't counted on was her own swift response. Sure, he'd gotten the best of her in the wine cellar, but she'd written it off as a result of not having had sex since her last "friend with benefits" had done the unthinkable and actually wanted an exclusive relationship. She'd had to cut all ties and hadn't found a suitable replacement in the last six months.

Tonight, she'd only meant to tease and torment Jake, give him a taste of what he wanted but couldn't have. Now she wasn't so sure she'd be able to stick with that game plan. The memory of her gut-wrenching orgasm pulsed through her, her nerve endings dancing along her skin with no more than his hand caressing her stomach and his cock grinding against her rear. His broad palm slid up until his long fingers brushed the undersides of her breasts, barely covered by the thin silk of her top.

She was vaguely aware of Sabrina raising a knowing eyebrow as she moved over to dance with one of the other groomsmen.

Without thinking she raised one arm, hooking it around his neck as she pressed back against the hard wall of his chest. Hot breath caressed her neck before his teeth latched gently on her earlobe. The throbbing beat of the music echoed between her legs, and she knew she wouldn't be able to hold him off, not when he was so good at noticing and exploiting her weakness.

"Let's go," he whispered gruffly, taking her hand and tugging her toward the edge of the floor.

She wasn't *that* easy. "What makes you think I want to go anywhere with you?" she replied, breaking his hold and shimmying away.

A mocking smile curved his full, sensuous mouth. "Wasn't that what your little show was all about? Driving me crazy until I take you home and prove to you exactly how good it could be between us?" To emphasize his point, he shoved his thigh between hers until the firm muscles pressed deliciously against her already-wet sex. "What happened earlier was just a taste, Kit. Don't lie and tell me you don't want the whole feast."

She moaned as his mouth pressed hot and wet against her throat, wishing she had it in her to be a vindictive tease and leave him unsatisfied, aching for her body.

But her body wouldn't let her play games, and she was too

smart to pass up an opportunity for what she instinctively knew would be the best sex of her life. Jake was right. She wanted him. Wanted to feel his hands and mouth all over her bare skin. Wanted to see if his cock was as long and thick and hard as she remembered. Wanted to see if he'd finally learned how to use it.

And why not? She was a practical, modern woman who believed in casual sex as long as her pleasure was assured and no strings were attached. What could be more string-free than a hot vacation fling with a guy who lived on the opposite side of the country? And this time she'd have the satisfaction of leaving *him* without so much as a good-bye.

Decision made, she grabbed his hand and led him toward the door. "Let's hope you haven't oversold yourself, cowboy."

"Baby, I'm gonna give you the ride of your life."

Outside, downtown Cabo San Lucas rang with the sounds of traffic and boisterous tourists. Jake hustled her into a taxi van's back row, and in rapid Spanish he gave the driver the villa's address and negotiated a rate.

Hidden by several rows of seats, Kit had no modesty when he pulled her into his arms, capturing her mouth in a rough, lusty kiss. Opening wide, she sucked him hard, sliding her tongue against his, exploring the hot, moist recesses of his mouth. Her breath tightened in quick pants as he tugged her blouse aside and settled a hand over her bare breast, kneading, plumping the soft flesh before grazing his thumb over the rock-hard tip.

Muffled sounds of pleasure stuck in her throat. She couldn't ever remember being so aroused, dying to feel his naked skin against her own, wanting to absorb every hard inch of him inside her. She unbuttoned his shirt with shaky hands, exploring the rippling muscles of his chest and abs. He was leaner now than he'd been at twenty-two, not as bulked up as he'd been when he played football for UCLA. The sprinkling of dark hair had grown thicker as well, teasing and tickling her fingers,

312 / Jami Alden

reminding her that the muscles that shifted and bulged under her hands belonged to a man, not a boy.

Speaking of which . . .

She nipped at his bottom lip and slid her hand lower, over his fly, until her palm pressed flat against a rock-hard column of flesh. The taxi took a sharp curve, sending them sliding across the bench seat until Kit lay halfway across Jake's chest. He took the opportunity to reach under her skirt and cup the bare cheeks of her ass, while she seized the chance to unzip his fly and reach greedily inside the waistband of his boxers.

Hot pulsing flesh filled her hand to overflowing. Her fingers closed around him, measuring him from root to tip, and they exchanged soft groans into each other's mouths. He was huge, long, and so thick her fingers barely closed around him. It had hurt like a beast when he'd taken her virginity. But now she couldn't wait to feel his enormous cock sliding inside her, stretching her walls, driving harder and deeper than any man ever had.

She traced her thumb over the ripe head, spreading the slippery beads of moisture forming at the tip. Her own sex wept in response. Unable to control herself, she reached down and pulled up her skirt, climbing fully onto his lap. She couldn't wait, her pussy aching for his invasion. God, this was going to be good.

If anyone had told her twelve years ago that someday she'd be having sex with Jake Donovan in a Mexican taxicab, she would have called that person insane.